PRAISE FOR TH

"[Briggs] spins tales of werewolves, coyote shifters, and magic and, my, does she do it well . . . If you like action, violence, romance, and, of course, werewolves, then I urge you to pick up this series." —USATODAY.com

"A terrific saga." —Midwest Book Review

"Interesting, fast-paced urban fantasy . . . [An] imaginative writer who always leaves fans anxiously waiting for the next tale." —Monsters and Critics

"Patricia Briggs is amazing . . . Her Alpha and Omega novels are fantastic." —Fresh Fiction

"Easygoing-yet-immersive writing style, well-drawn characters, and excellent world-building." —Dear Author

"Patricia Briggs has that special something that makes me feel so happy and contented to slip into her world and read any one of her books." —Badass Book Reviews

PRAISE FOR THE MERCY THOMPSON NOVELS

"I love these books." —Charlaine Harris, #1 *New York Times* bestselling author

"In the increasingly crowded field of kick-ass supernatural heroines, Mercy stands out as one of the best." —*Locus*

"[A] dazzling world of werewolves, shapeshifters, witches, and vampires. Expect to be spellbound." —Lynn Viehl, *New York Times* bestselling author

"Mercy is not just another cookie-cutter tough-chick urban fantasy heroine. She's got a lot of style and substance and an intriguing backstory." —*Library Journal*

Titles by Patricia Briggs

The Mercy Thompson Series

The Alpha and Omega Series

Graphic Novels

Anthologies

DEAD HEAT

AN ALPHA AND OMEGA NOVEL

PATRICIA BRIGGS

ACE BOOKS, NEW YORK

ACE

An imprint of Penguin Random House LLC
375 Hudson Street, New York, New York 10014

DEAD HEAT

An Ace Book / published by arrangement with Hurog, Inc.

ISBN: 978-0-425-25628-2

PUBLISHING HISTORY
Ace hardcover edition / March 2015
Ace mass-market edition / February 2016

PRINTED IN THE UNITED STATES OF AMERICA

10 9 8 7 6 5 4 3 2 1

Cover illustration © Daniel Dos Santos.
Interior text design by Kristin del Rosario.

Penguin
Random
House

To the lovely people who've made the journey with the Arabian horses so much fun: Brenda, who was there at the beginning; terrific travel companions Ed and Adriana; Alice, Bill, and Joan of Rieckman's Arabians, who made the trek before I did and tendered useful advice along the way; Dolly, Doug, and Peggy at Orrion Farms, who provided a jump start and guidance; Deb, Kim, and Portia at High Country Training for turning my ponies into good citizens; Robert and Dixie North, who love the horses as much as I do; and Nahero, my big Arab gelding, who has been my companion these twenty-eight years. But mostly to my very patient husband, who is particularly gifted at making dreams come true.

ACKNOWLEDGMENTS

No book is written in isolation. My thanks to the following people who helped me to make Anna and Charles's story real: Doug Leadley and Maegan Beaumont for their help with Scottsdale; Linda Campbell, who knows more about my books than I do; Collin Briggs, Mike Briggs, Michelle Kasper, Ann Peters, Amy J. Schneider, and Anne Sowards for editorial service above and beyond; and to Daybreak Warrior and his fascinating YouTube videos about the Navajo language and culture. As always, any mistakes are mine.

PROLOGUE

DECEMBER

The fae lord stalked back and forth in his cell of gray stone. Three steps, turn, four steps, turn, three steps. He could do it all day. Had, in fact, done it for two weeks.

His boots were soft and he made no sound as he paced. Sound distracted him unduly from his purpose—which was to bore himself to the point where he no longer thought about anything.

His clothes, like his boots, were practical, but still representative of his position as High Court Lord—though he no longer remembered much about that part of his life. Even so, his long red hair was confined in a complicated series of braids that trailed on the floor behind him, a court fashion of at least a millennium ago. Doubtless if there were still courts, still High Courts, he would be considered out of fashion entirely.

He'd worn High Court dress for the first week he was here, but there was no one to impress, so he'd left them off and exchanged them for the more comfortable clothing. He could have put on jeans, he supposed, but he was losing that long-ago lord a day at a time, and the clothes served as a reminder of what he had once been—though some days, some *years*, he could not remember why it was that remembering what he had once been was so important.

There was a knock on his door, and he hissed in irritation because he'd nearly succeeded in numbing himself to the imprisonment. Immortality was a curse because no matter how powerful you were, there was always someone more powerful. Someone to obey. Someone who stole what was yours and left you with the dregs of what you once had. Then they took that, too, and here he was in this prison while his gut ached with need and his body missed magic like meat missed salt. Without magic, he had no savor.

The knock sounded again. He'd pissed off whoever it was because his whole prison shook with a noise that hurt his ears and his heart. Wonderful. One of the Powers had come to call upon him. He almost didn't answer—what more could they do to him than they had already done?

He stopped in the middle of the room, because, of course, there was *always* something worse they could do. It didn't do any good to speculate upon what. He said, "Come in, then."

The woman who stepped in was neat and small. She almost stirred that beast inside him. But then she spoke and the illusion was gone.

She was the spiritual archetype of the evil queen in the fairy tales, partially because she'd participated in quite a few of the actual events that had spawned the tales. She adored causing misery and pain to the short-lived humans. All those centuries of power lived in her voice, even if she liked to hold the appearance of helplessness.

"Underhill will become anything for you," she said, her lip curling as she looked around his current home, "and you chose a prison."

He straightened warily. "Yes, lady."

She shook her head. "And they want *you*?"

She didn't say who "they" were, or what they wanted him for. He didn't ask because he still had some sense of self-preservation.

She walked around the small room. "They say you have imagination."

She folded her arms as she walked, twisting her torso first so as to see the ceiling stones and then turning until she got the proper angle to see the subtle bend in the wall that made his hiding place less noticeable. She loosened the granite block, the only one without mortar. "They say you know how to hide from humans, from fae, from other creatures who might hunt you because your glamour is so very good."

He wanted to stop her, to keep her from finding his treasure. He wanted to destroy her. But they had taken away his power and he was left with nothing. But that was vanity speaking; he knew that even if he'd had his power, it would have done him no good against one of the Gray Lords.

He watched as she pulled out the block and found the cubby it hid. She took out the doll he kept there and straightened the pretty yellow skirts, her fingers lingering on the faded tearstains.

A child cries with her whole heart, keeping nothing back. A child lives in the present, and that gives her pain an endless quality. Magic-shorn as he was, he could taste the power of those tearstains from here.

She put the doll back and replaced the block thoughtfully. Then she looked at him. "They tell me you were a skilled magician, subtle and powerful. Once the flower of a powerful High Court—later the bane of it, the first dark root of destruction. Able to hide from the best trackers."

"I don't know who they are or what they say," he told her truthfully, trying to hide his temper.

She smiled. "But you don't argue with the sentiment." She walked toward him and touched his face with her left hand.

His glamour fell away, the illusion that truly represented the lord he had once been. But as his magic had twisted and fouled, so had his true form twisted and fouled over the years. He waited for her to recoil; he was not good to look upon, but she smiled. "I have a gift for you. A gift and a task."

"What task is that?" he asked warily.

"Don't worry," she said, putting her right hand on the side of his neck. "You'll enjoy the job, I promise."

And his magic came back to him, flooding his body like the heat of the dead. He screamed, dropped to the floor, and writhed as the beautiful agony enveloped him.

She bent down and whispered in his ear, "But there are rules."

"Okay," said Charles Cornick, younger son of the Marrok who ruled the werewolves in North America and also, Anna had come to believe, the rest of the world. De facto if not officially. If Bran Cornick said, "Sit up and go *there*," there was not a werewolf in the world, Alpha or not, who wouldn't obey.

Charles had inherited a lot of the dirty work that allowed his father to keep their people, their werewolves, safe. The fallout when a good man was forced to commit heinous and necessary acts was that Charles's emotions could be mysterious even to himself.

For instance, he'd just said "Okay" when Anna could tell he was anything but okay with the topic at hand. She knew that from the way her husband got up abruptly from the stool where he'd been playing and put his battered old guitar up on the wall hook. Restless, he wandered across the hardwood floor to the big window and looked out at the February snow falling down. There was a lot of it: it was winter in the mountains of Montana.

If he had been a little less self-disciplined, she was pretty sure he would have hunched his shoulders.

"You said I should look into it," Anna told him, feeling her way. She knew Charles better than anyone, and still he was sometimes impossible to read, this wonderful and complex man of hers. "So I did, starting with your brother. Samuel tells me he's been working on the problem of werewolf babies for a long time, though not quite from our angle. Children apparently were something of an obsession of his before he found Ariana again. Did you know that werewolf DNA is just like human DNA? You can't tell the difference unless the sample is taken when we are in our werewolf form—*then* it's different."

"I did, yes," said Charles, apparently happy to talk about something, anything, else. "Samuel told me when he figured it out a couple of decades ago. Not the first time having a doctor in the family has been useful. I think that a human scientist published that data last month in an obscure journal; doubtless it'll make the newspapers sooner or later."

The alternative subject allowed him to relax enough to give her a wry smile over his shoulder before looking back out at the snow. "My da was overjoyed. Because of that, there is no way to use a blood test to see if someone is a werewolf or not—unless you're testing the actual wolf, in which case the point is moot. I'm not sure he'd have ever brought us out into the open if it were so easy to identify us."

"Okay." Anna nodded. "It's a good thing. Mostly. Except that there's no way to tell if an embryo is human, genetically, or werewolf, if we want to go with a surrogate."

"A surrogate," he said.

She had hopes for the surrogate card. Charles's mother had died giving birth to him. She knew that part of his objection, maybe his whole objection to having children, was the risk to her.

"If I can't carry a baby to term because I have to change every full moon, then a surrogate is the obvious option. No one has done it before—so far as we know, anyway."

He didn't say anything, so she continued, laying out the

issues for him. "Because there's apparently no way to tell which embryo is werewolf, human, or some combination of the two, there's still a good chance of spontaneous abortion, the same problem human mates of werewolves have. And then there's the issue of what happens to a human woman who carries a werewolf baby for nine months. Will she become a werewolf? Samuel said we ought to consider a surrogate who *wants* to be a werewolf. That would eliminate the risk of catching . . . um . . . being infected . . ."

He said, very dryly, "Feeling diseased, Anna?"

No. But she wasn't going to let him distract her.

"It would eliminate problems if such a pregnancy does make her Change, if our child is a werewolf instead of human," she said with dignity. This wasn't going at all well. "We don't know if carrying a werewolf baby and giving birth would infect the mother—or if so, when. No one but your mother has ever carried a werewolf baby to term. If the surrogate wanted to Change in the first place, that would eliminate one part of that problem. The other being if the surrogate is Changed before the baby is viable."

His back was now all the way toward her. "It sounds like we are offering a bribe. Carry our baby and we'll let you Change. With the implied corollary—whatever we say or deny—that if you don't carry our baby, we won't allow you to Change. And there is also the truth that most people die during the Change, and fewer women survive than men."

"Yeah," she agreed. "It sounds ugly when you put it like that. But there are a lot of surrogate births every year—and normal pregnancy is a life-and-death risk, too. If the surrogate goes into it knowing what might happen, and she's still willing to make that deal in exchange for money and/or the chance to be Changed, I don't have a problem. It's still a risk, but it is an honest risk."

"So we can risk someone else for this, can we?" he said, the hint of a savage growl in his voice. "Because they know as much as we know about what might happen to them, though we really don't know anything."

She opened her mouth to tell him about the things in the

thick file Samuel had sent her, but she reconsidered. Maybe if she went at the problem from a different direction she'd get better results.

"Alternatively," she said, "because science is having trouble with magic, I thought maybe someone who dealt with magic would have some ideas. I called Moira—"

He turned back to her, and some chance of light brought out the bones of his face and outlined his shoulders. He was so beautiful to her. His Salish heritage gave him bronze skin and rich, almost-black hair and eyes. Hard work and running as a wolf gave him the muscles that defined the contours of his warm skin. But it was the core of integrity and . . . *Charlesness* that really made her heart beat faster, that swamped her with knee-weakening desire.

Not just lust—though who wouldn't lust after Charles? She savored the whole of him and thought again, *Who wouldn't lust after Charles?* But she was consumed with the desire to claim him, to wrap herself in his essence.

Charles allowed her to understand the line in the marriage vows about "these two shall become one flesh." That sentence had annoyed her immensely when she was nine or ten. Why should she give up who she was for some dumb boy? She'd taken her objections to her father, who had finally said, "When and if 'some dumb boy' loses his mind and agrees to marry you, then doubtless he'll also be happy to take that phrase out."

Anna had taken out the "obey" part when they married. She didn't want to lie. Listen to, yes—obey, no. She'd had enough of obeying for ten lifetimes. She had, however, left in the part about "one flesh."

With Charles she didn't lose herself, she gained Charles. They were a united front against "the slings and arrows of outrageous fortune." He was her warm, safe place in the storm of the world, and she . . . she thought that she was his home.

She wanted his children.

"Absolutely not," he said, and for a moment she thought he was reading her mind because she had lost track of the conversation. But then he said, "No witchcraft."

She wasn't stupid. He was throwing out any obstacle he could find. She would have backed off except for the deep belief, born of the mating bond they shared, that he wanted a child even more than she did.

"Don't fret," she told him. "I won't do it the way your mother did." *Unless there are no other options.* "I actually thought that Moira might have some insights for Samuel. I thought it only fair to call and warn her that I've sent him after her . . . He sounded quite *intense* about the whole thing."

He raised his head like a panicked horse. "Ah. I misunderstood. Good."

Charles liked children. She knew he liked children. Why did he panic over the thought of *their* child? She considered asking him. But she'd tried variants of that; he'd given her a series of answers that were true as far as they went. She was pretty sure that he didn't know the real answer. So it would be up to her to discover it.

Once she figured it out, she would be able to see if there was a way around it. The panic she could work around—and if he honestly didn't want children, well, she'd deal with that, too. But it was the sadness that lingered behind the panic, the sadness and longing her wolf knew was there, that made her dig in and fight. Anna style.

"Okay," she said brightly. *She who fights and runs away, lives to fight another day.* "I just thought I'd give you an update." She picked up her bundle of information and tucked it under her arm.

She walked over to the window and looked at the falling snow that had frosted the deep green trees and coated the not-so-distant mountains, making the world seem clean and new. Also cold.

"Have you decided what you're getting me for my birthday yet?" she asked.

He liked giving presents. Sometimes it was a flower he'd picked for her—other times expensive jewelry. He'd gradually learned that really expensive gifts, which he liked best, freaked her out. He now left those for important occasions.

He put his arm around her, his body relaxed against her. "Not yet. But I expect I'll figure something out."

CHARLES COULDN'T KEEP his mind on the numbers, so he closed down his computer. Money was power, and in the long run it could keep his people safer than his fangs and claws. After a hiatus, pack finances were his to protect again.

His gaze fell on the yellow sticky he'd put on the top of his monitor—Anna's birthday, her twenty-sixth. He needed to find her a present. His preference was for jewelry—which, as his da pointed out, was sort of marking his territory for the other males in the vicinity.

My mate, the ring on her finger told them. And when she ventured to wear any of the necklaces and earrings he'd gotten her, they said, *And I can provide for her better than you.* After his da made him aware of the reason for his need to bedeck Anna in jewels, he'd begun to work on presents that she did want.

Anna wanted children.

He stared at the bright-colored Post-it note.

It was perfectly reasonable that she'd want children. He understood the urgency of her drive even if she didn't. She'd been a college student when Justin, the Chicago Alpha's hit man, had taken away nearly all of her choices; she'd spent the better part of the time since then taking them back. Reclaiming her life from those who would have taken it from her entirely.

His phone rang and he picked it up absently—until he heard the voice on the other end.

"Hey, Charles," said Joseph Sani, once the best friend he had in the world. "I was thinking of you today. You and your new bride."

"Not so new," Charles said, not fighting the happiness rising up. Joseph affected everyone that way. "It's been three years—a few months more than that. How are you?"

"Three years and I haven't met her yet," Joseph said, his tone asking, *Why not?*

Years slipping away without notice, Charles thought. *And the last time I saw you, you were an old man. I don't want you to be old. It makes my heart hurt.*

"I couldn't come to your wedding," Joseph was saying, "but you didn't make mine, either. We're even."

"I didn't know about yours," Charles told him dryly.

"You didn't have an address or a telephone that I knew about," Joseph said. "You were a hard man to find. I admit you sent me an invitation to yours, but it was through *Maggie*—and I didn't get it until the day before."

Yes, he'd rather thought that Maggie wouldn't pass it on. "I'm surprised you got it before the wedding at all," he said, acknowledging his own culpability. "But we didn't send out invitations through the mail. Just called. I tried three times and got Maggie twice. The second time I just left the message."

Joseph laughed, and then coughed.

"That's quite a cough," Charles said, concerned.

"I'm fine," Joseph said lightly. "I want to meet your wife, so I can see if she's good enough for you. Why don't you bring her down?"

Charles worked the numbers in his head. He'd met Joseph when he'd been twelve or thereabouts, back shortly after World War II. Joseph was in his eighties. The last time he'd seen him face-to-face he'd been in his sixties. Twenty years, he thought in dawning horror. Had he been so much a coward?

"Charles?"

"Okay," he said decisively. "We'll come." His eyes caught on the Post-it note again, and that gave him an idea. "Are you and Hosteen still breeding horses?"

THREE DAYS LATER

Chelsea Sani parked her car, pulled off her sunglasses, and got out. She patted the oversized sign that declared that Sunshine Fun Day Care was a place where children were happy as she passed it. The fenced-off play areas on either side of the sidewalk were empty of children, but as soon as she pulled the heavy door of the day care open, the cheerful blast of kid noise brought a smile to her face.

There were day cares closer to her house, but this one was clean and organized and they kept the kids busy. With her kids, it was always best to keep them busy.

Michael saw her as she peeked into his class of fellow four-year-olds and hooted as he dropped the toy he was playing with and double-timed it to her. She scooped him up in her arms, knowing that the time was soon coming when he wouldn't let her do it anymore. She blew against his neck, and he giggled and wriggled down to run to the wall of coat hooks where his backpack was.

The teacher in charge waved at her but didn't come over to chat as she did sometimes. Her assistant helped Michael with his backpack, grinned at him, and then was distracted by a little girl in a pink dress.

Michael held Chelsea's hand and danced to music he heard in his head. "First we go to pick up Mackie and then we go home," he told her.

"That's right," she agreed as they walked down the hall. She opened the door to Mackie's classroom and found her sitting on the time-out chair with her arms folded and a familiar stubborn expression—a look that Chelsea had seen on her husband's face more than a time or two.

"Hey, pumpkin," she said, holding out her free hand to give her daughter permission to get up. "Bad day?"

Mackie considered her words without leaving the chair and then nodded solemnly. The new teacher, who was maybe twenty, hurried over, leaving the rest of the kids with her assistant.

"Sharing time didn't go well," she said, a little grimly. "We had to have a talk with Mackie about being kind to others. I'm not sure it took."

"I told you. She isn't *hozho*," said Mackie stubbornly. "It's not safe to be near someone who isn't *hozho*."

"And she is old enough to speak clearly," continued the teacher, whose name Chelsea couldn't remember.

"She *is* speaking clearly," piped up Michael, always ready to defend his sister.

"*Hozho* is a Navajo word," Chelsea explained as Mackie slid off the chair, finally, and took her mom's hand in a fierce grip. *Ally amidst enemies*, that grip said, which meant that Mackie didn't think she had done something wrong. She never looked for help from her mom when she'd misbehaved. "Their dad or grandfather teaches them a little now and then. *Hozho* is"—complicated and simple, but hard to explain—"what life should be."

"Happy," said Michael, trying to be helpful. "*Hozho* is like picnics and swing sets. Happy little trees." He twirled around in her hand without losing his hold and half danced as he chanted. "Happy little breeze."

"Navajo?" asked the teacher, sounding surprised.

"Yes." Chelsea gave the teacher a sharp smile. No one could look at Chelsea, whose ancestors had sailed on dragon-headed ships, and think that *she* was responsible for her children's warm-tinted skin and eyes dark as a stormy night. *If you make my children, make any child, feel bad for who they are, I will teach you why people fear mama grizzlies more than papa grizzlies. I will teach you that if a child parented by Martians comes into this room, they should still be safe.*

"That's so cool," said the teacher, unaware of her danger. "We're planning on studying Native Americans in a couple of weeks. Do you think their father or someone you know who is Navajo might be willing to come in and speak to the kids?"

The wind pulled out of her defend-her-children-to-the-death sails by the new teacher's enthusiasm, Chelsea silenced her inner Viking and said, "If you wait to ask him until the end of the month. His family raises horses and there's the big show coming up. The whole family will be at sixes and sevens until it's over."

A little girl caught her eye. The child was standing in the

middle of the room, oddly alone in the chaos of excitement caused by the beginning of the arrival of the parents.

After picking her kids up every day, Chelsea knew the faces of most of the children in their classes. She'd seen this one before, too. This girl and Mackie had built clay flowers together and given them to Chelsea and the other girl's mother for Christmas a couple of months ago. Both girls had been giggling like triumphant hyenas as they'd tried to explain how they made the flowers. She was named for a gemstone. Not Ruby or Diamond . . . Amethyst. That was it.

Today, though, Amethyst was watching Mackie intently, and there was no sign of the giggling child she'd been. As the teacher talked about her own childhood pony with enthusiasm, the little girl shifted her gaze from Mackie to Chelsea. Green-gray eyes met Chelsea's eyes briefly and then the girl turned away.

"I ride a little," said Chelsea, half-distracted. "But I don't usually show the horses. My husband does, and he has a couple of assistants, too."

"Cool," said the teacher. "I'll remember to ask about getting your husband to come in after the show is over." She looked at Mackie. "Bye, sweetie. We're going to build pinwheels tomorrow. I think you'll like it."

Mackie considered her solemnly, then nodded like a queen. "All right, Miss Baird. I will see you tomorrow." The teacher, it seemed, was provisionally forgiven.

Mackie was strong in her likes and dislikes. She liked Ms. Newman, who'd been her teacher last year and was Michael's this year. She did not like the principal, the janitor, or Eric, one of her much older brother Max's friends. Eric had quit coming over because Mackie had made him so uncomfortable. Eric seemed like a perfectly nice boy to Chelsea, and she had deep reservations about Ms. Newman.

Mackie tugged on her mother's hand and led the way out of the day care. While Chelsea seat-belted Michael, Mackie belted herself in. Mackie had been belting herself in ever since her hands could work the buckles.

"Independent" was an understatement, Chelsea thought

ruefully. Mackie got that from her mother, as well as the managing nature. Both served Chelsea quite well in the business sector but would probably ensure that this wouldn't be the only time the new teacher was going to have trouble with Mackie.

Speaking of which . . . "What happened?" Chelsea asked her daughter. She rubbed her temples because she was starting to get a headache. "Why did the teacher put you in timeout?"

Mackie looked at her with a contemplative expression.

To her dad, Mackie would tell the complete, honest truth if he asked. But he seldom did, being more interested in her handling of the situation rather than the particulars of the incident. Had she done the right thing? Could she have chosen a different path that would have led to a better result? Those were the things that were important to Kage.

Chelsea, on the other hand, would be given what Mackie thought her mom needed to hear. Not because Mackie was trying to avoid getting into trouble, but because, Chelsea firmly believed, Mackie made a huge effort to spare her mom any burden of pain or sorrow.

Mackie worried her mother. Both of her boys, Max and Michael, were joyous, healthy spirits. Mackie was born solemn and watchful, a hundred-year-old soul in a barely fiveyear-old body. She had moments of lightheartedness, but her usual state was wary. Kage said his daughter had the soul of a warrior.

"The girl I was supposed to share crayons with was *chindi*," said Mackie, finally, which didn't make sense. Chelsea was pretty sure, even with her mere bits and pieces of Navajo language, that *chindi* were evil spirits of the dead. "But not *chindi*," added Mackie, even more obscurely.

"You aren't supposed to say *chindi*," said Michael direly. "*Ánáli Hastiin* says bad things will happen to you."

"Okay," Chelsea said, abruptly cranky with trying to interpret what had happened at day care. Kage could talk to Mackie about it when he got home.

It was February and usually there was some rain this time

of year, but today the skies were blue and the sun beat down and made her eyes ache along with her head. Chelsea didn't have any pain reliever in the car, so she had to get home to find any relief. Any relief from anything.

"I think I'm going to have to talk to your grandfather about what he is teaching you," she said.

"Not Granddad," said Mackie. "Ánáli Hastiin."

Ánáli Hastiin meant grandfather. But they only used the Navajo term for Mackie's great-grandfather, Hosteen.

"Fine," Chelsea said. "I will have a talk with Ánáli Hastiin about what is appropriate to discuss with five-year-olds and what is not." She shut the back door of the car with a little more force than necessary and started the drive home.

"SO FAR THIS trip," said Anna with wry amusement that would carry just fine through Charles's headphones, "we've talked over current stock market trends and why they are good for us and bad for lots of other people. We've discussed the problems with using military tactics for police-type problems. We've talked about the literary license used when filming classic fantasy novels and whether the results were enjoyable or heinous. We've agreed to disagree, even though I'm right."

We have not discussed the topic that we really need to talk about, my love. My mother used to say that no one does stubborn like a Latham, and I will prove that to you. We have time.

So she brought up the other topic he hadn't been willing to cover. "Are you ready to tell me about where we're going?"

Charles smiled, just a little.

She gave a huff of amusement. "I'm just trying to decide if it's a birthday present or a job." It would be a birthday present, she was sure. Her birthday was two weeks away, but Charles was *never* playful about work assignments from his father.

"Okay," Charles told her agreeably, and she gave him a mock punch on his shoulder.

"Careful, now," he told her, waggling the wings of the airplane just a little. "We might crash if you keep hitting the pilot."

"Hmm," she said, not worried. When Charles did something, he did it well. "Where are we going? Besides Arizona." He'd already told her Arizona, sometime between the discussion about police work and the one about movies. "Arizona is a very big state."

"Scottsdale," he told her.

She frowned at him. She knew only one thing about Scottsdale. "Are we going golfing?" Her father enjoyed golfing on his infrequent vacations.

"No, we're doing the other thing Scottsdale is famous for."

"Going to a resort and hanging out with celebrities?" she said doubtfully.

"We are going to find you a horse."

"Jinx is my horse," she said immediately.

Jinx was a mutt that was, Charles had told her, probably mostly quarter horse. He'd acquired the aging gelding at an open auction, outbidding the meat buyer.

Anna had learned to ride on him.

"No," Charles said gently. "Jinx is a great babysitter, but you don't need him anymore. He's a good horse to learn on, but he is lazy. He doesn't like the long rides or being asked to speed up. You need a different horse. I have a good home in mind for him. He'll be carrying kids around very slowly: he'll be ecstatic."

"There aren't any horses that would suit me in Montana?"

He smiled. "I have an old friend who breeds Arabians. I talked to him on the phone the other day and it got me thinking about your birthday and about how it is time for you to get a different horse to ride."

Anna sat back. An Arabian. Visions of *The Black Stallion* danced across her mind's eye. She couldn't stop her happy little sigh.

"I like Jinx," she said.

"I know you do," Charles said, "and he likes you."

"He's beautiful," she said.

"He is," agreed Charles. "He'll also see you saddle up another horse with a sigh of relief and go back to sleep."

"Arabians look like carousel horses," Anna said, still feeling as though she were betraying the amiable gelding who'd taught her so much.

Charles laughed. "That's true enough. The Arabians might not suit you; they don't suit everyone. They are like cats: vain, beautiful, and intelligent. But you deal well enough with Asil, who is also vain, beautiful, and intelligent. Still, if they don't have a good match for you here, we can find a horse nearer to home that suits you."

"Okay," Anna said, but in her heart of hearts she was riding a black stallion without bridle or saddle along a beach on a deserted island, and they were galloping full speed.

Charles must have heard it in her voice because he smiled.

Then a nagging thing—that she hadn't immediately pounced on because she'd been dazzled by the horse part of what he'd said—suddenly caught her attention. "An old friend," he'd said. Charles didn't have many friends. Acquaintances, yes, but not friends—and he was very careful in what words he chose. The people he was close to were numbered on the fingers of one hand—Anna; his brother, Samuel; and his da. Probably Mercy, the coyote shapeshifter who'd been raised in his pack, would qualify. But that was it. Charles was nearly two hundred years old and he'd collected very few people to love.

"Tell me," she said, "about your old friend."

For a moment his face grew still and her stomach clenched.

"Joseph Sani is the best horseman I've ever seen or heard of," Charles said slowly. "He's a daredevil with no sense of self-preservation." Most people would not have heard the half-despairing, affectionate admiration in Charles's voice. "The more dangerous something is, the more likely he is to throw himself in the middle of it. He sees people—all the way through them—and he likes them anyway." *Cares about me* went unspoken, but Anna heard it just the same. This Joseph was a man who knew her husband and loved him.

You love him, too, Anna thought. *And I've never in three years heard you mention his name.*

She didn't say it out loud, but his eyes flicked to her and then away, so she thought he might have caught her thought through the mating bond that sometimes startled her with its usefulness. Hard to keep secrets from your mate, harder to stay angry when you can feel the other person's pain . . . and love. Their bond seemed to communicate their emotions better than words. But it sometimes slid the words in, too.

"Yes," he said. "Until I met you, he was my best friend. I haven't seen him for twenty years because the last time I was there, I suddenly realized that he was getting old. He is human, not werewolf." He stared out at the blue sky. "I didn't stay away on purpose, Anna. Not on purpose. But visiting him wasn't a . . . good thing anymore. I counted on him keeping me . . . level. What you do for me now, when Da's assignments are bad." He let out a shaky breath. "I don't say good-bye very easily, Anna. Not gracefully or prettily. Good-bye tears your heart out and leaves it a feast for carrion birds who happen by."

She put her hand on his thigh and left it there until the plane touched down.

CHELSEA'S HEADACHE REDOUBLED on the way home, and after a few sharp interchanges the children fell silent. She craved home in a way that she hadn't since she was ten years old, returning from a very long, very bad summer camp.

When she turned the car into the driveway, there was no magical surcease from pain. She got the kids out of the car and into the house. She should have . . . done something with them, but she worried that in her current state she might hurt their feelings . . . or worse.

She left them to their own devices while she stumbled through her bedroom to the bathroom beyond. If she could just get rid of this headache, she could regain her balance.

She took three painkillers when the directions told her to take two. The pills were dry and stuck in her throat; she took two more and then put her mouth to the faucet and drank water to get them down.

Too many, she thought, but her head really hurt. She felt like she should take more. Her hand went up to the medicine cabinet where there were some leftover painkillers from when she'd had a root canal done a few months earlier. She hit the glass toothbrush holder, and it fell into the sink and shattered.

She cleaned it up, but her headache made her clumsy. She sliced her finger on a shard she was throwing away. It wasn't a bad cut. She stuck the finger in her mouth and stared at herself in the mirror over her sink. She looked . . . wrong. She put her hands to her face and pulled the skin back, flattening her nose a little, but it didn't change the stranger in the mirror where she was supposed to be.

She washed her face in cold water, and that seemed to help the headache a little. Her finger had quit bleeding.

A glance at the clock showed her it was nearly time for Max to be home. More than ten years older than his half brother and sister, he had . . . what sport was it? Basketball. He had basketball practice after school.

And if he was almost home, she'd been in the bathroom an hour, left a four-year-old and a five-year-old without supervision for an hour. She hurried out and down the stairs. The sound of the TV led her to the family room, where the kids were watching a cartoon. Michael didn't look up, but Mackie gave her a wary look.

"Sorry," she told them. "I have a bad headache. Will you two be okay for a while more? I have to get dinner started."

"Okie-dokie," said Michael, without looking away from the TV.

Because he couldn't be bothered. TV was more important than his mother.

Mackie didn't say anything. Just watching her with her father's eyes and judging what she saw, always judging her and finding her lacking.

Chelsea turned and went to the kitchen. She got random things out of the refrigerator with shaking hands: carrots, celery, summer sausage, and radishes. The cutting board hadn't been put back where it belonged and she had to search for it. She found it among the pots and pans instead of in the narrow cupboard next to the stove, and by then she was in a fine rage.

Max came in the kitchen door, letting it bang carelessly against the wall. He took after her, tall and blond, rather than her first husband, who'd died in a car wreck, leaving her to raise her two-year-old son on her own. For a moment Max's presence cleared her head like a breath of fresh air.

"Hey, Mom," he said cheerily, sounding so much like his father that it sometimes made her heart ache. She loved Kage, but that didn't mean she hadn't loved Rob, too. "What's for dinner?"

He was always hungry these days. Always expecting her to feed him when he was old enough to get his own food. She clenched her fingers around the chef's knife, so cool and powerful in her hand.

"Would you do something for me?" she said through gritted teeth, unable to look away from the bright silver promise of the knife.

"Sure," Max said, snitching a carrot from the bag she'd put on the counter.

Bad manners to steal food before the cook was ready. Bad.

ANNA BLOCKED THE tires while Charles finished tying down the plane to the anchors he'd driven into the ground. The plane wasn't that small, but it was designed to fly. That meant that a strong wind would move it unless it was tied down. They'd done this enough times now that Charles didn't have to tell her what to do or how.

A battered truck charged up the dirt road in a cloud of dust and stopped next to their airplane without slowing much in between. The driver was young, Native American, and dressed in a cross between cowboy and First People: jeans, boots, cowboy hat, T-shirt, turquoise necklace, earrings. He held up his pants with a leather belt decked with silver and turquoise.

Young meant that he was not the man she and Charles were coming to see.

Charles didn't look up from his task as the stranger rounded the end of his truck and walked toward them, his steps rapid and businesslike. If this man had been a stranger, Charles would have looked up.

The expression on the approaching man's face was a bit grim, as if he was engaged in a necessary but not enjoyable task. He watched Charles until he came within easy talking distance and then glanced, almost absently, at Anna. He staggered, rocked back on his worn boot heels, and let out a gasp of air like a man hit in the stomach.

He was a werewolf, Anna divined more from his actions than from his scent, as he was downwind. A dominant werewolf, if his reaction was anything to judge by. Less-dominant wolves tended not to react so strongly to her presence.

Omega werewolves were rare as hens' teeth. Anna knew of one other Omega wolf in Europe. As far as she knew, they were it. Bran said it was because there weren't many werewolves crazy enough to attack and so Change a person who had the qualities of an Omega. Samuel, Charles's brother, called her "Valium for werewolves."

Charles, satisfied the plane would be there waiting for them when they came back, looked at the stranger and raised his eyebrows. She knew he was amused at the other man's reaction to her, but she didn't think that the stranger would notice—most people didn't. A lot of Charles's expressions were more . . . micro-expressions, especially when he was in public.

"Hosteen," Charles said, "this is my mate and wife, Anna. Anna, this is Hosteen Sani, full-blooded Navajo, Alpha of the Salt River Pack, and breeder of fine Arabian horses for the past three-quarters of a century, give or take a decade."

Sani meant that he was related to Charles's Joseph. Anna was going to sit her husband down as soon as she got him in private again and make him talk.

"Good to meet you," Anna said.

Hosteen inclined his head but didn't say anything, just

stared at her while Charles tossed their bags into the back of the truck. Her mate didn't seem to be worried about Hosteen's lack of response, no matter how awkward. He opened the passenger door in open invitation for Anna to sit in the middle.

Anna got in and watched as Hosteen walked thoughtfully around the front of the truck with no sign of the get-things-done stride he'd had before he met her. He opened the driver's-side door as Charles got in beside her, but then Hosteen stood in the shelter of the door as if he were reluctant to sit next to her.

"Navajo?" Anna asked, trying to make things easier on him with a little conversation. "I thought the Navajo in Arizona mostly live north of Flagstaff."

Hosteen narrowed his eyes until she thought she'd said something wrong. Then he muttered something in a foreign language that she didn't quite catch, nodded to himself, and hopped into the driver's seat.

He didn't say anything more until they were headed down the bumpy, unpaved road.

"Yes," he said. "Most Navajo live in the north, in the Four Corners region. There are a few Navajo here, because there is work here, but you are right, mostly it is Pima, O'odham, Maricopa, with a dash of Apache or Kwtsaan to liven the mix."

She read the atmosphere in the truck as strained, but that might only be two dominant males in a small truck. Or more of Hosteen's reaction to her. She honestly couldn't tell whether Charles liked Hosteen or not. They certainly knew each other well; otherwise two dominant wolves would never have gotten into the same vehicle together.

She decided to keep quiet and let them figure things out.

After five minutes or so of silence, Hosteen gave a jerky nod as if in answer to some question only he heard. Then he put an end to any image of the laconic Native American; an image that Charles, for instance, could have been the poster boy for.

"There is a long story to how I ended up here, away from

the lands of the Diné, the Navajo," he told her. "When I was Changed, a hundred years ago, more or less, I thought I must be a skinwalker. I had never heard of werewolves, you see, and neither had anyone I knew. You know what a skinwalker is?"

Yes, but she'd learned that it was better to plead ignorance because sometimes what she thought she knew about the supernatural world was wrong or incomplete. "A little."

"Skinwalkers are evil witches who take on the shape of animals—usually it is animals—they skin. They delight in destruction, suffering, and pain. They spread illness and evil. I thought that was probably what I was—though I didn't *feel* more evil than I had before I was attacked." He smiled at her, inviting her to enjoy the joke on the young man he had been. She thought it was more horrific than funny—too close to her own experience.

When she didn't smile back, he regarded her thoughtfully, then turned his eyes back to the rough dirt track they were following.

"I didn't skin an animal for its shape. But even an ignorant boy such as I was could see that changing into a wolf, a monstrous wolf, gave me something in common with the witch people," he said. He seemed to relax as he settled into the story, his voice drifting into a cadence that made her think that he had told this story more than once. "Those who follow the witchery way are evil, so I figured I must be, too. My parents loved me, but I was dangerous to them and to my family, so I left. This is where I ended up."

"California is where you went first," said Charles, and the way he said it made Anna think that he was encouraging the other man to tell stories. "Hosteen is a movie star, Anna."

Hosteen smiled—and it changed his whole demeanor. Anna saw that she had been wrong when she'd thought he was a little grim. There was delight and innocence in that smile.

"You'll see my face in a few movies," he conceded almost shyly. "But only if you like the old silent movies. No real parts, just Apache number two, Hopi number eight, that sort of thing. When they found out I was good with horses, I moved pretty quickly into horse wrangling. Worked on *The Son of the Sheik*."

And Anna realized that Charles had prodded Hosteen because he knew that she'd enjoy this story.

Charles kept telling her that just because a wolf was old didn't mean that he'd ever met a famous person from the past. She and her brother had spent a lot of Saturday afternoons eating popcorn and watching movies with her father. He liked either very old black-and-white movies, though usually with sound tracks, or kung fu theater.

One afternoon, her father had rented a whole bunch of Valentino films and they'd watched them, one after another. The finale had been *The Son of the Sheik*.

"Rudolph Valentino's last film?" Anna asked.

"Yes," Hosteen said. "I wrangled horses for a few of his movies. Valentino was a horseman. He was famous, but he didn't mind stopping to talk to the Indian who was handling the horses. I liked him."

Hosteen had answered her question, but he kept talking. Either he sensed her continued interest, or he liked to tell stories. Maybe a bit of both.

"They brought in a small herd of Arabian horses for the movie. Rented them from Kellogg, the guy who invented cornflakes." Hosteen laughed to himself as if something about the deal amused him. "Anyway, they brought in a number of Arabians—prettiest horses I'd ever seen. Valentino liked this big gray the best. But Valentino was too valuable and Jadaan, he could be unpredictable. The producers were worried Valentino would get tossed, so he mostly rode other horses for the film. Valentino was furious and insulted." He pursed his lips. "They were idiots, those producers; Valentino could ride."

Hosteen fell silent, and Anna tried to think of a question to get him going again. Before she did, he said, "That Jadaan. He had terrible front legs. But he was as good as Valentino himself at striking a pose. Cameras loved him."

They bounced on over the rutted dirt road.

"They brought in a stunt double to do the dangerous stuff," Hosteen said after a while. "Carl Schmidt, he was a good horseman. Later, he changed his name to Raswan and wrote a lot of books about the Arabian. A good horseman, but a ridiculous person—like that singer who changed his name to a symbol instead of a word. Carl Raswan." He snorted. "Raswan was a horse. Still, Carl was a good rider, did most of the shots with Jadaan and anything that required more speed than a canter. No one on the set, except perhaps Valentino because he was a nice guy, would have missed Carl if he'd broken his fool neck, so he was a good choice for a stunt double."

He laughed a little to himself again. "Now you see. Just ask me a question, any question, and it all comes back to horses. But you asked what I am doing here. I met Fowler and Annie McCormick, big money people, in California when they brought a couple of their horses to me to train. They had a place out here and were willing to guarantee me some work. I wanted to breed Arabians, and so I moved here. Bought a hundred acres next to their ranch and started my own operation." He glanced at Charles. "About the time we first met, eh? Just before the Second World War."

"How's Joseph?" Charles asked, in an apparent non sequitur, and Hosteen sobered.

"Still human, and will apparently die that way. Eighty-two, stubborn as a mule." Hosteen looked at Anna and then the road. "I wish you would change his mind about that."

"I've offered before," Charles said.

"Yes," said Hosteen. "I know." He kept his eyes straight ahead. "Maybe you could do more than offer."

The atmosphere in the truck chilled to below zero, even though, Anna was pretty sure, it was close to seventy degrees outside.

"No," said Charles.

"You go see him," said Hosteen with a sudden growl in his voice. "You go see my son, that bright spirit who is trapped in a body that is dying around him. You see him—and then you look me in the eye and tell me that again."

"Hosteen," said Charles carefully. "If Joseph had at any

time in the last twenty years changed his stance on the matter, he would have asked you or me. I will not, and you will not, force him. A wolf who Changes an unwilling victim must himself die, by the Marrok's word."

"Your father would not kill you for it," said Hosteen, but the fire of his anger was gone. "He would kill me—have you kill me—but you he would spare."

"If you think that," Charles said, "then you don't know my father very well."

CHELSEA TRIED NOT to look at the blood when she called her husband.

"Kage, Kage, Kage," she chanted in time with the rings.

"This is Kage Sani," his voice said in her ear, and she could have cried. "I can't answer right now. Please leave a message and I'll get back to you as soon as possible."

"The children," she said. "Kage. The children." She wanted to tell him about the children, but she screamed instead. When she caught her breath, and silence fell, she could only whisper, as if another loud noise might wake something evil. Again. "I was so angry, Kage. This knife. Blood. Hurry. Hurry. Hurry. Blood." When Kage's phone beeped to signal that it had stopped recording, she was still chanting into the mouthpiece.

2

The road switched from dirt to blacktop without warning. Anna couldn't figure out why there was a paved driveway in the middle of nowhere, but then the house suddenly appeared.

The lines of the house blended into the surrounding sand and various desert plants and backed into a small rocky formation too big to be a swell and not big enough to be a hill. Between shape and sandy color, the house seemed to grow out of the desert.

Charles, seeing her surprise, said, "The Badlands of the Dakotas are like this, too. Things are hidden pretty easily out here. There's a lot more relief to this land than your eyes tell you—that's one of the reasons the landing strip is so far away. That's where they had to go to find flat land without bringing in bulldozers."

"Lots of flat spaces in Scottsdale," Hosteen said. "But out where we are the landscape is more interesting."

Hosteen pulled the truck into an empty slot in a line of covered parking spots designed to protect vehicles from the desert sun. A woman came out the nearest door to the house.

She could have been anywhere between sixty and eighty, and she carried a broom in one hand.

"Welcome to our home, Anna Cornick," she said graciously. Her voice sounded like it should have belonged to a fifteen-year-old—soft and birdlike, without the quiver that age can bring. She pulled herself up straighter, raised her chin, and looked Charles in the eye, searching for something that she evidently found. Her voice grew husky. "Welcome home, Charles."

Anna couldn't help but glance at her husband, but if there had been an expression on his face, she was too late to see it.

Briskly the old woman said, "Hosteen, take those filthy boots off before you come into the house. Please." The "please" was an afterthought.

"Yes, Maggie," said the Alpha, his voice soft. "And who is it that gave you a broom?"

She raised an eyebrow at him and thumped her broom on the stone of the walk in front of the door. "No one gives me a broom in my own house, Papa. I *took* it from Ernestine. She is a good girl, but she doesn't get the edges where the floor meets the wall. Usually it doesn't matter, but today we have visitors." She looked at Charles and her face softened.

"It's good to see you again," she said, then ducked her eyes away almost shyly. "Joseph apologized for missing your arrival, but he takes an early lunch and then naps in the afternoon on most days. He would love to see you later."

Charles took the old woman's hand in his and kissed it with a gallantry Anna had seldom seen him use with anyone but her. "I look forward to speaking with him."

Joseph, Anna thought, was not the only one Charles felt affection for in this household. She was a little wary of this turn of events. Clearly she should have pinned her husband down and forced him to disgorge more information.

Warned by Maggie's scolding of Hosteen, Anna pulled off her shoes and put them on a mat near the door while Charles pulled off his boots.

"You two haven't been playing in the horse manure all morning," said Maggie. "You can leave your shoes on."

"It is no matter," Charles disagreed. "Shoes come off and on without trouble."

The interior of the house was full of white plaster walls and high, dark-beamed ceilings with big fans designed to help keep the air moving. Though it was February, outside it had been pleasantly warm—especially compared to Montana, which was still in the middle of a deep freeze. Being a werewolf, Anna didn't mind the cold, but she didn't mind being out of it, either.

The floors were hardwood. Anna knew oak floors, and these had a different grain, with the worn patina that comes with decades of foot traffic and the gleam that comes with cleaning. She couldn't help but check, but she didn't see any hint of dirt against the wall.

"Maggie and Joseph and I are the only ones living here right now," Hosteen said. "Ernestine, Maggie's great-niece, comes in on the weekdays to clean and cook for us. Ernestine's sister Libby does the same on the weekends."

"Which is a waste of money," muttered Maggie. "I am perfectly capable of caring for two old men for two days a week." It had the sound of an old argument—all the heat gone.

"Kage knows you're here," Maggie told Charles. "He called from the barn to say he'd be up in an hour or so. They are shorthanded because one of the stable girls quit last week and my son is picky about the people who touch his horses. We'll feed you a late lunch and then he'll take you out to look at horses." To Hosteen she said, "Why don't you wash up, Papa, and I will show Charles and his wife to their room?"

She didn't wait for Hosteen to say anything but turned and, summoning her guests with a gesture, led them through a large living room designed for entertaining. Anna recognized a pack house when she saw one. This room, with its multiple levels and conversational groupings, could hold twenty or thirty people, a whole pack, and still feel comfortable rather than crowded.

"That old wolf," said Maggie as soon as they were alone,

"is pleased as punch and flattered that you are shopping among our horses. Don't let him make you think otherwise."

Anna heard a huff of laughter coming from behind them somewhere. Maggie might think that they were out of earshot, but Hosteen's ears were a lot better than an old human woman's.

As she led them to a set of mission-style stairs, Maggie stopped and gave Anna a good once-over. Then she said something in a foreign tongue, almost staccato in its rapid use of short syllables, but the consonants were too soft. Pizzicato.

Charles narrowed his eyes. Whatever Maggie said, he didn't like it. "Yes, she is." His voice was soft. "It is impolite to talk in a language that your guest doesn't understand. And even more impolite when you are talking about her."

Maggie looked at Anna. "I told him you are beautiful and young." She made it sound like a bad thing. "He will run over the top of you and never notice."

"He is beautiful, too, don't you think?" said Anna, big-eyed. She was unable to resist the urge to respond to the disapproval in Maggie's face. She was tired of being misjudged, and more tired of people who thought that Charles would marry a doormat. She put all the earnest sweetness in her voice that she could manage. "And he makes me so happy. I would never dream of disagreeing with him. Why would I? He is strong and so much wiser than I am." She reached out and ran her hand down his arm.

She was afraid she'd overdone the last sentence, but evidently not. Maggie frowned at her, missing the fleeting grin Charles gave Anna's meek little speech of adoration. The old woman turned to Charles and let loose a flood of words.

"You know that she is Omega," Charles said finally, when she had run to a stop. "Hosteen knows; Joseph knows, and it is something that he would tell you."

She said something more, and her frown turned into a scowl.

Charles laughed, the quiet happy sound he made only when he was among friends. "Omegas aren't submissive,"

Charles told Maggie. "Some of them even have a sense of humor and tease well-meaning people who worry about them when they are hanging around big bad wolves. Don't worry, she argues with me a lot. She even holds her own with my father."

"With Bran?" Maggie looked at Anna as if she'd grown horns.

Anna said modestly, "My father-in-law could use more people who will argue with him. It would do him good."

"I misjudged you," Maggie said. "I'm sorry."

She didn't sound sorry. Charles might think that Maggie had been worried about Anna, but Anna knew better. She knew jealousy when she saw it.

She knew a number of very old people who looked as though they were twenty-five instead of two hundred or however old they were. One of the lessons that had been drummed into her was that no matter what a person looked like on the outside, who they were on the inside could be quite different. Lurking inside Maggie was a woman who still had feelings for Charles.

"People tend to look at me and think I'm a lightweight," Anna acknowledged. "You aren't the first." She understood loving Charles, and since it was she who had him, she could make an effort to be gracious. "But you were worried, which was kind of you. It's all good."

She and the old woman exchanged equally insincere smiles. Anna had the distinct urge to roll her eyes and stick out her tongue.

Maggie ushered them into a suite of rooms with a sitting room, bedroom, and bathroom. "When you've freshened up, come down to the kitchen—you still remember where it is, Charles?"

"I do," he said. "And we will."

Anna used the bathroom, washed her face, and went back to the bedroom. Maggie was gone. Charles headed to the bathroom, presumably to do the same.

When he reemerged, she said as neutrally as she could, "Maggie likes you."

He understood what she meant.

"We dated once upon a time," he told her somberly. "Though 'dating' is too formal a word for it. Flirting is better, but too lighthearted. We didn't suit in the end—and she and Joseph were married. 1962, I think. Though I could be off a year either way."

Anna heard it all in his voice. The sorrow of friends who grew old and died when you did not. She hadn't experienced it herself yet, but she knew that the probability was that she would live to see her father and brother grow old and die while she still looked like a woman in her twenties. Charles, she knew from talking to his father, had made a point of never getting involved with human women. Until Anna, he'd pretty much steered clear of any kind of real relationship with any woman. Maybe, she thought, Maggie had been one of the reasons why.

CHARLES KNEW THE way around the house—it hadn't changed much in the last twenty years. A few new pieces of art, different throw rugs, but mostly it was the same.

Despite what she'd said, Maggie met them at the top of the stairs. He could see her younger self superimposed in his imagination. Her fiery eyes were the same, and the straight spine that made people give way when she passed by.

Charles let the women lead the way down to the main rooms of the house, Maggie first, her back stiff and hostile. He was not unaware that Maggie had decided she didn't like his Anna, a very unusual reaction to his Omega wife. Since it didn't bother Anna, he let it ride. She had taught him that despite Brother Wolf's determination to protect her from anything that would cause her discomfort, *Anna* was perfectly capable of protecting herself.

Brother Wolf had bowed to Charles's belief that to protect Anna from everything would cause her more harm than good. It didn't stop his wolf from being very unhappy with Maggie.

"I can't find my phone," said a half-familiar man's voice

in the kitchen. "I had it this morning. Have you seen it any-where?"

"I don't keep track of your toys, Kage," said Hosteen. "But if I did, I might have seen it in the laundry room this morning."

"I found it and put it on the phone table in the hallway," Maggie announced as she entered the kitchen. "I thought you'd look there first. I'll get it."

Charles put a hand on Anna's shoulder and walked into the capacious kitchen beside her.

Seeing a forty-year-old version of Joseph made Charles feel like a horse had kicked him in the stomach. The last time he'd seen Kage, he'd been a young man and the resemblance had not been so obvious. His attention on his mother, Kage grinned Joseph's grin. "Thanks, Mom. I knew I could count on you. Now, as Chelsea likes to tell me, if I could only find my common sense, I'd be all set."

Maggie shook her head. "If you had any common sense, you'd have left this place to be a banker like your older brother. And you'd have been as unhappy for the rest of your life as he would have been if he'd stayed here. Be content that your phone is found." She patted his shoulder and left by another doorway, presumably to get the phone.

"You find your rooms all right?" Hosteen asked them.

"Beautiful," Anna answered for them.

Kage looked toward his visitors for the first time and stiffened warily. "Charles. Hosteen told me your names, of course, but I didn't make the connection to you. I don't think I ever heard Dad use your last name." Charles wasn't aware of anything he'd done to make Kage wary of him, but people often feared him. He had a sudden flash, an image of Kage as a young boy peering at him from around his mother's back as Maggie sobbed, accusing him of . . .

He didn't remember anymore.

Maggie was another reason that it had been such a long time since he'd last visited. It had not been her fault nor his, but his presence brought tension between Joseph and his wife. Oddly, the trouble wasn't from Joseph, whom she had picked second. It was Maggie who couldn't let the past rest. She had rejected Charles, but she was still possessive of him.

Anna smiled. "Lots of people named Charles around," she said.

"Kage," Charles said. "This is my wife, Anna. Anna, meet Joseph and Maggie's son, Hashké Gaajii Sani. He goes by Kage."

Anna smiled and moved forward, holding out her hand. "Pleased to meet you," she said with the warmth that was so much a part of her. "I understand that you're going to show us some horses."

"That's the plan," Kage agreed, his face relaxing under Anna's influence. "I just need to grab my phone—"

Maggie slid back into the kitchen from another direction and handed him an old-fashioned, battered flip phone.

"Thanks, Mom. Do you prefer mares or geldings?" Still paying attention to Anna, Kage flipped the phone open and glanced at the screen.

"I don't know," Anna said. "Mostly I've ridden geldings."

"I understand you have a couple of weeks," Kage said. "The big show starts in three days and I'll have to spend most of my time there. I have a few horses in mind. I'll show some to you today and then I'll take you out on a trail ride tomorrow."

Anna shot Charles a startled look, probably at the "couple of weeks." But Charles needed time with Joseph. If the tension between Maggie and Anna got worse instead of better, they could find a hotel. Besides, choosing a horse was serious business; it was important to take the time to do it right.

"I've missed some calls from my wife," said Kage with a frown. "She gets nervous when I don't pick up. She rides pretty good for a city girl, but she knows that horses are big and things happen. I'll give her a call and then we'll go down to the barn."

He hit a button and waited as the phone on the other end rang directly to a message. "This is Chelsea Sani. Please leave a—" He cut the message off and gave his phone an irritated look. "I have four new messages since this morning. I'm sorry, I'd better listen to them."

"No trouble," said Anna. "We have a couple of weeks. A few minutes isn't going to make any difference." She hesitated. "You should know this already, since Hosteen is a werewolf. But if you listen to the messages here, Charles and I will be able to hear them, too. So if they are private . . ."

He grinned at her. "No worries. We have a teenager and two younger children. There is no way either of us would leave private messages on our phones."

"Kage, damn it. Pick up." The voice was the same woman as before. But instead of being professional and cool it was irritated and . . . Charles didn't know this woman well enough to do anything more than pick up some intense emotion.

The second message was more troubling. "Kage. You have to come home, please. I don't feel well. Headache from hell." She gave a laugh that was more like a sob. "And there's a knife. It's shiny and sharp."

Kage was frowning when he called up the third message. This time his wife was whispering. "Something is wrong with me. Can you help me? Help them?"

The fourth message had them all bolting out of the house, all besides Maggie. She was left behind by an aging body that didn't allow her to run with the rest of them. Brother Wolf grieved, but Charles was more worried about Kage's children.

"I'll drive," Hosteen said shortly.

There wasn't room for the four of them in the cab, and with a glance at Anna, Charles changed his direction and leapt into the truck bed. Anna landed gracefully beside him an instant later. Hosteen put the truck in reverse and burned rubber backing out of the parking area. He stopped and threw open the passenger door for Kage, who, human slow, was the last one to the truck.

It took them under ten minutes before Hosteen stopped in front of a pale stucco two-story house. A maroon BMW was parked in the driveway. As they all bailed out of the truck, Hosteen held one hand up. He looked at Charles and gestured toward the back of the house.

Brother Wolf hesitated but decided it was okay to take

orders in this situation because it was Hosteen's family in trouble. Hosteen would know best how to organize the hunt.

Anna, ignored by Hosteen, had chosen to come with Charles, and she had no more trouble than he did hopping to the top of the eight-foot cement wall that separated the public front yard from the private back. She waited on top of the wall with him while he took a quick but comprehensive impression of the situation.

The backyard was not extensive, consisting of a couple of small areas of arid-appropriate plants and a tile walk that surrounded a moderately large swimming pool. There was no sign, to any of his senses, that anyone was nearby. The nearest people were several kids playing in another swimming pool several yards to the west.

What he did notice was that someone was playing cartoons overly loudly in one of the upper-floor rooms in Kage's house. He stood up and walked along the wall until he was fairly near the house. Someone had been safety conscious enough that there were no windows within easy human reach from the wall. But Charles had never been merely human.

He jumped toward the house, catching himself on the sill of the window and doing a chin-up so he could see inside the room the sound was coming from.

The bed was against the wall the window was on. He could see the backs of the heads of three people who were seated on the floor using the bed as a support. Two of them were young children cuddling as closely to the third as they could. One of the littler bodies still vibrated with the results of a bout of tears.

"Dad is coming, right?" asked one of the youngsters.

"Dad is coming," said the one who was adult size. His voice was more hopeful than definite to Charles's ears.

"Is she still out there?" asked the other child. "She quit knocking on the door."

"I don't know," the older one told them. "It'll be okay. You just stay in here with me, Michael. I'll keep you safe."

Charles dropped soundlessly to the ground and then went back up to the wall, where Anna waited. "The kids are up in that room. I don't think any of them are hurt, but one of us needs to get in there and make sure they stay okay. You're less scary than I am."

He kept his voice quiet, well below the range anyone in a room with the TV blaring could hear.

"Do I go through the window, or open it?" she asked.

The window was modern. He'd have had to break the latches or go through the glass. Anna had another option.

"Why don't you see if you can get the kids to open the window?" he said. "Save breaking the glass as a last resort. I'll see you safely inside. Then I'll go down and into the house from the back."

He jumped back to the ground and stepped out of immediate view. Anna's leap to the window was graceful, and she chinned herself up just as he had. But she kept going until her upper body was clearly visible, and then she knocked on the window.

"Excuse me?" she said.

He had to imagine the first reactions of a group of kids who had locked themselves in a bedroom to hide from . . . from something. He hoped that the older boy wasn't armed. But the room was decorated for a young girl, not a teenage boy. If the boy had a gun, it was probably in another room.

"Who are you?" asked the older boy's voice hostilely.

"I'm a werewolf like your great-grandfather," Anna said, sounding cheerful and utterly normal, as though she hung by her arms outside windows all the time. "My husband and I were at the ranch when your father got a call that sounded . . . odd. He and your great-grandfather are coming in the front door. My husband is going in downstairs from the back, but he thought you might like an ally in here. I'm tougher than I look. But you'll have to open the window first."

There was a clicking noise as the latch released and the window opened inward. People did things for Anna. It wasn't like when his father ordered people, and they just did what he told them before they had a chance to think about it. People *wanted* to do what Anna asked them to do.

"Thanks," she said, swinging her legs up and over. "I was

beginning to feel a little silly. My name is Anna, but I don't know yours. Charles and I rode in the back of the truck on the way over here and I'd just met Kage, your dad, so there was no chance to get the details. You'll have to introduce yourselves."

She chattered at them as if everything were normal. Charles tuned her out and dropped to a crouch as he approached a pair of French doors he intended to use to gain entry. Inside the house, Kage called his wife's name, but there was no response.

Charles eased the nearest door open and slid inside without wasting time.

ANNA PUT HER back against the wall, just to the side of the door, between the human children and whatever made this room smell of fear. They were as safe as she could make them at the moment.

"Okay," she said. "Michael, Mackie, and Max. Tell me what happened. All we got was a few odd phone messages from your mom." She kept an ear out. Kage was calling for his wife in a soft voice that she didn't think the kids could hear. His wife was not answering.

"I got home from practice," Max said. "Mom was in the kitchen and the kids were in the family room watching TV. She seemed a little off, but I figured she was tired—she works hard." He glanced down at Michael, who had decided that the exploits of a lost little fish on the TV were more interesting than the woman who had climbed in the window.

Reassured that he wasn't going to freak out his brother, Max continued in a calm voice designed, Anna thought, not to attract Michael's attention. "She was chopping carrots on the cutting board and I reached out to take one." He hesitated, looking at the youngest boy again. His sister patted his hand.

"Chindi," she said in a very small voice.

Max nodded back at her. *"Chindi."*

"What's *chindi*?" Anna asked.

"Wild spirits, evil things, wrong things." Max gave a nervous shrug. "It's a Navajo word."

"I'm not supposed to say it," Mackie said in a small voice. "I said it, and then Mom got angry. It's all my fault."

Max huffed. "That's just superstition. It's not real."

"Ánáli Hastiin says not to say that word or the evil spirits will come get you," she told him.

"Ánáli Hastiin . . ." Max swallowed whatever he'd been going to say. "Look, pipsqueak, you didn't cause any of this. Kage—your dad says that a lot of what Ánáli Hastiin says is make-believe. You can ask your dad, but he'll tell you the same thing. You did not cause anything bad to happen."

"You promise?" she asked distrustfully.

"Promise." He raised his hand, trapped his pinkie with his thumb, and left three fingers straight in the air. Anna thought it might be the Boy Scout sign, but it could be the sign of the flying spaghetti monster for all she knew. She'd never been a Boy Scout or any other kind of scout.

Mackie evidently knew what it was because she heaved a big sigh. "Okay."

"So your mother was chopping carrots?" Anna asked Max.

"And I reached out to grab a carrot out of the bag and she—" He swallowed and looked very young. He mimed someone holding a knife and bringing it down with speed and force. "She meant to get me, but she changed the direction at the last moment. She"—he made sure Michael was still occupied, but he spelled it out anyway in the manner of older brothers with too-young-to-be-literate siblings the world over—"s-t-a-b-b-e-d her own hand and screamed at me to get the kids and lock us in a room and not open the door until Dad came home. Not to let her in under any circumstance."

He looked at Anna with great big puppy eyes and whispered, "She was bl— b-l-e-e-d-i-n-g. Her hand was stuck to the cutting board and I just left her there. Left my stupid cell phone in my backpack with my laptop and there aren't any landlines in the house except in the kitchen. I couldn't call anyone for help." He looked away and blinked hard as his nose reddened.

"How long ago?" Anna asked, to give him something else to think about.

"Fu—" He quit speaking, wiped his face on his shoulder, and looked down at his sister. "Freaking feels like hours, but this movie is about an hour and a half long and we are only about two-thirds of the way through."

"The *chindi* who looks like my mother knocked on the door," Mackie told Anna solemnly from the shelter of her brother's arms. "She screamed at Max to open the door. And then she cried. And she tried to be nice—and Max turned up the movie so we didn't listen."

Chindi indeed, thought Anna. It was as good an explanation of the events Max had described as any. She was a musician, not a psychologist, but she was pretty sure that mothers didn't go crazy and stab themselves out of the blue.

"Max is very brave," Anna said.

Mackie nodded. "Yes. Yes, he is. When I grow up I am going marry someone like Max and make him hunt *chindi* with me." Her belief that saying that word would cause problems was allayed, evidently, by Max's honest scout sign, because she said it without hesitation.

Max gave a choked laugh. "You do that, squirt." To Anna he said, "Someone let her watch *Supernatural* and now all she wants is to go out and fight evil magic."

Mackie frowned at Anna. "You said you are a werewolf. Like Ánáli Hastiin."

Anna nodded. "If that is your great-grandfather Hosteen, then, yes, I am."

"You can come hunt *chindi* with me," she said with authority. "Max can't because he'll be an old man by then. Michael is too loud and clumsy. He gets scared and he will make mistakes. The bad things will eat him. And then what will I do without a little brother?"

"I don't know," Anna said slowly, as if she were considering the invitation. "My husband doesn't like to be left behind. But if we take him with us, the bad things will all run away and it won't be any fun."

"Your husband is a werewolf, too?"

"Yes."

"If he scares away our prey, he'll have to stay home," Mackie said.

Anna grinned. "Right. He'd ruin our fun. But maybe it would make him feel bad not to be included."

"If he cries, you just have to explain it to him." Mackie said wisely.

"Mackie," said Max reprovingly.

"Max," she said in the same tone.

"Both of you shut up," Michael told them, still staring at the TV. "The shark is coming."

Anna heard feet traveling upstairs in a rush and, just outside the door, Kage whispered his wife's name and tried to open the door.

All of the kids came to alert (shark or not), but no one said anything. Maybe the whisper freaked them out—urgent and stressed. They'd already had one parent scare the bejeebers out of them today; apparently they weren't trusting the other one not to do the same.

"No," said Anna, unlocking the door, but staying ready just in case whatever had affected their mother was catching. "Not Chelsea. But all the kids are here with me and they are okay."

When the door opened, Kage brushed past her to drag the kids into his arms, then pulled back to check each one to make sure they were okay. There was no difference in his urgency when he grabbed Max, whose coloring suggested that he was a stepson and not Kage's own child. Hosteen watched them, his face cool, his attention focused outside the room. He knew that this was not over.

"There's a fog of fae magic on the first floor of the house," he told her. "Where's Charles?"

"Downstairs," she told him. "He sent me up here to make sure nothing happened to the kids."

"There's a pool of blood just outside the door," he whispered, stepping aside so Anna could see it while the kids were preoccupied. "Chelsea's blood. I can't scent her through the stink of fae magic that is coating this house."

"Charles will find her," she said. "He—" She couldn't complete the thought as her wolf surged forward with the urgency of the message Charles sent her through their mating bond. She knew that her usually brown eyes were pale, icy blue when she looked at Kage and said, "Choose."

Kage looked up from his children. "What?"

She gave him the only words she had. "Choose. Choose now."

CHARLES INHALED BLOOD and magic. Blood he'd been half expecting, at least until he found the children all apparently safe. So the blood was not surprising. It was the fae magic he felt carelessly caressing his skin that changed the game.

There weren't supposed to be fae out and about. They had, with great fanfare, locked themselves away on their reservations, declaring themselves free of the laws of the United States. For the last several months they'd made no appearances outside the reservations that he was aware of.

But he knew magic, knew the feel of fae magic. Brother Wolf rose and abruptly colors dimmed a little, and the shadows revealed their secrets to his eyes.

There was no one in the room he entered. It was a typical family room with a big-screen TV on one wall and bookshelves filled with trophies, photos, books, and games on the other. But the blood was fresh and nearby. He angled his head to see if he could pick up where the scent was coming from without making a large movement that would be more likely to attract attention if something was waiting for him.

Upstairs the TV was still blaring. If there weren't so much noise, his ears would be of more use. But the noise would make it more difficult for any enemy to hear him, too.

The floor creaked somewhere in the house. He thought it was to his left, but it was difficult to tell. He moved quickly to that side of the room, staying low, pausing next to the wall. He didn't trust walls—he'd broken through a few too many in search of prey himself. Sheetrock and two-by-fours didn't stop a werewolf, and a lot of fae were just as strong. But as a visual barrier, a wall worked okay.

He put his head cautiously around the corner. It was the laundry room. There was blood all over the floor here, some of it splattered, and then drag marks that slid around the appliances and out of sight. He paced cautiously forward, past the washer and dryer—and found himself staring into the eyes of a wild-eyed woman who was crouched in the bathroom hidden on the far side of the room. He froze where he was.

She was sitting on the floor, legs crisscrossed, with a damn big knife in her hand, and that hand was shaking as though she had palsy. The motion could have been caused by blood loss, shock, or both.

Long bloody slices, some deep and others shallow, decorated both of her arms and her legs through what had been a very nice pair of slacks. She bared her teeth at him.

"The children must bleed," she gritted out, and the knife shook in her right hand. "Bleed out the bad—" She dug the knife into her thigh and he winced. But she didn't push it deep, just slid it along her leg parallel to the other wounds that bled there. "Something in my head wants me to kill my children," she said in a hurried whisper, very different from the voice she'd started speaking with. "You have to stop me."

Brother Wolf snarled at this enemy he could not fight with tooth or claw; fae magic surrounded the woman. Charles needed to figure out how to help Kage's wife. The magic clinging to her meant he was better equipped to do it than anyone else here. Not that it wouldn't have been helpful to have a witch or someone else to back him up—his da would have been useful.

"Chelsea Sani," he said with a push of his own magic, trying to give her something to cling to.

It wasn't enough.

She paused and rocked forward, falling until she was on her hands and knees, and she started to crawl. Not toward him, he didn't think. He wasn't her target.

"There are bad children here . . . little boys who steal

food, little girls who don't play well with others, little boys who . . ." She dropped all the way to the ground then and writhed as she groaned.

"*Chelsea,*" Brother Wolf demanded, pulling on his pack, on his da's power. Icy with the cold of winter, the power came to his asking and hit the woman with his call.

She stopped making noise, stopped moving except for the heaving of her ribs. Then she rolled her head until she could see him. She met his eyes, opened her mouth, and shut it. She sliced open her hand, leaving the knife in the wound. "Blood makes it easier to fight. Who are you?"

"I'm Charles. A friend of Joseph's. Can you tell me what happened?"

He edged closer, calling upon gifts given to him by both his da's and his mother's blood. His skin warmed and tingled uncomfortably, but he could see the spells that encompassed her. Where fresh blood flowed onto the steel of the knife, the magic was drawn more tightly, never quite touching the cold iron. It pooled uneasily around the open wound, thinning around the rest of her body.

Witchborn, he thought, for her blood to have that kind of power. But not trained, or she'd have broken the geas.

She gasped, and a tremor shook her body as though she were freezing to death. "Werewolf. Charles? You are Joseph's werewolf?" she half asked, half demanded.

"Yes. I'm here to help you."

She laughed breathlessly. "Too late for that. Too late for me. I sent them to a room with a door they could lock against me, but they need to get out. *You* go take my babies away somewhere safe." There was a command in her voice that he found himself shaking off with an effort. Brother Wolf found *that* very interesting.

"They are safe," he assured her.

Her eyes widened, fae magic flared, and he realized, too late, he'd made a mistake.

Some of the fae are quick, and whatever magic had done to her, it gave her better-than-human speed. But Charles had been edging toward her, and that gave Brother Wolf time to move even faster and catch the hand that held the knife just before she shoved it up under her jaw.

It had been a two-part geas, then, forcing her to kill her children, and when that was done—or if that wasn't possible—to kill herself. Her death would make it more difficult to find the fae who had done this to her.

She fought him, fought to control the knife with strength that was not her own, and he finally drove the blade into the floor, through the linoleum tile and into the wooden floorboards below. He sank it deep so he didn't have to break her arm.

Sobbing, she tried to pull the knife out, but suddenly, between one breath and the next, the scent of fae disappeared and she collapsed, her breathing thready.

"Safe?" Chelsea Sani whispered. "Tell me again."

"They are safe," he told her, and her body went limp, as if she'd used the last of her strength. And he knew what had broken the geas.

He took a good look at the blood on the floor, the way her last wound was not bleeding as it should. Her heartbeat was irregular. She'd lost too much blood—and was losing more through every cut she'd made in her own body in the effort to keep her kids safe from the magic driving her. It had been an incredible feat of willpower and quick thinking for a woman who was only human. But it had come at a cost.

She was dying. Even if they were at a hospital, it would be unlikely that they could save her in this condition. She was dying, and that satisfied the geas.

We could Change her, Brother Wolf told Charles. *She knows how to fight.*

It would be skirting his da's law. He didn't have his da's approval, but desperate times were a gray area, judged case by case. As his da's right-hand man, he had more leeway than other wolves. He'd had nothing to do with the incident that brought Chelsea to this end; his actions would be seen as impartial. Brother Wolf's clear judgment would weigh in his da's sight, if not anyone else's. All he needed was her consent.

Charles knelt beside her. "You are dying. Do you understand? I can Change you if you wish it."

She said something, too faint for even his ears to hear.

It must be now, said Brother Wolf. *And we must be in wolf skin.*

She couldn't give permission, but there was someone here who could. Brother Wolf's shape came over him—the wolf had dictated the change. It was so simple, the change from man to wolf, this close to the full moon's call when he had not walked on four feet for days. As the wolf shape became his, Charles sent his will to his mate.

Tell him to choose for his wife. Do I let her die—or do I Change her?

CHAPTER

3

The hallway behind Brother Wolf filled with people, some he knew, some he didn't. But Anna was there; she was the one he needed.

He stared at her, and she turned to the human who was the dying woman's mate.

"Your wife is dying," she said. "Charles says she is strong-willed and courageous. He is willing to Change her—but she is not in any condition to make that choice."

"No," snarled Hosteen suddenly. "Not her. It's not sup-posed to be her. If Charles won't Change my son, he doesn't get to decide to Change *her* instead. Not her."

Quiet filled the hallway as Brother Wolf met Hosteen's eyes and drove the Alpha to his knees. It was not for that one to tell him what he could or could not do.

"Grandfather?" asked Kage from behind Brother Wolf. That one had bolted for his mate as soon as he'd seen her, ignoring Brother Wolf's presence.

"He's fine," said Anna grimly. "He just forgot who is in charge here, and Brother Wolf—Charles reminded him. You have a decision to make, Kage, or it will soon be made for you. Would your wife accept life as one of us? You know how we are regarded by the rest of the human race."

Charles had some other things for Anna to tell Kage.

She listened and then said, "Charles wants me to point out that if she dies, we are unlikely to find out why a fae bewitched her into attacking her children. It will be difficult to find that fae and bring them to justice, leaving Chelsea's attacker free to continue killing. Your wife fought the magic, saved the children at great expense. Is that enough for her? Or would she want to stop her attacker?"

The woman was fading, and Brother Wolf shot an impatient look at Anna.

"No," said Hosteen, without getting up or raising his eyes. "Not Chelsea."

"Why not?" asked Kage. "Because she isn't the wife you wanted for me? Because she doesn't like you? That is your fault, old man."

"She is witchborn," hissed Hosteen. "Witches are evil."

I am witchborn, Brother Wolf told Anna.

She nodded at him but didn't interrupt. She was better with people than he or Charles. If she thought that fact would not be useful now, she was probably right.

"Her grandmother was a witch," Joseph's son said in a reasonably snarly voice for a human. "*Chelsea* has no power at all."

That was not true. Without power she would never have defeated the geas laid upon her. In fact, the closer to death she drew, the more easily Brother Wolf could smell witch. That probably meant she had some way to hide it, and now that she lay dying her magic was dying with her.

He glanced at the children, at the small girl who looked at him with a steady gaze though her hand was grasping the bottom of the shirt of the young man standing next to her. That one smelled like something more. Witch.

Hosteen hissed between his teeth, unsatisfied. "Witchborn should not be werewolf."

"Mama?" said a small voice. Brother Wolf saw the youngest child grab hold of the teenage boy's hand. "Mama?"

"It'll be okay, Michael," said Kage, his face ravaged as he knelt beside his wife. "Yes, Charles, yes. Change her. Grandfather, take the children away, please."

"I'm not leaving," said Hosteen.

"Stay," said Anna decisively. "I'll take the children. Hosteen should stay."

He'll make her angry, Anna's voice rang in his head. *Make her fight to live.* "I have to leave because I'm not useful at this stage."

She gathered the children despite the young man's protests and left the room. That was right, Brother Wolf thought. The Omega soothed. Surviving the Change was a battlefield, and this woman who lay at his feet needed to remember how to fight.

He waited until Anna left the room.

"What do—" began the woman's mate. He might have been talking to Hosteen or to Charles. It didn't matter to Brother Wolf.

He sank his teeth into her thigh, tasting old blood and, faintly, detergent from her clothes. He shook his head to tear flesh and let his saliva flow into the damaged tissue. He had not Changed many people—his job was to kill. More often than he'd like, it was to kill in the most gruesome manner possible to discourage others from following the choices that had led to his victims' deaths. This was better.

Inexperienced or not, he knew how it worked, had stood witness to hundreds of Changes and nearly that many deaths in the days that followed. He knew what not to do. He didn't bite her near her head or heart. She needed both to function for the Change to take place. The thigh was meaty with lots of little blood vessels to take his magic and spread it through her body.

Her mate cried out and would have tried to interfere, but Hosteen, who had Changed a lot more people than Charles had, stopped him with an arm around his shoulders. He dragged his grandson away from Brother Wolf and his charge, out of the bathroom and into the laundry room where they could watch from a distance.

"If you want this," Hosteen said heavily, "and if you don't want to join her in death or Change, then leave the wolf to his work. He won't allow your interference, not now. She won't hurt long, one way or another."

Brother Wolf did not like Hosteen—though he knew that Charles did. They did not always share the same opinions, even though they shared their existence. Though what Hosteen told the woman's mate was not meant to be comforting, it was truthful.

Brother Wolf released her leg and considered. She needed to be dying from a werewolf bite—not blood loss. His next bite was to her soft belly. He let himself taste the sweetness of her flesh, let the flavor of it stimulate his saliva glands— and then he did something he'd seen his father do once.

He slashed his own leg and bled into the wound, letting the pack magic seep in, binding them together: temporary pack. It was an awkward feeling; he wanted to make her his. His to protect, to lead, to live with: to make her family. But Charles did not want to lead a pack. Brother Wolf rejoiced in the understanding that they belonged to the Marrok and felt no need to rule his own pack. It was not his place to bring a wolf into the Marrok's pack. So he let this magic lie uneasily and temporarily between them.

Then he reached with the extra senses that were his because he was the Marrok's son, and therefore witchborn as his father was witchborn, and found the connection created by his blood and hers. He asked the dying woman, *What do you live for?*

Kage was fighting his grandfather now, fighting to stop what he'd begun without really understanding what it meant to be Changed. Had he thought it would be without pain or cost?

Mine, the dying woman said.

His ears flattened in pleasure because he heard more than words. She meant those she considered hers. Her children, her mate—*hers*. Here was a woman who would be dominant. Maybe more dominant than Hosteen. And wouldn't that get in the old wolf's craw?

Will you fight for them? he asked her, inviting her to hear her husband's angry voice.

Yes. Not a simple answer but a warrior's battle cry.

While her response was still vibrating through him, he bit the calf of the leg he had not already bitten, letting his teeth slice through flesh and scrape bone.

Then fight! he roared at her with so much more power than sound could have conveyed—sending energy down the temporary bond he'd made between them, energy that grabbed her and held her to her dying flesh and *made* her live.

Only once had he seen his father force the Change on someone this way. Charles had been, perhaps, the only one who could fully appreciate what the Marrok had done. He'd waited until later, until they were alone in his father's library, to ask why that one and not others.

"He is needed," his father said. "He was willing and he will make a fine wolf. But mostly he is needed—we have so few submissive wolves. He will stabilize his brother's pack, stabilize his brother, too, and that will save dozens of wolves." He'd frowned at the book he had been reading, then set it aside. "It is not such a gift to be a werewolf. I had it forced upon me, and I was angry about that for a long time. I would not do that to another person. If they don't want life badly enough to fight for it, who am I to argue? Life is hard; dying is easier and kinder. But Neal is willing, and he was very near to making it on his own. I just gave him a boost." He sighed. "It was probably still the wrong thing to do."

So every October, when people who wanted to be wolves died under the Marrok's fangs when they failed to survive the Change, only Charles and Brother Wolf knew how deeply and why his father grieved.

When they had to carry out the more horrible task of killing those who Changed but could not control their wolf, Charles understood that his father was wise. If a person could not fight through the Change on their own, what chance did they have to control their wolf nature? Neal had managed, but it had not been easy for him.

This woman was hampered, not by her nature but by the

blood she had shed to protect her children. Brother Wolf knew that she would be a fine werewolf, so Charles used what his father had showed him and pushed her through the Change.

He bit her again—an arm this time, while her mate clung to his grandfather and wept. Hosteen watched Brother Wolf over Kage's shoulder with rage hidden in his eyes. He dropped his gaze after a moment because Brother Wolf was the dominant wolf in this room.

"WHAT HAPPENED?" ASKED Max, still angry that he'd been ordered away.

Anna had hauled the kids all the way out of the house and up the street toward where Max told her there was a park. Changing someone wasn't painless and generally involved screaming and other scary noises that no kid needed to hear their mother make. Max had been especially angry when she'd made him leave the house.

"Fae magic," Anna said; she'd gleaned a little from Brother Wolf.

"What does that mean?" muttered Max, kicking a rock off the sidewalk. He caught his wandering brother by the hand and tugged him out of the road. "No, Michael, you walk next to us. Stay on the sidewalk, no matter how cool some rock might be."

"Wasn't a rock," said Michael with dignity. "It was a penny."

"Sorry, buddy, you need to stay with us." Max let out his breath. "So. Let's assume 'fae magic' doesn't mean anything to me; what does it mean to you?"

"Charles says that someone, some fae someone, put a magical compulsion on your mother."

"When did he tell you?" Max asked sharply. "Mackie, put that down, you don't know where it's been. Tell me, Anna, did you know that when you came in through the window? Because it takes a werewolf fifteen minutes to half an hour to change to a wolf. And he was a wolf when we went downstairs."

"He is my mate," Anna told him, patient with his sharpness. His blistering anger was caused by worry and frustration that he couldn't protect his mom. "We can communicate without talking."

"Telepathy?" Max's voice was scathing.

"Look," she huffed in exasperation. "Werewolf. Me. Magic darn near strong enough to make your mother try to kill you—and you are balking at telepathy. Charles is my mate, and that means we share a spiritual bond. Far as I've been able to find out, that bond works a little differently for everyone. Charles and I can find each other in the middle of an Atlantic hurricane—and we can communicate some things."

"Men," said Mackie smugly, reacting to Anna's tone rather than the content of their conversation. "Can't live with them, can't live without them."

"Shut your piehole, punk kid," Max said, thumping her on the head with the palm of his hand.

"I'm telling Mama you said 'Shut your piehole,'" Michael said. "'Shut your piehole' is a bad word."

"'Shut your piehole' is three words, Michael," said Mackie.

Undaunted, Michael said, "I'm telling Mama you used three bad words."

"You do that, kid," Max told him, sounding subdued. "I hope you do that." He glanced at Anna and said, "So tell me about this fae magic that made my mother try to kill us. I thought the fae were all locked up."

Anna snorted. "They locked themselves up. I don't know who got your mom or why; maybe she can help with that when she—"

"Don't you mean if she—" He didn't complete the sentence.

"It could go wrong," she admitted. "Lots of people don't make it. But your mother has courage and willpower. She fought to keep you safe. Apparently she could stave off the compulsion by hurting herself; that's why she was so cut up, why she stabbed herself before telling you to take the kids away."

"But she made it," Max said. "Why didn't they just call the ambulance? Why Change her?"

"She saved you," agreed Anna. "But it took us too long to get here. By the time Charles found her, she was dying from blood loss."

He swallowed.

"Mom is dying?" asked Mackie.

Darn it, thought Anna. *Forgot the little ones were listening in.*

"I thought she was turning into a werewolf like Ánáli Hastiin," Mackie said. "Dying is like Mrs. Glover. Dying is gone forever." Her voice rose and wobbled.

Her little brother picked up on it and started to cry. "Mrs. Glover was nice. I loved Mrs. Glover. She gave me candy."

Max looked overwhelmed.

Anna gathered herself together and said, "I don't know who Mrs. Glover is, but your mother is strong. Brother Wolf told me so, and he never lies."

"Who is Brother Wolf?" asked Max.

She hadn't meant to bring Brother Wolf out in the open. His presence confused people who had been werewolves for centuries.

"He's the big wolf," said Mackie. "The one who made Ánáli Hastiin listen."

Anna tilted her head at the little girl who smelled like witch—witchborn and observant, too.

"That was Charles, Anna's husband," said Max.

"You are both right," she said. "That was Charles and Brother Wolf."

"You call your husband Brother Wolf when he is in his wolf shape?"

Anna decided that a technical discussion would lower the emotional distress and possibly give the kids some useful information. Charles wouldn't mind; Brother Wolf wasn't a secret.

"No," she said. "I call Charles Charles. And I call Brother Wolf Brother Wolf. It has nothing to do with the shape they wear, or that they share the same body."

"I'm lost in an episode of *Doctor Who*," said Max without even a hint of humor. "Explain that to me."

"Werewolves," Anna told him, "have two natures. The human part and the wolf part. But the wolf isn't like a real wolf—it's a lot more angry than that." How did you tell a kid his mom was going to be a monster? Maybe she should have thought this through better.

"Like the Incredible Hulk," Mackie said thoughtfully. "Nice Mommy and Werewolf Mommy. We're not supposed to bother Ánáli Hastiin when he's grumpy."

Anna looked at her for a moment. "Exactly. Most werewolves learn to control the wolf, the Hulk part, in a year or two."

"Does Great-Grandfather have a Brother Wolf?" asked Michael.

"I don't know," Anna told him. "Most werewolves don't actually think of themselves as two people, not like my husband does. But he was born a werewolf and it made him strange in a lot of ways. To him, his wolf is a separate being who lives with him inside his body."

"I thought werewolves weren't genetic," said Max. "Kage isn't a werewolf and neither is Joseph, even though Joseph's father is."

Anna nodded. "You are right. Except in Charles's case. His mother was Flathead, one of the Salish tribes, a wisewoman with magic of her own. Werewolf women can't have babies, but she did anyway." *As I will.* "She died when Charles was born."

"I could be a werewolf puppy," said Michael thoughtfully. "Then no one could steal my toys."

"That happened a long time ago," said Mackie impatiently. "Don't be a baby. Mrs. Glover made Joshua give you back your robot and say 'I'm sorry.'"

Michael's bottom lip stuck out. "I liked Mrs. Glover." Tears gathered.

"Mrs. Glover was *my* teacher," Mackie said. "She liked me better than she liked you."

"Shut up, you freaks," snapped Max. "Shut up."

"'Shut up' is a bad word," said Michael, incipient tears interrupted by the chance to point out his older brother's fault.

"Just shut up anyway."

Anna touched his arm. "Who is Mrs. Glover?"

"My teacher," wailed Mackie. "She died and never came back."

"She did too like me," said Michael, crying in earnest.

"And now Mommy is dying," Mackie said. "Everyone is dying."

"Stop it," said Max tightly. "Just stop."

"Your teacher where?" Anna asked. Mackie might be old enough to go to elementary school—but Michael wasn't.

"Preschool/day care," said Max. "They both go. Different classes. Mackie is five, but she was born after the September deadline, so she'll go into kindergarten next year."

"So your mom leaves work, picks up the kids, and then goes home, right?" Anna said.

"That's right," Max said. "I get home an hour or so after they do. Hey, Mackie, was Mom okay when she picked you guys up at the day care?"

Mackie had been bickering with Michael, but Max's question made her fall silent.

"Mackie?"

"Mackie was in the time-out chair," said Michael. "Her teacher was mad at her, but Mommy wasn't."

"Yes, she was," said Mackie in a small voice. "She didn't sound like it when she talked to Miss Baird, but when Mommy was talking to me in the car, she got mad. She didn't talk to me at all, and then she sent us to watch TV."

"That's unusual?" Anna asked.

Max nodded. "Mom doesn't do the silent treatment, not ever. My grandmother—her mom—abused it. Mom swore she'd never do that to us. She yells."

"Once she threw dishes at Daddy," Michael said. "But she hit the floor instead of him. Then he laughed and cleaned up the glass. I didn't touch the glass."

"She wasn't trying to hit him, just make a point," said Max. "But yeah, Mom is loud. She doesn't do the silent treatment, and she doesn't like the kids to watch TV by themselves."

"Half hour a day," said Mackie. "Michael gets a show and I get a show, unless we're at Granddad's. There's the park."

"And Mom or Kage or I watch those shows with them," Max said. "She'd never just send them in on their own." He glanced at Anna and gave her a half smile. "Especially not after Grandma let them watch *Supernatural*; Michael had nightmares. She says she can't control what they watch at their granddad's house, but she can make sure they're not watching grown-up shows at home."

The park was small and carefully tended without a single bit of plant life. It was beautiful anyway. There were two fountains on either side of a play area that was covered with a giant roof held over the playground equipment on painted steel poles. It was pleasantly warm right now, but Anna expected that anything left out in the sun in high summer would be hot enough to burn skin.

A comfortable number of children were playing on the equipment, with a few adults sitting on the ubiquitous benches set around playgrounds to encourage parents to watch over their children. One woman talked with extreme animation into her cell phone while a man of approximately the same age was deeply engrossed in a book.

Michael and Mackie bolted for the play fort as soon as their feet hit the sand of the playground at the edge of the sidewalk. Evidently that was where walking with grown-ups was no longer necessary.

"Tell me about your mother," Anna said. "Where does she work?"

"She's a trainer like Kage," he said with a wry smile. "But instead of training horses, she trains people to sell things. She's very good at it. She's part owner in a company that sells that training to other companies. And because she really *is* very good at selling things, lots of companies hire her company.

"People like her," he said. They'd stopped on the edge of the sidewalk, right where Mackie and Michael had taken off. But now Max walked with quick determination toward an empty bench. "She says everyone likes her because she's good at selling herself, too."

He swallowed and said without humor, "Except for Hosteen. Kage says that if she really *were* selling herself, she'd have the sheiks at her feet with piles of money. Then she says, 'There's that one who came to buy a filly from you. He'd have bought me, too.' And then Kage says . . ." He looked at Anna. "It's not going to be like that anymore. You can't bring people back from the dead—they come back different."

Anna pursed her lips and then nodded. "Life changes people more than death does, in my experience. Ten years from now you wouldn't see her the same way you do now, any more than you see her the same way you did when you were Michael's age."

Max's face flushed. They'd reached the bench, but he didn't sit down. "You don't have to patronize me. I understand you're a million years old like Kage's grandfather and that means you know *so* much more than I do. But this is different from being a child looking at a parent. I've seen Hosteen when he isn't playing human, and I don't want to look in my mother's eyes and know she's thinking how good my liver would taste."

"I'll be twenty-six on my next birthday," Anna said mildly. "That gives me ten years on you. Take it from me, *anyone* who lives with you is going to occasionally wonder how your liver might taste, and not because they are hungry. It comes with being a teenager—you inspire violence in the hearts of those who love you. It mostly goes away when you hit twenty."

He laughed reluctantly.

Seriously she said, "Your mother's basic nature won't change. She is quick thinking and fierce. She will probably still throw dishes at Kage and hit the floor with them to make a point. She'll have to learn to pull her throws, though, or she'll leave marks on the floor. She loves you, and respected you enough to know that you were capable of protecting those two kids until Kage could get home to help you. None of that will be different."

He dropped down on the bench.

"This would never have happened if she hadn't married Kage," he said bleakly. "Our lives were normal until she met him."

"It's a little too early to look for causes," she told him, deciding to respond to the logic of his statement instead of the emotion.

She sat down beside him and looked at the fountain instead of at him. "It might have been an attack aimed at your great-grandfather and his pack. Or maybe your mother was in the wrong place at the wrong time. Although I admit when someone connected with werewolves is attacked by supernatural means, my first thought is that it has something to do with the supernatural elements in the victim's life. What do you know about Hosteen's pack? Have they done anything recently that might attract the attention of the fae?"

"I don't know anything about the werewolves," Max said. "Hosteen Sani hates my mother. He did not attend the wedding. He hates her because she . . . because we're white and Kage divorced his proper wife and married my mother. He doesn't take it out on the munchkins—but he and I don't have anything to say to each other."

"I can't address how Hosteen feels about the color of your skin or his son's previous marriage. I don't know him that well," Anna told him. "But I can tell you that today, the thing that bothered him about her is that she's witchborn."

In the house, steeped in the magic of the fae, she hadn't been able to smell it as well. But out in the open air, sitting next to him, she could smell the scent of witch faintly. She didn't smell magic as well as Charles, but witches had a distinctive odor, a sweet, almost-floral tang that emanated from their skin.

He snorted. "She isn't a witch. It's just a story that my grandmother liked to tell, my mother's mother. She ran away from home when she was a kid. She never did tell anyone where she came from. She made up a story about a wicked witch for my mother so that my mother never went looking for them."

"Nope," Anna said. "Sorry to blow your worldview, but you can't afford to be ignorant on this issue. There are witches, good and bad witches. There isn't much worse than a bad witch. If her mother was a wicked witch, your grandmother was smart and lucky. I can smell it, a little, on you. I expect that Hosteen can smell it, too."

She contemplated that a moment. Being married to Charles had given her impetus to read up on the native peoples. "Hosteen is Navajo. The Navajo have a healthy fear of witches and their ilk. My understanding is that there have been, and still are, some very evil Navajo witches. Maybe Hosteen doesn't like it that your mother isn't Native American—I don't know him well enough to tell—but it was the witch blood he was objecting to when Charles offered to Change your mother."

Anna met Max's eyes. "The Navajo and Hopi, of almost all of the Native American cultures, have preserved their identity the best. They walk close to the earth and remember what our modern society likes to forget: that normal humans are at a grave disadvantage when they run into the nastier things that live hidden in this world. Hosteen was taught as a child that anyone who dabbles in magic is evil. It is hard to put aside such teachings, no matter how old you get, especially when you have real evidence that they are mostly true."

"I'm a witch?" he asked, sounding more intrigued than alarmed. Which just meant that he really didn't know anything about witches. Anna hoped he never had to learn.

Anna shrugged. "I can only tell you what I smell. But witch blood doesn't always mean you can work magic. My understanding is that the power doesn't beget power—two witches can have ten children and none of them have power, only to have it show up generations later. The men in the family are usually a lot weaker than the women."

"Could a fae know that Mom's descended from witches? Could that be why someone tried to kill us?"

"I'm not an expert in the fae," Anna said wryly. "All I know is that some of them are freaking scarily powerful and some of them—well, not so much. Guess which ones are the most likely to be horrible."

"Yeah," Max said. "It's easier to be horrible if you can squash everyone who tries to stop you."

They sat in silence for a little while.

"How long before we can go home?" asked Max.

"I don't know," she said. "Someone will come for us, or Charles will let me know. It might be a few minutes or a couple of hours. Magic is unpredictable. No news is good news, though."

He nodded. "Okay. So Mom was fine this morning. She worked in her office today, ate lunch there. I know because she took her lunch with her this morning. She drives directly from her work to the day care. And the spell— Do you say 'spell'?"

"Works for me," Anna admitted.

"So the spell hit her sometime after she left home this morning."

"Michael and Mackie disagree about how she felt about finding out that Mackie had gotten into trouble," she said. "Is he good at reading people?"

"He is observant," Max agreed. "And Mackie was feeling guilty. But if Mackie thought she was mad at her later, she was probably right."

"So if she wasn't upset at Mackie when she picked her up in the classroom, but that changed in the car . . ." Anna stopped and shook her head. "I don't know enough about the fae to even hazard a guess. Maybe the spell was laid on her a year ago and a day because she cut off someone in traffic."

"We're just speculating," Max said after a minute. "It doesn't matter if we're wrong or right. So let's say it happened on the drive home from the day care."

"How far away is the day care?"

"About three miles. Maybe four."

Anna focused on the children playing some sort of tag

that was growing to include most of the kids who were past the toddler stage. Something was nagging at her.

"Mrs. Glover," Anna said.

"What?"

"Tell me about Mrs. Glover. Something evidently happened to her."

"She was Mackie's teacher at the day care. She killed herself a couple of weeks ago. It was bad, really gruesome. She lived in a house with one of those two-story entryways. She hanged herself from the banister of the upper floor. Apparently someone forgot to close the door when the police got there and photos hit the Internet." He scuffed his foot. "People who work with kids need to think about the kids before they do something like that."

It was probably not connected. People committed suicide all the time. Still.

"Did she leave a suicide note?"

He shook his head. "No note. The police looked pretty closely at her husband the first couple of days. Maybe they still are. But I heard he was across the country giving a lecture to a room of engineers when she died." He paused. "I saw her the day before she died because Mom sent me to pick up the kids. She was smiling and cheerful, just like always. She told me that Mackie needed to bring an old shirt for a painting smock for a class project they were supposed to start the next day."

Anna thought about it. People did commit suicide in all sorts of ways. Hanging didn't seem like an impulsive thing, like shooting yourself with a gun. Hanging would take more time, and it would give someone a fair chance to reconsider. Find a rope. Figure out somewhere to hang yourself. Climb over the banister and hope that you don't slip. If you fall before you've tied yourself properly, you might just hit the floor below and break a leg or something.

"Anything else unusual happen at the day care lately?" she asked. Mackie swarmed up the rope net, then paused and climbed back down so she could help Michael up. "I'm talking about disappearances, deaths, anything like that."

"Not that I know of," Max said. Then he called out, "McKenzie Veronica Sani, don't you try climbing up there on the outside. Whatever you do, Michael will do. You'll both break your necks."

Like Mrs. Glover.

"There was that boy," he said. "In Mackie's class. He died in a car accident last month. He and his two brothers and his mom were hit by a semi when his mom crossed into the oncoming traffic. There was a rainstorm that day. Mom says Scottsdale drivers can't drive in the rain."

Anna's phone rang, and she answered it.

"Might be useful if you came back," Charles said. "Kage is helping his wife to clean up a bit and then we're all going to be staying at Hosteen's place for a while." He hung up without saying anything more—a sign that all was not going well.

"You heard that?" Anna asked Max.

He shook his head. She was getting too used to being surrounded by werewolves.

"Charles said gather the kids and head back," she told him. "Your mom is over the first hurdle. We're all going back to Hosteen's ranch."

He closed his eyes briefly and heaved a sigh of relief.

"I'll gather the rug rats," he said, standing up. "Why are we all going to the ranch?"

"Because a new wolf needs help controlling herself," Anna told him. "A more dominant werewolf can help her keep her impulses in line until she can do it herself. You might be staying there for a few months—at least your mom might be staying there for a while. Also, I expect, they want to keep an eye on all of you until they figure out if there is likely to be another attack on you and your mom."

"Great," Max muttered. "Mom will be ecstatic. She and Ánáli Hastiin are the best of friends." He got up, took a step toward the play fort, and then said, "Mom's going to be okay?"

She wouldn't lie to him. "I don't know. This means that she made the Change. But she's still got to prove that she isn't a risk to anyone, that she has the willpower to control the wolf."

He gave Anna a half-worried smile. "Kage says my mother has more willpower than Mahatma Gandhi. He's not usually happy about it, but I'm thinking it might mean that she'll be all right."

Anna smiled. "Go get the kids."

THEY GOT BACK to the house and Charles, on his own two feet, was standing outside with a clearly fuming Hosteen. The latter noticed the kids and altered his body language to neutral. She could still smell his ire, but the kids were human and they would see only what he wanted them to.

"Is Chelsea okay?" she asked Charles.

He nodded, though the grave expression on his face wasn't reassuring. Either he was worried about Chelsea still, or he was unhappy with Hosteen.

Hosteen looked at Mackie and Michael and schooled his voice into something gentle. "You are all coming to my house for a little bit, until we find out what happened to your mom."

"It is *chindi*, Ánáli Hastiin," said Mackie, and Hosteen winced.

"There are some words that should not be said," he told her.

"Don't start that," said Max loudly. "She said it today and she thinks that's what caused Mom to go nuts. So don't start with that."

Hosteen's eyes flashed yellow, and he showed his teeth. "Careful, boy," he said.

"Stop," Charles told him. "Now is not the time. Listen to his words, old man, and let the rest go."

Hosteen shot Charles a look that raised the hair on the back of Anna's neck.

Charles looked at Mackie. "Your Ánáli Hastiin is right. It is not wise to speak the name of evil where it might hear you.

But you didn't call evil spirits to your mother. They don't listen to children."

Charles was intimidating at the best of times. Mackie stepped behind Max and peered out at him warily. "You are Brother Wolf?" she asked.

He shook his head. "Brother Wolf is sleeping. I am Anna's husband, Charles."

"The *chindi* are afraid of you," she told him. "Anna says."

"Is that what Anna said?" he asked. Anna could tell that he was smiling, though his lips never moved. "Then it must be so."

"You can't come hunt *ch*—" Mackie stopped and glanced at Hosteen. "You can't hunt evil things with Anna and me. You'll take away all of our fun."

"You are planning on hunting down the bad guys?" Charles asked.

"When I am grown-up," Mackie confirmed.

He nodded. "All right, I'll stay home. But only if you agree to wait until you are at least your brother's age"—he tipped his head at Max—"before you go looking for trouble. Otherwise your Ánáli Hastiin will follow you to protect you. The evil things are even more afraid of him than they are of me."

She slid around Max and caught up Hosteen's hand. "Okay. I don't want to hunt bad things today, anyway."

"Let's go pack," Hosteen said to her. "You and I and Michael, hmm?"

"Yes," she said. "Max is coming, too."

It wasn't quite a question.

"Max is coming, too," Hosteen agreed, without looking away from his granddaughter. "And so are your mom and dad."

"So Max should come with us to pack," she said with more authority.

"I can pack on my own, squirt," Max told her.

"So can I," she told him as she followed Hosteen and Michael into the house. "I am just helping Michael."

"I don't need help," Anna could hear Michael complain.

Max let the door close behind them, took a deep breath, and then headed in.

"I wonder what made her say *chindi* before her mother got angry," said Charles thoughtfully.

CHAPTER

4

Anna drove with Charles and Max in the truck. Charles rode in the middle, which wasn't comfortable for him; his long legs didn't fit easily anywhere. But better, she thought, than forcing poor Max to squish between virtual strangers. Charles could have driven, of course, but he had just shaken his head when she'd suggested it. At a guess, Changing Chelsea had left him pretty raw. He wouldn't say it, though, in front of Max.

Hosteen had packed the two youngest children, Kage, and Chelsea, pale but freshly showered, in the BMW. Anna followed them through the streets of Scottsdale.

"Mom looked okay," said Max, not looking at Charles.

"It varies from person to person," Anna said. "But I suspect she's got about two hours before she sleeps like the dead for a good long while. She'll wake up for a couple of hours and sleep the rest of the day for two or three days. Then she should be mostly back to normal."

Charles grunted assent, and that unfriendly sound shut Max down completely. Rather than start more awkwardness, Anna chose to keep quiet, and they drove to the ranch in silence.

Maggie was waiting for them at the door with a tiny woman who was more or less Anna's age. She had Navajo features and skin tone but honey-blond hair. Maggie followed Hosteen and Kage into the house, but the other woman waited for them.

"Ernestine," said Max with relief and uncomplicated affection. He trotted over to her and gave her a hug.

"How's the hoops?" she asked, returning the hug.

"Okay," he said. "Is there food?"

"Isn't there always?" she said. "Go on into the kitchen and help yourself."

After he'd retreated, she greeted Anna and Charles. "How are you? You must be the Cornicks. Charles, I doubt you remember me, but I met you once when I was about Mackie's age. I'm Maggie's great-niece Ernestine. I'm usually only here from six to four every day, but today I'll be here all day, all night, and all tomorrow. They've called me in as the heavy reinforcements." She grinned and opened her arms to showcase all hundred pounds of her. Then she stepped forward, and from the high ground of two steps up she leaned forward and kissed Charles on the cheek.

"Chelsea is my friend," she said when she was done. Her cheeks were a little red, but she spoke with dignity. "Hosteen would have let her die, so I know who to thank."

Charles didn't say anything, so Anna smiled. "Always glad to be of service."

THEY RETREATED TO their room. Charles heaved a sigh of relief as soon as the door closed behind them.

"Tough day at the office, sweetheart?" Anna asked.

"Better than it could have been," he told her. "Nobody died. Any day with no deaths is a good day. I need to call Da and let him know what's happened."

When Anna came back from the bathroom, where she'd scrubbed off some blood she hadn't realized she was wearing, he'd already put his phone away.

"That was a short call," she said.

"He didn't answer," Charles told her. "So I left a message for him to call me back. If you're done, I'm going to shower."

He had more blood on him than she did. Not on his clothes, which had returned clean, as usual, when he'd changed back. And he'd washed his hands and face at Kage's house. But there were rusty stains just under his collar.

"That would be good," she said, and he smiled at her.

He came out fifteen minutes later, freshly shaved with his hair damp. He didn't have a great deal of facial hair, but enough that he shaved every day. His eyes looked tired, but he'd lost that grim edge.

"I wonder," he said, "if Joseph is around."

They tracked down Ernestine in the kitchen. She glanced at the clock. "He's usually awake by now. He's still got the same suite as he was in the last time you were here. Do you remember how to get there?" She shook her head. "Don't know what's going to become of this family once he's gone. He's the glue holding everyone together. Kage and Hosteen have always paced around each other like a pair of game-cocks, but since Kage and Chelsea got married, the feathers fly a lot more often."

Beside Anna, Charles went still.

"Gone?" asked Anna tentatively. "Is he sick?"

"Dying," said Ernestine surprised, then a little horrified. "I thought you knew. I thought that's why you came. I'm so sorry. He was diagnosed with lung cancer about five years ago. He fought it off with chemo for a while, but it came back with a vengeance a few months ago."

Charles didn't say anything, just turned and headed back through the kitchen door.

THE HOUSE SMELLED of wolf and sage, but as they proceeded, the smells became more astringent. Disinfectants. Medicines. And beneath it all the scent of illness and dying. Charles's face didn't change, but his hand tightened on hers.

He knocked lightly on a door.

"Come in, come in," said a shaky voice.

This suite was bigger than the one she shared with Charles, a full apartment within the house. The first room was a sitting room decorated in a sleekly modern Asian style—simple furniture built of glass and steel and dark wood. Here as throughout the house, the floor was a dark wood, but instead of throw rugs and the occasional Persian rug, there was a huge handwoven wool rug in a traditional Navajo pattern.

The walls were painted a slate gray that matched the shade in the rug too well for accident. On the wall opposite the door was a large framed black-and-white photograph of a young man on a bucking horse.

The horse was a dark dappled gray and all four of his feet were off the ground, back feet headed left and front feet right. The hooves were a little ragged, and no horse that was in Charles's barn ever was that ungroomed. But on this horse, all the ragged hair was appropriate and oddly beautiful: he wasn't a pampered pet, he was something wild. There was joy and power and grace in the thousand-pound animal as he was caught floating in the air.

On his back was a young man, a sweat-stained cowboy hat on his head and a foot-long black braid floating in the wind. His boot-clad feet were just ahead of the cinch that held the saddle on the horse, heels down. One hand was up in the air and the other gripped a thick rope that connected his hand to the bosal on the horse's nose. The hat shadowed his eyes, but his grin was fierce and as wild as the horse he rode.

On the bottom right corner of the photo, someone had written "July 24, 1949." The rider wasn't Kage, obviously, but the resemblance was marked.

Charles had gone ahead while she paused to look at the photo, and she jogged through the rest of the room and caught up to him as he went through the next doorway.

The bedroom had been decorated with the same serene feel as the sitting room, but all that peace couldn't compete with the hospital bed that squatted in the middle of the room. Various medical devices stacked around the bed wheezed and beeped and flashed lights, presumably doing their jobs.

A skeletally thin man lay in the center of the bed, his head raised so he could see intruders as they came in. His hair was iron gray, worn as Charles sometimes did, in two neat braids that lay over his shoulders. His face was layered in wrinkles, like a shar-pei, features obscured beneath the straps that held his oxygen tubes below his nose.

"Joseph," said Charles softly.

The man in the bed moved his head and his eyes opened. For a moment he blinked foggily, as though he'd been lost in dreams, and then his gaze sharpened. "Charles."

The voice was so quiet Anna didn't know if a human would have heard it. "I should have told you, I know. But I didn't want to make you come if you didn't want to. Or I didn't want the only reason you came to be because I was dying. Pride, you know."

He spoke in rapid groups of words with pauses between to breathe. Charles didn't say anything, but fathomless sorrow gathered in his eyes. Anna knew that Joseph really was his friend because he saw it, too.

The old man smiled. "I intended to be one of those sweet old people, you know the kind, who do exactly what they're told and eventually they lie down and die when it's convenient for everyone."

"I remember," said Charles, and his face softened into a reluctant smile. "As I recall, it was when you were getting on that rank stallion at the Half Moon on a dare. I told you that I'd feel bad burying you the next morning."

"I rode that horse," Joseph said.

"And herded cattle with him the next week," Charles said. "It was still a stupid thing to do."

Joseph started to speak, but he had to stop and breathe for a minute. Then he said, "Too much pride and stubbornness, you said."

"More than once," agreed Charles.

"You'll be"—Joseph grinned—"happy. I'm proud and

stubborn, as always. Won't go to the hospital as Maggie
wishes—too many evil spirits from all the dead people. I will
die here and haunt this house until the old man lets Maggie
burn the place down."

He coughed lightly. "In the old days they'd have kissed
my cheek and then left me in the desert to die. Then my
family would hire some Hopi or white man too stupid to
know the dangers of handling the dead to go deal with the
body. Now we're caught between modern ways and the old.
If I die here, only fire will keep my evil ghost from making
everyone miserable, and they are too rational to do that." He
laughed, a sound that tried hard to be a cackle, but he didn't
have the air to make that much noise.

Charles rocked back on his heels. "I could take you out
to the desert, Joseph, but I don't know about the kiss."

Joseph laughed again. Then he started coughing and suddenly all sorts of equipment squealed and beeped. Charles
gave the machines an irritated look and they all shut up.
Anna, half-horrified, hoped that they had just gone back to
their jobs of monitoring Joseph and pumping him full of
medications for whatever he needed. But she was afraid not;
their silence felt very permanent.

Charles waded through the wires and tubes to put his
hands on Joseph's chest. Joseph stiffened as his eyes met her
mate's, not a gentle stiffening, but like a person who'd stuck
a table knife in a wall socket. All that was missing were the
sparks and the smoke.

Charles narrowed his gaze and started chanting softly in
a language that no one except for him had spoken for nearly
two hundred years, a dialect of the Flathead tongue that had
died when his mother's tribe had succumbed to one of the
sicknesses that the Europeans had brought with them to the
New World, when he was a very young man.

He could have been saying anything, but Anna's wolf
stirred, called to attention by the sharp ozone breath of the
sacred that Charles occasionally could tap into when, as
Charles put it, the spirits so moved him.

Joseph stopped coughing eventually, leaving Charles's

soothing voice the dominant sound in the room. There were no plants here, but Anna could smell pine. Some impulse urged her to touch Charles, so she did. The back of his neck was the easiest skin to reach, so she put her fingertips there. She closed her eyes and felt his voice sink into her bones. Unable to resist, she lent her song to his.

She didn't have the language, so she hummed an alto descant to his bass almost-song. The chant was Native American, so it didn't follow European chords or patterns. But that didn't bother her. She'd accompanied Charles when he played or sang the songs of his childhood before, though never had it summoned magic. As she found the right notes, it seemed to her that the chant grew stronger.

Charles stopped singing abruptly, and she fell silent at the same time. She may not have understood what he was doing, but the connection between them had told her when the song was finished. On the bed, Joseph's breathing was no longer labored. He was relaxed and his color was better.

Anna let her arm fall away from her mate and flexed her fingers to rid herself of a last sharp tingle of some sort of magic that had nothing to do with pack and everything to do with her husband's odd and possibly unique heritage of witch, shaman, and werewolf.

"What did you do to me?" Joseph asked in a hushed voice. His eyes were wide.

"I have no idea," admitted Charles. "You know how it is when the spirits kick me in the direction they want me to run. Whatever it is, it probably won't last long." He paused. "Or do anyone here any good."

"You have always been such an optimist," said Joseph, amusement lighting his eyes. "I remember that about you."

Charles frowned at him. "I didn't heal you. If you didn't want to die of lung cancer, you could have quit smoking fifty years ago, when I told you to."

Joseph laughed, but there was compassion in his expression. "I am eighty-odd years old, my friend. Something is going to kill me soon, it might as well be cancer." Then the laughter left his face. "Unless you've been listening to my father and intend to change that."

"Being a werewolf is not a panacea to death," said Charles. "Quite the opposite, in fact. I would never force it upon anyone. Even if I were so lost to right and wrong to try, such an act carries a death penalty. Being my father's son means I have no defense against charges of Changing someone against his will."

"My father thinks that you need no such defense, since you *are* your father's son."

Which was almost what Hosteen had said to Charles when he'd driven them in from the landing strip. How terrible, Anna thought, to watch your child die, knowing you had the means to save him and he wouldn't let you do so.

"Then he does not know my father," Charles said as he had to Hosteen. "I am the last person he would make allowances for. Because I am his son, the Marrok could not allow me to break his laws."

"Yes," said Joseph. "So I told him. But I also know you, and not even a death sentence would stop you from doing what you think is right."

"You don't want this," said Charles, gesturing to himself. "You never did. If you have changed your mind, I'll be very happy to help."

Charles had offered to Change Joseph before. Neither man said it, but Anna heard it all the same.

There was a little silence, and then Joseph, who had relaxed against the pillow, gave a small smile. "So you are here to buy a horse for your wife's birthday."

"I have come here to see my old friend," Charles said. "To introduce my wife to him, and to say good-bye."

Joseph sighed deeply. "First good breath I've drawn in months. Thank you." He took a deep breath, held it, and let it out. "My father is a good man. I love him. He tries to do what is best for everyone—and he leads his family and his pack with his heart. But he also thinks that he is right and doesn't always give weight to the opinions of others. I will die when my time is here, and it is very near. What you have done for me does not change that."

It wasn't a question, not quite.

Charles said, "No."

Joseph said, "I can feel death's wind in my face, and I heard an owl cry every night this past week. My father's will cannot change that." He drew in another breath and smiled directly at Anna. "Enough of my drama, I am tired of it. Charles, you have not introduced me to the pretty lady."

She hadn't felt ignored. Both men had been aware of her; Joseph had been studying her. But they had had unfinished business to wade through before bringing her into it.

Charles nodded gravely. "Anna, this is my good friend Joseph, who pulled me into more mischief than he should have been able to. Joseph, this is my mate, Anna, who is a gift an old foolish wolf like me doesn't deserve."

"Heaven forbid that we should get what we deserve," Joseph said, examining Anna. "You have a beautiful song in your heart," he said at last. "I am grateful that my old friend would find such as you because he is too often alone. Don't break his heart or my ghost will haunt you for the rest of your days."

"It isn't me who is breaking his heart right now," she told him.

Joseph nodded. "But that is the dual gift of love, isn't it? The joy of greeting and the sorrow of good-bye." He narrowed his eyes at Charles. "You came here to buy this woman a pretty horse? Something exotic? A horse that will be living art?" He didn't sound like he approved.

"Arabians," said Charles, following Joseph's conversational trail without protest, "are the cats of the horse world. Anna doesn't need to dominate. She will enjoy having a partner rather than a servant."

"An Arabian," said Joseph to Anna, "can be your best friend. He will not desert you when you need him. He will come to your call and be the wings that take you where you need to go."

Charles laughed. She'd thought he laughed like that only

with her, and she was grateful to be wrong. How terrible to live centuries and never laugh with your whole body.

"Wasn't Jasper an Arabian?" he asked. "Your 'best friend' dumped you by the roadside to walk home plenty of times."

Joseph grinned, but said, "Hush. I'm making a point. If you spend time with them and treat them with justice, they will reward you." He cleared his throat. "Jasper excepted."

"I can do justice," Anna said.

"My father likes horses," Joseph confided to Anna. "But he also likes money. There's a reason this farm kept making money after the market for Arabs crashed in the eighties and breeding farms were abandoned to banks by the dozens. He knows that Charles can afford to indulge you. Unless you want to show, you don't need a twenty-thousand-dollar horse, which is what he'll try to sell you. My son, Kage, he loves the horses. He loves the five-hundred-dollar geldings as much as the million-dollar stallions. You listen to my son, Kage, about the horses we have, and not my father."

"All right," she agreed.

Joseph's eyes closed. "It's been a long time since I had no pain. It's hard to sleep when you hurt."

"Go ahead and sleep," Charles told him. "You won't die today."

Joseph nodded but opened his clear eyes to meet Anna's. "Don't let Dad talk you into Hephzibah. She's a witch who only looks like a horse."

"I thought Arabs are all friendly except for Jasper," said Charles.

Joseph grinned—and it was the same expression that he'd worn when someone had taken a photo of him as he rode a bucking horse. "Hephzibah will kill someone someday. There's something wrong with her spirit." He shut his eyes again and his voice slurred. "Maybe the evil dead have touched her. Maybe she is really a skinwalker. You keep your wife away from her."

"I'm a werewolf," Anna said. "I'm not in danger from a horse." But Joseph was already asleep.

Maggie met them at the door to the hallway.

"It is good that you've come to see him," she said to Charles. Anna suddenly realized that Joseph's apartment had been entirely masculine. Didn't Maggie share the apartment with him? "Are you going to do as Hosteen asks now? Do you see what has happened to Joseph? He is gone already, that man I married." She brushed an impatient hand over her face, and Anna realized Maggie was crying.

"No," Charles said, but he said it gently. "Joseph does not want to be a werewolf. He has no need to live forever. And whatever the rest of us feel like we need, that is, it must be, *his* choice."

She grabbed his arm, swift and sudden. Anna instinctively moved to intercept her but caught herself before Maggie noticed.

"I don't want him to die, Charles," Maggie told him intensely.

"Neither do I," he said in the same gentle tone. "But everyone dies, Maggie. This is not the worst death I have seen. He is not afraid, not of death, anyway."

She let go of him and took two steps backward. "Joseph has never been afraid of death," she agreed. "I think it surprises him that he has lived this long."

The intense intimacy of their conversation faded, caused by some trick of Maggie's body language: she was once again the gracious hostess.

"Food is ready downstairs," she said. "Kage said that after dinner, he'd take you to see some horses." She smiled suddenly. "He is grateful for Chelsea, and my son can see no greater reward than to take you to see his horses." She started down the hallway. "In that way, he and his father are just alike. Horse-mad idiots."

"You, too," Charles said, his hand on the small of Anna's back as he followed. "Remember that poor skinny pinto you saved from that pair of cowboys, Maggie?" He looked at Anna, his eyes smiling. "One woman against two armed men, and she took after them with a broom for the way they'd half starved a mare. Only it turns out, when the dust settled, that they'd just bought that mare from another guy because they didn't like the way he wasn't feeding her."

"I apologized and fed them my burritos," Maggie said. "They didn't care about a few bruises after that."

"Won't it be too dark to ride?" asked Anna.

"The main barn has lights," Maggie said shortly. "You won't have any trouble seeing."

THEY ATE IN the big dining room because there were too many to fit around the kitchen table. Ernestine had roasted a huge beef brisket and topped the meal off with corn bread and a green salad. She ate with the family, deliberately sitting next to the kids and helping Max and Maggie keep a normal conversation going.

Anna sat next to Charles and watched everyone (except for her husband) try not to stare at Chelsea.

Chelsea, when she was not dying on a bathroom floor, was a strikingly attractive, if not beautiful, woman. She was tall, half a head taller than Kage, and built like an athlete. Her hair was a Nordic blond that complemented her icy-gray eyes and was cut very expensively to frame her expressive and rather bony face.

Max had given Anna a picture of a charming and funny woman. But Chelsea didn't engage with anyone, not even when someone spoke to her directly. She would eat a few bites quickly, then set her utensils down as if they were puzzle pieces she had to fit into place. Then she would take a gulp of water, stare at the wall or the table or her hands—and then suddenly grab her silverware and eat another two or three mouthfuls with ravenous intensity. Every once in a while she'd try to eat something besides the meat, and Anna could see her fight to get the food down.

It was probably something from the Change, Anna thought. She didn't like to think about the weeks shortly after she had been Changed. There were large gaps in her memory—

She curled around herself shivering, cold and hot by

*turns. The bars of the cage burned her skin, but without
something against her back she felt vulnerable to attack.
She smelled grease from a fast-food box . . .*

Okay, so some things she remembered just fine, but she
could choose not to dwell upon them. There was no cage here,
no one to throw a cardboard box of fried chicken at Chelsea.
To this day, Anna couldn't eat chicken from that particular
chain.

There were no rapists here.

Suddenly Chelsea's eyes met Anna's from across the table
and held them. Icy gray became even more pale, and Chelsea's nostrils flared.

"Who hurt you?" she asked, slicing through the two other
conversations going on at the table.

"He's dead," said Charles, his hand sliding up Anna's back
reassuringly. "I killed him. If I could, I would bring him back
to life so I could kill him again."

Chelsea turned her gaze to Charles for a moment. "Good,"
she said, before she had to drop her eyes. Her intensity faded.
"That's good."

Charles put his lips against Anna's ear. "He's very dead."

Anna nodded jerkily. "Sorry."

"No," he said, his breath warm against her neck. "Don't
be sorry. Just know if anyone ever tries to hurt you again—
they will be dead, too."

And some people had tried, hadn't they. And yes, she
realized, they *were* all dead. Charles was a big warm presence at her back, better than a solid wall or bars.

She picked up her fork and took a bite of brisket. "Okay,"
she told Charles.

They cleaned the table collectively, Ernestine directing
traffic. Anna found herself in the kitchen washing pots and
pans as Maggie put them away.

"Do you suppose Ernestine made us work together on
purpose?" asked Anna.

"Undoubtedly," Maggie agreed.

She didn't say anything more for a moment. It wasn't
exactly private—people were in and out with food and dishes.

Max had taken up the post at the dishwasher, where he scraped and loaded dishes.

"I loved your husband once," said Maggie.

"I gathered that," Anna said. "He cares a lot about you." She forced herself not to add *and Joseph, too.* It was true, but it made her sound as though she were jealous. She wasn't. Territorial, yes. Jealous, no.

"I was not as courageous as you," Maggie said. "Twenty or thirty years later I would not have made the same choice, but I was young and he frightened me when I found out what he was." She glanced at Anna. "I was about your age. Werewolf side effects aside, Joseph said that Charles is buying you a horse for your twenty-sixth birthday. You were younger than I was when he found you. And you weren't afraid of him."

It was a big concession, implying that Anna was somehow better than Maggie for not running away.

"Yeah. I had already met the real monsters," she told Maggie. "It gave me some basis for comparison."

"If I had not been afraid, I would have picked Charles," Maggie said. She headed off to a pantry space with a handful of pots. When she came back, she said, "Joseph suited me better. Charles and I are both too serious. Even now, Joseph is a breath of pure sunshine. I'll send you home with my recipe for burritos. Charles and Joseph both love them."

And after that they finished up the pots and pans and serving dishes in utter harmony.

"Hosteen is pretty distracted," said Max, when the dishwasher was loaded and running. He took the big pan out of Maggie's hand with a smile. "He wouldn't have let Ernestine put you to work if he'd been paying attention. Why don't you let me finish this and go sit down as though you'd been doing it all along?"

Maggie exchanged a grin with him and left the kitchen to younger hands.

"Hosteen has been more protective of her since Joseph got sick," Max told Anna. "She knows he's feeling bad, so she indulges him." He smiled. "She's a tough old broad, is Maggie.

He'd better lay off because she's going to get tired of it pretty soon."

WHEN THE KITCHEN was clean, Hosteen organized a war council. He began by evicting the innocent bystanders.

"Hey, kids," said Ernestine in response to Hosteen's raised eyebrow. "Why don't you come watch some TV with me up in the gold guest suite?" She took Michael and Mackie by the hand. "Coming, Max?"

Max gave Kage a half-pleading, half-defiant look. "I think I'll stay," he said.

Kage nodded. Ernestine smiled at Max and then led the children away as the rest of them reseated themselves around the dining room.

"I'm proud of you," Anna overheard Kage tell Max. "You've been extraordinarily useful today. It's always hard to be on the support staff when there's action elsewhere. Thank you for taking care of the kids this afternoon."

"I did it under protest," said Max, apologetically.

"But you did it well," Kage replied. "Good enough for me."

Hosteen sat at the head of the table and looked down its gleaming surface at Chelsea. "We need to know what happened to you," he said, not unkindly. "Are you up to answering questions?"

She nodded. "I don't know how much help I'll be."

"You are witchborn," said Charles. "Did you sense anything wrong? Do you know when you were bespelled?"

She shook her head. "I don't have much training. My mother taught me how to hide myself, but that's it."

"When did you notice something was wrong?" Hosteen said, his voice a little impatient.

"In the bathroom," Chelsea said, sounding a little lost. Kage scooted his chair nearer and put his arm around her. "I was looking for something stronger, for my headache. I knocked the toothbrush holder into the sink and it broke. It cut my hand when I cleaned it up, and I could think for a moment." She looked at Kage. "That's how I figured it out, that I could stop myself if I was bleeding."

"That's why you stabbed yourself in the hand?" Max asked. Chelsea's left hand still had a scab on it.

She nodded. "You or me," she told him. "I picked me."

He nodded and then said, "I'm not a kid anymore, Mom. Next time—pick me, okay?"

"Not going to happen," said Maggie. She was sitting next to Max, and she patted his hand. "Nothing to do with your age. Mothers protect their children."

"When did the headache start?" asked Charles.

"After I picked up the kids, I think," Chelsea said. "That's when I noticed it anyway. I left the kids on their own and ran up to take something for it." She paused. "I took too many pills and then went looking for something stronger. If I'd found the pills instead of getting a cut, would the kids have been safe?"

Anna said, "Pain is a distraction; it can be used to break down your will." She knew that. "So can certain drugs. Tylenol won't do it—but what kind of stronger were you looking for?"

"I had some leftover Vicodin," she said. "But I was just trying to stop the headache."

"Vicodin would have made it harder for you to fight the geas," said Charles. "But now we are talking a very complicated magic. 'Kill your children and then yourself' is, essentially, two commands. 'Kill your children if you can, and if they are dead or if you fail to kill them, then kill yourself' is more complicated. And the geas absolutely tried to make you kill yourself after I told you the kids were safe. If the magic drove you to do something that made you a better vessel to carry out your task . . . we're getting into magic that is above the ability of most fae."

"How long would it have taken to put such a spell on her?" asked Hosteen.

"A Gray Lord with the right magic could do it in an instant," Charles said. "Or it could have taken hours."

"The only time I lost was while I was in the bathroom," Chelsea said with some certainty. "I work off a schedule. I'd have noticed any gap through the day."

"I went through the house," Charles said. "There was fae magic in plenty, but there was no fae in your house."

"Could they have put the spell on her earlier?" asked Max. "Left it inert for a while until the right conditions were met? Like Sleeping Beauty's curse?"

"Absolutely," said Charles. "But if that's what happened, it's unlikely we'll easily figure out who did this and why. So we should concentrate on scenarios that are more useful."

Chelsea frowned. "There was something odd—"

"What was that?" asked Kage.

She put one hand to her head and reached to the table with the other and collapsed. Hosteen jumped over the table and pulled her chair away so they could get to her.

"Mom?" Max said.

"It's all right," Anna told him at the same time Hosteen said, "It's about time."

Kage picked his wife up from the floor. Hosteen said, "Take her into the apricot guest room." He put a hand on Kage's shoulder. "I know that's not your usual rooms—but the kids are in your suite and we need to keep them safe. Probably there will be no trouble, but the Change is disorienting and werewolves are dangerous."

"What's wrong with her?" asked Kage.

"Her body is undergoing a lot of changes at the same time," Charles said. "It's pretty normal for her to seem to be fine directly after the Change heals the wounds that allowed the Change to take place. But after a few hours—sometimes a few days—everything will catch up with her."

"Anna told me about that," Max said. "I just forgot."

MAX HAD GONE up to help Ernestine with the kids.

Hosteen settled into Chelsea's room with a book, and so had Maggie. When Hosteen tried to send her off to bed, she'd given him a sharp look. "You quit trying to make me into a useless old woman, Papa. I can sit with Chelsea while she sleeps. I've got a good mystery to read."

Kage hesitated, and his mother shooed him off. "You go on now," she told him. "I know that you need to go *do* something. So take these two nice people out to the barn and give yourself something else to think about. Chelsea's not going anywhere in the next few hours."

Kage looked at Anna and said, "Assuming you are really interested in looking at horses . . ."

"Yes?" she said hopefully.

Behind Kage's back, his mother caught Charles's eye and nodded at Kage, then at Charles. He bowed his head.

Kage was examining Anna's face. "Not much of a poker face," he said.

"Take her to Vegas and she'll come back with a small fortune," suggested Maggie warmly. "If she starts with—"

"A large one," Charles agreed, and ducked meekly when Anna pretended to hit him.

DESPITE THE SLURS on her poker face, Anna decided to adopt an air of casual interest. She didn't really know how she felt, anyway. She was excited, yes, but an odd unsettled feeling vied with excitement as they drove out to the barn.

She'd never ridden much before she met Charles. Since then she'd ridden a million miles—well, a couple of hundred at least—in the mountains. They were a long way from the mountains. In a few minutes she was going to take her meager skills and demonstrate them.

Sitting in the front passenger seat of the utility vehicle Kage drove, Anna felt the odd unease grow stronger as they approached a glorious building that could have been a luxury resort. It didn't resemble any image of a "barn" that she held in her head. The rough topography had hidden the barn from the house, and supposedly there was another barn around somewhere, too. She was more impressed by the Arizona desert's ability to make things disappear, because they weren't more than a half mile from the house and the barn was huge.

Spanish-style elegant, the massive structure sprawled in gracious lines that were lit like some gigantic Christmas tree with hundreds of small white lights. *Behold,* the expensive and tastefully illuminated xeriscaped combination of stone and exotic desert plants seemed to say. *Here are the kings and queens of equines; prepare to bow down and worship them.*

Anna looked down at her battered riding boots, identifying that second, unhappy emotion. She was more excited than she'd have thought to be getting a horse of her own, but she had the sinking feeling that she was not good enough for these horses. Having her ride a horse that lived in a barn like this would be akin to a sixth grader playing a priceless Lupot cello.

"Fancy," said Charles from the backseat—he'd insisted on her riding in front—in dry tones. Kage laughed, pulling into a parking spot right next to an identical vehicle.

"Yeah, Hosteen thinks it's an eyesore, but it makes people spend more money than the tin mare motel that he claims he'd be happier with." Kage looked at Anna and explained, "A mare motel is a metal roof that sits over a series of small runs. It looks horrible, but it keeps the sun and rain off the horses. Hosteen likes to gripe, but he made us build it a third larger than Dad had originally planned, and he was right. We are nearly at capacity."

Kage turned off the engine and tapped the steering wheel. "You saved my wife," he told Charles without looking at him. "As far as I'm concerned, you are welcome to any horse in the barn."

"Not necessary," said Charles. "Besides, I do know Hosteen. I may not have seen him in two decades, but no one changes that much. He'd wash your mouth out with soap if he heard you offer to give a horse away."

Kage smiled when, Anna sensed, usually he would have laughed. He struck her as a man to whom laughter came easy, as if his natural state was happy—when no one was trying to kill his wife and children. Good for him. She hoped that he'd find his balance again soon.

"Okay," Kage said, hopping out of the utility vehicle. "Just keep my offer in mind. I am not afraid of the old man. If what you want is over budget, we can talk. Dad says you're mostly looking for a trail horse, sensible and pretty."

Charles held out a courtesy hand to help Anna down. She didn't need the help, but the reassurance of his hand on hers made her stomach settle down.

"Anna has been riding a couple of years," he told Kage. "Trail riding in the mountains. Maybe she might find herself interested in something else down the line, though, so we won't rule anything out. But whatever else she decides to do with her horse, we do ride in the mountains. Anna has light hands and a decent seat. She doesn't need a beginner's horse—just nothing too apt to spook at shadows."

Kage laughed. "You know what they say about Arabs, right? They all spook. And half Arabs spook exactly half as much." He looked at Anna. "It's not really true, but they *are* easily bored. Most of the shying and other drama happens when they are looking for something interesting to do. They think they're doing you a favor by making things a little exciting."

He shook his head. "When I was a kid, Dad had this mare he was going to by-golly turn into a kid's horse for me. But the more he worked her in the arena, the more she shied and snorted. One day he got so frustrated he took her out on the trails for a week—a trial by fire, he said. He rode her through creeks, over hill and dale—they even got buzzed by some idiot on a motorcycle and she didn't turn a hair."

He looked at Charles.

"She was bored," Charles said.

"She taught me to ride," Kage said. "A fire truck with sirens and lights blazing didn't bother her a bit, but let a piece of straw blow across her path? I learned to pay attention and stay in the saddle."

Kage led them through the front doors, through an airy reception room decorated Southwestern casual complete with an Old West–style wet bar. Glass double doors took them to a viewing stand that looked out over a large arena two-thirds the size of a football field. There was a tractor wetting down the arena with a water tank and spray rig. The woman on the tractor waved to Kage and continued working.

"Pretty late for chores," said Charles.

Kage nodded. "Staff is usually done by five, except for the foaling managers, who rotate on twenty-four-hour shifts this time of year. But we're gearing up for the big horse show. Lots of people come to the show specifically to buy horses. We'll have a presentation or ten out here during the show, so we've got to get the barn ready and groom all hundred and sixty horses and not just the thirty we are showing. That means overtime for everyone."

He looked at Charles. "You ought to take her out to the show. It's not as over-the-top as it was thirty years ago." He grinned at Anna. "We had all sorts of celebrities and entertainment industry people then, and people came to look at them as much as the horses. Millions changed hands both in real money and on paper to dodge the tax man, and the Arab industry attracted a different crowd. But the show is still spectacular. Lots of pretty horses and horse-mad people."

They entered the stabling area. It smelled of cedar shavings and horses, with a faint tang of urine and leather. On the inside of the three of them, when Anna turned the corner she was next to the first stall.

A copper-colored horse thrust his head toward her, and she found herself nose to nose with him.

Not just any horse, either, but a fairy-tale horse. Every hair in his mane and forelock lay as though someone had separated them from each other and put them exactly where they would look best. The narrow stripe that ran from between his eyes down to between his nostrils looked as though someone had powdered it with baby powder to get it white-white, except for a small triangle of pink on the end of his nose. His chestnut coat was flame-brilliant, and, when she reached out to touch his cheek, the skin under her fingers was soft and sleek.

"Careful," cautioned Kage. "He's only a two-year-old and a stallion, which means he's lippy. He's not mean, just looking for handouts. But he will bite if you aren't watching."

"Like you, boss," someone shouted from a nearby stall.

"And I fire people who get above themselves, too," Kage called back with a grin.

"Yeah, I'm worried, boss," said the same guy. He was hidden somewhere in the row of stalls. "If you fire me, you'll have to muck out twenty stalls before you can go to bed. I've got job se-cu-ri-ty."

"You go on thinking that way, Morales," said someone else. "If you want more security, you can clean my stalls, too."

Anna petted the colt's velvet cheek and sought out the spot just behind his ear to scratch. It was the right spot because he pressed his neck into her hand hard enough to bang it against the side of the stall opening, then twisted his neck to make her fingers hit exactly where he wanted them. His eyes closed and his lips waggled in ecstasy.

"Why aren't horses more afraid of us?" Anna asked. "I mean, if I were a grizzly bear, he wouldn't be asking me to rub his neck, right?"

Charles's stance had relaxed the moment they'd entered the stables; she didn't think he knew it. Her man loved horses the way he loved music.

He smiled, but it was Kage who answered. "Horses are adaptable. I mean, I go out to some poor, half-grown colt smelling like the steak sandwich I ate for lunch. I throw a piece of dead cow on his back and tell him it won't hurt him. Pretty amazing that they'll let us get anywhere near them."

He reached out and rubbed the other side of the horse's face. "If you were in wolf form and all snarly and ready to attack, I suppose they'd freak, all right. This one might just try to trample you—he's not got a lot of fear in him. Hosteen says they just think you smell like a funny kind of dog, and they know about dogs." He paused. Looked at Charles. "So what do you think?"

"Pretty horse," he said dryly. "Tippy ears."

Kage choked back a laugh. "Dad said you'd do that." He

looked at Anna. "Gives a compliment that you know is an insult. Right now the Saudi billionaires are bolstering the Arabian market. They don't care about bodies or legs, but they pay a lot for a pretty head."

"Not just the Saudis," grunted Charles. "The judges are rewarding longer and longer necks, taller and taller horses. If you reward the extremes, that's where the breed heads.

"Long necks"—he nodded at the chestnut—"usually mean long backs. A lot of taller horses just have longer cannon bones, which weakens their legs. The Arabs I rode herding cattle with your father in the fifties and sixties would do a full day's work for twenty years, seven days a week, and retire sound." He snorted. "The drive now is for pretty lawn ornaments. The Arabian horses were originally bred as weapons of war, and now they are artwork. Those old Bedouins are rolling in their graves."

"Nothing wrong with artwork," growled Kage, really offended now.

Charles was doing it deliberately, Anna thought. Goading Kage into what? She narrowed her eyes at her husband, who looked back at her blandly.

Kage reached over and snagged a halter from where it hung on the wall next to the stall door. "Yes, he's got a pretty head and neck, and that makes him valuable. Like those little tippy ears you're so annoyed with. But you can have your cake and eat it just fine."

Anna backed out of the way as Kage slid the stall door open and brought the two-year-old stallion out to stand in the broad aisle under the lights. She was watching the man, not the horse, though. He'd been wounded, she thought, from what had happened to his wife today. Stoic, but wounded. The anger burned all that away.

And her husband said he wasn't good with people.

"You tell me that those old-time, round-barreled, cow-hocked Arabs had *anything* over this horse," Kage growled as he somehow cued the colt to freeze in place and stretch his neck out and up. The irritation he'd demonstrated dropped away as he looked at the colt, too. Anna thought he couldn't hold anger and the way he felt about the horse at the same time.

Passionately, Kage said, "This one would take you over the desert sands, sleep in your tent, and stand guard over your body. You *look* at him and you tell me his back is too long or his legs are weak."

The horse looked spectacular to Anna, but she was no judge. The young stallion's copper coat gleamed even in the artificial light. Large, dark eyes looked at them with arrogance, a healthy dose of vanity . . . and humor, she thought.

His body looked balanced to her and he had a nice slope to his shoulder that was echoed in his hip. His mane was pale and thick and emphasized the arch of his neck, and his tail would have reached the ground if it hadn't been braided and wound up in a bag.

"What's with his tail?" asked Anna. "Is there something wrong with it?"

"No," Kage said with a wary look at Charles.

"Because even in a stall, a horse will rub and wear down his tail to a useful length instead of letting it grow long enough to trail behind him like a bridal veil," Charles told her, but his real attention wasn't on his words but on the horse. "Judges like a tail dragging the ground in the show ring."

He paced around the horse slowly, stopping to pick up a foot. The longer he looked, the more smug Kage was. When her mate finished his examination, what Charles said wasn't a judgment, but a question. "You're taking him in the ring at the big show?"

"That's our intention," Kage said. "We didn't show him last year because he was still going through the yearling fuglies. His butt was four inches higher than his withers. This year . . . he's got a good chance. He certainly won't look outclassed in his age group."

"I don't know about Arabian horse judging," said Charles, raising a hand in surrender. "But I do know horses. This one is seriously good—assuming he has a brain between those tippy little ears." He smiled at Kage. "Tragic if he ends up a lawn ornament or a piece of artwork brought out to make a rich man's guests ooh and ahh." He gave Kage a long look. "You've successfully defended him and your breeding program. Feel better?"

Kage gave him a sharp look, hesitated, and then said, "You picked an argument with me so I'd feel better?"

"Yes," Charles said. "I also picked an argument with you so you could quit treating us like customers and talk to us about Chelsea. Your mother is pretty sure you won't talk to Hosteen about her, and she thinks you need to talk to somebody."

Anna couldn't help letting her eyebrows climb up. Charles had gotten a lot of information from no more than two seconds of voiceless communication with Maggie.

Kage frowned at Charles. "She does, does she? I am very grateful to you for saving Chelsea, Mr. Cornick. But I assure you I'm fine."

"Chelsea isn't," said Anna.

"Chelsea," Kage said. The stallion butted him with his head, and he rubbed the horse's forehead. He looked around and lowered his voice so that the people working around them wouldn't hear what he said. "Her mother taught her that her witch blood taints her. And Hosteen never lets up about it. The idea that she's a werewolf now and has to obey my grandfather, with whom she has been painfully feuding for eight years, hasn't caught up with her yet. But it will. She is never going to forgive me."

"If that's the only problem, you'll do okay," Anna said. "If she honestly can't stand him, then move. There are other packs."

"And with your reputation you can get a job in any Arab barn in the country," added Charles.

"Maybe so," Kage said. "But she's very big on being independent. I just changed her life without consulting her."

"There was no way to bring her into it," Charles pointed out. "I tried that first. If she really didn't want to Change . . . It's a lot easier to give up, Kage, than it is to fight for your life."

"She's not going to buy that as an argument," said Kage, but at the same time, for the first time since he'd picked up his cell phone and heard his wife's messages, he looked like he'd caught his balance. "You think that she would have made that choice herself? I didn't force it on her?"

"If anyone forced it on her, it would be I," corrected Charles. "But no. If I thought she really didn't have a choice in the matter, I would not have done it even if you begged me to. She chose to die for her children, and she chose to live for all of you."

"What about my dad, then?" Kage asked. "By that argument you couldn't Change him unless he secretly wanted it. Which we all know he doesn't. So why is Hosteen still after you to Change him, anyway?"

"Because he believes that he saw my father force a man through a Change. That man wasn't unwilling, just unable, which is different. He thinks that I can do the same," Charles said.

"Can you?"

"Chelsea needed a little help, but I did not force her," Charles answered. "She saw a chance for survival and she wanted it."

He wasn't lying, Anna knew. But there was a sick feeling in her stomach. That was what Justin had said when she'd survived the Change—as if she'd wanted what was done to her and all that followed.

"Use that," she told Kage, "to comfort yourself, because it is true that she had to fight to live. But don't tell *her* that. Tell her you love her and need her. Tell her the kids need her. Tell her you tried to make the choice she might make. Tell her that you thought she'd want us to find the fae who did this to her so he couldn't kill anyone else. But don't tell her that her survival means that she really wanted this." When she said "this," she motioned to herself. Werewolf, she meant, werewolf and all the things that went with it.

Kage's voice was compassionate. "The voice of experience?"

"Yes." Anna took in a deep breath. "Truth has many facets. Choose the ones that make her happy to be alive instead of the ones that make her want to smack you."

"Are you happy?" he asked her.

"Yes," she said with total conviction. "But it took a while. It might take her a while, too."

"Yes," he said, but he didn't sound nearly as upset about it as he had been when he'd started talking. "I expect it will."

"It could be worse," Charles said thoughtfully. "She could be dead."

Kage nodded. "Yes. This may be difficult. That would have been unbearable. Difficult is better."

CHAPTER

5

"Market's back up, is it?" Charles asked dryly, looking at the sales list Kage handed him.

"Sort of up," said Kage. "The very top-tier horses, the ones that will win at Scottsdale, nationals, or Paris, they sell as high as they ever did. Higher maybe. Last year a stallion sold to Saudi Arabia for five million dollars, but he was a freak of nature. The second-tier horses, good pedigree and nice horses that aren't quite topflight—those are harder to sell and make a profit on." He grinned at Charles. "Those are the ones I'm going to be showing you. Before we start, though, you'll notice Hephzibah on that list."

"Yes," Charles said, his eyes crinkling in humor. "Her price has a negative sign by it. Does that mean he'll pay me to take her?"

Kage laughed. "I won't sell her to anyone. Hosteen put her on the list. My wife loves that mare. Only horse that Hosteen's ever failed to ride. I think that's why Chelsea likes her. Too crazy to sell, too healthy to put down. Beautiful enough that the temptation to breed her will someday over-whelm us all. A nastier horse I've never been around. She is all sweetness and goodness, until she goes after you." He sobered. "She put two of our grooms in the hospital and nearly killed another. Only Hosteen or I handle her now. Treacherous. Her sire, to my knowledge, has never sired another horse with a bad disposition. Her dam was an old mare we got in trade, and Hephzibah was the only foal she had for us."

A Hispanic man came up to them. "Hey, Kage. These the folks who wanted to look at horses?"

"Mateo—" Kage started to introduce him and paused. "Where is Teri?"

"She's getting the first horse saddled. You wanted them in the small ring, right? You head over there and we'll bring them to you."

"Good. Mateo and Teri are going to wrangle horses while I do the salesman thing." Kage grinned. "We'll use the little ring because the big one is being prepped, as you saw. Mateo is our senior trainer, but like all of us, he steps in where we need him. Teri is one of our apprentices and she rides for us in shows."

"Lots of people working for you these days," said Charles.

Kage nodded. "It's because we do the whole thing: breed, train, show. And we show in whatever class the horse is suited for. That means lots of people on the payroll, but we're diversified. Right now the halter horses are bringing in the biggest money, but Hosteen thinks too much specialization is bad for business."

And Hosteen would always run this place, would never grow old and gradually let his grandson take over. Anna wondered if that bothered Kage.

As they walked to the smaller arena, all along the barn aisle horses put their heads out over the stall doors—stalls that were both cleaner and fancier than a lot of hotels Anna had stayed at. As they walked, Kage chatted lightly—to Anna and Charles and to the horses.

"We train our horses, but we train other people's horses, too. *Heyya, Bones, are they feeding you enough?* Most of the horses I'm going to show you are ours. But a couple of them belong to other people. *That's my girl—aren't you lovely today? No carrots, sorry.* What you are primarily looking for should not be an expensive horse. Show horses, good show horses, are expensive—so mostly what I'm going to present to you are horses unsuited, in one way or another, to the show ring. But Hosteen put a few show horses on the list, just in case. *Are you my good, great beastie? Yes, you are.*"

The small pen was a round arena about a quarter of the size of the big arena they'd walked by. The fence was made from plywood sheets that were scarred and battered—though still solid. Kage ushered them inside; before he closed the gate, a tiny woman who was rawhide and leather led a small-ish bay mare, already saddled with a western, silver-bedecked saddle, into the ring.

"This is Honey Bay Bee," Kage said. "She's twelve. We showed her halter at the regional level when she was a yearling and then hunt seat for a year as a futurity horse. She is no longer breeding sound, so we've put another year of riding on her and are selling her as an amateur prospect."

Anna tried to look like she knew what he was talking about, but he lost her at "regional" and "hunt seat."

"Go ahead and ask," said Charles.

"Hunt seat?"

"English saddle," said Kage. "But horses trot long instead of high like they do in the English classes. You'll see what I mean."

Teri hopped up gracefully and walked, trotted, and cantered the mare around the pen. Teri had a big smile on her face; the horse looked vaguely annoyed.

She felt annoyed, too, when Anna mounted much less gracefully. She walked, trotted, and cantered for Anna with as much enthusiasm as a kid doing homework. Her ears weren't pinned, but they weren't up and eager, either. *Bored, bored, bored,* they said.

At least she didn't shy at anything.

Charles shook his head before Anna got off.

"She gives me a baseline," Kage said. "But no."

Anna rode four horses that night. By the third horse, she

lost most of her shyness about riding in front of virtual strangers who knew a lot more than she did. Which was good, because the fourth horse they brought for her was a tiny gelding who was "English pleasure but not quite a park horse," whatever that meant. Mateo rode him for them first. Anna saw immediately what Kage had been saying when he'd told her English was up instead of out. The tiny powerhouse snapped up his knees and hocks with enthusiastic energy.

"Could I ride him in a western saddle?" she asked.

"English saddles suck if you are riding in the mountains." Kage grinned. "Of course you can. Heylight won't care. He's all about getting down the road and having fun."

Evidently they weren't going to get the western saddle now, though, which was kind of what Anna had been asking. Anna eyed the itty-bitty scrap of leather that was missing the horn for her to grab on to.

"Don't worry about it," Charles said as he adjusted her stirrups. "Western or English style, it doesn't matter. Ride balanced. The seat support is still there. Your rump will know it even if your eyes tell you differently.

"The turn signals for English are like steering a bicycle: turn by pulling his nose a little in the direction you want to go and give him a little more rein with the other hand so you aren't just pulling back." He demonstrated with his own hands, moving them together. "You'll still steer mostly with your body and legs—just like at home."

"If I screw up on the steering," she told him, "we'll just go round and round in circles, anyway."

He gave her a quick grin and stepped back. She asked the gelding to move off.

The little gelding had stood perfectly still when she got on, but the minute her calves put pressure on his sides, he powered off at a trot instead of the walk she was expecting. It wasn't the gentle slow trot her usual mount had, either. She bounced around like a rubber ball until she found her seat a little farther back than she was used to. After a few more minutes she settled in and felt a big grin cross her face.

He was probably going slower, as far as distance traveled, than the first mare had been with her long striding gait, but it felt like they were flying. The gelding was like a high-performance sports car. The faster he went, the more responsive he got. The best thing about him was that although speed was always available, so were slow and stop.

Reluctantly she slowed him and brought him to the middle of the arena, where Charles, Kage, and Mateo watched.

"Usually we post that trot," commented Kage with a grin when she stopped. "Not many people would try to sit it."

"Is that bad?" she asked.

"Heylight's ears are up, so you weren't hitting him in the back—but it's a lot of work to sit a big trot like that."

She wasn't sure he'd answered her question until she glanced at Charles, who gave her a nod—it was a compliment.

Charles walked all the way around the horse and then asked, "Does he even make fourteen hands?"

"Wasn't it you who was just complaining because we're breeding Arabs bigger and bigger?" asked Kage. "Yes, she could take him in a pony class. Still, she doesn't look too big for him. I wouldn't have brought him out for you. He could carry you, but it would sure look funny. We'd have to put wheels on your stirrups or they'd drag in the dust. How big is he, Mateo, do you know?"

Mateo shrugged. "I've put a measuring stick on all the horses. I can get his real height from the office if you want me to. But it's easier to categorize horses as small, medium, and big. Most people can't tell the difference between fifteen hands and fifteen two anyway, so why confuse the issue? This horse is size small with a size big heart."

Anna patted the horse and laughed when he leaned into her hand.

Kage put his hand on the horse's forehead and rubbed lightly. "I kept waiting for this horse to grow. It shouldn't be about size, but this guy really just isn't tall enough to compete in the big ring. He also has the problem that in an English class his gaits are sometimes too big and he gets penalized. In a park class his gaits usually aren't big enough and he gets penalized. We could maybe fix that if we grew his feet out to the maximum and stuck the heaviest shoes that are legal for the show ring on him. But his right front foot is soft and the big shoes don't stay on it. So we're selling him as a junior-to-ride horse: English pleasure. He's not nationals quality, for the reasons I told you, but he could take a regional championship with a good round and a judge who didn't care about size. That's why his price is as high as it is."

"Have you ridden him outside a ring?" asked Charles.

Kage nodded. "Well, not me. Hosteen took him out on one of his weeklong treks into the desert last fall. Said he did fine after the first couple of days. It was just the once, but he also has two years of showing, too. That will sack out a horse but good."

"Sack a horse out?" Anna asked, picturing people beating on a horse with paper sacks.

"Desensitize him to the kinds of things that could make a horse spook," Charles said. "They used to take feed sacks and rub them all over the horse until it quit being frightened. The sacks were handy—and scary because they were light-colored and noisy. Showing exposes horses to all sorts of situations, and they learn not to be afraid every time they run into something new."

"Most of them do," said Kage. "Eventually. But he's honest and brave. Mackie's riding him in the show, and I wouldn't trust my girl to just any horse."

"We'll keep him on our likely candidate list," said Charles.

Anna slid off reluctantly. "Don't I get a say in it?"

"The big grin on your face already said a mouthful," Charles told her. "Mere words are not necessary."

"You might try her with Portabella," said a breathless voice just outside the arena.

"Dad?" Kage sounded shocked. "What are you doing down here—you should be in bed."

Sure enough, Joseph Sani stood watching with both hands on the upper surface of the arena fence. "I'll have plenty of time to lie down when I'm dead." He nodded at Anna. "Portabella is full of fun like that. She'd like to spend her days in the mountains up there in Montana. She'd like that."

"You named a horse after a mushroom?" asked Anna.

"Her name is Al Mazrah Uhibboki," Mateo said. "We had to call her something pronounceable. Her grandsire is Port Bask—so Portabella."

"Her real name is what?" Anna asked.

"Al Mazrah is the stud farm that bred her," Kage said. "Uhibboki means, we think, 'I love you.' So Al Mazrah Uhibboki. Al Mazrah stud is in Indiana and no one there speaks Arabic. No one here speaks Arabic, either, so I don't know for sure. And we are probably pronouncing it wrong anyway."

Joseph laughed, and then he coughed harshly a couple of times.

"Dad," said Kage.

"Don't fuss," Joseph said. "When I'm dead, you can fuss. I needed to smell the horses again." He closed his eyes and took a shallow breath. He opened them and said, "Better than medicine for an old man. And I need to talk to Charles. Ernestine said you were at the barn."

"How did you get here?" Kage asked.

"I took the last UTV," he said. "But I think I'll let Charles drive me back up. We can talk on the way." He glanced at Kage. "You and Mateo might want to show Anna some of the new babies. I hear that our Kalli had a filly yesterday that everyone is over the moon about."

CHARLES WAITED AT Joseph's unspoken request while Mateo and Kage took Anna off to look at the foals. When they were out of sight, Charles said, "Do you need me to carry you? Won't be the first time."

Joseph laughed. "That's for damned sure. There was that one week I was determined to drink every bar in the town dry."

"I don't remember that," said Charles gravely. "But I was

thinking about when that mustang dumped you and you broke your leg twenty miles from anywhere. Horse made it back and your dad and I finally went out as wolves to find you. He ran back for help and I carried you halfway home before help came."

"Really?" said Joseph tentatively. "You don't remember?"

"Someone asked me not to," said Charles. "And I told him I would oblige him. So no. I don't remember."

Joseph nodded. "You know, I think I could make it back to the UTV, but I'm sure that if I did, I couldn't talk with you and that's important. I'm too old for pride."

Charles picked him up with considerably less effort than he'd used to carry Joseph on that long-ago walk into town, because a frail old man weighs a lot less than a wiry cowboy. Charles wondered if the reason his dad did not associate much with humans was that they grew old and died. He did not enjoy the sorrow, but he would not have missed the years that he and Joseph were friends, either. Such joy was worth a little sorrow.

The lights were off in the big arena, and no one saw Joseph being carried out to the utility vehicle. The old man had pushed himself too far. Even if the spirits had granted him strength, muscles that had lain in bed for three months were not as able as they could be.

He didn't say any of that, because Joseph knew it as well as Charles did.

He put Joseph in the passenger seat and climbed into the utility vehicle beside him. "You're going to have to tell me how to start this thing," he said.

"You don't use ATVs or UTVs up in those mountains of yours?" Joseph asked. "I thought there was a lot of country too rough for trucks in Montana."

"That's what horses are for," Charles told him, and Joseph laughed, though Charles hadn't meant to be funny.

With the old man's help, he got the vehicle started and heading the right way.

"Chelsea," said Joseph in a low voice. "Was that because I wouldn't let you change me? My father thinks it is."

"Chelsea was because of Chelsea," Charles told him. "If she had not belonged to your family, I'd have done the same thing." And because it was Joseph, he shared the full truth, shameful as it was. Consent was important; it ought to be necessary. "I'm glad I knew she was Kage's wife, that I could contact him to get permission. My wolf admired her toughness. There aren't many people who can face down a fae geas. I think that he would have insisted we Change her no matter what Kage had said."

Joseph listened, and said, "That's pretty messed up. But it will probably work out okay."

"I hope so," Charles said.

"Brother Wolf isn't going to try that with me?" Joseph's voice was wary.

Charles laughed, a small laugh that sounded like it could have been something else. "Brother Wolf is already in mourning for you. He'd roll over and die for you, but he won't do something you'll hate him, hate me, for. You're safe."

They drove for a little while.

"I like Chelsea," Joseph said, breaking the comfortable silence. "She stands up to Hosteen when everyone else backs down. She is tough." He paused. "I would not have chosen this for her, though. Death is a gift, Charles."

"When you are ready to go," agreed Charles. "But not when you have three young children who need you. Do you think *she* would have chosen death over being a werewolf?"

Joseph didn't answer. It was a big question, and he liked to take his time with those.

"HE'S SOFTER THAN I remember him," Kage said as he drove Anna back to the house. "Your husband, Charles. Dad would be so happy when he'd come visit, but he scared the pants off me. Mom would get this funny look and do her best to find some reason to go visit relatives. Sometimes she'd take me with her. He always looked at me like he was deciding how best to kill me."

Anna couldn't help but laugh. "I've seen that look," she

said. "If it helps, I think it's his default when he's worried about something. Not usually murder." *Usually when he kills, his face is very quiet. It doesn't look like he's thinking at all.*

"But he wasn't like that today," Kage said.

She made a neutral noise and then caught herself. She didn't talk about her husband to people, but he was right, Charles had been softer with him. "You know what his job is, right?"

Kage nodded. "Bran's troubleshooter and assassin."

"That's right," she said. "It means that he can't care about anyone, you know? Because that might be the guy who goes nuts and starts a bloodbath Charles has to finish. It was worse after the werewolves came out because it meant that little bit of gray area that allowed him not to kill every-freaking-body who didn't toe the line disappeared."

Kage stiffened.

"Chelsea's not home free," she told him. "But she's tough and she controls herself, right? I've seen her kids; they've grown up with rules tempered with love. That's a good place to start if you become a werewolf."

"But he could be the one called to take care of her if something goes wrong," he said.

"Probably not," she disagreed. "That would be your grand-father."

"Hosteen?" Kage swallowed. "He'd kill her just because."

She started to protest, then swallowed it. She didn't know Hosteen; she couldn't offer reassurances about what Hosteen might or might not do.

They bumped along quietly for a little and then, when the lights of the house were visible, Anna said, "Anyway. Charles is hard. He has to be. Justice and law, right? Because without those he cannot function. He doesn't get close to people—just his father, his brother, his foster sister, and me. And Joseph. That makes you important to him."

He looked at her like he couldn't figure out why she'd told him that.

"You can go to him for help," she said. "That's why he made you get mad at him—so you'd know he was safe.

Hosteen has issues with Chelsea. If you think things are getting out of hand, you call us, okay? Charles isn't soft. He can't afford to be soft. But he is always just." She smiled. "And he's not afraid of Hosteen."

Kage nodded. "Okay. I'll keep it in mind."

They pulled into the parking area next to the house. Kage walked back to the bedroom where his wife was, and Anna walked with him.

Chelsea slept, curled up in the corner of the bed. They'd left the lights on because nothing short of a nuclear explosion was going to wake her up.

Maggie was seated in a rocking chair, reading a book that she'd set down as soon as Kage appeared. Hosteen had a book, too, but his brooding unhappiness was strong enough that Anna's wolf took a decided interest.

Maggie watched her son and then stood up. "Anna?" she said. "Could I have a word with you?"

"*DO* YOU THINK I did the wrong thing? Changing Chelsea instead of letting her die?" Charles asked, again. They were coming up to the house, but Charles drove past the turnoff for the driveway.

"Do I? Yes." That was his friend. Blunt to the point of rudeness, but only with Charles. "Does she?" Joseph made an ambiguous sound that might have been a sigh if he'd had more air. "I think that in the heat of the moment, she would have fought for her life. Any kind of life. I think if you asked her right now, she'd say she was grateful. What she will say in five years or ten?" He shrugged.

"Did you know she was a witch?" Charles asked.

Joseph nodded. "She told me before she married my son. She wanted Maggie and me to understand what we were getting ourselves into. Black witches hunt down people like Chelsea; untrained witches apparently can feed them a lot of power. She's pretty sure that her first husband was killed by a witch hunting her. She changed her name, bundled Max up, and moved from Michigan to Arizona. I told her that we already had werewolves; a witch would be a welcome change."

"And Maggie?"

Joseph said, "It was the worst argument we ever had—and I don't think either of us said a word about it." He shrugged. "My father likes to argue, to use words. I think his way is better—but it is not Maggie's way. So we were silent for a while and things went back to normal. Maggie likes her now."

"But not Hosteen."

Joseph frowned fiercely. "He keeps the old ways so alive he forgets what is true and what is false. He believes witches are evil because the Navajo stories of witches are all about evil witches. He still believes in the monsters in the stories his mother told him and her mother told her."

"Navajo witchcraft is such that Navajo witches are evil. If they are not evil, then they are not witches," Charles said. "And your father is right about the monsters. I've met a few of them. The worst monsters hide in plain sight."

Joseph frowned at him. "Monsters here?"

"I've seen skinwalkers who wear the skins of dead men so they look like the person they have killed. I have seen the Cold Woman," Charles said. He'd forgotten how easy it was to talk to Joseph. "So have you. Do you remember that woman in that old bar in Willcox? The persistent one who tried to get us both to come home with her?"

"Yes," Joseph admitted. "You were pretty adamant that we had to wait for a friend we didn't have."

"Two men went missing that night and were found dead in their car a few weeks later a couple hundred miles away," Charles said.

"She was the Cold Woman," he said. "How did you know?"

"I didn't know then, just knew that she didn't smell human. She was gorgeous. In a room full of richer-looking, certainly better-looking men"—Joseph nudged him with an elbow—"she picks two dirty, tired cowboys? Felt like a trap. I figured out who she was after the bodies turned up. There were no wounds. Just two dead men sitting in a car in the middle of a pleasant spring day, frozen all the way through. The coroner figured someone had murdered them in an ice locker or commercial freezer, then staged the bodies."

"The Cold Woman . . . why didn't you tell me?" he asked.

"By the time I figured it out, you'd met Maggie. The Cold Woman wasn't as important as other things."

"I think I'm glad I didn't know," Joseph said.

"Too much knowledge can make you paranoid all the time," Charles agreed. "It can also make you a target." They came to the junction where the Sani road met the highway. He turned the UTV around and headed back to the ranch house.

"So if my father is right about everything—is Chelsea evil?"

"Hosteen is not right about everything." Charles grinned at Joseph's ironic tone. "And Chelsea is no more evil than you or I." He paused thoughtfully. "Than I am, anyway. I don't know about you." More seriously he said, "There is a scent to black magic—I would smell it."

"Ah, good," Joseph said. Then he said, in the same tone, "My wife will ask you to Change her after I'm dead."

Charles had no time to prepare. No warning to brace himself, and he felt as though he'd been punched: Maggie.

He had loved her once. She was a fiery warrior, Maggie. Tough and smart and funny—and unexpectedly tender. If he closed his eyes, he could still see her, her beautiful bright eyes wet and luminous. There were many things in his years on earth that were faded by time, but not that night. That night was clear as cut glass.

"IF YOU WOULD have me, I would be yours," Maggie said, moonlight softening her fierce young features into something more accessible.

He knew how hard those words were from this proud woman who did not believe in making herself vulnerable for anyone. Her childhood had been hard and hadn't made it easy for her to trust.

The night air was crisp—spring in the desert. The wooden

boards of her porch were uneven under his feet. He could hear the wild-caught horses in the corrals moving idly a dozen yards from the little house. Could hear the soft sounds of Joseph's sleeping breath.

Her roughened hands reached out slowly, and he did not back away. They touched his face and he closed his eyes, allowing himself the comfort of her touch. To be touched with love was uncommon in his life, and he treasured it, absorbed it.

She was beautiful, but that had nothing to do with why he loved her. He loved her for her refusal to give in to a world that twice judged her wrongly, first for the color of her skin and then for her sex. He loved her for the joy she took in the sun on her back and the horses she rode. He loved her for the laughter she found in danger and storms.

And that was why he'd let it go this far. Far enough that she risked her battered heart—and he'd done it knowing that he would break it. There was no name for the depth of hell he deserved for doing that to a woman he loved.

He pulled back gently. "You don't know me, Maggie. If you knew what I am, you would not touch me." But he knew her. And that knowledge gave him no hope to cling to—no excuse for letting her think that they might be more than what they were.

"I know you," she said, trying to hide her hurt. She couldn't hide from him, but he didn't let her know that. Her pride he would protect as well as he could; it was easier than protecting her poor heart. His poor heart.

"We may have known each other for only four months," she continued. "But those have been four months of sixteen-, sometimes eighteen-hour days. I know you, Charles Smith."

You don't even know my name, he thought in despair. *And I don't dare give it to you.* He wanted to take what she offered, wanted to drown himself in her until he wasn't alone anymore.

"I am not who you think I am," he told her. *I am a liar. I have lied because I could not bear for you to turn away from me.*

"If you tell me you're a murderer," she said stoutly, "I'd say

that whoever you killed deserved it. If you tell me you are a
thief, I'd not believe it. Thieves don't work as hard as you do,
and I should know. My dad was a thief and a murderer—he
killed my mother as surely as if he'd shot her. I know evil,
Charles. And I know a good man when I see him."

His father's rules rang in his ears. *No one must know
what you are.* Charles had lived long enough, seen enough,
to know that his father was right—and still. She thought
that he was a good man when he wasn't a man at all.

"You know a good man, do you?" he asked, feeling anger
sweep up and make him light-headed. *"Do you?"* asked
Brother Wolf, hurt and enraged that he would be the cause
of such tragedy. Brother Wolf loved her, too, but he knew
that she could not love him. Would not love him. "Then see
me, Margaret. See me and tell me again that you love me."

In despair and anger then—knowing what would happen
because even though she did not know him, he did know
her—he did what he'd sworn he would not do. He let Brother
Wolf's shape take him, glorying in the odd quirk of magic
that let him shift swiftly, faster now because it had been so
long since he'd allowed Brother Wolf to stand out in the real
world.

Maggie froze. For a moment there was no expression on
her face at all, and then it went blank with fear. She screamed
and stumbled away from him, falling to the ground and curling into a ball. Not physical fear, but fear of what he was,
what he might turn her into. The Navajo had more experience
than most with the ugly side of magic.

Joseph barreled out the front door and saw Maggie and
Charles. He'd always been quick; he took in everything at
a glance. Joseph, the son of a werewolf, knew what Charles
was, had known what Charles was from the first.

But Joseph was also the son of his mother, who had been
so frightened when she found out what it was she had
married that she'd left them and gone back to the reservation. Joseph understood the terror that had stricken Maggie
silent, too.

Joseph knelt and gathered Maggie into his arms and

made soothing noises. She quieted, her head buried against his shoulder so she couldn't see the wolf. Joseph looked up at Charles.

"Give her some time," he counseled. "Let her see that the wolf is still you."

If he'd listened, maybe his life would have been different, and so would Joseph's. But he hadn't listened; he'd left at a run, knowing that she'd be safe with Joseph. When he came back a year later, he had not been surprised to learn that Joseph and Maggie were married.

"DID YOU EVER think about what might have happened if you hadn't left that night?" said Joseph.

It didn't surprise him that Joseph understood what Charles had been thinking about. Dying left a man very close to the whole spirit of the world, and odd things made it through. As long as he didn't draw Joseph's attention to it, Joseph wouldn't even notice.

"Yes," Charles said.

Joseph laughed. "You ever lie?"

"Not unless lives are on the line," he told his old friend.

"Yeah, I remember a few of those times," he agreed. "Now that you mention them." There was a natural pause. "The stories I've heard about you and Anna—they tell me that you've learned to fight for what you want."

Charles let that ride for a moment, trying to frame the truth. "I think I've learned what I wanted. Maggie could never have loved Brother Wolf the way we needed her to. In a stupid way, I think that's why I wanted her so badly."

"Man, that's twisted," said Joseph. "You loved her because she only loved your human half." He thought a moment. "Is that, like, sibling rivalry? Does that mean you have a ménage à trois now, you old rogue, you?"

Charles found himself smiling. "Maybe *à quatre*, don't you think? Anna has a wolf side, too."

Joseph fell asleep as Charles drove up to the house. He slept while Charles carried him up to the door. Maggie opened it before he needed to worry about how to get through it without waking Joseph up. She followed him silently up to Joseph's apartment and watched as he tucked Joseph in. The host of medical equipment had been pulled to the side of the room and stood like a grim, silent reminder that this chance to talk with his old friend was a finite thing.

"You don't sleep in here?" he asked. Because this room was all Joseph.

"He sent me away," Maggie told him. "Right after the cancer came back. Told me I needed my sleep." She leaned against the wall and looked at Joseph. "He probably meant it. But the pain makes sleep very hard for him to find; mostly he dozes because he can't really sleep. I move in my sleep, I always have. He can't sleep with me in his bed." She pushed off the wall and walked to the bed.

"You could sleep with him tonight," he told her. "He's exhausted, and the pain shouldn't be too bad."

"An effect of your magic?" she asked. "It's good that something could stop the pain." She looked at Charles. "I know it's not permanent, but it is hard not to hate you for leaving him alone when you could have helped. He's been in so much pain."

He opened his mouth to tell her that it wasn't his magic. That he had no idea why the spirits had decided to relieve Joseph of his burden for a while. That they probably wouldn't have helped earlier. But he closed his mouth without speaking. She didn't need truth. She needed someone to be angry at because anger was easier than pain. He could give her that.

She sat down on the bed and turned her attention to Joseph, who slept like a child.

"Silly old man," she said, brushing his hair with her hand. "Think a little magic is going to turn back the years? So you can go out and break mustangs and women's hearts again?"

It can, Charles thought. Because he'd lied to Kage. He could pull Joseph through the Change whether or not his old friend wanted him to. Chelsea had taught him how to do it.

In his heart, he ached more for this man than he ever had for Maggie, and his heart had ached plenty for her.

"What am I going to do with you?" Maggie asked her husband.

Joseph didn't answer her, and neither did Charles.

"Go away," she told him finally, her hand on Joseph's cheek. Just as she had touched him once.

A long time ago.

He left, closing the door carefully, and pretended he didn't know she was crying.

6

After putting Joseph to bed, Charles checked in with Anna, who was sitting in the rocking chair in Chelsea's room working on her current knitting project. Hosteen was in the room, too. Chelsea would need a dominant werewolf around for a while, until they were certain she could control her wolf. The most dangerous time would be when she woke up after the first deep sleep.

"Maggie needed to take a break," Anna said, looking up at him. "She went up to check on Joseph." She paused, but he thought it was because she'd done something wrong to her knitting while she was looking at him, because she pulled out a few stitches before continuing.

"She's up there now," he told Anna. "He's sleeping. We tired him out."

"I told her that he'd come down to the barn," Anna said. "She wasn't pleased. We sent Kage away, though. Chelsea's been showing signs that she might be waking up. Have to get the fragile humans out of the room, just in case."

"I told Anna that one person watching another sleep was plenty," said Hosteen. "Maybe you can persuade her."

"I'm just fine," said Anna. "I have to get this knitted before Christmas, anyway."

"It's February," said Hosteen.

"Yes, I know," his Anna deadpanned. "I should have given myself a little more time. Now I have to speed up my knitting to compensate."

She didn't want to leave Hosteen alone with Chelsea, thought Charles. He saw Maggie's touch in this, but Maggie knew Hosteen better than Charles did. If she thought it would be good not to leave the Salt River Alpha alone with Chelsea, she was probably right.

"I need to call Da, anyway," Charles told Anna. "You stay here and knit. I'll come back when I'm done." He didn't tell her to be careful. His da used her all the time to help wolves who were awaking from that first sleep. She knew the dangers, and she was better equipped, even than Charles or Hosteen, to deal with any trouble.

He kissed Anna on the cheek and headed up to their rooms. His father needed to know how closely Charles had walked the line of the law they all lived by.

"YOU CHANGED HER without her consent," the Marrok said softly when Charles finished. "Without talking to me. And she is witchborn."

His da was just repeating what Charles had already told him, so he saw no reason to say anything more. He also knew it would annoy the Marrok, and decided it served him right for the implied chastisement. Da knew that Charles wouldn't Change someone lightly.

Silence played loudly between them. Until he heard his father take a deep breath and release it. When he spoke he sounded more willing to discuss the matter.

"You are certain she was bespelled by a fae?"

"Absolutely," Charles replied. And that was the real cause of his da's temper.

When Bran spoke again, he didn't sound happy, but he wasn't playing the chastising Alpha, either. "You got her husband's consent, which will appease the worst of the letter-of-the-law crowd. Most of them are old enough to believe that a husband's word is good enough for his wife. I will give my retroactive permission—it was an emergency situation. The witchborn part can stay between us. It may not be against our law to Change a witchborn, but it is frowned upon. There is no sense in making a nasty monster into a nastier one."

Charles listened for irony, but he didn't hear it. That didn't mean it wasn't there. Bran was witchborn and he certainly considered himself a very nasty monster. So did Charles. He'd glimpsed what lurked inside his da, and if he never saw it again, it would be too soon.

"She's not a black witch," Charles told his da, because that was important. "She hid her witch blood pretty well. I got only a faint scent until I tasted it in her blood. It might have been what attracted the fae's attention to her, though. Or she might have seen something that a human would have overlooked, and the fae tried to get rid of her."

"It sounds as though the fae was trying to get rid of her children."

Charles grunted. "That's a fae thing, going after children. But she was supposed to kill herself, too."

His father sighed. "I suppose you're going to go looking for the fae."

There was a long silence, because Charles seldom bothered answering stupid questions.

His da swore, taking a good long time about it. That he used Welsh made it softer sounding—and might fool someone who didn't know him about just how frustrated he was. The drop into Welsh meant he was really unhappy.

"It took us a long time to hammer out that agreement," he complained, his voice a little bitter. "And it's been in place not even six months. My whole intent was to keep our people safe."

"It attacked *children*," Charles said. He wasn't pleading, not really. Because whatever his da said, he was going after it.

"*Mortal* children," growled his father harshly. "*Human.*"

When he heaved a big sigh, Charles knew he'd won, even before his father spoke. "The first trespass was theirs. They attacked the great-grandchildren of the Salt River Pack Alpha. You won't be breaking the treaty because they already did. Maybe I can salvage something from this. Find out who it is and stop them."

"By whatever means necessary," Charles clarified.

"This is a fae capable of making a woman kill her children," his da snapped. "Assuming that she didn't have a hidden desire to kill them?"

"No," said Charles. "Quite the opposite."

"Then this is a powerful fae. Mind control, forcing someone to act against their nature and perform a specific task, especially a task repugnant to them, is rare. At least outside Underhill it is rare. Leaving such an enemy alive is stupid. Find this one and kill him if you can." He snorted, and his voice was full of self-directed amusement. "I'll deal with the Gray Lords. You go kill whatever is attacking children. And tell Hosteen that I authorized it." He muttered, "Not that he'd wait for my approbation, either."

The Marrok ended the call.

Charles loosened his shoulders to lessen the tension of Brother Wolf's eagerness. "I told you he would not object," he murmured. They would hunt, but it would take patience and care. Hunting a fae was different from hunting a deer or elk. More challenging—and more satisfying.

Then his phone rang.

"You couldn't tell she was witchborn until you tasted her blood?" asked his father.

"YOU CAN LEAVE," Hosteen told Anna. He'd been pacing for the better part of the twenty minutes that had passed since he'd driven Kage and Maggie out of the guest room, with a brief pause when Charles had come in.

He stopped moving, possibly accidentally, between Anna and the bed where Chelsea lay in the comalike sleep that marked the Change from human to werewolf. He put his hands on his hips, stared at Anna, and waited for her to obey him.

Alphas were used to people obeying them.

Anna raised her eyebrow at him and continued to knit, rocking herself in a dark wooden rocking chair that was a lot more comfortable than it had looked when she sat down in it. Knitting was new for her.

She'd started with quilting. She loved the feel and looks of the fabric. It was like making stained-glass pictures with cloth, and it was an effective gateway drug. Weekly lessons with one of the people who kept the little craft store in Aspen Creek had led her into a whole world. She'd found knitting particularly useful because it let her wait without being restless.

"I'm not going to hurt her," Hosteen said, nodding toward the bed.

"Okay," Anna said, continuing to work on the sweater she was making for Charles.

The last one had not turned out very well, and she was determined that this one would be better. It was red, his favorite color. She wasn't ready to try any kind of fancy pattern yet, but so far the sweater was looking like the picture in her how-to book, so she was encouraged. Except, that is, for those weird little holes that crept in here and there.

"*Go,*" Hosteen said with power.

She gave him a chiding click of her tongue, though it wasn't diplomatic. But she wasn't feeling very charitable toward him because he thought she was stupid. Anna could tell when someone was trying to lie with the truth. It didn't tingle her magic werewolf senses, but her plain old body language skills were plenty adequate. Sure, he wouldn't *hurt* Chelsea: death can be painless.

The idea that Hosteen would kill Chelsea would never have occurred to her. For one thing, murder was murder, even among werewolves. But Kage had been worried, and Maggie had been emphatic. Hosteen's actions since then weren't exactly subtle. She didn't know Chelsea, but she wasn't going to let anyone be murdered on her watch.

"Charles asked me to stay here," she said, rather than confronting Hosteen with his lie. "You aren't *my* Alpha—and even if you were, he can't *make* me do anything, either." She tapped herself in the chest with one of her needles and half sang, *"Omega. Me."* Dropping into her own voice, she said, "As an Omega wolf, I don't have the urge to obey you. At all. Not even the tiniest bit. Don't worry, it makes the Marrok crazy, too." There was another of those funny holes in the row of otherwise neat stitches she'd just finished.

"What do you think I'm going to do to her?" he asked. "She's the mother of my great-grandchildren."

Anna met his eyes. "Then why do you want to be alone with her so badly?"

He flinched from her gaze. "Two wolves aren't necessary," he said. "I can keep her wolf in line, and you are, forgive me, not family."

"I can help her keep herself in line," she told him, "because I am an Omega wolf." She quit speaking, holding up her knitting again. There was another stupid hole. "But that's not why I'm here. I'm here to protect her from you."

He turned his back to her altogether. Anna wasn't sure why. Alphas, she'd noticed, had weird reactions to Omega wolves. He could be ashamed, or he could be fighting off his temper.

"Witches are evil," he said without turning around. He was telling the truth as he knew it. Mostly as Anna knew it, as well.

"So I've noticed," she agreed.

He turned back to her, his surprise evident. Some idiot had been arguing that point, evidently. Anna hadn't been in the supernatural world long, but the scariest person she'd encountered (other than the Marrok himself) had been a witch.

"Most of them, anyway," she continued. "But you can tell when they've turned." She tapped her nose with the end of one of her needles and went back to work.

"All witches are evil," he told her.

She pursed her lips. *"A fructibus eorum cognoscetis eos."*

"By their fruits shall you know them?" He didn't have

any trouble with her Latin—she must be getting better. "She tried to kill her own children. That is her fruit."

"No," she said patiently, though she didn't know exactly why she was arguing with him. Kage had been married to Chelsea long enough to have two children. If his own grandson hadn't changed Hosteen's mind, she probably wasn't going to be able to. Her job was just to keep Chelsea safe. "You know that. She *didn't* kill her children, though she was under a strong fae compulsion. Charles thinks that it was her witch blood that let her resist. The fae don't break their spells with 'blood and spit,' that's a witch thing. She bled herself nearly to death to *keep* from doing evil. That is, in my book, the very opposite of evil."

After a moment of silence, Hosteen came over to her and sat on his heels in front of the rocking chair, putting his head level with hers. "You're doing it wrong."

She raised an eyebrow.

"The knitting," he told her, his face still serious. He indicated her beginning-of-a-sweater-for-Charles with a jerk of his chin. "You have holes. You've been letting your yarn get in front of your knitting. That's why you aren't getting a solid pattern."

Anna brought her knitting up where she could examine it, as if she hadn't already noticed the stupid holes—seven of them scattered irregularly.

"You aren't paying attention to your yarn," he said. "We all do it once in a while, pay so much attention to making things right that you make mistakes in the simple things. If the yarn is in front, between your needles while you're knitting, you're actually purling where you should be knitting. It leaves a hole. It's a legitimate stitch, actually; it's called a yarn over."

"Son of a gun," she said. "That's where those little suckers are coming from."

He laughed, sounding tired.

"You know how to knit?" Anna asked. She was going to have to unravel it down to the first few rows to get rid of them all.

Hosteen nodded. "My mother taught me to weave. I enjoy it; most of the rugs you see in this house are mine. But weaving takes a loom and sometimes it is good to have something to do with your hands. So I learned to knit and crochet and cross-stitch."

"I thought that traditionally weaving was a woman's thing among the Navajo?"

He snorted. "Navajo men did what there was to do—just as Navajo women did."

Anna sighed, looked at the inches of sweater she'd managed, and then pulled on the loose yarn to unravel it.

Hosteen sighed, too, his sigh quieter than Anna's had been.

"You think," Anna said gently, "it might just be possible that you may have been paying so much attention to the duty that requires you to keep your pack and your family safe that you might have made a little, very important misjudgment?" she asked.

Hosteen said, "In my experience, either witches are evil, or they are victims waiting until one of their kind notices them and comes hunting. At which time many people who cared about the white witch die as well."

"Okay," agreed Anna easily, watching the unraveling piece in her lap instead of looking at Hosteen. She didn't want to make him uncomfortable now that he was actually talking to her, but she wasn't going to make a big thing about dropping her eyes for him, either. No sense in letting him think that he was her boss.

"I mostly agree," she continued. "I know exactly four exceptions to that rule: Charles, the Marrok, Samuel, and a witch I know in Seattle."

"Bran and his sons don't count. If a witch has power enough to defend herself, she has sacrificed someone for it," Hosteen said unequivocally.

"Sacrifice, yes," Anna conceded. "But the witch I knew paid the price for her power herself rather than hurt anyone else. She isn't evil, and she is very powerful." It was discouraging how quickly the beginnings of a sweater turned into a

loose pile of yarn. She took the ball and began winding, careful not to stretch the yarn out as she put it back on the ball.
"Why do you think the Marrok and his sons don't count?"

"They are werewolves," he said, taking her bait.

She'd learned to argue from her father, a very good lawyer. "Let them argue themselves into your court if you can
manage it," he'd told her. "They'll do a better job of convincing themselves than you ever could."

Anna looked up at the Salt River Alpha blandly. Then she
looked at Chelsea, who was beginning to look younger. The
crow's-feet were fading from around her eyes, and her skin,
formerly Arizona tan, was paler. She couldn't see any of the
cuts Chelsea had made; most of those had been on her body
and were covered with a quilt. But if the lycanthropy was
healing the marks of aging, Anna assumed it would have
already healed the other marks, too.

Anna didn't state the obvious.

"Old werewolves," he snarled. "Not new made."

"Who were once young werewolves—witchborn," she
told him. "And not evil."

"Evil is going against the nature of things, the way things
should be," he told her with painful exactness. "Evil twists
and turns and smells of blood and disease and death. I am
evil, too. I fight it every day, the evil inside me. But I fear
that it has a hold on my heart, tempts me to force my son so
that I won't be alone. I fight it. But I don't know if she will.
How can anyone fight two monsters in their heart and win?"

He looked faintly surprised at his own words, but more
dismayed that he'd told her so much. Anna had, well, not
grown used to the peculiarity of having normally taciturn or
repressed wolves suddenly spill their inner thoughts to her,
exactly, but she was no longer surprised. They talked to her
of their pain or sorrow because their wolves *knew* that she
was no threat.

Looking at Hosteen's dismay, she decided that in addition
to quilting and knitting, she needed to learn something about
counseling, too. If people were going to air their darkest sor-
rows to her, she ought to know how to help them. All she could

do now was run with her instincts and gather the wisdom her twenty-odd years on the planet had given her to counsel a man five times her age.

"We all carry within us the seeds of the child we were," she said slowly. "The ideas of right and wrong and proper behavior. Charles will not speak the name of the dead if he can help it." For Charles, she fervently believed, that taboo was a good one. His ghosts were dangerous. "The ways of the culture we were born into stay with us, even if we live as long as Bran or the Moor have. Some of those ideas are right and good, but others are modes of survival outdated by the passing of time. Like the idea that men shouldn't weave or knit, or . . . wear pink and flowers unless it's on a Hawaiian shirt. The trouble seems to be sorting one from the other."

"You think the monster I see in Chelsea is a remnant of some outmoded cultural leftover," he said neutrally.

"Oh, no," Anna said, her voice so definite she almost winced. She continued more carefully. "Most people carry a monster within. Not just werewolves or fae, most *people*. That monster has nothing to do with our wolf except that the wolf makes it more dangerous. It's a monster born of our own selfish desires and the wounds that life leaves on all of us. Whether those lives are a couple of decades or a couple of centuries long, living means that we get hurt, and some of those wounds don't heal or they don't heal completely."

She had her own monster, didn't she? Her own darkness that she tried to keep out of sight. A monster that would surprise her mate with its ferocity. Born of helplessness that was made worse by the understanding that there had been help just waiting for her if she'd known how to reach for it.

She hid that monster from everyone because it would hurt Charles if he knew that she carried those scars still. But since she was admitting her weaknesses here, if only to herself, she also worried that it would interfere with his image of the person he thought she was. He thought she was brave and true and good, and she wasn't. Inside, she was dark and ferocious. If he truly understood that she had this twisted and broken part, maybe he could not love her.

But this wasn't about her. Hosteen needed to see what she carried, so he'd understand he was not alone. And so he would not remember this conversation and feel humiliated because he'd told her so many things and she had not left herself as vulnerable to him. So she let that darkness fill her and looked him in the eye.

He stepped back, involuntarily.

She stopped it, swallowing her broken pieces until she had them tucked out of sight, where she kept them unless she needed to draw on that rage and viciousness.

"We *all* fight to be better than our base instincts, Hosteen," she told him, her voice a little rough.

"What happened?" he asked. She saw the protective instinct that made his Alpha kick in: it wasn't the response she'd expected.

"Do you think that Charles would not have taken care of any problems I might have faced?" she asked.

He nodded solemnly. "Chicago. I heard that Charles killed Leo over his treatment of a newly Changed wolf." He paused. "That's what he was talking about over dinner."

She was losing control of the conversation; time to put it back where it belonged. "Leo didn't fight his monster. It is not only witches who are tempted by darkness. When we werewolves fail to contain that monster, then it is up to our pack to make sure we don't hurt anyone. Up to our Alpha, really. For Chelsea, that will be you."

He nodded. His responsibility. Alphas, she had noticed, were very responsible people. That was it, that was the key. The reason he felt he had to take care of Chelsea, in the hit-man sense of the phrase.

"But we don't all fail, do we?" Anna said softly. "Too many of us, yes, but not all." She looked at the unconscious woman. "Brother Wolf doesn't think that she will fail. That's why Charles Changed her. It was not impulse, it was inspiration that drove him. His inspiration is more accurate than most people's."

Hosteen rose to his feet and looked down upon his daughter-in-law. "She is strong-minded," he said, then smiled a little. "I've never had anyone argue with me by listening before. You must drive Bran wild. You listen and tug a little, and listen and push a little, and in the end you persuade me not to do—"

"—something you never wanted to do." Anna finished winding her yarn and began knitting again, paying special attention to which side of her knitting the yarn fell on. "My dad always says it's easier to convince someone of something they already want to believe."

"She saved Kage's children." He reached out and touched Chelsea's cheek. She stirred under his touch and then quieted. He left his hand there.

Anna tensed. She was too far away to stop him, assuming she could stop him. But she didn't think she'd have to.

He bowed his head and then looked over his shoulder at Anna. "You—" His voice broke. Probably because the Marrok was talking to him, too.

Anna, get out of there. The witchborn don't always make the transition from witch to wolf easily. If she was strong enough to hide herself from Charles's wolf, then she's strong enough to be dangerous. Strong enough to hide if she is a dark witch. Charles is coming, but you and Hosteen get out of there right now.

She couldn't respond to him. The Marrok couldn't hear her if she talked back to him.

Hosteen looked at her. *"A fructibus eorum cognoscetis eos,"* he quoted back at her softly. "How strongly do you believe that, now? What do you think the Marrok told Charles to do to her? What can he do that you and I could not?"

Anna put her knitting down and walked over to the bed. Chelsea had been restless for the past half hour or so. Bran's message had spiked the adrenaline in both Anna and Hosteen, and that was enough. Chelsea's heartbeat was picking up; Anna could smell fear and helpless frustration in a growing wave. That first deep sleep often reset the newly rising werewolves' memories to the moments right before they were bitten. That was why it was such a dangerous moment.

She took one more deep breath just as magic, a lot of magic, flooded the room. Bran was right; Chelsea Sani was not a weak witch. Not at all.

Chelsea sat up in one explosive movement, staring at Hosteen without recognition or sanity in her eyes. Panicked, she rose to a crouch, crying out involuntarily, a harsh wolflike sound. The magic, which had been strong, suddenly made it hard to breathe in the room, as if the magic had replaced the oxygen.

Anna met Hosteen's eyes and then showed him what being an Omega really meant as she flooded the room with her own particular and peculiar power.

CHARLES JUMPED RATHER than ran down the stairs, conscious of startling Kage when he landed beside Joseph's son at the foot of the stairs with more sound than he usually allowed himself. But just now Charles was more interested in speed than stealth.

He threw open the door to the room where Hosteen had stashed Kage's wife. And jumped back like a scalded cat almost before he felt the touch of Anna's magic.

"Heyya, Charles," slurred Hosteen as though he were drunk. He was leaning against the wall on the far side of where Anna had dropped her knitting in a deep red tangle of yarn and needles. "Come join the par-ty." Then Hosteen giggled.

Anna gave Charles a helpless look, her back to the werewolf and the bed.

Charles grinned at Anna through the open door, but he didn't approach any closer. Brother Wolf wanted to go in and roll in her power like a cat in catnip, but Charles kept him back. If the attack on Chelsea had been directed at the werewolves, then someone needed to be prepared to defend the people in this house. It wouldn't be Hosteen, not for a few hours anyway. If he entered the sphere of his wife's influence, it wouldn't be Charles, either.

Kage came running down the hallway, not werewolf fast, but human-athlete fast. He gave Charles an odd look but didn't slow as he ran into the room.

Kage was human. He'd probably be okay. Anna's most deadly weapon worked best on dominant werewolves, especially a dominant werewolf whose wolf was kept tied up in little knots because his human half was still, after a century of being a werewolf, convinced that the wolf was something evil. At least Charles thought that might be why Hosteen's reaction was this extreme.

"Grandson," Hosteen intoned solemnly. "I've decided to let your wife live until she does something evil."

A woman whom Charles couldn't see from his hallway position snickered. It wasn't Anna, who grimaced at Charles because she knew that there would be hell to pay for this tomorrow. They both knew a wolf like Hosteen wouldn't forgive her lightly for doing this to him.

"Evil," said the other woman, who could only be Chelsea, though she sounded quite different from the woman he'd heard talk at dinner. She spoke dramatically with a touch of comic flare that might or might not have been intentional. "I'd like to do some evil to you right now, you old bastard. But mostly I'd like to do something evil with my sweetie." Her voice was relaxed and smoldering.

"Chelsea?" said Kage, in a poleaxed voice.

Charles couldn't see the woman from his vantage point, and he wasn't getting any closer until the effect lessened a bit. Hosteen's stress level could explain the giggling Alpha, but Charles thought Chelsea had been hit hard, too. It was always possible Anna had put more oomph than usual into her "Omega superpower," as she liked to call it.

Anna cleared her throat. "Sometimes people wake up from the first sleep after the Change and feel a little aroused. Nothing to worry about and it usually goes—"

There was a flash of motion that had Charles moving forward, even though he knew the danger of getting too close to Anna. But Chelsea fell onto the hardwood floor, finally in Charles's line of sight. She fell softly, muscles relaxed, and lay where she'd landed, looking up at her husband with a pleased smile.

Charles recovered and retreated.

"—away," continued Anna valiantly, "when they try to move and realize that they have to learn how to deal with muscles that are stronger and respond more quickly than they're used to. It's a good distraction, because sex is not a good place to experiment with augmented strength. Most people are back to normal in a day or so."

Kage crouched down beside his wife and touched her cheek. Charles couldn't see his expression but had no trouble reading the love and relief in the bend of his head and the softening of his shoulders.

"Hey, little rabbit," he said huskily. "You okay?"

Chelsea blinked up at him, and then her whole body tightened. "The children . . . I . . . the children. Kage?"

"They are fine," he told her. "Freaked-out. But fine. They are asleep as of ten minutes ago. Ernestine is staying in the suite with them tonight."

Chelsea fought to stay focused, but Anna's power was too much. It said something about how dominant her wolf was going to be that Anna affected her nearly as much as she affected Hosteen. Or maybe Anna was getting stronger. Chelsea's body grew looser and her face softened into a smile. "That bastard wanted to kill me," she said, pointing a wobbly finger at Hosteen. "I heard him."

"*Didn't* want to," said Hosteen; he sounded as though he were talking to himself. "Never a good thing when you have to kill the mother of your great-grandchildren. Could scar them for life." It didn't sound as though it bothered him much. "But it's like knitting and purling. I don't have to. Not until you do something evil, witch."

Kage's head turned and he looked at Hosteen, hostility in every line of his body.

"Actually," Anna said quietly, "I think he was trying very hard to find a reason not to kill her. Very hard. He wouldn't have been so easy to talk out of it otherwise."

Hosteen giggled again. "The Marrok told me to do it. After

I decided not to. Spoke in my head. I hate it when he does that; creepy. I thought, 'Geez, old man, if you want someone to do your dirty work, you get Charles to do it. I'm not going to follow orders and destroy my family for you.' " He sighed, a happy, contented sound, and slid down the wall until he was seated on the floor, his feet stretched out until they nearly touched Chelsea's hair.

He looked at Anna and tried to frown. "What did you do to me, little girl? I haven't felt like this since . . . since . . . since I was six and my father gave me a glass of whiskey to drink before he set my wrist. Got tossed off a horse and we lived out in the wild country. My ma, she didn't trust those white doctors in town, anyway. They didn't know about the evil spirits, didn't know how to sing them out of a body. So my dad, he set it. Used to ache something fierce some days. But not since I became a werewolf."

"What happened to him?" Kage asked Anna. "I've never seen him like this. I thought werewolves couldn't get drunk."

Chelsea reached up, grabbed her husband by the back of the neck, and dragged his startled head down to hers.

"Charles Cornick," said Maggie in a soft voice from just behind him.

Charles realized that he'd stepped too close to the room because Maggie caught him by surprise. If he hadn't been affected by Anna, no one, especially not a human, would have been able to sneak up on him. He turned his head to see Maggie with an odd expression on her face.

"I don't think I've ever seen you laugh like that," she said.

ANNA WOKE UP blearily, her knitting needles on her lap. It took her a moment to remember why she was sleeping in a rocking chair with Charles, in wolf form, curled up at her feet.

Chelsea slept on. She'd been awake for less than an hour, spending most of that time eating. When she'd fallen back asleep, Kage escorted his still-giddy grandfather upstairs.

Maggie had gone back to Joseph's room as soon as she was certain there was nothing to worry about.

Kage had come down to check his wife, and Anna had driven him gently back to his own room.

"No sex," she'd told him, again. "Not until Chelsea truly understands her own strength. And that means separate beds, because the Change will increase Chelsea's libido by a lot."

He'd nodded, touched his wife's face, and smiled when she moved toward him without opening her eyes. "You'll watch over her?"

Charles said wryly, "Since Anna's incapacitated the only other person who could do that, yes, we'll stay here."

"How did you manage that?" Kage asked.

She shrugged. "I'm an Omega wolf. I have a tranquilizing effect on other werewolves, but I have to admit I've never seen anything like what happened to Hosteen."

"I've never seen anything like that, either." He hesitated at the door. "She'll be okay?"

Charles nodded. "For tonight, all is as it should be."

He'd left then. She'd turned out the lights and Charles changed into Brother Wolf's form, settling himself by her feet and keeping them warm with his dense fur. She knitted for a while; her eyes were good enough for it even in the dark. Eventually she must have fallen asleep.

Charles stirred, standing up and stretching.

"I hear them," Anna assured him, because the sounds of someone getting serious in the kitchen was what had awakened her in the first place. She checked Chelsea, but the new wolf was sleeping deeply.

"Is it safe to leave her long enough to change and freshen up?" she asked Charles.

In answer he led the way out of the room and up to their own. While she showered, he changed and dressed in his preferred fashion statement of battered jeans and bright-colored T-shirt. This one was pumpkin orange and clung to his bone and sinew and made her want to pet him.

Instead she braided her damp hair and dressed herself.

"Wear something comfortable," Charles told her. "We'll probably go out to the barns again this morning."

THEY WALKED INTO the kitchen just as Ernestine put a tray piled high with bacon on the table. Kage, his three kids, and a stranger were already seated at the table.

"Good," said Ernestine. "I was about to send Max to find you and see if you wanted to come down. You can sit where the clean place settings are."

"Good morning," said Kage. "This is Hosteen's second, Wade Koch. Hosteen brought him in to help with Chelsea. Wade, this is Charles and Anna Cornick."

"I know Charles," Wade said. "I'm pleased to meet you, Anna. I've heard a lot about you."

He was a soft-spoken man, neither tall nor short. His eyes were intense when he looked at her.

"Wade," said Charles, his tone of voice telling Anna that he liked this man.

"I'm going to call Chelsea's work this morning," Kage said. "Do you know how long it will take before she's ready to go back to work?"

Charles shook his head. "That depends on her, and how stressful her work is. Not this week, but maybe next week." He hesitated. "I'd keep all the kids around here for a week or so. Not because of Chelsea, but because whoever bespelled her in the first place is still out there."

"That work okay for you and school, Max?" asked Kage.

Max nodded, swallowed, and then said, "I was going to stay home for the first few days of the show anyway. It's only another couple of days on top of that. Most of my teachers post their assignments on the computer. You'll have to call it in for me, though."

"Okay," said Kage. "I'll make the calls, and then if you'd like, we can go out and try a few more horses."

"Where's Hosteen?" asked Charles.

"That man got up about two hours ago, saddled a horse,

and rode off into the desert," said Ernestine. "He told me he had some thinking to do." She looked at Charles. "He said you were to keep his family safe until he got back."

"He did, did he?" said Charles softly.

Ernestine had been walking toward the table. She stopped.

"Do you remember exactly what Hosteen said?" asked Kage.

"He said that the family would be safe with Charles here," she said slowly. "He told me to ask you to keep an eye out for them."

Charles nodded. "That's fine." He went back to eating.

Ernestine gave him a cautious look that he didn't see. Anna smiled at her. "This is very good," she said. "I don't know when Chelsea will get up, but she'll be hungry again. It might be a good idea to put together some food for her. Well-fed werewolves are easier to deal with than hungry ones."

ANNA RODE THREE more horses. Her favorite of the morning was a quick-moving gelding named Ahmose who had a long scar down the length of his shoulder.

When Anna, Charles, and Kage, sweaty and smelling like horses, got back to the house, Chelsea was sitting at the table and eating ravenously. She looked up when they came in.

"Hey," she said. "I've been thinking about yesterday. I felt just fine driving to the day care. But by the time I was belting the kids into the car, I had a killer headache. I don't get headaches as a rule, and it seems to me that it was part of the whole compulsion that eventually pushed me to try to hurt the kids."

"You are witchborn," said Charles. "Trust your instincts. It happened at the day care?"

"Yes."

"There've been some other bad things happening at the day care lately," Anna said. "I had a long talk with Max about it yesterday. He said that they had a teacher commit suicide. And they also had a family killed in a car wreck."

Chelsea nodded. "People do commit suicide, and they die

in traffic accidents, but I am not naturally inclined to kill my children and then myself. If one of those was a spell, maybe all of them were?"

"I think," said Charles, "that Anna and I will go visit the day care. If there is a fae there, one of us should be able to figure out who it is."

"Should be?" asked Kage.

"This fae is strong," Charles answered. "A powerful fae can disguise itself from a werewolf."

"I'll stay here," Wade said. "I've taken the next few days off work."

CHAPTER

7

There were kids everywhere. Kids slid down miniaturized slides and climbed plastic play forts in bright colors, and a few plastic play forts in dull, sun-bleached colors. Kids in sandpits dug with plastic shovels or threw sand on one another. One little boy in jeans and a pale blue T-shirt was running as fast as he could as two little girls chased him with death on their faces. Anna hoped he could run fast or he was in for it.

Adults fluttered among the chaos of children. Some of them brought order with them like the best Alphas did. Some of them elicited excitement and happiness. Some of them made the kids scatter before them like chickens in front of a fox.

She left her hand on her husband's arm, feeling the tension in him, knowing it was her fault. She would never do anything to harm her husband in any way—not on purpose.

Yet she was unwilling to sit around and wait a hundred years for the opportunity to have children. It wasn't impatience, no matter what Charles thought. Werewolves could live forever, but on average lived far shorter lives than their human originally could have expected to.

Charles did not live quietly. More even than the Marrok, he lived with a target painted on his chest. As the werewolves crept further out of the shadows and into the daily lives of ordinary people, the list of his enemies increased.

Anna hadn't died the day she'd been involuntarily Changed, had in fact been made less mortal rather than more. But she had lost her old self as surely as if she *had* died, and it had taught her not to be complacent. She was not impatient, but she no longer trusted life to be good. She had become more conscious, not less, that people died: that she might die, that *Charles* might die. Death was real to her in a way that it had never been real when she had been human.

She was a long way from defeated. His arguments that any child of his would be a target were unassailable. Within the supernatural community, Charles, as the Marrok's son and hatchet man, was very well-known. Eventually even the humans would know about him. Any child of his would be perceived as a weakness. She could not argue that point, but she did not feel as though that necessitated refusing to have a child.

His other stated objection, that there was no current possibility for them to conceive, was more open to argument. She didn't want to argue with him, shouldn't have to argue with him. She'd thought that he'd been willing to listen to the possibilities.

The key, she thought, was to pick through her husband's complicated and mostly unspoken issues with children or with his own children or being a father. She didn't know exactly where his absolute refusal was finding its power. When she found something real, she'd work at the knot of his resistance until she had it unraveled. Then she would go back to the next tangle and do the same thing.

Her brother didn't call her Anna the Relentless for nothing.

She needed a loose end, and so far she hadn't been able to find it. His father might know, but it seemed dishonest and possibly damaging to go to someone else for insight without knowing what kind of a tangle she was working with. Better to get it herself if she could.

Two months of effort had resulted in nothing except the tension in Charles's arm as they walked through the safety zone of the sidewalk.

"Even if they were to choose to attack," she murmured to him, "they are safely caged behind that vinyl chain-link fence. I think you can relax."

"Vinyl doesn't do anything to stop magic," Charles murmured back. "The steel wire beneath might have some effect, but it is best to be prepared."

Under the circumstances it was difficult for her to tell whether he was being funny or serious. Neither of them was under the illusion it was the threat from the fae that was causing his tension.

Still, he had a point about being prepared to face a hostile threat from the fae here. It was time she turn her attention away from having her own children and start trying to discover who had sent Chelsea off to murder hers.

The kids took no notice of a pair of uninteresting adults wandering up to the main doors. Surely if a fae were among them, he or she would notice that Anna and Charles were a little different from most people, but maybe not.

When Charles drew a deep breath of air through his nose, Anna followed suit. She didn't smell any fae—though her experience with fae was fairly limited. She wasn't sure she would detect one right under her nose. Charles didn't say anything, so she assumed that he didn't scent anything, either.

Hosteen had rendered his power to be of assistance moot by his absence. Charles had turned down Kage flatly—one human was as easily bespelled as another. Probably more easily, since Kage was not witchborn like his wife. Wade had been easier because Hosteen's orders were that he was to help with Chelsea, so leaving him home hadn't incited rebellion.

That left Anna and Charles to go check it out. Anna was

pretty sure that being a werewolf wasn't an automatic defense, either, but Charles wasn't worried about confronting a fae. She put her trust in him.

Anna winced as someone blew a shrill whistle on the playground. Charles didn't even twitch as he held the door open for her. She wondered how he managed it.

THERE WAS A big sign on the door immediately to their right as soon as they entered the building. It said PRINCIPAL EDISON—ALL VISITORS PLEASE CHECK IN. It amused Charles. A day care was really just an efficient way to provide baby-sitting and not actually a school.

Anna knocked on the closed door and Charles stepped back to let his wife interface with the public. People liked her, and, as a bonus, she didn't scare them. People talked to him because they were intimidated. Anna could usually get more and better information from people because they honestly wanted to make her happy.

The woman who opened the door of the principal's office looked tired and a little startled to see them, though she tried to cover it over with a big, and mostly sincere, smile.

"Hello," she said, recovering. "You must be Mr. and Mrs. Smith. I'm Farrah Edison. Welcome to Sunshine Fun. You said you have a four-year-old and a five-year-old, right?"

"We'd like to talk to the teachers of the four-year-old and the five-year-old classes," Anna said.

Charles took the opportunity to sample the air in the principal's office. He didn't notice that it smelled particularly of fae-anything. But he wouldn't, because the principal wore Opium, one of the perfumes that tended to kill his ability to scent things.

Anna looked at a ragged piece of paper she carried. "We'd like to see Miss Baird and Ms. Newman. You told us this would be a good time to speak with them both."

Anna's voice rose at the end, as if she weren't sure they were here at the right time, seeming to allow Ms. Edison a graceful way to reschedule things if she needed to. It was a tactful response to the surprise Ms. Edison had displayed; she'd obviously forgotten they were coming.

"Yes. You can talk to Ms. Newman first. Her children are in music for another fifteen minutes. When they get back, Miss Baird's students will go and you can sneak over to her room."

Students and *teachers* at a day care? Charles weighed the vocabulary. He supposed children *were* learning a lot between the ages of two and five. He pursed his lips and regarded the sign again. Maybe this *was* a school.

As they followed the principal down the hallway, she told them about how they planned the meals they served, their hours, and their rates, which were very high. She assured them, without looking at Charles, that they did not discriminate on the basis of race or religion. Every teacher had an assistant teacher for every ten children.

She told them about weekly outings to nearby parks, and that once a month each age group went to a local private swimming pool, where the students would learn to swim. Two-year-olds en masse at a swimming pool sounded to Charles like a disaster waiting to happen. Maybe the remarkable thing was not how many children, teachers, and parents associated with this school had died, but that there had not been more.

Ms. Edison talked a lot, and he rather wished she'd chosen different perfume. He trailed behind Anna and the principal in order to save his nose. Generally the more expensive the perfume, the better it smelled; most chemical re-creations of scent smelled like their chemicals to him. Opium, the perfume Opium anyway, smelled fine; he just couldn't scent much of anything else after he'd been around it very long.

Just before she opened the door, Ms. Edison gave Anna a sharp look. She'd avoided looking at him, Charles had noted, though that might have been because he followed about ten feet behind them. More probably it was the usual response people had around Anna: as long as he didn't draw attention to himself, they grew so focused on her that they forgot about him.

"As I'm sure you know, Miss Baird is new to us this month. Who gave you her name in particular?"

"My sister-in-law," lied Anna smoothly. "But it was a friend of a friend of hers who had children in your day care. I don't know their names, I'm sorry. Just the names of the teachers."

"In all honesty," said Ms. Edison somberly, "I should tell you that we have given her notice. She is new and on probation and there have been some unacceptable disruptions in her classroom."

"I see," said Anna. "I'd still like to speak with her."

"Yes, that's fine. I just didn't want to mislead you."

Anna smiled. "I appreciate that."

Ms. Edison introduced them to Ms. Newman, an Energizer Bunny of a woman wearing too much makeup and perfume that made Brother Wolf sneeze in disgust. It only smelled bad, though, and wouldn't keep him from detecting other scents the way Ms. Edison's did.

Ms. Edison's phone buzzed; she glanced down at a text message, frowned, excused herself, and then abandoned them to their fate with the teacher of four-year-olds.

Ms. Newman talked at them for fifteen minutes without letting Anna get a word in edgewise. In contrast to Ms. Edison, Ms. Newman had no trouble at all paying attention to Charles. Ms. Newman told them, or rather told *him* because she ignored Anna, about her BS in child psychology and about her philosophy of education. While she was doing that, she managed to sneak in a lot of information about her divorce three years ago and how it was so hard to find nice men who weren't already in a relationship.

Anna cleared her throat.

"I believe," said Ms. Newman, still without so much as looking at Anna, "that children benefit from order. Every day they come into my class exactly at seven thirty and we all get out our crayons and set them on the tabletop for inspection. They have to tell me what color each crayon is and something that is that color."

As she described her very regimented schedule for the

children, Charles found himself feeling sorry for them. Children should run and play, not have learning shoved down their throat for their own good from the moment they hit the day care until they left. But Kage's boy had seemed to like this woman, so maybe she knew more than he did.

"I have been on staff for ten years and have more experience than any other teacher here," Ms. Newman told Charles in a voice someone might use to impart state secrets. "When Ms. Edison is ill or when she has to travel, like when she was called away for a death in the family before Christmas, I'm the one who keeps an eye on things." She breathed deeply, drawing attention to an asset that wouldn't help her in her job.

Was it acceptable to wear low-cut shirts to take care of children? he wondered. The mores of the world tended to change more often than he paid attention to them, but her clothing didn't seem to be entirely appropriate.

Ms. Newman looked at him until he felt like a side of beef she was thinking of eating for dinner. Like Ms. Edison, she was scared of him. He hadn't been able to smell the principal's fear, but he'd heard her heart rate speed up. But unlike with the principal, fear seemed to excite Ms. Newman. Brother Wolf much preferred Ms. Edison's avoidance to Ms. Newman's flirtation.

A bell rang from somewhere in the building, and Ms. Newman's face fell. "That's my cue, I'm afraid. It was very nice talking with you," she said to Charles. "I look forward to seeing you again when you bring your child in."

"Ms. Newman," said Anna in a low voice.

Ms. Newman dragged her attention off Charles. Anna put her hand on him and leaned toward the other woman, who stepped back; smart woman.

"You need to understand something," she said intensely. "Charles is my husband. You can't have him. Mine. Not yours. There are lots of nice, unattached men out there, I'm sure. Pick one of them and you might live longer." Then her body relaxed and her voice regained its usual cheeriness. "Thank you for your time, Ms. Newman."

As they left, Charles turned back toward the teacher and

shrugged helplessly. Then he put on his meekest face and turned around to follow Anna.

"I saw that," she muttered at him.

"Saw what?" asked Charles in mock innocence. Brother Wolf was pleased with her claiming of them. So was Charles.

She gave him a look that made him smile, then knocked on the door of the room that bore a temporary paper sign that said MISS BAIRD in big block letters. Behind the door, decorated hopefully with spring flowers and bright green leaves, the strains of cello music wafted out. Charles recognized a recording of Yo-Yo Ma that he often listened to himself. The soon-to-be-unemployed Miss Baird had good taste in music.

The woman who answered Anna's knock looked sad underneath her warm smile. She was very young, a little younger than his wife, he thought. Like Ms. Newman, she smelled entirely human.

Her ash-blond hair was cut short to reveal the bright purple elephant earrings that were the same color as her bright purple shirt. The bright colors only served to emphasize the depression that weighed down her shoulders. She wasn't wearing perfume at all—which meant he already liked her better than Ms. Newman.

"Hello," she said cautiously. "Ms. Edison told me to expect you. She also said she told you that I'm leaving at the end of the week."

Anna nodded. "Yes. We'd still like to speak with you if you don't mind."

Miss Baird's look sharpened, but she backed up and opened the door to invite them in. Her room was not as big as the very-available Ms. Newman's, but it was decorated with art obviously created by her five-year-old students.

One student was washing a whiteboard with a spray bottle and an ink-stained rag, her back to them. She seemed totally engrossed in cleaning the board. There was a stiffness to her movements that didn't please Brother Wolf, who always looked for things that were ill or off.

The teacher saw his glance.

"Amethyst is choosing not to sing today, so the music teacher sent her back here. Choice is fine, but it is a choice between music and work, not music and play."

He'd thought initially that she was a submissive person, and that would indeed mean trouble while she was trying to run a class of young children. But that firm voice was plenty dominant. So her defeated greeting of them probably had more to do with the temporary nature of her employment than her usual personality.

"This is the five-year-olds' classroom," she said to him and Anna in the same tone she'd used on Amethyst. "It's the smallest class until later in the year. The children who are five in the fall started kindergarten, so we only have the children who were five after the beginning of September. This class will grow as the four-year-olds in Ms. Newman's class turn five. The kindergarten kids, who go to public school for half the day, go in an entirely different classroom. We do have an after-school program for older children divided by grades—first and second graders, third and fourth graders, fifth and above."

She looked at them both, shoved her glasses more firmly on her nose, and said in a faintly accusatory tone, "But you aren't here for that, are you?"

She glanced over her shoulder at the girl cleaning the whiteboard and lowered her voice. "I thought you looked familiar, but I only just this moment figured out why," she told Charles in a voice that would not carry across the room over Yo-Yo Ma's cello. "My stepfather is"—another glance at the girl—"one of you. When I was ten, you came to talk with him about his . . . friends. We lived in Cody, Wyoming. I know who you are and I know you don't live in Scottsdale. Your moving away from Montana would have been big enough news that my stepfather would have told me."

He didn't remember her, though he had indeed gone to Cody about a decade ago and removed an Alpha who had lost control of his wolf. He'd gone to talk individually to all of the wolves in the pack. Some of them had been married, with human families.

"You don't live here," she said. "You don't have children. So why are you here?"

He took in a deep breath, to make sure, then turned at Brother Wolf's steely determination to face the child who was still wiping down the same board, which had been clean for a while.

"We are here to speak with her," he said.

The child froze. Then straightened and turned awkwardly around.

Beside him, Anna, too, had stilled.

"This doesn't concern you, wolf," the child said in the voice of a five-year-old.

"Chelsea Sani belongs to the grandson of the Alpha of the Salt River Pack," he told her. Miss Baird already knew about werewolves, and about secrets. She would not tell other people of Chelsea's connection to the pack. It was important to let the fae know where it had erred. The pack was a deterrent that would keep Chelsea and her children safe. "You picked the wrong victim, protected by the pack and by the Marrok."

The creature's face twisted in an expression that didn't belong on a child. "No werewolves. That's the only rule. Mackie's mother is not a werewolf. Mackie is not a werewolf. Mackie's brother is not a werewolf."

"They belong to us," Charles said, noting that the fae was more interested in Chelsea as Mackie's mother than as a person herself. That indicated the attack was actually focused on Mackie. He walked toward the child, keeping her attention on him and not his mate or the human woman who was more vulnerable than either of them.

He could smell fae magic; it permeated this room, where this fae had apparently been playing at being five years old. But the smell didn't get stronger as he approached her. Also, he detected only magic and not the fae herself. Had she disguised her scent somehow? But then why not disguise the magic, too? And what was she doing with the magic he could feel as a steady presence?

She snarled soundlessly, backing away from him before he got within touching distance. "No. She wasn't a werewolf. Fair game. Fair game. Witch but not werewolf. I could kill her, the rules say." She still sounded like a five-year-old.

"Amethyst?" said the teacher, sounding afraid.

"Amethyst is mine," said the child in a sharp bark of anger. It was said with the same degree of possessiveness that Anna had just used with the four-year-olds' teacher. "You can't have her. She's mine."

Charles knew what it was. It had given the game away with its last two words.

If Amethyst wasn't the one who was talking to them, there was only one thing a creature who looked and spoke like Amethyst could be. The reason he could not smell the fae was that there was *only* magic here.

"Riddle me questions," Charles said, chanting the old words slowly. "Riddle me rhymes. Riddle me swiftly, I've said it three times. By threes and by custom you dare not deny. I bind you to answer and compel your reply."

"Riddle say, riddle say," it said, as it had to, being what it was. "Riddle say me, and I will answer thee." Fae magic and the fae themselves were constrained by rules that allowed magic to exist in a world where magic was a rare thing. Riddles needed to be answered.

"What walks like a child and talks like a child and is left by the fae in the child's right place?" Charles asked in a singsong voice that was part of the draw of the riddle. "What curdles cream, makes sick the cows, what makes a mother moan? What hides like poison and rots away family and home?"

"A fetch! A fetch! A fetch!" it answered, and as soon as the third response had left its lips, the child disappeared and a bundle of sticks fell to the ground. Worn ribbons tied the sticks in a semblance of a human figure, arms and legs and head. There was a scrap of hair banded top and bottom and shoved into the body of the thing.

The smell of brimstone and vinegar overwhelmed his

nose and sent him into a paroxysm of coughing. Behind him he could hear Anna doing the same thing. The smell didn't bother the human, though.

"Amethyst? Amethyst?" Miss Baird hurried over to the board and then looked back at Charles. "What happened to Amethyst?"

"When did you last talk to her parents?" Anna asked hoarsely. He turned to see that she had covered her nose with her arm.

"This morning," Miss Baird said. "Not her parents, though. Her mother dropped her off and is supposed to pick her up. Her parents are in the middle of a nasty divorce. After the third incident, we have this list to tell us who is to pick her up on which day." Her voice trailed off.

"Where is she?" Miss Baird asked very quietly. "What happened to her?"

Anna looked at him, and he pulled out his cell phone. "I think this has gone beyond my sphere of authority," Charles said. He hit the button that dialed his father.

TO SAY THAT the police were displeased with them when Charles and Anna refused to talk was an understatement. Miss Baird talked to them until she was hoarse while Amethyst's parents watched in unrelieved apathy. Miss Baird, who knew about werewolf secrets, didn't tell them anything about werewolves, just that Charles and Anna were there interviewing the teachers at the day care.

"It's a fetch," Miss Baird told the police officer for the fifth or sixth time. "Not a child all. He didn't turn a child into a bundle of sticks, he just made it admit that's what it was. No. I don't know why it worked or what he did."

Anna didn't know why she and Charles weren't talking to the police. Except perhaps the obvious reason, which was that Miss Baird was not having any effect on their disbelief. Why should their reaction to what Charles or Anna had to say be any different? If no one would believe the truth, then why say anything at all? But that didn't seem very Charles-like. Bran hadn't told them to maintain silence when Charles had called him.

Bran had listened to Charles's careful recital of the exact events from the moment they walked into Miss Baird's classroom. When Charles was finished, he told them to call the police. They were to wait at the school until help arrived, with the implication that help would be a while in coming.

Then Bran had ended the call and they'd spent most of the afternoon waiting. First with Miss Baird, then the police arrived. Eventually, Ms. Edison had wandered in; finally Amethyst's parents, the Millers, who had arrived separately, joined them.

The Millers were pretty subdued for people whose only child had turned into a pile of broken sticks. From Miss Baird's description of warring parents, Anna had sort of expected more hostility. More energy. They sat near each other, not touching—or communicating in any other way, either. They hadn't said much when Miss Baird tried to explain to them what had happened. Unlike the police, they hadn't tried to argue with her, though they hadn't seemed to believe, either.

They looked . . . faded. She thought they waited with the rest of them because no one told them to go home, rather than out of any curiosity. They hadn't been angry, or disbelieving, or any of the things they should have been. Either children made you as crazy as Anna's own father claimed, or the changeling had been doing something to them. She thought about Charles's riddle and how poison could be spiritual rather than just physical.

The police officers were officially skeptical that a child had turned into a bundle of sticks. They were inclined to write Miss Baird off as a stupid mark willing to believe anything. Either Charles and Anna were con artists in the middle of some muddled game that involved kidnapping Amethyst, or they were stupid marks, like Miss Baird, who had the bad luck to witness some flimflam trick. That she and Charles weren't talking to the police made them more inclined to believe the first than the last.

The police officers in Scottsdale were evidently not used to dealing with the supernatural. They would have dismissed everyone and gone home themselves if it weren't for a call they received from someone they "yes, sir"ed who had asked them to hold the witnesses at the day care and wait for an investigator who was coming.

Ms. Edison could have gone home after the children had cleared out, but she was "disinclined" to leave Miss Baird to fend for herself. That made Anna like her better, and she'd been inclined to like her in the first place.

The Cantrip agents came next, Marsden and Leeds. Cantrip was the federal agency that dealt with the supernatural. It surprised her, given the attitude of the police, that there was a Cantrip presence in the greater Phoenix area.

Anna didn't recognize either of them, but her experience with Cantrip was not vast. Nor was it a happy experience, either. She couldn't tell from his reaction if Charles knew who they were, though he had extensive files on Cantrip, since Bran viewed it as a danger. The Cantrip agents weren't, she was pretty sure, the help that Bran had promised.

"So you are Mr. and Mrs. Smith," said the Cantrip officer to Charles. She was pretty sure it was the one named Marsden, not Leeds. Whichever one he was, he managed a credible sneer. "And you were here when the child turned into a pile of sticks?"

Cantrip seemed to attract a variety of people, from the true-believer geek to the rabid "kill 'em all and let God sort 'em out" kook and most everyone else in between. Leeds, Anna thought, was of the geek variety, but Marsden seemed to be a disbeliever. That didn't make sense. Why would someone who didn't want to believe in magic become an agent of Cantrip?

No one had touched the sticks so far. Anna thought it hadn't been Charles's soft-voiced warning that it wasn't always safe to deal with faé magic, even spent faé magic, that had kept the police from messing with it. She thought it was because no one wanted to be the one who collected the bundle as evidence, and thereby also collect harassment from everyone in the department for listening to a bunch of crazy people.

To date, the fae had been too good at appearing powerless and telling people that the stories of Tuatha Dé Danann, who could level mountains and raise lakes, were make-believe.

The truth was, humans wanted them to be stories. They didn't want to be afraid, didn't want to believe that their ancestors who huddled in stone crofts and wooden huts had been right to hide. So they listened to the fae weave a fictional story out of truths and the people believed.

The sole exception to that image was the day Beauclaire had beheaded the son of a US senator in front of a Boston courthouse several months ago. And that had been more a show of strength rather than a show of *power*, really.

She was sort of surprised that a Cantrip agent would take that attitude, though.

Charles looked at Marsden and said, as he had to the police, "We only want to tell the story once. We're waiting for the proper authority to tell it to."

Maybe Bran had told Charles who he'd planned on calling in to help in one of his one-sided only-in-your-head conversations, though Anna doubted it. Bran tended to include her in most of those unless there was some urgent reason not to. Charles sounded cool and certain that someone else was coming, though.

Marsden frowned. "We *are* the proper authorities, Mr. Smith. Cantrip is in charge of anything that looks as though magic is involved. Are you saying that there was no magic?"

"There was no magic," said one of the cops, deadpan. To be fair, she whispered it to the cop next to her. Anna was pretty sure that anyone who wasn't a werewolf wouldn't have heard her.

In a land where the police didn't believe in the supernatural, at least not in their jurisdiction, a pair of Cantrip agents must be bored stiff.

The attitude of the police department also told her that Hosteen Sani was a very good Alpha. That none of his wolves—and this was a fair-sized pack of twenty-seven plus

Chelsea—had had a run-in with the law was unusually good discipline. Even Bran could not claim that, though his pack . . . her pack, too . . . tended to have a lot of the more dangerous wolves, the ones he could not trust in the care of another werewolf.

Marsden's little speech didn't have any effect on Charles, but Miss Baird finally hit the end of her tether.

"Idiots," she snapped. "No wonder he's not talking to you. You're supposed to be experts in the supernatural and you don't even recognize the signs of a fairy kidnapping when it slaps you in the face. It's a fetch. A mannequin spelled to look like a child and act enough like a child that people who do not know what to look for believe it is a child." She scowled at the Cantrip agents. "A fetch is the word for a changeling left in the place of the real child."

Gradually all the rest of the conversations in the room stopped as Miss Baird's voice grew a little shrill. She was tired; they were all tired.

Leeds, Anna was almost certain he was Leeds, wasn't paying any attention to Miss Baird or anyone else. He'd been wandering around the room for a while, letting Marsden take point. Anna had seen him check out the artwork (as done by five-year-olds) on the walls and peer into the shelves of games and toys. He'd gotten to the part of the room where the sticks and ribbons had dropped to the floor. In the middle of Miss Baird's definition of a fetch, he dropped to the floor, too, right next to the bundle that had once looked like a little girl. He stared at the mess and then tilted his head.

No one but Anna was watching him, she thought, though one could never tell with Charles.

Miss Baird was still ranting. She swept her hand toward the silent couple who were seated incongruously on the small chairs usually occupied by children. They were huddled together and silent. "Ms. Edison, two other teachers, and half the day care children can tell you about the nasty fight these two had a week ago right in the hall. With the changeling gone, just look at them. It's like they're comatose or something. They haven't even processed that the Amethyst who came to school today is gone, let alone that she wasn't really their daughter at all. A family with a changeling in it suffers and dies, gentlemen."

"And how do you know so much about the fae?" asked Marsden in a nasty voice.

"I *read*," she snapped. "Which is something I recommend you learn to do." She looked at Charles. "I hope whoever you are waiting for is not a complete moron."

Leeds, still on the floor, laughed.

Marsden looked at his partner, who said, "He's in Cantrip, Miss Baird; 'moron' comes with the territory. No offense, Jim. I think we've both been morons about this."

"Have we?" Marsden asked in an altered voice. He sucked in a breath and then looked at the small contingent of police officers in the room. "Tell you kids what. Shift change is coming in half an hour. We've got this. Looks like they're going to stick by their claim that it's magic, so we'll give your department our report. If one of your superiors is upset, you know our names and numbers. We'll take it from here, and you folks can all go home."

"You got it," said the officer who apparently was in charge. "Let's pack it up, boys and girls. Hey, Marsden, you and Leeds on for softball on Saturday?"

"Yessir," Marsden said. "Ten a.m. sharp."

They waited until the police filed out.

"Okay, they're gone," said Marsden. "This is real?"

His partner, still on the floor, said, "There hasn't been a case of a fetch since we first found out that the fae were real. Standard changelings, where a fae disguises itself as a human child, those we've had a few of. But a fetch, an inanimate object spelled to mimic real life, that's a new one."

Marsden sucked air. "Leeds. Pay attention. Is it a real case?"

"We've been looking at a series of oddities in this neighborhood, right?" Leeds focused on Miss Blair. "I overheard you are new. Did you get this job because the previous teacher—I'm sorry, her name escapes me just now—hanged herself? I remember reading about a teacher here who died recently."

She nodded.

"So," said Marsden slowly. "It is a real case."

"And that odd car wreck, Jim," Leeds continued as if he were talking to himself—even though he addressed Marsden. "This is the right area of town and there were some kids in the car that were the right age for day care." He caught Miss Baird's eye again. "Someone in your classroom recently die in a nasty car wreck with their family?"

"No," said Miss Baird.

"Yes," said Ms. Edison. "About three days before Mrs. Glover's unfortunate death. Henry Islington. His mother crossed the median and she and her three boys all died. Henry was the only one who was a student here." She paused. "There was an incident the day before he died between him and one of the girls in the classroom. I don't know if it was Amethyst."

"It was," said Amethyst's mother in a dull tone. "Mrs. Glover gave us his written apology after he died."

"If Henry was in this classroom, he was five years old," Anna said. "He *wrote* an apology?"

"Mrs. Glover wrote it, of course," Mrs. Miller said. "He signed it—his *r* was backward. Then he died and it was horrible. And now Amethyst . . ."

Ms. Edison walked over to her and patted her on the shoulder. "I know, Sara," she murmured.

Amethyst's mother wiped her eyes, but not because she was crying. Maybe they were too dry. "Amethyst and Henry were best friends from day one. She talked about him all the time. And then, out of the blue one day, he punched her."

"Henry said she said something bad," Ms. Edison told them. "He wouldn't tell us what it was, and she just smiled." She paused. "In retrospect, it was very odd behavior for Amethyst. It didn't strike me that way at the time, but she is usually a gregarious, cheerful child."

"Amethyst?" said Miss Baird. "Cheerful?" She shook her head. "But we weren't dealing with Amethyst, were we?"

"It's real, Jim," said Leeds.

Marsden stared at him a moment, then took a good long look at the bundle of sticks on the floor. "Do you know how many fake calls come in? We've been stationed here for a year, and the most excitement we've had was when some kids swore a demon was eating their dog's food every night. Twelve hours of stakeout turned up a half-grown coyote. Then there was the lady who saw a unicorn, which turned out to be her neighbor's kid running around in last year's Halloween costume. My brain's a funny thing—it tends to atrophy if I don't use it. Real, huh?"

Leeds nodded. "Real."

Marsden waited a beat. "Okay, then." He pulled out an electronic notebook and said, in a cool professional tone, "Can I get everyone's name and what their relationship to the missing girl is?"

Anna leaned on her husband and raised her eyebrows. He narrowed his eyes at her, but she thought he was smiling a little. It was hard to tell.

Marsden started with Miss Baird.

"I've been teaching here for two weeks," she told him, her feathers still ruffled. "Probationary period. I was informed this morning that they would be terminating my contract because there had been too many incidents in my room and parents were complaining."

"Fourteen in two weeks," Ms. Edison said. "Our average is about once a month for the whole school." She gave Miss Baird a half smile. "We need to revisit that decision, I think. All of those complaints revolved around Amethyst and for some reason none of us, myself and our board members, even thought twice about that. And I assure you that is something we normally do. If one student causes more than three incidents in a month, he is on probation and the next time he is gone. Under normal circumstances Amethyst would have been served notice and then asked to leave."

"Your name is?" Marsden asked. His partner, evidently satisfied that he'd gotten Marsden on the right track, was back to examining the bundle of sticks.

"Farrah Edison," Ms. Edison said. "I run this lunatic asylum. I stayed because what I know might help. Cathy, Miss Baird, has only been here for a short time." She took a deep breath. "I've been sitting in this room for going on four hours, and every hour it feels like my head clears a little more. Amethyst used to be a cheerful, gregarious girl, and she came back from Christmas break totally different. I intended to call her home, but Sara, her mom, came in to talk to me before I managed it. She told me that she and her husband were thinking of divorce. Then they—I'm sorry, Sara—they started to have some loud altercations when they would come to pick up or drop off Amethyst. I decided that was an adequate cause for Amethyst's sudden change in personality."

Marsden nodded. "Okay. Thanks. And you are Amethyst's parents, right? Names, please?"

Amethyst's parents were Sara and Brent Miller. She was a bank administrator, he was a doctor. No, they hadn't noticed anything different about their daughter. Not when she'd had the fight with Henry. Not any time.

"When did you two begin to fight?" asked Anna, her eyes on their clasped hands.

Sara looked up and just blinked at Anna, but her husband's eyes sharpened. "It was just before Christmas," he said slowly. "We were going to go visit my parents, it was their turn. But the day before we were supposed to go, Amethyst said she didn't want to go. Then Sara was adamant that she didn't want to go, either. My parents aren't always kind to her. But over the years she's always just dealt with them. But not this time." He cleared his throat. "I'm babbling."

The slowest babbling Anna had ever heard, though maybe he was talking about coherence and not speed.

"They're not so bad," said Sara suddenly. "Your parents. I like your dad. He's funny when your mom isn't in the room."

Marsden was watching Anna but typing on his notebook as fast as he could anyway.

Charles stepped in then. He didn't ask a question so much as make a statement. "Dr. Miller, you've had a run of bad luck since Christmas."

Miller opened his mouth, then nodded abruptly. "Two car wrecks—the second totaled my car. Our six-year-old cat died. It seems like we can't keep an appliance up and running longer than a week." He gave a half laugh and a shrug.

"I can't bake bread," said his wife. "Not since Christmas. The dough just won't rise."

"Most of it is centered in your home?" Charles asked. "It hasn't followed you to the office, right?"

The Millers nodded.

"That's right," Sara Miller said. "Just at home."

Marsden looked Charles in the eye and said, harshly, "Okay, buddy. Just who are you?"

Anna felt Charles stiffen against her at the challenge, but he kept his voice steady when he replied. "I am Charles and this is my wife, Anna."

"Smith," said Marsden.

"That will do," Anna said. "We were asked to come and talk to the teachers here on a related matter, having some experience with the fae. We expected to find a renegade fae who had escaped from the Nevada reservation. If that had been so, we'd have been in and out with none the wiser. This"—she indicated the bundle on the ground—"was unexpected."

"A related matter?" Marsden asked.

"A friend of ours gave us reason to believe that there was a fae problem here," she said.

Ms. Edison smiled thinly. "Was that the friend of a friend of your sister-in law? No wonder you wished to speak to Miss Baird even though I told you she was only temporary." She looked at Marsden, effectively dismissing Anna. "So you believe a fae stole the real Amethyst and replaced her with a . . . simulacrum?"

"Correct," said Marsden grimly.

"So what happened to our daughter?" asked Dr. Miller.

He didn't sound like he thought it would be good. A doctor would know all about not good, Anna thought.

"That depends on what kind of fae we're dealing with." A lean, muscular black woman dressed sharply in a dove gray suit stepped into the room. "Special Agent Leslie Fisher, FBI. Sorry I'm late."

8

So that was who Charles had been waiting for. Anna frowned at him. How had he known? He smiled at her, just a crinkle at the corner of his eye. He hadn't known, just made a very good guess. She was almost sure.

"Leslie," said Anna. "It's very good to see you. Tell me you didn't fly all the way over here from Boston."

Leslie smiled. "Hey, Anna. Charles. Not from Boston, thank goodness. I'm stationed in Nevada now, in a town of two hundred that just happens to be the closest town to the James Earl Carter Jr. Fae Reservation. Apparently our little run-in made me one of the FBI's experts in fae relations, so they moved me out there."

"I'm sorry," Anna apologized. That's how Charles had known. He'd kept track of Leslie. Knowing that she was living nearby, he'd have figured she'd be brought in.

"Yeah, well." Leslie shrugged without losing her smile. "That's what it means to be FBI. We go where we're needed."

"How did Jude take that?" She had liked Leslie's husband, a huge man with a sense of humor and a backbone of steel. He'd been a linebacker in college headed for the pros when an injury had changed the direction of his life. He taught elementary school.

"He was torn up about leaving his kids." Leslie smiled, a private smile. "But he got a job right off. Apparently there aren't a lot of teachers willing to live where it gets to be a hundred and twenty degrees in the shade and the nearest restaurant I would consider eating at is a four-hour drive. The kids out here need him a lot more than the kids in Boston did. Once he saw that, he was okay. Moving him out of there when the time comes is going to be harder than moving him in was."

"I take it you both know Agent Fisher?" Marsden interrupted.

"Yes," Leslie agreed. "We've worked together before. I haven't met you, though."

"Agent Jim Marsden, Cantrip, and this is my partner, Hollister Leeds. This is our investigation. What is the FBI's interest here? We're not even sure if we have a kidnapping."

Leslie gave a quick, professional smile that was remarkable in the amount of information it imparted: *I'm sorry, I respect you and the job you do, but I am competent, too, and this time you have to back me.* It was such a good expression that the words felt like an afterthought.

She used them anyway. "Sorry, gentlemen. The DOJ has determined that this is part of a larger terrorist operation, and that puts me in the driver's seat. I would be overjoyed to have your assistance."

Marsden paused and looked at Leeds, who was still on his knees by the bundle of sticks. He'd taken out a sketchbook and was drawing it.

"Terrorists?" Marsden asked. "How do you figure?"

She smiled at the civilians in the room. "Did these gentlemen already take your statement?"

"Come, Miss Baird," said Ms. Edison. "I think we are in the way. I'll send Miss Baird home, but I have some work to do in my office. Please let me know when you leave and I'll lock up."

"That would be terrific," Leslie told her. "Thank you."

Miss Baird raised her chin. "That child was in my class," she said. "I feel responsible for what happened. Is there any way I could be informed what happens?"

"Of course," said Anna before anyone else could refuse her. She pulled out her card, the one with nothing but the name "Anna Smith" in calligraphic writing on it and an e-mail address, and handed it to her. "E-mail me, and I'll tell you what I can."

"This is Dr. and Mrs. Miller," Anna told Leslie, not quite comfortable saying, *I don't think they are competent to get themselves home.* Hopefully Leslie would notice on her own. "They are our victim's parents. I think they've been questioned enough."

"Maybe Ms. Edison and I should see them home," said Miss Baird. "I'm not sure either of them should be driving." She looked at Ms. Edison. "If you drive them, I'll follow and bring you back here."

"I think that would be a very good idea," said Anna, relieved. She made sure that the Millers had cards for the Cantrip agents and Leslie so that they could call with any questions and walked the four of them down the hall and out the door.

"She's really gone." Sara Miller looked up at her husband. "Our little girl is gone."

He put his arm around her and said, "She's been gone for a while."

"We need to get her back," said his wife earnestly, but not as though the full impact of her daughter's disappearance had really hit her.

Dr. Miller looked over his shoulder and met Anna's eyes for an unsettling moment. "Yes," he said.

"Dr. Miller, we cannot promise that," Anna said. "I can promise that we will find the person responsible and make sure that it never happens to anyone else."

Ms. Edison stopped to frown at Anna. "How can you promise that? It's a fae. You don't even know what it can do."

"I've worked with Special Agent Fisher before," Anna said. "And my husband . . . Charles gets things done." She turned back to the Millers. "We'll find out what happened to her, and we'll take care of the fae who took her."

"Okay," said Dr. Miller. "Okay." He led his wife out the door.

"I'll be back," Ms. Edison said after the doors closed behind the Millers. "But the doors are all locked from the outside, so if you need to leave before I get back, just make sure the door is latched."

"TERRORISTS," LESLIE WAS saying when Anna returned, "are people who commit violent acts against people with the purpose of coercing a population or their government. Hey, Anna, welcome back."

"They're off to see the Millers safely home," Anna said. "Did they bring you up to speed?"

"Yes," Charles said.

Leslie nodded and then looked at Marsden. Leeds, Anna saw, was sliding the fetch-bundle into a large evidence bag.

"Marsden," Leslie said. "I've done my homework on you, on both of you. You're innovative and capable, even if the thing you're best at is ticking off the higher-ups. It was your people, Cantrip analysts, who first alerted *us*—that would be the FBI—that the fae are sending out . . . a few individuals who have particularly nasty histories and letting them loose on the general population."

Charles made one of his noises, and Leslie nodded at him. "Hah. I thought you might have noticed what the fae were doing. The FBI has been hoping that you people would contact us so that we can work together. Or at least talk about working together."

He didn't say anything, and Anna abided by his judgment. Marsden was staring at Charles like he was a puzzle.

Join the club. Anna hid her smile.

Leslie, apparently deciding she wasn't going to get an answer yet, continued. "The fae want to get our attention. We took out someone . . . something in Florida, a kelpie we think. It was eating people who swam in its lake. There have been other incidents, too. Our analysts think it's probably a negotiation tool, a 'look what we've been saving you from all these years; you humans better start thinking about how the negotiations are going to proceed' kind of thing. That's the optimistic view. The pessimistic view is that this is the first wave of a war that we're not sure we can win because the only thing that we know about the enemy comes from folktales and what they themselves have told us. They might not be able to lie, but they left a whole freaking lot out."

She looked at Charles again and asked, "What do you know about it?"

Charles angled his face a little, considering her question. Finally he said, "About what you do."

That was news to Anna. Though, to be fair, she wasn't actively involved in everything he did for the packs or his father. She wasn't honestly certain that Bran would be upset about the fae attacking regular people. She might love her father-in-law, but she was not blind to his faults. He was focused on the werewolves to the exclusion of anything else.

There was also the possibility that Charles hadn't been aware of the attacks until Leslie told them. Some of his reputation for awesome cosmic powers came from not telling anyone how much he knew about anything. Thus leaving it to other people to assume the answer was "everything." The rest of his reputation was wholly deserved.

Charles glanced at Leeds or maybe at the remains of the fake Amethyst Miller. "There was some question about what side we'd come down on, if any."

"That's what I thought," Leslie said. She waved her arms around the room. "I'm hoping that your presence here means that you've decided to help?"

"All right, who *are* you people?" Marsden waved his hand vaguely at Charles and Anna.

"This thing is really pretty cool," Leeds announced from the floor, as though he had entirely missed the conversation going on ten feet away. "I never thought I'd see one of these in person. Just think of the kind of power that can take a mannequin—something, anything, shaped to look vaguely human—and make it walk and talk and act human. Well, mostly human, anyway. And it fooled people for *months*. I suppose it could have been a doll or a clay figure, but a bundle of sticks is traditional. I think that this ribbon must have been something the original child wore. I also think, though I can't swear to it without taking it apart, that there is some hair here as well." He spoke with the intense enthusiasm of a miner discovering gold for the first time.

Leslie gave Leeds an assessing look. "Him I want on my team, especially. Geeks are really useful."

"So am I," said Marsden. "How do you know the Smiths, Special Agent Fisher? And who are they?"

"I worked with them last year—you probably heard about the case," she said. "It culminated in Beauclaire, Prince of the Elves, beheading the son of a US senator. Charles and Anna Smith were sent to help in the investigation."

Marsden frowned, but he wasn't slow on the uptake. "Werewolves. There were a couple of werewolves called in to consult on that. They testified under pseudonyms by special dispensation—" He looked at Charles. "Mr. and Mrs. Smith," he said. "I should have caught that."

"Werewolves?" said Leeds, distracted at last from the now safely contained bundle of sticks.

Charles smiled at him, the smile that had teeth. "Werewolves, yes, both my wife and I. What you should know is that this fae launched a barely failed attack on a couple of children under the protection of the local Alpha. We were available, so we volunteered to see if we could find the culprit. We walked into the room with Miss Baird and found the fetch. It didn't take long to realize what Amethyst, the thing wearing Amethyst Miller's shape, had to be."

He looked at Leslie and his face softened. "And yes, that the fae attacked some of ours means that we have chosen to work with the humans against the fae, in this instance. I cannot say that alliance will last, or that we won't retreat back to being a neutral third party when this incident is resolved. My experience with the fae leads me to believe that such a retreat would be useless. I will convey my belief to . . . those higher up."

"Who were the children who were attacked?" asked Marsden, prepared to write it down. "We should go talk to them, too."

Charles just looked at him.

"No need to be rude," Anna told Charles. To Marsden she said, "We know the details and we'll tell you if anything would be useful, but mostly they just led us to the change-ling. Some of the werewolves are out to the public, but some of them have chosen not to be. This is not our pack. I don't know who is out and who is not, and we will not give their names out unless it becomes necessary."

There was an awkward silence as Marsden clearly wanted to push the issue, but Charles was at his intimidating best. She could almost see the moment when Marsden remem-bered he was dealing with a werewolf, and that it wasn't a smart idea to meet a werewolf's eyes unless you were pre-pared for a dominance battle. Once he dropped his eyes from Charles's, it was too late to push.

"So do you know what we're dealing with?" asked Leslie.

"Fae," said Charles. "But you know that much."

"One that can build a fetch." Marsden indicated the bundle of sticks with his chin.

"I thought that a fetch is an exact duplicate of yourself that warns you that you're about to die," said Leslie.

"Or kills you," added Anna.

"Or a bundle of sticks that is magicked to look exactly like a child," said Charles.

"Another word for 'changeling,'" said Marsden.

Leeds shook his head. "No. Well, yes. But a fetch is spe-cifically a changeling that isn't a real living thing—" He pointed to the sticks. "Most changelings are fae who make themselves look like the child who's been stolen away. That takes very little magic, just a variant of the glamour they use to appear like normal human beings. But this, this is very rare. I've seen six . . . seven changeling cases. None of them involved a fetch."

Anna looked at Charles. She hadn't known that the fae had been that . . . active before Beauclaire had killed his daughter's attacker and then retreated with the rest of the fae behind the walls that everyone had believed to be jails. Those jails, as it turned out, were really fortresses. He gave a subtle shake of his head. He hadn't known, either.

"Seven?" Leslie asked. "I haven't heard of any."

"Oh, two of them weren't real. One was some parents who thought it would be convenient if the child they beat to death wasn't really theirs. Another was, oddly enough in this day and age, an actual case of babies switched at birth. Resulted in a heck of a lawsuit and a lot of work running down just which babies had been switched and switching them back. But five changelings—" He gave them a wry smile. "One was me. My parents never knew. They died in a car wreck when I was twenty or so. I didn't find out for a long time afterward, when I volunteered for a DNA sample to . . . let's just say my human family has a number of people who would bring up the ratings of one of those Dr. Phil analogues. Turns out I'm half-human, half-fae. My human half has nothing in common with either of the people I always thought were my parents." He looked down at the floor and muttered, "I found it to be kind of a relief, really. Not the being-half-fae part, but not being related to the people who raised me? That was outstanding."

Marsden put himself between them and his partner. Anna didn't think it was a conscious move. But he positioned himself in such a way to let them all know that anyone who wanted to take a potshot at his partner would have to go through Marsden to do it.

No one said anything. Leeds smiled gently at his partner's back and shrugged. "My bosses give the changeling cases to me, for obvious reasons. The last one, the boy who was beaten to death, landed me in Phoenix. I was apparently more blunt than necessary."

"Scared them into confessing," said Marsden. "Useful, but not the approved method of coaxing the truth into the open."

Leeds looked kind of harmless to Anna. Harmless people don't scare people into confessing to murder.

"The changeling targeted my friend's grandchildren," Charles said. "Will the fae who made the fetch know what the fetch did? Does the fae use the changeling for ears and eyes?"

Leeds shook his head. "I don't think so. Assuming the fae isn't here, too. Everything that I've been able to dig up on them is that a fetch operates on its own. It is an inanimate object given intelligence and purpose."

They all considered that a moment.

"How many of the stolen children were recovered?" asked Leslie.

Leeds sat back on his heels and gave her a half smile full of sympathy. "None of them. But then the ones I've seen, like me, were all adults when it was discovered. As far as I know, this is the first stolen child in two decades. Still, the fetch is really a hopeful sign, not that I'd have said so in front of the Millers. I don't like to give false hope."

"Why hopeful?" asked Leslie.

"Because a fetch costs a lot of magic, right?" Leeds told them. "And what is the primary purpose of a fetch?"

"To disguise the fact that a child is missing," said Anna.

"And why disguise it, if not to keep people from looking for the missing girl." Leeds nodded. "If she were dead, a body is easy to get rid of, easier to hide than a living child. The thing is, unlike a living changeling, a fetch has a finite life . . . animation period. Presumably, if Charles hadn't forced the issue, it would have continued in her place until the real child died."

"It could have been left to keep people from looking for the fae who stole Amethyst," said Charles.

"And that right there is why I didn't say anything while the Millers were here," agreed Leeds.

He looked at Marsden. "If Special Agent Fisher is right, and the fae are really letting loose their bad guys upon us, you know what that means."

"No," Marsden said.

Leeds sighed. "Who are their favorite prey?"

"Children," said Anna, a cold chill running down her spine. "It's the children."

"**WE SHOULD GO** to the Millers' house," Charles said to Anna as they walked toward their car. They'd borrowed it from the Sanis, and so they'd parked it in the parking lot of a strip mall a mile or so from the day care. It would be stupid to give the Sanis up to the fae, the FBI, or Cantrip with a license plate.

"Can you get their address?" she asked, and was rewarded by her mate's smile.

"Will they let us in?" she asked.

"Their daughter is missing," he said. "Now that they're coming out of the fog of the fae's spell, they will be looking for help from whoever offers it."

IT WAS DARK by the time they found the right street. Every light in the house was on. Anna thought about how she'd feel knowing her child had been missing for months, hurting and afraid if not dead. And the whole while they'd believed that the fetch had been their daughter.

"It's important they have hope," she said, pulling into their driveway.

"We won't take it away from them," promised Charles.

Dr. Miller opened the door before they knocked.

"Who are you?" he asked.

"My husband and I are specialists of a sort," Anna said. "Fae, werewolf, whatever. We get called in. We thought, if you don't mind, that we might find something here to help find your daughter."

"She's dead," he said heavily. "She's been gone for months.

Twenty-four hours is the usual time frame for recovering kid-napped children alive."

"Maybe," Anna said. She'd been wrong, she saw. There was no chance of taking away hope that wasn't there. Maybe it was cruel to give it back to them, but she couldn't help her-self. "If she'd been abducted by humans, almost certainly. But the fae are funny creatures when it comes to children. Some-times they kill them, but some kinds of fae take children to keep as their own. We don't know enough about this one to know what happened to Amethyst."

"Let them in," said Mrs. Miller from behind her husband's back.

Dr. Miller hesitated, then opened the door to welcome them inside. "Don't hurt her," he told them earnestly, and he wasn't talking about Amethyst.

"Life hurts," Charles said gently. "But we won't lie to you or to your wife."

Amethyst's room was neat as a pin. Toys were organized by size, then by color on the white shelves along one wall. The bed was tidy and Anna suspected she could have bounced a quarter off the bedspread.

"Was she always this tidy?" Anna asked.

Sara shook her head. "No. I didn't even notice when it changed. She'd get started on something and get distracted. So her bed would be half-made. She'd color part of a color-ing book page."

"She'd have one shoe on," said Dr. Miller. "Because she remembered she wanted oatmeal for breakfast before she found the other shoe."

Charles had his head tilted and his eyes half closed, a sure sign he was smelling the room.

"How could I not have noticed?" Amethyst's mother said. "What kind of mother doesn't notice that her child's been replaced by a . . . a *thing*?"

"Fae can fog your perception," said Anna. "If you started noticing something wrong, the fetch would have distracted you." When Mackie had noticed something was wrong, the fetch tried to kill her.

"Is there something that Amethyst kept close to her?" Charles said. "A favorite toy she slept with? Something that the fetch didn't associate with too much?"

"Something a dog could use to get a scent to track her with," Anna supplied.

"You're going to use dogs?" Dr. Miller frowned.

"We'll use whatever we can," Anna said. "Some of our methods are unorthodox—magic. And it would help to have something that belonged to Amethyst."

"Her bunny," Sara said. She went to the bookcase and picked out a grubby, one-eared rabbit and handed it to Anna. "Will this do?"

Anna held it to her forehead, as if she were a TV psychic. Her nose told her that if the fetch had touched it, it hadn't been very often. Children didn't have as much body odor as adults, but they also didn't disguise it with soaps and perfumes the way adults did.

"This will do," she said. "Do you have a plastic bag I can put it in?"

Sara looked as though she wasn't sure she wanted them to take it.

"I promise we'll bring it back," said Anna.

"Go get a bag from the kitchen," Dr. Miller told his wife gently.

As soon as she was out of the room, he looked at them. "Werewolves?" he asked.

Anna smiled at him. "We're not psychics. Yes."

"My wife would be afraid, if she knew," he told Anna. "But I've had dealings with your people, when I was in the army, a lifetime ago. Why are you helping us?"

"Because children deserve to be safe," Charles said.

CHARLES AND ANNA got back to the Sanis' ranch well after dinner. Kage met them at the front door, making Charles think he'd been watching for them.

"Hosteen is still out riding somewhere," he said, ushering them inside. "Dad ate better than he has in months and fell asleep. Chelsea has been sleeping most of the day." Kage continued with his dogged recitation. "Kids are up in the TV room with my mom and Ernestine, watching some TV show about serial killers, zombies, or something equally healthy for them."

Kage waited, but when it became obvious no one else was going to say anything, he continued. "There are leftovers from dinner in the kitchen I can fix if you need food." He took a breath. "That's what's going on here. From you I get a text that says not to expect you for dinner. Not exactly helpful. Did you find out anything?"

"Fae," Charles told him, pulling off his boots and setting them where all the other people's shoes waited.

Anna rolled her eyes at her husband with, he hoped, a little fondness to go along with her mock exasperation. "Food would be lovely, thank you. We actually found out a lot— not enough, but a lot. Why don't we go eat and I'll tell you what we know."

"Anna uses actual words," murmured Charles tranquilly, holding her arm as she took off her shoes, too.

"Useful," said Kage, leading the way to the kitchen.

"Some people think so," Charles agreed, and Anna bumped him with her hip.

Dinner was fried chicken, biscuits, and a huge salad. Wade, Hosteen's second, came in before the food was on the table. He was one of those quiet people who instilled order in those around them. He was obviously at home in the house, and he helped Kage pull out food and dishes. When Anna tried to help, Wade waved her off before Kage could.

"I'm the hired help," he said. "Even with all the desperate life-and-death drama, you're also here to look at horses, right? That makes you clients—sit down."

"Wade has a real job," Kage explained as they all settled around the table. "But his family has been in the business of breeding and showing Arabs nearly as long as mine. He comes and catch-rides for us when we need an extra rider in a show."

"There was a changeling in Mackie's class," Anna began

as soon as people were eating. "Apparently Mackie half figured out what she was and the changeling decided to get rid of her."

Charles ate and listened as, between bites, Anna did her best to give Kage and Wade a thorough update. Wade had the right to hear it. The attack had been on his Alpha's family, and the victim who suffered the most was likely to become a permanent member of the pack if Hosteen got his act together.

But as Charles listened, he also watched the other two men's faces as they relaxed into his mate's storytelling. Tension left Kage's shoulders and Wade laughed helplessly as Anna described Leeds's fascination with the bundle of sticks that had been a little girl, while everyone else was deciding who was in charge. She did it without making anyone think less of Leeds, because she clearly didn't. Sure it was serious business, but humor in the face of evil robbed evil of some of its power. His Anna understood that better than most.

"You're going to look for the missing girl, right?" asked Kage. But not like he was sure of it.

Anna nodded. "Charles and I stopped in at her house. The only real connection to the day care was the fetch. If we're going to find the fae who took the girl, our best trail should be Amethyst's. But she was taken so long ago. Charles says that from the faintness of her scent in her room, it's been months. We also took a walk around several blocks near her house, but neither of us caught scent of a fae."

"So what's next?" asked Wade.

"The FBI, Cantrip, and a number of unlucky police officers spend the next few days sorting through police incident reports until they come up with something," said Anna. "Leslie is going to call us if they need our help."

"That sounds—"

"Like they are taking over the investigation and throwing us out of it," growled Wade.

It was the pack's hunt, as he would see it—as Charles saw it, for that matter. The entrance of the human organizations, useful as they were, annoyed him as well. He understood the necessity, but that didn't mean he liked it.

"They have access to information we don't have," Anna soothed, articulating the reason Bran had decided to bring them in. "Let them do the legwork. Besides, we're trying to keep the pack out of it. It's likely there'll be some publicity when this is all over—one way or another. I know the FBI agent and, better, she knows us. She'll call for help when they have anything we can be useful for."

"Cantrip? Call on a werewolf?" Wade looked like he wanted to spit on the floor.

"I know, right?" Anna nodded sympathetically. "But Special Agent Fisher, of the FBI, will call us in whether Cantrip wants us or not. Not many humans are really equipped to deal with a fae who has decided to prey openly upon humans. And, though Leeds is half-fae, I'm not sure they have anyone who can detect a fetch." She tapped her nose.

"And because the humans want the werewolves at their back if the fae decide that this is war," Charles said, getting up and scraping his plate before putting it into the dishwasher.

There was a little pause and Wade said, "Are we? Are we at war?"

"My father spent weeks in negotiations to ensure that we were not brought in on either side." Charles paused, not wanting to criticize his father in public.

Bran saw humans as "other." He was so far from his own days of being human that Charles doubted he could remember them without effort.

Charles, who had never been human, had nevertheless grown up surrounded by his mother's family. The uncles and grandfather who helped raise him, aunts and grandmother who clothed him and indulged him. He understood, in a way that was a gift of his grandfather's view of the world, that werewolves, humans, and fae were all a part of a greater community.

If a war broke out, everyone would lose. The fae were not

fond of humans, and worse, they were contemptuous of them. That meant that war with humans scared only the more perceptive and less arrogant fae—which meant not many.

But the werewolves, the werewolves were respected. Not many fae would want to declare war if it meant fighting werewolves, too. So Charles forcing his father's hand might have some unexpected benefits.

Charles sighed. "Look at us here in this room, in this house. We are human and werewolf, waiting to go deal with a fae who attacked the great-grandchildren of a werewolf. Most of us are connected to the human community with ties of love and loyalty that no treaty will stand up to. There is no question we'll be drawn into any conflict. We cannot be separated from those we love because they are human—as in most ways are we."

Kage smiled a predator's smile. "Fair enough. As long as whatever hurt my Chelsea is made harmless, I don't care if it's us, werewolves, or Canadian Mounties. Though I'd like to have a hand in it."

He put food back in the fridge and said, "This isn't an attack on Hosteen or his pack, though. It sounds like Chelsea was a random victim. Or if she wasn't, it was because of her witch heritage and nothing to do with werewolves."

"Chelsea is Hosteen's granddaughter by marriage," growled Wade. "It is an attack on the pack whatever the motive of the fae."

Charles nodded. "Agreed."

"And," said Anna, "if we had been aware of any child stolen by the fairies, we'd be out looking. Human child, witch child, or werewolf child."

He heard the bone-deep protective instinct that drove her—instincts that had nothing to do with being a werewolf. She would, he acknowledged wistfully, be a wonderful mother.

Wade grinned at her fierceness. "You tell it like it is. Count me in."

"At any rate," Charles told Kage, "I think that the attack on Chelsea was directed at Mackie, not at the pack. A matter of opportunity and necessity rather than planning. However, the fae are notoriously persistent. I would not count your family safe until we find the perpetrator."

Kage grunted. "I'll keep the kids here, where Hosteen can keep an eye on them." He paused. "When he gets over his snit and comes back, anyway. Chelsea . . ." His voice trailed off.

"Our pack will watch over Chelsea," said Wade. He smiled at Kage's carefully neutral grunt. "Hosteen occasionally ties himself up in knots, but I've known him a long time. He'll get his head out of his—" He glanced at Anna and rephrased. "He'll come through. He always does."

"Yeah," said Kage without conviction.

"**DO YOU THINK** we'll find her?" asked Anna as she emerged from the bathroom, ready for bed.

"Yes," Charles said after a moment. "Because we won't stop until we do, even if we have to take this town apart stick by stick."

She froze, then turned to him. "You feel it, too?"

"She's five years old," he said. "And the very best case is that she's been in the hands of a fae for months. The very best case."

Anna nodded. "I feel as though we should be out looking some more. But I don't see that it would do any good because after we didn't find anything at the Millers' or the day care, there's no place else to look."

"Come here," he said.

She crawled onto the bed and into his arms.

"We'll find that fae," he promised her. "I don't know if we'll be in time for Amethyst. But we'll be in time for the next one."

She burrowed against him. "Okay," she said. "Okay."

He felt Brother Wolf's joy in his mate's fierceness. He would never take the gift of her presence in his life for granted. He'd been alone so long, so certain that there would be no one for him. He scared even other werewolves. And a part of him—of Charles, not Brother Wolf—hadn't wanted to find anyone. He'd understood that caring for another person the way he cared for Anna would leave him vulnerable. His father's hatchet man could not afford any weaknesses. And one day, there she was, his Anna: strong and funny despite the harm that had been done to her. She had tamed Brother Wolf first, but before he'd been in her presence ten minutes, he'd known that she would be his. That he needed her to be his.

"You're growling," she said, her voice drowsy. "What are you thinking?"

"That I love you," he said. "That I am grateful every day that you decided to let me keep you."

She hmmed and rolled over on top of him with hard-won confidence. "Good," she said. "Gratitude is good. Love is better." She paused, her mouth almost touching his. "I love you, too."

He told her, "The day I met you was the first day I ever felt joy."

She drew in a surprised breath. "Me, too," she said, her truth making his eyes burn. "Me, too." Then her lips traveled the few millimeters that lay between them.

They made love. To his amusement she grabbed his hand and put it over her mouth to muffle the noises she made. He left it there until she was too involved to remember it, and then he used that hand, too.

She didn't want anyone to hear her cries, but in this house, with Chelsea and Wade, the only werewolves, a full floor away and on the other side of the house, there was no chance of it.

When they were finished, she lay limply on him and slipped effortlessly into sleep. He lay awake awhile, listening to the rain pouring down outside.

The rain would have a salutary effect on Hosteen's ruminations, he was certain. *That's right, old man, you think before you blow up at my wife, who saved Chelsea. Not her fault that it affected you like alcohol did your father, awakening old demons. Put them back to bed, old wolf.*

And you get ready to welcome Chelsea into your pack with a whole heart. Or else you will lose your grandson and your son in the same year, because if Chelsea has to leave, he will, too. He's as stubborn as either you or Joseph.

Charles never had the knack for sending his words into other people's heads, except for sometimes Anna's. But he figured that the rain would do the job for him.

Anna stirred in his arms. "We have to find her."

He kissed the top of her head. "Yes," said Brother Wolf.

9

Leslie called them at seven in the morning. Anna answered Charles's cell because Charles was just emerging from the shower.

"I heard you stopped in at the Millers', about an hour before a pair of my FBI agents stopped in," Leslie said. "Did you find anything?"

"Yes and no," Anna told her. "We confirmed that Amethyst has been missing for months. We have one of her stuffed animals that Charles and I can use for scent if we get close enough. No one who lives nearby is a fae. Or else they're hiding their scent trail all the time, which Charles assures me is unlikely. Most fae don't expect to have werewolves on their trail."

"Okay," Leslie said. "I'd have preferred you talk to me before you go off hunting on your own."

"Okay," said Anna, deliberately unspecific about what she was okay about.

Leslie laughed tiredly. "So I have people doing background checks on anyone who has worked at the day care, but that's not a priority. I think that the day care trouble was caused by the fetch. All of the people who died were connected in some way to Amethyst."

"That's what we think, too," said Anna.

"What we have been doing is compiling two lists. The first is weird things that have happened in the vicinity of the day care. For the second, Leeds suggested that maybe the fetch was not the first or the last this fae has made. So we've made some calls to local counselors, psychologists, and anyone else we could think of, asking about children who have had sudden personality changes. We still have some calls coming in on that. What we'd like to do is have you ride with me for the weird things and Charles ride with Leeds and Marsden looking into the kids. I know you usually work together, but neither the Cantrip agents nor I could tell if someone was fae or fetch if they spit on us."

"Leeds can't tell if someone is fae or not?" Anna asked.

"He says he's hit-and-miss, and we can't afford a miss. We have eleven calls to make; with luck we can do most of those today."

"Fast work," Anna said. She heard a huff of breath that might have been a laugh, hard to tell over the phone.

"We have a kid in danger, Anna. We take that seriously. Lots of folks have been up all night putting this information together for us."

"Yes," said Anna. "So where do you want to meet up? I don't know this area, so I'll need a real address."

When she hung up, she looked at Charles, who was toweling off his hair; he'd heard most of the call. "We get to go and make people talk."

"Sounds good," he said. "I'll try not to scare some poor kid so badly he can't talk for a year. You try not to get attacked by some fae who doesn't understand how dangerous you are because you look so soft and sweet."

She thought about her reply for a moment because his voice was just a little too neutral.

"Nah," she said casually, answering him as if she thought her reply didn't matter. "You scare adults pretty good— you've got that 'I could kill you with my little finger' thing going for you. But the kids or the adults who are hurt . . . you are safe and they know it. Doesn't mean they aren't shy with you, but they know they're safe." She'd known it.

Sure he'd scared her when she first met him—she wasn't stupid. He was big and she knew all about how even between werewolves, big counts. But her instincts had told her that this one, this one would stand between her and anyone who would hurt her. That aura of guardianship—that was what made her mate such a powerful Alpha.

Charles just stared at her.

"You know that, right?" she said. "Most people stay out of your way, but the defenseless ones, the hurt ones, they just sort of gradually slide into your shadow. Not where you'll notice them too much—but you keep the bad things away."

He still didn't say anything. She buttoned her jeans and then took the two steps to press against him. "We know," she whispered to him. "We who have been hurt, we know what evil looks like. We know you make us safe."

He didn't say anything, but his arms came around her and she knew that she had told him something he didn't know—and that it mattered.

CHARLES HAD ONE of Kage's people drop them off at the airport, where he rented a car as Mr. Smith. He took out the fake driver's license with the credit card he kept for Mr. Smith. Anna watched him fill out the fake address without hesitation.

When they were walking toward the elevator in the parking garage that would take them to their car, she whispered, "For an honest man, you lie pretty smoothly, Mr. Smith."

He gave her one of his eyes-only smiles.

There were four cars to choose from, identical except in color. Charles raised an eyebrow at Anna and she trotted around them, pondering.

"Gray, white, and silver would all blend in," she told him.

"By all means let's take the metallic orange," he agreed somberly. She grinned at him.

She drove the orange car and he navigated. Brother Wolf didn't like traffic, didn't like driving at all, and was unpredictable enough in his road rage that Charles didn't like to drive, either, if he could avoid it. And both of them trusted Anna, he'd told her.

She knew that she wasn't a spectacular driver; the best she could do was steady and law-abiding. She didn't take chances and she laughed about the rude drivers. Even Brother Wolf had to work to get upset about someone making Anna laugh, Charles told her.

She sincerely hoped that over the next few days they didn't meet the guy who'd flipped her off as they left the airport. Only by slamming her brakes hard had she avoided hitting him. Why was it that the people who made idiots of themselves immediately felt it necessary to compound their sins by flipping off the people who saved them from possibly fatal mistakes?

Yes, she hoped that the moron didn't come anywhere near Charles anytime soon.

With Charles running the car's navigation system, they made it to the coffee shop exactly on time. They managed greetings all around—and coffee in great big cups.

"If I could get a permanent IV of this stuff into my veins," Marsden murmured as they all filed out of the coffee shop and into the parking lot, "I'd go into a happy coffee coma and never come out again until I died of sheer contentment. Not just any coffee, you understand, only extra-dark mocha caramel from this shop." He cupped it in both hands like it was something precious to him.

Leeds sipped his apple cider and looked at Anna. "I know I'm weird," he said. "But I was preoccupied and didn't notice what the rest of you were discussing. You'll have to forgive me if I ask you something you already answered for him. You said you and your husband are both werewolves?"

"Yes," she agreed.

"How did that happen?" he asked earnestly. "Did he fall for you and then bite you? Or did you bite him? Or did you go to a werewolf dating site? I didn't know there were actually women werewolves at all. The only ones you see on TV are men."

Marsden thunked him gently on the back of the head. "I can't leave you with anyone, can I? I *like* having you as a partner. It's refreshing working with someone who can speak in whole sentences, and I can use words of more than one syllable. Please, for my sake, make an effort not to irritate werewolves. New partners are a crapshoot."

"No," said Anna, laughing. "It's okay. We met because I got myself into trouble and I called for help." She glanced at Leslie. "Like your bosses did in the Boston case. Charles came and cleaned up my trouble neat as you please. I thought, 'Hey, I could use a guy like that.' So I kept him."

"You didn't get yourself into trouble," growled Charles. "You got yourself out of it."

Leeds looked at Charles, and Anna saw it in his eyes as he looked at her husband. He was one of the ones who'd been hurt, one of the ones who saw that her Charles protected the helpless. Interestingly, Marsden saw it, too. The hand that had been resting on his partner's shoulder tightened. Leeds glanced at him and smiled.

"That's why I'm taking you with me," Leslie told her quietly. "You see a lot of things that happen without words." In a carrying voice, she said, "Okay, you goons. Go find our perp. We'll rendezvous here at sixteen hundred hours if no one finds anything worth calling each other about."

As it turned out, Leslie and Anna had identical rental cars, parked several spaces apart. Anna glanced at Leslie and laughed. "Guess we're going to have to use the fob to see which car is which?"

"No," Leslie said after a moment. "Mine has a scratch on the driver's-side door. It's the closer one. You might as well leave yours locked," she continued in a no-argument tone. "I'm driving."

Anna rolled her eyes. "The mommy voice doesn't work on me," she informed Leslie. "I was raised by my dad, a very logical, calm man who explained things in a normal tone. When he swore, it was in Latin, mostly directed at my brother."

Leslie assessed her. "The only person I trust besides me to get my butt where it needs to go in safety is currently teaching second graders how to multiply by twos. Do you mind if I drive?"

"See," asked Anna, walking around to the passenger seat, "was that so hard?"

"Anna," said Leslie, "I think I could learn to get along with you just fine. Go through those files and see what you want to start with."

There was a stack of files tucked in between the seats. Fourteen new in various colors and one faded and battered. She opened the battered one and said, "1978?"

"Five-year-old boy—attempted kidnapping except that the boy had a big dog who heard him cry out. And—" She stopped. "You read that file and tell me what you think."

Anna read. And thought. "This sounds right. The fae don't like to move." Bran had told her that once. There were a few that moved all the time, but most of them found a place and stayed if they could. "Most of them, anyway. They don't age. And they don't change their rituals, not unless they're High Court fae." And to think just a few years ago the only things she'd known about the fae had come from Disney movies. "They can't."

"That's what Leeds said. He said we were making this perp too human. He's the one who went digging in older files. Found four cases that fit, but that one was the only one where the kid escaped. This kid grew up and still lives in the Phoenix area. Teaches higher mathematics at Arizona State." She gave Anna a challenging smile. "Why don't you call him and see if we can make an appointment."

AS IT TURNED out, Professor Alexander Vaughn had just finished his two morning classes and had the rest of the day free. Did they want to meet him at his house? He'd be delighted to entertain an FBI agent and her consultant—they should reach his house in Tempe about the same time.

Anna assured him that would be lovely.

"He didn't ask what it was about," Anna observed after hanging up.

"Could be a crime groupie," said Leslie. "Lots of people are. Could be he is bored or lonely or anything. No speculation until after we talk to him."

"FBI policy?"

"My policy. Assumptions drive an interview away from interesting places."

"All right," Anna said. "We'll go talk to the professor."

Leslie pulled up to a house that had been built in the fifties. Evidently they had beaten the professor there. Leslie did not obey speed limits as well as Anna. She arrived fifteen minutes earlier than the car's navigation system's estimate.

The house was large and most notable because it was not built in the Southwest adobe style Anna's eyes were getting used to. Nor was the yard xeriscaped with the conscientious water conservation she saw everywhere. Green grass covered the very small front area and huge old trees surrounded the house. Likely the shade from the trees was how the grass survived summers here.

A Volvo, older but in pristine condition, purred into the driveway and disgorged an athletic man with a military-short cut that managed to tone down his bright red hair. He shut the door and took his time looking at them. Anna returned the favor. He looked a little younger than someone who had been five in 1978.

He walked toward them slowly and said, "Can I help you, ladies?"

"Professor Vaughn?" asked Leslie.

He shook his head. "No. Who are you? Why are you looking for Alex?"

The roar of an engine distracted them and a big truck pulled into the driveway beside the Volvo. The truck was painted black with bright pink flames and jacked up high enough it wallowed when it turned.

The door popped open and a mad scientist hopped out, looking very out of place in the redneck vehicle.

"It's okay, love," he called out. "If you answered your cell phone, I'd have updated you."

The red-haired man turned to the professor, tilted his head, and said, "I don't talk while I'm driving. And you shouldn't call while you are driving, Bluetooth or no. I don't want to get that phone call."

The mad scientist nodded, kissed the big man on the cheek, and patted his shoulder. "I'm Alex Vaughn and this bulldog is my partner, Darin Richards of the Phoenix Police Department. He worries, that's his job. Dare, these are the FBI, they want to talk to me."

Darin's head jerked first to his partner and then to the two women. His eyes narrowed. "ID," he said.

Leslie showed him her badge and he examined it. He frowned and said, "I don't know you. I work with the local FBI office a lot."

"They brought me out especially for this case," Leslie said.

He looked at Anna, and she raised both hands. "Don't look at me, I'm just a consultant."

"And you are here to speak with Alex."

"With Dr. Vaughn," Leslie said. "Yes."

"Dare," said the mad scientist. "It's okay."

"Maybe," he agreed, without agreeing at all. "Why are you here?"

"We have to do this on the lawn?" asked Leslie, not losing her smile.

"Dare," said Alex gently. "What are they going to do? Shoot me? Let's go in and have some coffee and talk." He looked at Leslie. "I have a stalker, a former student. She quite often calls in complaints and we have police officers come to investigate strange noises, screaming, shots fired. You name it. The Tempe PD knows her, but occasionally she gets one through to a rookie. The fire department was here last week at two in the morning because she reported a fire. I guess she got tired of not getting a response."

"We are definitely not here because someone called in a complaint," Leslie said. "We'd like to interview you about an attempted kidnapping—yours—that happened in June of 1978."

Both men's faces went blank with surprise.

Darin recovered first. "You never told me you were kidnapped. Freaking damn it, Alex. You'd have been six in '78. June. You'd have been *five*."

"Attempted." Dr. Vaughn sounded shell-shocked. "I don't think the police even believed me. My dad installed a security system and my mom fed the dog steak every day for a week."

"No one believed in fairies back then," Anna said. "We're all clapping our hands for Tinker Bell now, though. We have a missing child who lives four blocks from where you grew up. Would you mind talking to us about what happened?"

"Sure," he said. "I guess. I was five, though. And it's been a long time."

"How about I go next door and see if your mom is home," said Darin. "That woman has a mind like a steel trap. She'll remember what you told her when it happened."

"You think it was a fae?" asked Dr. Vaughn.

"He was green and hairy. His hands had six fingers with claws on them," Anna said matter-of-factly. She'd memorized the words on the first reading—it hadn't been hard. The boy's terror and the police officer's skepticism rang through in the dry words typewritten on paper older than Anna. She continued, "His voice was funny—like on TV sometimes. He had a long yellow tongue and he called you a barn. He said, 'Come here, barn.'" She looked at the police officer. "If someone reported it now, Darin Richards, instead of years before the fae admitted their existence, what would you say it was?"

"Barn," said Darin. "'*Bairn*' means child, right? If he was in Scotland instead of Scottsdale."

"Yes," said Leslie.

"You go in and have some coffee," said Darin. In a gentler

voice he said, "That sure explains some of your nightmares, Alex. You take them in and I'll be right back."

THE MAD SCIENTIST—well, mad mathematician—paced back and forth in the house even though he'd seated Leslie and Anna at the table and put coffee in front of them. He had that kind of kinky hair that never lies down right, and it was about two inches too long or ten inches too short to look good. Especially if it belonged to the kind of person who grabbed it and twisted or pulled when he was nervous.

Anna thought he was adorable. She wanted to adopt him as a big brother and give him a big hug to calm down his rising anxiety.

"My dad was a cop," he said.

Leslie nodded. "That was in the report."

"If he hadn't been a cop, there wouldn't have been a report," Dr. Vaughn said. "He believed me. By the time I was ten, I didn't know why. Hell, I kinda don't believe me now. I mean, this thing looked like it was eight feet tall, and it ran away from my dog and a horseshoe I threw at it?"

"That dog impressed whoever wrote the report," Anna said. There hadn't been any photos of the dog in it, but she had a pretty good idea that "BFDog" in the report (complete with exclamation point and a penciled-in remark that read "I'd have run from that thing, too") meant it wasn't your average run-of-the-mill dog.

"Yeah." Dr. Vaughn quit pacing and grinned. "My dad brought him home from work one day a few years before the . . . incident. I don't remember it, but it's one of those family stories, you know? My mom was scared of him and wanted Dad to take him back where he found it. Then that big dog walked up to her and put his nose on her foot and sighed. He stared at her until she fed him. She was a goner after that."

He smiled at the memory, then sobered. "We only had him for another month or so after that. One day, he just wasn't around. Maybe he was hit by a car or something. I think Dad knew exactly what happened because he never went looking for him. And hit by a car is the kind of thing you might not tell a kid. Hey, I ran across a photo of him the other day."

He booked out of the kitchen, the speed an indicator of how grateful he was for the distraction, and Anna could hear him in another room opening and shutting drawers.

Leslie started to say something, but Anna shook her head. She could hear people talking just outside. In a moment Darin opened the door and escorted a tiny female version of Dr. Vaughn into the kitchen.

She frowned at Leslie and Anna and sat down opposite them with regal suspicion. "Darin tells me that you are here to ask about the time something came into our yard and tried to take my son away," she said.

"We think it was a fae," Leslie said. "It sounds like a fae. It acted like a fae. And a fae took a little girl and left a changeling, a fetch, in her place. We are trying to find that little girl. She is five years old. The attempted abduction of your son is not far from where we think our girl was taken. Thirty-odd years might be a long time for us, but it's a minute to one of the fae."

The stiffness left Dr. Vaughn's mother's back, and she softened. "Thirty years doesn't feel that long ago to me, either." She looked up at her son's partner and said, "Sit, sit, Darin. I gather that Alex never told you about this."

"No, ma'am," he said.

"Well, I think he wanted to believe it didn't happen."

"What do you think?" asked Leslie.

"I think my son never exaggerated or lied about a thing in his life, no matter how uncomfortable it made him. He was twelve when he told us he liked boys instead of girls. That was right after some friend of his got kicked out of his home for doing the same. Stupid people tossing away the most precious thing God saw fit to give them, I say." She looked at Leslie. "So yes, I believe him. I also believe we have not been introduced. I am Mary Lu Vaughn."

"FBI Special Agent Leslie Fisher," said Leslie as Dr.

Vaughn came into the room and put a photo on the table with an air of quiet triumph.

"Anna Smith," said Anna, staring at the photo of two small children trying to tug a rope from an enormous black animal, "special consultant. And that is a werewolf."

CHARLES SAT IN the front passenger seat, since Leeds had taken one look at him trying to fit in the back and said, "Hey, man, that is just not going to happen, is it? No worries, I'll catch the backseat."

Charles wasn't thrilled with having a stranger behind him, but even Brother Wolf couldn't make that man feel like a threat, so he figured it would be okay. He didn't like Marsden's driving, either. He drove too fast and he didn't have a werewolf's reflexes. But if there was a wreck, Charles figured that he, at least, would walk away, so he kept his comments to himself.

"So we've concentrated our efforts in Scottsdale because Leeds thinks that this fae probably doesn't have a huge hunting ground. The ones that steal children tend to get attached to one place even more than the usual fae."

He waited, so Charles said, "It sounds like a reasonable way to make an impossibly big search smaller."

"Okay," Marsden said. "The first place we're going is a foster home to visit with a fourteen-year-old girl. The girl's parents gave her up to the state, said they couldn't deal with her anymore. Claimed she was possessed, things flying around the room with no one touching them, which is why we are visiting even though she's older than the girl who was taken. Her parents said she was dangerous, but the counselor who gave us this one said she was uncommunicative but showed no signs of violence. The foster mom says we're okay to talk to her as long as we do it with the foster mom in the room."

"Why isn't she in school?" asked Charles.

"Yeah," Marsden agreed. "I don't know. But we'll ask."

The house they drove to looked pretty much like all the

rest of the houses on the street. This was not an upscale neighborhood, but it wasn't poor, either.

The woman who met them at the door was a human in her midfifties, if Charles was any judge. She introduced herself as Judy White, examined Marsden's and Leeds's badges, and frowned at Charles. She wasn't unhappy about them, but she was careful.

"Consultant," said Leeds. "No official ID."

She looked grim. Grimmer. But just nodded. "Blair's not going to talk to any of you," she said. "She came here two weeks ago and she hasn't spoken a word to anyone. She doesn't eat much. If I could have a word with her parents . . ." She sucked in a breath. "Well, don't stand out here. Come in."

She led them into a house that smelled of . . . Charles shut his eyes to get a deep breath. Cookies, recently baked. Fresh homemade bread. A man, a woman, three children, and someone in between; that would be the girl they were looking for. Sorrow. This house had seen a lot of sorrow, but there was a warmth to it, too. Nothing smelled like the fetch, which had carried hints of greenwood, magic, and darkness.

He shut the door behind him and tried not to feel like an invading giant when the woman led them to a room with two couches and a couple of those soft squishy chairs, the kind that could unfold with footrests. Charles would let himself be shot before he sat in one of those. They always felt like they were trying to swallow him, and they were impossible to get out of quickly.

He was still trying to decide where to sit when the woman brought in a tall girl of about fourteen wearing clothes that would fit a woman twice her size. She didn't look at any of them, just sat on the edge of one of the person-swallowing chairs, a pale-skinned, pale-haired girl who was little more than skin and bones. The word that occurred to him wasn't "starving" but "fading." This was why no one sent her to school. Even blind humans must be able to tell that she was mostly gone already.

Judy White introduced Marsden and Leeds but made no mention of Charles—and he was fine with that. He watched as Marsden and Leeds did a fair job of good cop/bad cop, Leeds unexpectedly playing bad cop. The girl saw them all right, but she said not a word and gave no reaction to anything they said.

She is abandoned, something whispered in his left ear. Into his right, something else said, *Her true name is sorrow.*

He did not always act upon the things the spirits told him. They were interested in this girl. They hovered unseen, even by him, in the air around her.

She could be anger, they told him. *She could be vengeance, for she has much to be angry about, much to avenge. Those who should have cared for her acted for themselves when they rightly should have acted for her. She has been much sinned against.*

This, he thought, this half child, half woman was where the sorrow that was trying to enfold this house was coming from. He'd told the Cantrip agents he wouldn't talk, but he couldn't let this lie. Someone needed to help her before she chose to leave this existence. He had the sure feeling that she would be needed somewhere in the future, that terrible things would happen without her. But that was not why he chose to act. Brother Wolf liked her.

He knelt on the floor at her feet, interrupting Marsden trying to coax her to speak. Judy White leaned forward as if she would have put herself between them, then paused as she realized this was no attack.

Tempering his usual fierceness not at all, Brother Wolf said, "Little sister. What makes your eyes weep with dry tears and your bold heart ache with pain? What service can we do for you? We will stand for you in any way you need us." And because it was Brother Wolf speaking, Charles felt the words reach through the barriers she had erected between herself and the world.

She blinked at him, and no one in the room said anything as he waited for her to speak.

She cleared her throat. "I'm not your sister," she said hoarsely.

But she was confused, not rejecting them, so Charles and

his wolf waited. They were here to serve her, not to pull information from her, not to take. Too many people had already taken from her.

"My baby," she said, finally. "They made me . . . and I thought, what could I do with a baby? Her father didn't want her and my parents didn't want her. So I let them. I should have stopped them. I should have protected her. She didn't have anyone else. She's dead, she's dead before she had a chance to be born and no one cares. They wanted to pretend that nothing was *wrong*."

And when she said the last word, no more than a whisper, an entire shelf of children's games fell off the bookcase they'd been on with a crash.

ABOUT AN HOUR and a half later, Charles belted himself back in the Chevy and waited for Marsden to drive. But they just sat there with the engine running for a little.

"How did you know?" Marsden said.

"I'm a werewolf," he told Marsden. "I know about all sorts of things. Wizards, humans who can manipulate the physical world, aren't common, but they happen."

"Frightening for her," said Leeds. "To find out that when you get mad things fly around. Do you think the woman you recommended her foster mother talk to might help her?" He sounded like he knew all about being alone with funky powers.

"I wouldn't have given her the name if I didn't." Charles wondered what Leeds's fae blood had left him with as a legacy. But as long as he wasn't stealing children, Charles didn't care. He considered that for a moment, but he could smell Leeds's fae blood quite clearly and it bore no resemblance to whatever had bespelled Chelsea or stolen the child.

"Fourteen," said Marsden. He swore with feeling. "Whoever was watching out for her should have been shot." He paused. "That baby's father died—did you catch that? Hit by a car in a freak accident."

"I hope it was her," said Leeds, then, almost contradicting himself, "and I hope she never knows it."

"That was powerful," Marsden said. "What you did in there, Charles." He rubbed the steering wheel. "It should have been absurd—you know. But it was powerful."

"He is a dominant werewolf," said Leeds. "When he submitted himself to her will . . . of course it was powerful. What if she had asked you to kill her parents? The ones who abandoned her, abandoned her twice, by my accounting."

"Her name was sorrow," said Charles. "All she needed was for someone to hear her so she could mourn."

"But what if?"

He didn't owe Leeds that answer, especially since Brother Wolf was insulted that he would ask.

Still.

"What do you think?" Charles said softly.

After a moment, Marsden drove away from the curb. "Could you tell me the address of the next one, Leeds?"

THE NEXT ONE was another girl, Helena, age thirteen. Her parents and counselor insisted on staying for the interview. They also answered every question Marsden or Leeds asked Helena. The upshot was that they, parents and counselor, were certain that she was possessed by a demon.

"Meth," said Charles quietly into Marsden's ear.

Marsden extracted them quickly.

"We need help," said the counselor. "You folks are supposed to know how to deal with this."

Marsden frowned at them. "Meth isn't demon possession. You change her friends and get her into a rehab program. I shouldn't have to tell you that." He glanced at the parents. "You should also get her a better counselor."

THE THIRD CHILD, another girl, Iris, was five. Her single-parent father, who introduced himself as Trent Carter, was over his head and looked it. Knew it, according to the notes the counselor had given them.

The girl's mother had committed suicide when she was only a toddler. Her father, in sweatshirt and jeans, looked exhausted and underweight. The little girl was dressed in a similar outfit, but in pink, and she had her hair up in lopsided pigtails.

Charles let Marsden and Leeds question both parent and child without saying anything at all. The little girl was happy to talk to them, even though she bowed her head shyly when they asked her a direct question. Eventually, she showed them bruises on her wrists and legs and told them she was clumsy and fell down stairs. Her father paled and looked away.

When Marsden finally looked at Charles, he shook his head. She wasn't fae. Not what they were looking for at all.

Reluctantly, the Cantrip agents left the pair sitting on opposite sides of the room.

"Damn," said Marsden. "Did you see those bruises? We got referred by a counselor, right? Why didn't they get that girl out of there?"

Leeds looked at Charles. "Why aren't you angry? I mean, when that first girl came in . . . the ethereal temperature of the room dropped into the subarctic zone."

"Sometimes," Charles said, "anger, though I am well acquainted with both it and its useful cousin vengeance, is not the appropriate response."

Marsden opened his mouth and Charles said, "Where to next?"

He got in the car and shut the door. After a pause both agents did the same. They drove sedately away from Iris and her father.

"And that, gentlemen, is an actual demon possession," Charles said once they were well on their way.

"The man?" asked Marsden. "That's why he hurt his daughter?" As if he couldn't imagine anyone hurting his own daughter otherwise.

Charles hadn't wanted to like either of these men, though he deemed them useful and perhaps necessary for his hunt.

The other Cantrip agents he had dealt with . . . But these men were decent people.

"The fingerprints on the bruises were too small," said Leeds suddenly. "Those bruises, she did them to herself. I thought there was something off about her." He paused. "Is there something we can do for them? Do you know someone you can send them to for help?"

"I'll look into it," Charles promised.

"Okay, then," said Marsden. "This next one is a boy, a teenager, and he's a long shot. He fits neither our profile nor our neighborhood. But the counselor for this one is quite insistent that there is a problem . . ."

"WELL, YES," SAID Dr. Vaughn's mother mildly. "Sid's great-grandfather or some such. His human wife had just died and the whole family was concerned about him; he wasn't eating or drinking. We thought that his Alpha might just put him out of his misery. So Sid drove over to his house in his squad car, told him he was coming home with him. And when Archie turned into a wolf to discourage him, Sid said, 'Fine. Be a wolf. But you are coming home with me.'"

She looked at Anna. "He just loved our kids, Archie did. Let Alex's older sister dress him in whatever pink and frilly thing she wanted. Pulled a wagon for the kids and saved my Alex's life, I think. He was cantankerous as a human, but he was the best dog this family ever had."

"I can't believe no one ever told me he was a werewolf." Alex let out a laugh. "Do you remember the Christmas turkey? No wonder you were so mad." He paused, then looked at his mother with horror. "The flea bath. You gave a werewolf a flea bath. He was *not* happy about it. No wonder Dad was so upset when he got home."

"He had fleas," she said primly. "I wasn't letting him sleep in your room with fleas."

"So what did happen to him?" Dr. Vaughn asked.

"His Alpha came and got him, finally. Told your dad that it wasn't healthy for a werewolf to stay in wolf form for that long. He went back to his house. Apparently the pack had kept it clean and the bills paid while he lived with us. He visited a couple of times, but he eventually had to move for work. I think that living in his house just wasn't good for him." She pursed her lips. "We never heard from him after that. I know your dad was unhappy, but there wasn't much we could do. Werewolves don't let humans interfere with their pack. Matters are less tense now, of course, because everyone knows about werewolves. But then? I think we had a wolf watching us for a while, just to make sure no one was talking."

She looked at Anna. "Are you a werewolf, dear?"

"Yes," said Anna. She didn't mind, but the unexpectedness of the question caught her off guard.

"Mom," said Dr. Vaughn. "Don't *do* that."

"Do what, dear?" she asked.

Darin chuckled. "I love you, Mary Lu. And I need to recruit you for the PD. Our confession rates would go way the hell up."

"Do you know this werewolf's full name?" Anna asked. "He saw the fae and he wasn't a five-year-old kid. Maybe he can help us if we can find him."

"Archibald Vaughn, dear."

"I'M THINKING YOU'LL have an easier time finding Archibald Vaughn than I will," said Leslie.

"Probably," Anna agreed. "Do you want me to start making calls?"

"Let's check out the rest of these first," she said after a moment's thought. "We scored big on the first one, maybe there will be a second."

"Okay." Anna picked out another file and read off the address. She called the phone number of the witness before she waded through the four-page report. No answer. She checked the paperwork and found no other phone number. She skimmed the report. This one was a clean printout on white paper.

"You've got to hear this," Anna said. She tried to keep her voice businesslike as she quoted the witness report for Leslie.

"It was a unicorn and two small dragons, no bigger than a poodle. Not the little ones. Well, not really the medium-sized ones, either. But you know, a big poodle. Standard. The unicorn was bigger. More like a black Lab, maybe. Or a big German shepherd."

"Why did we pick this one out?" Leslie asked.

Anna kept reading—this time to herself. "Oh. Here it is. She has been looking for fairies ever since she saw the green man living in her garden a couple of years ago. He never leaves and no one else can see him. Except for the dog who jogs past every day with his owner. The dog barks at him every time he passes our witness's garden."

"All right," said Leslie. "You try that number again and if he's not home—"

"She," said Anna. "Kathryn Jamison, age sixty-four." There was another report behind the first—it had another witness's name on it. She reported that her dog barked every day as they passed Jamison's garden. She didn't say anything about the unicorn and dragons.

"We can at least get a look at her garden the same way the jogging lady's dog does, right?"

They were spared the indignity of skulking around Ms. Jamison's garden fence. The second time Anna tried the number, the lady answered on the first ring.

"Call me Katie," she said, her voice slurring just a bit. "Kathryn was my grandmother. You want to come talk to me about a police report I made about the unicorn and dragons?" She laughed, her voice low and husky, a sexy laugh for a sixty-four-year-old woman. "It's been a long time since I had to worry about a unicorn, right?" She laughed again. "But those dragons might burn something down and that would be a shame, don't you think? That's why I thought I should report them. Sure. Come on over."

MS. JAMISON, "CALL me Katie," lived in Gilbert, another Phoenix suburb, about fifteen minutes south and east of Dr. Vaughn's house. Leslie pulled into the spotless, half-round

driveway and parked. There were two fountains in front of
the house, and the whole impression given was a combination of beauty and money, both flaunted with equal abandon.

Anna looked back at the road left and right and saw no
sidewalks for jogging. The house, huge as it was, was set
between two other houses that varied in architecture if not
in stucco color.

"How'd a jogger see into the yard at all?" Anna asked.
"Where would a jogger run?"

"Maybe the jogger knows the unicorn and the dragons,"
murmured Leslie. "And flew over the stone wall and looked
into the garden with her dog." She put on a practiced smile
and headed for the door.

"I'll get you, my pretty," murmured Anna in her best
wicked-witch voice. "And your little dog, too."

MS. JAMISON WAS tall and had muscle under her tanned
and well-cared-for skin. Her chestnut hair was cut short and
expensively. She looked closer to forty than sixty. Some of
that might be surgical, but not all of it. She wasn't stunning,
but she was memorable.

She was also wearing a holey pair of jeans with dirt on the
knees and a very ratty old ASU football jersey. She smelled
like alcohol, for which she apologized.

"I was out gardening and drinking when you called," she
told them. "And now I'm a little drunk. I don't usually over-
indulge, but my divorce from husband number three just
came through. My sister told me he was just after my money,
and she was right."

She sighed. "I knew she was right. But he was *thirty*. He
could keep up with me. Men my age . . ." She shook her head.
"But, as I told her, that's what a prenup is for. I guess he
believed that if I thought he loved me, I'd be stupid in other
ways, too. Caught him red . . . well, red-assed if the truth be
known, and I have the photos to prove it. So he went and took
nothing with him except for the liposuction on his stomach
and two years of luxury living. I'd have paid a gigolo more

for his services. But I'd have probably gotten better services."
She looked pensive.

"Do you want us to come back later?" Leslie asked.

"No. It's all right," she said. "Waiting would only waste
your time and mine. I only had two shots—okay, three. But
I did it on a full stomach and I've been drinking water since
you called."

Leslie looked doubtful, but Anna said, "Look. We're not
after her. We are not going to use this testimony in court. If
we need real testimony, you can come back and get it."

"You're sure you're okay?" Leslie asked. "We can return
later."

"That stupid jogger set the police on me. Her uncle is a
judge, I think. Now she's set the FBI. Sure. Come talk to me
about unicorns and dragons."

10

They followed her into the house, which smelled like cinnamon and vanilla in a combination not quite strong enough to cause Anna distress, though she'd be glad to leave. The entryway led them into a huge circular room with hardwood floors trimmed in stone around the smallish fountain in the center of the room and around the fireplace on the wall opposite the entryway.

Other rooms opened off the main room. Anna caught a glimpse of a kitchen, a dining room, a weight room, and a room where everything had been torn out down to the studs. The drywall, shreds of carpet, and bits and pieces of furniture were left in an untidy pile on the floor.

"My ex-husband's office," Katie caroled as she walked by. "I did the demolition myself. Better than therapy. But my contractor is sending people in the next few days to redo it. And clean up the mess." She paused, then looked at Anna and winked. "He put that carpet in for me, right after we got married. When he came in to give me a bid on repairs, he asked me what had been wrong with the carpet." She smiled. "I told him there wasn't any blood on it."

Katie led them into her own office, bright and airy with a view of a swimming pool dominating a huge backyard. Other than the pool, it was mostly xeriscaped but with patches of green hidden under fruit trees. The back fence was eight-foot wrought iron with a gate leading out to a waterway and presumably, because Anna couldn't see it from the window view, a jogging path.

The office was big enough to swallow a desk and a couch and love seat with room left over. Katie plopped down on the love seat, tucking one sandal-clad foot underneath herself.

"So did she tell you that there must be a body in my garden because her dog barks at my yard all the time?" Her voice rose and sweetened. " 'Remington doesn't bark anywhere else, just at *her* garden. Remington is an intellectual genius and knows, absolutely knows, that there must be a body buried there. He's trying to tell us.' " She narrowed her eyes at Leslie, and when she continued, it was in her own voice. "Remington is a squat toad who pokes his nose in other people's business. If I were going to bury someone in my garden, it would have been my hushband. Husband. Ex. Ex-hushband. But he's still alive and living in sin with his girlfriend, who is the same girlfriend he'd just broken up with when I met him. Stupid dog. Stupid men. All of them should rot in hell."

"So the jogger's report was first," Anna said, suddenly understanding what had happened. "She has connections, so the police came to ask you about your garden."

Katie had been nodding, but she held up a finger to stop Anna. "Point of fact. They dug up my garden and it took me three weeks to get it back into shape. One of my yuccas is, I'm afraid, doomed."

"And so you told them that there was a fairy living in your garden," Leslie said.

Katie held up a finger. "No. I called them back at one in the morning and said that there was something dangerous here. Something. The police came and asked me what was dangerous. I told them I'd seen a unicorn and two smallish dragons running down the street. Which I had. My neighbors have a trio of delightful children who like to dress up in last year's Halloween costumes. I suppose they'd escaped the babysitter I saw chasing after them. Both of the dragons were carrying lighters—you know the kind I mean. Not the ones for cigarettes but the ones for lighting a charcoal grill. The unicorn was armed only with her horn." She paused. "I may have left out a few things in my story. And I might have called it in five or six hours after I first saw the unicorn."

Anna saw Leslie's face and didn't laugh, though she wanted to.

Leslie said coolly, "So you deliberately called police officers to your home because they inconvenienced you. And kept them here when they might have been needed elsewhere?"

Katie's eyes narrowed and she lost the soft, half-drunken act entirely. "No. I'm telling you that I called them on a possible threat. I never saw the babysitter actually corral the little hooligans, did I? Two ten-year-olds can do a lot of damage with fire lighters. It's not my fault that the police officer didn't ask the right questions."

Leslie sat up straighter, and Anna interrupted her. They were here for information. A lecture on the stupidity of crying wolf, no matter how well deserved, was not going to get them anywhere.

"We are not actually here about the unicorn. We're more interested in the green man in your garden," Anna said.

Katie stiffened more, and her scent spiked with anxiety that was not quite fear.

"You needed to distract the police from your garden," Anna said. "The unicorn and dragon story did that very nicely. They aren't going to want to come back here anytime soon, are they? But they've written you off as a kook." That had been quite a sacrifice for this woman who spent so much time and energy on her own appearance. "But that green man comment—just a throwaway, really—has the ring of truth and that's what brought us here. What do you have living in your backyard, Ms. Jamison?"

"I think I would like to call my lawyer," said Katie.

"We are here because we are looking for a five-year-old

girl who was taken by a fae who left a changeling in her place," Leslie said. "That fae kills children, Ms. Jamison."

"You can show yourselves out," she said stonily.

"Time matters," Anna told her, not mentioning that Amethyst had been missing for months already. "How will you feel when we find that child's body? Will you ask yourself if she might have survived if you had cooperated? Or will you be able to shrug it off?"

"He has nothing to do with kidnapping children." The older woman's voice was harsh.

"Maybe," Anna said. "But maybe he would know who does. Maybe he could help us."

Katie looked up and Anna caught her eyes. Anna was no Alpha wolf to force people to do things that they would rather not. But she was honest and stubborn. It was Katie who looked away first.

"If you put anything in writing, I will make you look like a fool," Katie said.

Anna tipped her head. "We have no intention of making you look foolish or getting you into trouble."

Leslie hesitated. "If this has nothing to do with the girl's disappearance, there will be no need to record anything more than that we checked out your story and found it not germane to our investigation."

Katie was quiet a moment. "All right. All right. Fine. I have a touch of the Sight. My mother did, too, and her mother before her. My grandmother was a healer and wisewoman. My mother . . . she had migraines during which she would see things. Some of them happened, some of them didn't. She thought she was getting glimpses of likely futures. Me? I can see the fae for what they are, whatever guise they are wearing. And I have hidden it from them because they don't like sidhe-seers. If you give me away, my life will be very short."

"Understood," Leslie agreed.

KATIE JAMISON STRODE past the big pool with its attendant fountains, hot tub and assorted pool chairs, bar and barbecue: a full-service pool. Instead she aimed at the small green corner in the back of her yard.

Three huge palm trees formed the upper canopy, and huge clumps of lavender nearly waist high lined the eight-foot stone wall that separated Katie's yard from the next house over. There was some kind of bush in between the lavender with pretty orange flowers. But there was no denying that the most spectacular plant was a huge orange tree, craggy with age.

It sprawled arrogantly over the wrought-iron fence into the jogging path, its branches laden with green fruits that were just starting to turn orange. It was obviously older than the yard it presided over, older than the housing development, the jogging path, and the three other fruit trees next to it, too. Anna, though no gardener, thought that the other fruit trees, though much smaller, were pretty old, too.

She paid attention to the messages that her nose was giving her. Over the faint scent of lavender, though most of the lavender was not yet in bloom, over the unripe fruit, and the orange-flowered whatsit, she smelled something wild, something magic, something fae.

"These people want to talk to you," said Katie, staring directly at the decorative and effective gate between the yard and the canal-and-jogging-path. "It's about a missing child. I don't think they care about you being here at— Yes. I know it was stupid, but *I* didn't torment that damned dog on purpose for months, either."

Apparently Katie was a sidhe-hearer as well as seer, because even Anna's enhanced ears couldn't hear the person she was talking to. Her eyes caught on the great orange tree and stayed there.

The trunk was bent and twisted with knots where limbs had been cut years and years ago. The oranges were plum-sized and green. Anna didn't know much about the vegetation in Arizona. A few quiet afternoons in Asil's greenhouse in Montana had given her a working knowledge of rare roses and a handful of flowers and plants that appealed to the old wolf. The only fruit tree he had was a waist-high dwarf clementine that Asil said was a tribute to his Spanish heritage and the oranges he used to grow on some farm he'd owned at one time or another.

Katie turned back to them. "He likes to play games," she said. "He told me that if you can find him, he'll answer three questions."

"Agreed," said Anna. She pulled her cell phone out and texted a quick message to Charles so he wouldn't worry when he felt her change.

"I'm not my husband," she told Leslie. "I'm going to change to my wolf shape. Unlike him, I probably won't be able to change back for a couple of hours after this."

"You can't just—" She tapped her finger to her nose.

Anna shook her head. "If it were that easy, he wouldn't be making a deal. Just remember to phrase your questions very carefully. Take your time. The fae always answer truthfully, but not always completely. If they can deceive you with the truth, they will. Don't ask rhetorical questions, because those will count."

She stepped to the side of the big tree, where she was hidden from the sight of people outside the yard, and began stripping her clothes off. "This will take a while," she warned them.

"What are you doing?" Katie said as Anna kicked off her shoes.

"I'm a werewolf," Anna told her. "I'm changing into my wolf. The wolf's nose is better and less easily confused."

The moon was almost full, so her change should have been easy. Pain, as her body rearranged itself, was now an old friend. It slid over her head with hot hands that dug in and cracked her jaw so forcibly that the pain of the rest of her body seemed gentle by comparison—until her shoulders slipped out of their sockets at the same time.

On a moon night, with the pack gathered together, pack magic shielded the sounds the changing wolves made in their pain, and the moon could sometimes change pain to ecstasy. But alone and in the full Arizona sun, Anna was obligated to make no noise that might attract attention. She was good at not attracting attention.

Some changes were better than others, regardless of the moon's phases, but this was much, much worse than any shift she'd done this near the moon's call. Before pain drove her to the single determination of *silence*, Anna belatedly recognized the wariness her wolf felt that drove her to speed the change. The wolf could not adequately defend herself while caught between forms. Anna had chosen to change in front of a virtual stranger and a fae she could not see and knew nothing about. A fae who could be the very creature they were hunting.

Anna trusted Leslie to have her back. But the wolf was more judicious in her trusts and Leslie was not pack, nor anyone they were long acquainted with. So speed was necessary and pain was a small cost to pay for safety.

When it was over, Anna lay winded and shaky, which wasn't exactly a safe thing, either. She rolled to her feet and shook off the last of the muscle twitches. She couldn't tell how long it had taken. Pain made time subjective.

She stretched, sliding her claws out until they dug into the soil. Satisfied that her body was working, she turned her head to look at the two women who stood carefully not looking at her.

"Are you all right?" Leslie asked when Anna moved around so she could look the FBI agent in the face. "That looked . . . that sounded like it hurt. We could hear your bones break."

Anna sneezed and let her tail wag. Katie looked at Anna, and then quickly away again. Her hand over her mouth. "It's not . . . it wasn't . . ." Her voice stuttered to a stop—and then she made a break for her house.

Anna sighed. Yes. Werewolves are monsters and the change isn't pretty. Unfair to ask the mundanes to deal with it. She'd had no choice.

"Can you find the fae?" Leslie asked. "I assume the deal is still in effect. If you find him and we can't communicate, I'll go back in the house and drag Ms. Jamison back out."

Yes. Finish this business, thought Anna.

She checked out the big tree first, though it was too obvious. It smelled of fae magic, no question. But to her wolf nose, the whole yard smelled of fae.

She trotted the circumference of the yard and played a little hot and cold with herself to make sure she was right that the fae was somewhere near that big orange tree. The scent of the fae, who did not smell like Chelsea's house or the day care, faded as soon as she got to the house end of the swimming pool. She quartered the yard around the pool and ended up back by the orange tree.

Not the butterfly bush, not the granite rock that was decorated with small pots of herbs where the sides of the boulder made natural shelves. Not the handful of tea rose bushes. Not the yuccas—which did indeed show signs of being dug up and replaced. Everything smelled of the fae, but not enough. Anna backed away and looked carefully for something she had missed.

Where? she asked herself, asked her wolf spirit. *Where is he?*

The wolf focused on one of the lemon trees, the smallest and scruffiest of them. Like the yuccas, it looked as though it was suffering from rough handling.

She closed in on it, shut her eyes, and let her nose lead her across the stone walkway and onto the gravel that covered the earth around the plants. Her ears picked up the sound of a door opening in the house, a car pulling up on the street, and Leslie's heartbeat twenty feet away. Her nose followed the elusive trail until fae was all she could smell.

She opened her eyes—and fear, visceral and unexpected, turned her joints to water and closed her throat so she could neither breathe nor make a sound. Justin stood before her, the werewolf who had Changed her and then made her life a living hell.

And all she could think was, *You're dead. You're dead. I saw you die.*

THE TEXT MESSAGE from Anna was simple. It said: Don't worry. I need my wolf nose to find a fae. As Charles finished reading, he felt his mate's shift begin.

She knew him. She was worried that he'd come looking

for her if she transformed to wolf, so she was reassuring him that she wasn't in harm's way. If she hadn't added the last bit, he'd have let her text message reassure him.

She was looking for a fae on her own? When the fae they were looking for was powerful and sophisticated enough to create a child from a bundle of sticks? Not without him, she wasn't.

"Pull over," he told Marsden, interrupting whatever the agent had been saying about the next place they were headed, *had been* headed.

"Excuse me?"

Impatient, Charles caught the other man's eye and said, low-voiced, "Pull over."

The car swerved out of traffic and came to a halt with a jerk.

"What the freak, man?" said Marsden, staring at his hands as though he couldn't believe what had happened. That he'd just obeyed orders.

Humans weren't used to following the hierarchy of the pack, but it still worked on them. At least it worked on them when Charles was giving the orders. It wasn't magic. But there was a reason Charles was usually the most dominant in his world that was filled with dominant wolves. Even humans had that primitive brain that drill sergeants around the world tapped into, the part of the brain concerned with survival. That part heard an order and just *obeyed*.

Charles got out and rounded the front of the car rapidly, so the spell of his order didn't have a chance to fade. He opened the driver's-side door and said, "Time for me to drive." When that didn't move Marsden, he met his eyes again and said, "Get out of the car, Agent Marsden. I'm driving."

"Jim?" Leeds said.

Marsden unbuckled and got out, too slowly to suit Charles, but it was done. Charles sat down and belted in. While Marsden got into the passenger seat, Charles played with the tablet mounted in the dash of the car until it gave him a map to look at. He hadn't used this particular version of a tablet before, but there was nothing related to a computer that didn't eventually spill its secrets to him.

Charles knew Phoenix of twenty years ago, but the new city and its suburbs were much changed. Anna's pain echoed in his head, shivering shreds that were worse than usual. He felt her wolf's anxiety, but Anna was okay.

That knowledge gave him the patience to wait until Marsden was beside him, buckled in. Then he hit the gas, crossed four lanes of traffic, and slid sideways through the police emergency road that connected one side of the expressway to the other. There was a car in the nearest lane and the Cantrip agent's car was undertorqued compared to his truck.

The siren control bar had a switch helpfully marked LIGHTS NO SIREN. He tripped it, crossed the highway in front of the oncoming car, and then pulled into the next lane over, ignoring the sounds his passengers made.

He put his foot down and wished the car had more power on the top end. He drove it a little slower than flat-out because he might need that extra speed to get them out of trouble. Every few minutes he glanced at the map on the.tablet. He didn't know where Anna was, but he could feel her and he headed that direction as quickly as he could.

"I thought you said you couldn't drive," said Marsden tightly.

In the backseat, Leeds was chanting fervently, "Not gonna die today, not today, Lord. Not gonna die today, not today, Lord."

Charles passed a four-car mobile roadblock by squeezing the car down the left-hand shoulder, which wasn't quite wide enough, and he had to muscle it pretty good to keep the soft sand from pulling them into the ditch. Leeds's half prayer sped up and got pretty loud until the car was traveling with all four wheels on the blacktop again.

"I prefer not to," Charles answered Marsden as he switched lanes over and back. "But it is better if I drive when my wolf is on the hunt." And then he quit talking, quit listening, and drove while his Anna completed her change, and her pain left him clearheaded.

She didn't need him. She was a werewolf and he'd spent the whole of their time together making sure she could take care of herself. She was tough and smart. She didn't need him to deal with a fae.

But he was coming anyway.

The Cantrip agents did pretty well, he thought, given that they were used to human reaction times and he was not human. The biggest limitation on their speed and the path he took was the car. He skidded it pretty good as they came off the expressway and onto the city streets because its suspension was for crap. He had to drop speed a bit, but not much as they rocketed through red lights and crosswalks with kids and little old ladies.

Leeds fell silent and Marsden closed his eyes with one hand on the oh-crap handle and the other braced on the dashboard. The quiet in the car was good. It allowed his ears to pick up the first hint of rubber slipping on pavement, even before he could feel it. That gave him a little more reaction time, so he sped up a bit.

Even with the map, he circled her location twice before he found a road that led to the house where the orange car was parked. He pulled in behind and took a deep breath, opening the car door, and that was when Anna's panic nearly dropped him to his knees.

He'd never been more grateful for his ability to shed his human skin for wolf in moments, in a breath, instead of the long drawn-out process his father and the other wolves had to go through. It hurt, it hurt, but Anna was frightened and that made the other of no concern at all.

On four paws, he bolted through the plate-glass window; the glass cut deeply, but he ignored the damage. He healed as he ran through the stone house, over a silly little fountain, and out the closed patio doors, shedding water, blood, and glass as he ran.

The graceful black wolf who was his mate crouched, hindquarters and tail tucked, at the far side of the yard. She was better at controlling her responses in human form. The only time he'd ever seen her look scared was when she ran on four paws.

Whatever she saw, and he didn't see anything in front of

her where her attention was focused, it really scared her. His Anna had the heart of a lion.

Whatever it was that frightened her, he needed to kill it and lay it at her feet. A gift of love, he thought whimsically as Brother Wolf calculated where the invisible and presumably fae creature had to be, based on Anna's body language and position.

Charles hit it hard. Brother Wolf had found their target. As it fell with him upon it, he dug in wherever he could. Two things happened when his fangs sank into flesh that tasted of bark, sap, and lemons. First, he could see the fae. Second, Anna's fear dissipated, and that quick dispersal felt like a spell breaking.

This is not our villain. There was no doubt in her thoughts. *He has been here a long time. He might know something about the fae we are hunting. Who better than another fae who is at large in the same vicinity? He has promised to answer our questions. If you kill him, we'll never know. Charles, you cannot kill him. Not before we find Amethyst.*

Anna wasn't hurt. But Brother Wolf wanted the fae to die; leaving your enemies alive was not smart. Any fae who frightened Anna was his enemy. Fear was a power the fae used to protect themselves, to freeze their prey, to kill. He knew that, understood that, if Anna did not. It was a weapon, and this one had used it against Anna.

Please, Anna said, breathing a little calmness to him. Not enough to influence him; he didn't think she had done it on purpose. Maybe she was trying to calm herself down and the effect had sifted through their bond.

But wherever she had aimed, it succeeded in allowing him to think. Anna wasn't hurt. Anna wasn't hurt, ergo he did not need to kill this fae. And, given that it had not hurt her, if he killed it, it would be because he wanted to. To kill when it was not a matter of defense or law was murder.

Woodland fae are too tough to kill easily, anyway, Brother Wolf grumbled at Anna.

Charles extracted his fangs and stepped back, letting the growl dwelling in his chest ring in the open air.

The wounded fae was definitely one of the tree folk but not a particularly dangerous one, not if he'd been too frightened to fight back when Charles had attacked him. His skin was more like tree bark and he had no flesh to soften the rawboned look. Yellow and red eyes, one each, blinked up at Charles in fearful horror.

Though Charles's strike would have killed a human, this fae was not much hurt, he thought. The fae were tough, the forest fae among the toughest. As Brother Wolf had observed, this one would not die easily under the fangs of a werewolf.

Beside him Anna shook herself, shivered, and shook herself some more. And even if she was not terrified anymore, she was definitely disturbed, allowing Charles to stay between her and the fae.

If not for the humans watching—the FBI agent, the Cantrip agents who were cautiously climbing through the remains of the patio doors, and the woman in the house who stared out through an upstairs window—he would have pressed against her, reassuring her that she wasn't alone. He would have done it despite the audience if she had still been frightened. But she was recovering and he wouldn't take that from her.

Charles circled the fae as it struggled back to its feet. The damage he'd done mended itself, the barklike skin flowing together until there was no trace of fang marks or hurt.

Leslie cleared her throat. "Hey, Charles," she said. "Quite an entrance." Her voice was steady, though he could smell her fear.

He glanced at her and then away. In his current state it wouldn't be safe for her if he caught her eyes. Excess adrenaline made it impossible for him to stay still, so he stalked back and forth like a lion in a cage and waited for someone to do something.

"All right, then," Leslie said. "Sir. I don't know your name. I think you have to agree that we located you. That's not a question."

The fae shuddered and took on human semblance—a bland-featured man of average height and average build wearing a sand-colored, double-knit suit fifty years out of date.

"It wasn't fair," he said. "It wasn't fair. I didn't know it was a werewolf. If I'd known it was a werewolf, I wouldn't have made that bargain. It wasn't fair."

"You didn't ask," Leslie said. "You should know better than to make assumptions."

"Not fair," he said again, pouting. "Spoiled the game."

If the fae was talking about playing games, Leslie might need a little coaching. Hostile fae could be difficult. Charles took a deep, deliberate breath and pulled his human shape out and donned it. He shook his head and a few shards of glass tinkled on the ground. He dusted himself off and got rid of a few more. His skin burned where the glass had cut deeply and the werewolf magic continued to heal him.

"Leslie," he said. His voice was still gravelly, but he couldn't help it with Brother Wolf so close.

She took a step away from him, caught herself, and stepped forward again. He could smell her fear, but she was not giving in to it, which was what he had come to expect from her.

"Fill me in," he said. "Let me help."

Marsden and Leeds came up and Leslie relaxed fractionally. She nodded at them and then turned to Charles.

"We came here investigating a report that Ms. Jamison filed about unicorns and dragons, and a green man in her garden. Most of it was a false report, camouflage for the truth that there was a green man in her garden. The deal was that if we found the green man, he gives us three true answers."

"First, it isn't a green man." Charles looked at the bland man without favor and pretended not to notice that Anna had moved close to him as soon as he stopped moving and was pressed up against him. You didn't reveal your mate's weaknesses before the enemy. He couldn't kill it until Leslie discovered if it could help them find Amethyst.

"Woodland fae, a tree man, related to the green man. Wearden, the old Anglo-Saxons called them. I have no idea what he calls himself. One of the lesser fae, which doesn't mean he isn't dangerous. Just not as dangerous."

The fae curled his lip up and hissed at Charles.

"Okay," Leslie said.

"Ask a question that requires a broad answer," Leeds said. "Don't use yes-or-no questions. Oddly enough those are pretty easily fouled up."

"What—" The fae leaned forward, just a little. But it cued Leslie in and she rephrased it. "Leeds, please explain that. Yes-or-no seems pretty cut-and-dried to me."

"Take the question every husband dreads." Leeds looked at the fae and then back at Leslie. "You know, the one about if pants make you look fat. A fae could say 'No,' which you would take to mean that you don't look fat, when in fact he means 'The pants don't make you look fat, your extra weight makes you look fat.'" Leeds cleared his throat and a flush rose up his face. "Not that you do look fat. It was just an example."

Leslie grinned at him but said, "Okay, thanks."

"Before you start, I can tell you some more things about this wearden to help direct your questions," Charles told her. "I am absolutely certain that this is not the fae who stole the child. He smells wrong and I doubt he has the ability to make a fetch as convincing as the one that took Amethyst Miller's place. He's the wrong kind of fae to have that sort of magic. The lesser fae's magic is very specific. He doesn't have the power to get Chelsea to kill her children, either. He is here because it is hard for the tree-tied fae to move. Those who could were moved into the reservations early on."

"Do you—" Leslie glanced at the fae again. She cleared her throat. "I don't mean to be giving orders, but they are better than questions under the circumstances. Given that he is tied to this place, tell me if you think he will know anything about our quarry. Please."

Charles shrugged. "The chances are pretty good; fae gossip like everyone else."

"Right."

A woman ran out of the house. She was older, Charles thought, but in impressive shape for a human of her age. In one hand she held a camera with a very big lens attached.

"Can I take photos?" she asked as she ran up to them, out of breath. She was looking at Anna, but she did not specify.

"Yes," said the fae, his voice suddenly mocking. "You can take photos, Katie, but I fear you *may* not. You'll have to ask the wolves." He looked at Charles and smiled. "That is question one. Two more."

The woman's face paled as she took in the whole tableau. "I screwed things up."

"Leslie, ask your questions," Charles said when it looked as though they were going to get bogged down in extraneous conversation that might include more irrelevant questions.

"I'm so sorry," said the stranger, but she subsided when Charles shook his head at her.

Leslie took a deep breath and then ran with it. She described in detail what they knew, told the fae about the missing girl, about the attempt to force Chelsea to kill her own children. She added a bit that she and Anna must have discovered, about an attempted kidnapping almost forty years ago. She didn't talk about the other things, the ones they weren't absolutely certain were related to their fae, the teacher who hanged herself or the car accident.

"My first question is, then, what exactly do you know about the fae who kidnapped Amethyst Miller and left a fetch, a changeling, in her place?"

The fae half shut his eyes, searching for a way out. It probably didn't matter to him how much he told, except that fae didn't like giving their secrets away.

"Once upon a time there was a High Court fae," he said finally. "Now, the fae of the High Court, they are great ones for stealing human children and teaching them to fetch and carry, to work and to give life to the below lands. This one, this one maybe loved children too much, or maybe the twist happened sometime during the very long time it took Faery to fall in the Old World. His kind take children, but this one, this one, he loved children, stole them from the humans and turned them into his toys until they died and he had to replace them."

The fae looked around slyly. "Humans are such fragile things. It was a hobby for him, but when the magic fell and rose and fell again, it took that part of him and twisted it into a geas such as we low fae must follow but usually the powered fae, like the High Court fae, do not." There was glee in his voice, though his human facade was still bland and doll-like. "So now he must have a child for his collection. He keeps them for a year and a day and then consumes them entirely, at which time he has to collect another. He feeds on the change that time brings upon them, see?"

He looked at Anna and smiled. Charles felt a rush of magic and put a hand on his mate's head. She raised her head and growled at the fae man, showing him her fangs.

He can't pull that trick on me twice. Anna's clear voice rang in his head. *Justin is dead. If the fae wants to wear his face, that is just fine.*

Rage, squelched earlier, rose like a phoenix. Brother Wolf would kill this one without a twinge of conscience. Not that wolves regretted much. Regret, like guilt, they mostly left to their human halves. He veiled his eyes because he knew that they had lightened to wolf amber from his own human dark brown.

Leslie started to ask another question, but Charles shook his head. "He's not finished answering the first question," he said. His voice was too rough again, but he couldn't help it. He looked the wearden in the eyes, and the creature took a step back and his magic sputtered and died. "And don't ask about High Court fae. I know of their kind and can answer any questions you have about them."

The wearden sneered at him. Charles just watched him back coolly.

The fae's expression gradually grew sulky again and finally he continued. "The humans in Scotland a century ago broke into one of his lairs. They called him the Doll Collector because the girls were dressed up like dolls. The one who was still alive would not talk. She died a few weeks later. But it became impossible for that fae to live in Scotland anymore. Like many of us, though later than some, he hopped aboard a steamer and came to the New World."

They waited. When Leslie would have said something, Charles shook his head.

Finally the wearden spoke again. "He lived here—" The fae gave an address that Leslie jotted down. "For a long time. But when the Gray Lords decided that it was necessary for the fae to reveal themselves . . ."

He rubbed his hands down the front of his shirt and looked around nervously. "I shouldn't be telling you this."

"I understand that bad things happen to fae who break their word," said Charles silkily. "The powers that be don't approve of lying."

The fae gave him a nasty look. "The Gray Lords went to the less publicity-friendly fae and forced them to behave. They went to the Doll Collector and took away his power. They froze his need, and his ability, to take the children and left him to his own devices. I did not hear of him again until the Gray Lords released some of the monsters they hold, and that one came back here hungry." He flashed Charles a look of intense dislike. "That is all I know about the Doll Collector, except for the information you have given me."

"What can stop him?" asked Leslie.

The fae grinned at her. Only his mouth moved, which looked odd. Either he was trying to freak out the humans, or this fae really had little experience trying to look human. "Death stops everything."

It dropped the appearance of humanity and stepped back among the trees in the corner of the garden and became a small, scraggly tree in the shade of the big fruit tree.

"Sorry," Leslie told Charles. "I guess I was hoping for Kryptonite, you know?"

Charles shook his head. "Your first question was good. It told us everything it knew." He glanced at Leeds, who had been writing as the fae spoke. "You have that address, right?"

"I have it. I've texted it to our research division. They'll have the ownership records and whatever else they can find, like house plans, back to us as soon as they can."

"Excuse me." The woman he didn't know, presumably the owner of the house, spoke to Leslie. "Do you think I might get a photograph of the werewolf? Photography is a hobby of mine and she is beautiful."

Leslie raised her eyebrows and looked at Charles. "What do you think?"

He was inclined to refuse. "Anna?"

She hopped on the big granite boulder and posed, looking graceful. And cute. Which was pretty amazing, because werewolves could be beautiful, but they were predators. Cute was not, usually, in the picture. But then, his Anna was amazing.

We have some time because we need to wait until we have a little more information on the address, right? Her voice inside him still felt new and wondrous. He was so grateful not to be alone. *We need to know if we're breaking into a fae's prison or the home of some poor slob who happened to buy the house in the last fifty years. And we owe Ms. Jamison. How much damage did you do to her house?*

He smiled at her. "Yes," he said to Anna, forgetting that everyone couldn't hear her. "I'll pay for the damage, of course, but a little PR repair might be in order."

11

Charles left a business card, one with only an e-mail address and a PO box, for Ms. Jamison to send the estimates for repairs. She wanted him to sign a release for the photographs, but he shook his head.

"I'm not the one you photographed," he said.

"Photos showing people's faces need release forms or I can't use them," Ms. Jamison complained sharply.

"Werewolves are in a gray area," he told her. "Use them. If someone gives you trouble about it, write to the address on the card and we'll take care of it."

Leeds's phone rang, and whoever was on the other end had news. The house at the address the wearden had given them was owned by the estate of a woman who'd died twenty years ago. It was cared for by a property management company for the past fifty years until, in fact, a few months ago when the renters had been asked to leave.

"Keep looking for the owner," Leeds told them. "We're headed over to that address. Three federal agents with two werewolves for backup. We'll be okay." He put his phone away. "Let's go check this out."

"Good luck," said Ms. Jamison. "I hope you find her."

CHARLES RODE WITH Leslie, who followed Marsden and Leeds since they were local and knew the area. Anna stretched out in the backseat of Leslie's car. She grumbled because there just wasn't room in the backseat for a two-hundred-pound werewolf to be both comfortable and secure.

"Not designed for wolves," he told Anna sympathetically.

Riding with Leslie was less troublesome than riding with the Cantrip agents. He liked them well enough, but Brother Wolf approved of Leslie, and she drove better.

They followed Marsden's dark sedan for a few more miles, away from upscale houses and into neighborhoods a few notches further down on the economic scale, before Leslie spoke again. "Her change was very slow compared to yours."

"We're all different," he said after a moment's thought. "But I'm more different than most. And yes, there is a more detailed explanation for it that I'm not at liberty to tell you."

She laughed unexpectedly. "My security clearance isn't high enough?"

"You aren't a werewolf," he said, half apologetically.

"Yes, Mr. *Smith*," she said. "Just remember, as many politicians can attest personally, secrets tend to come out at the worst possible time and blow up in your face."

"We're trying for a controlled release," he said.

She laughed again, and he wondered how well she sang. Maybe she'd like to sing with Anna and him sometime. If her singing voice was like her laugh, it would blend very well with Anna's. He was adding in Anna's cello and a little piano . . . or maybe even guitar to the song in his head when Marsden pulled over in front of a mailbox that fronted a piece of property with a tagged and crumbling eight-foot cinder-block wall.

On the corner of the block stood a run-down apartment building with a full parking lot of cars that showed signs of spending a decade or two in the unforgiving Arizona sun.

Next to it, across the street from where they had parked, was a small house with a fenced-in yard in which a puppy and two boys played a complicated game of fetch and tag.

"This is it," said Marsden. "We have a search warrant fast-tracked because of the terrorist angle and endangered child. Leeds called the management company and they say as far as they know it has been empty since they were asked to remove the renter. The lady he talked to said she thought they were still managing it but had no record of any maintenance or interaction with the owners since last December. She did not know why they cleared out the previous renters—only that the owners requested it. Her boss is on vacation in Florida. She's looking for the paperwork."

The wooden gates were half-opened. The left-hand gate drooped sadly to the ground.

Marsden would have led, but Charles stepped in. "Let Anna and me lead. We don't know what we'll find, and the two of us are less likely to get hurt if it's bad."

Marsden retreated with his hands up. "All right."

"And stay with us," Charles added. "If this is the fae's home, he is unlikely to run." This was why he didn't like working with humans: they died too easily. "Stay with us and we'll do what we can to keep you alive if it attacks."

Leslie pulled her weapon and held it down against her leg. "We'll do the same for you," she said dryly.

He smiled at her and then ducked through the person-sized gap between the tall gates, Anna at his side.

THIS WAS NOT the first dangerous situation Anna had strolled into at her husband's side. She was, if she felt like being honest, pretty humiliated by her performance with the fae in Ms. Jamison's garden. Big bad werewolf reduced to shivers by a wussy little garden fae. What was it Charles had called it? A wearden.

Humiliation was better than the shiver of horror that the thought of Justin called up. Funny, she didn't remember being that terrified of him while he was alive. Terrified, yes, but reduced to shivering like a jellyfish, no. Maybe the wearden's magic had done something to make her fear worse. But if so, why did her stomach still ache?

But she had a job to do, and she shoveled Justin to the dark dungeon in her mind where she kept him and he only bothered her in her nightmares.

Inside the walls, the yard was barren, not xeriscaped, but zero-scaped. Red soil with patches of dead vegetation provided no cover for anything to hide behind. She breathed in deeply but smelled nothing unusual: no magic, no fae, nothing but dust.

And yet . . . she put her nose down and half crept, half walked. Her ears drooped slightly in unease that was not, she didn't think, spawned from her earlier fright.

Do you have anything? Charles asked her.

Her lips pulled up involuntarily, a threat display of teeth for— *Nothing,* she told him, *and yet . . .*

She shivered in the warmth of the high sun. It was not summer, but in Scottsdale that didn't mean it wasn't warm, nearly eighty degrees. She could smell the others' sweat.

I let that fae spook me, she told him. *I'm overreacting.*

He shook his head. *No birds, no insects, nothing living here at all. There are ghosts here; they burn my skin with their breath. Stay alert.*

"In the front door?" asked Leslie.

"If he's in there, he already knows we are here," Charles told her. "Front door, back door, or down the chimney, we're not going to have surprise on our side." He added, "I don't smell anyone. Anna?"

She jerked her head in a negative, but a growl rumbled in her chest. *Do you feel it?*

"Yes," he said, putting his hand on her head. "The dead have a weight here. This place is haunted in the true Navajo sense. I can feel it try to cling."

"Don't try to give us courage, now," said Marsden dryly. "I feel so much better after that speech."

Her mate gave him a smile. He didn't usually give people

smiles until he had known them for a lot longer, at least not friendly smiles.

"I don't think we're going to find anyone alive here," Charles said. "Does that help?"

"Not really," said Leeds. "No."

"No," agreed Leslie.

The front door was locked. When no one answered Marsden's vigorous knocking, Leeds took a roll of handy-dandy lockpick tools out of his pocket and went to work on the lock.

Anna conceived an instant desire to learn how. It didn't look too complicated. Charles probably knew how. He could teach her.

"Get your nose back, ma'am, please," said Leeds. "You aren't in the way. But I have a hard time concentrating with a freaking werewolf breathing down my neck."

"She won't hurt you," murmured Charles.

"I *know* that," Leeds said calmly, still wiggling the delicate picks, one in each hand, his head tilted so one ear was nearer the lock than the other. "My brain does anyway. My gut says, 'Run away, run away, you freaking moron. That's a werewolf.'"

Anna backed up. She tried looking through the windows, but the blinds were down and turned so she couldn't see anything. She could positively say that no living creature had been on this porch for a long time. She got a faint whiff of perfume, presumably belonging to whoever had rented the house, but nothing else. If the fae had been to this door, it hadn't been for a long time.

The lock gave up and the door admitted them into an empty living room that smelled of dust and cleaners that made Anna sneeze. She trotted past Leslie and into the main house, which was as barren as the rest. She caught faint scents of humans who had once lived here: a girl in the pink room and someone who smoked cigarettes in the master bedroom. They'd had a dog, too. Helpfully, all of the doors were open, so she didn't have to wait for someone with hands to let her into anywhere. The bedrooms and bathrooms were a bust, as far as her nose went, anyway. From the sounds in the living room, someone had found something.

In the kitchen there was a ladder nailed into the wall, painted cream with mint-green, tole-painted leaves to turn it into a decoration. At the top of the ladder was a locked trapdoor in the ceiling with a note taped to it: RENTERS NOT ALLOWED IN ATTIC.

She put her nose on the ladder and smelled nothing. But it wasn't like the house was Hosteen's mansion. There weren't many places to hide things, and a locked door looked interesting. She climbed up to the trapdoor, digging her claws into the wood and leaving indentations behind. The narrow edge of the two-by-four ladder hurt her paws, and she thought maybe she should let one of the comfortably shod people try this. Not to mention, werewolf bodies were not exactly designed to climb ladders. It was an older house, and the ceilings were high, maybe ten feet or more.

She smelled nothing more up at the top than she had at the bottom. She pushed her nose against the trapdoor, and it wiggled a little. As soon as the edge of the door broke contact with the frame, scent wafted out of the attic only to disappear as soon as the door settled again.

But that was enough. She smelled the little girl whose grubby rabbit was in a plastic bag back in their room at the Sanis' ranch.

She dropped to the ground and ran to Charles.

In the living room they had pulled up some stone around the fireplace and were looking into a metal-lined hole filled with not much.

I found her, she told Charles, and then ran back to the kitchen, claws catching on the tile floor. This time she bolted up the ladder and hit the trapdoor with her shoulder as hard as she could. Wood cracked and she bounced down to the ground. When she looked up, the door was still intact. She ran up and hit it again and this time when she landed, the door landed with her, in three pieces with a fourth still attached to the ceiling.

The reek of death, old death and new blood, billowed

through the kitchen. Of the others, only Charles caught the full brunt of it.

He pulled his forearm up to his nose. "Stay down here," he ordered.

Anna didn't wait, though. There was a child up there who was bound to be hurt and scared, a child who had been held captive for *months*. She scrambled through the hole at the top of the ladder, ignoring Charles's impassioned "Anna!"

The attic space was stuffy and hot, a room of maybe twenty by twenty with a ten-foot-tall ceiling that sloped down sharply with the slant of the roof until on two sides it was only three feet high. The old-fashioned linoleum, marbled army green, was cooler than the air and reminded Anna of photos of her grandmother's house.

In the center of the room was a child's princess bed, a four-poster painted white and trimmed in gold leaf—Louis XIV style, Anna thought, or maybe Louis XVI. Gauzy white fabric was artfully tangled around like—she remembered Ms. Jamison—a fashion shoot of some sort. Pale pink, dried rose petals littered the fabric, the bed, the floor around the bed, and the little girl who lay like Sleeping Beauty in a gown of pale pink silk. Her skin was milk white and she was not breathing.

Charles climbed up beside Anna and then called down, "No. Stay down. This is a crime scene and there's not enough room up here. If you come up, too, we'll compromise the scene."

"What do you have up there?" asked Leslie. "I'll call it in."

"Multiple homicides," said Charles, his voice steady, but his horror bled into and blended with Anna's own. "I count twenty bodies, at least. All of them children. Most of them have been here awhile. At a guess, the murders took place before the fae came out and the Gray Lords put a stop to our Doll Collector's habits."

Bodies were stacked like cordwood against the three-foot wall between the floor and the ceiling along the edge of the room. Old bodies with skin like parchment and hair stiff and dry.

They looked more like the doll Anna's mother had made her out of nylons, stuffed and stitched, than the remnants of people, of children. Anna's nose told her the truth that her eyes wanted to deny. Some of the children were dressed in gowns like Amethyst's, satin gleaming through layers of dust. Others wore dark suits. It looked as if they were all dressed for a wedding.

Anna thought that from now on, whenever the air was warm and still and smelled like leather and dead things, she would remember these children. She pressed against Charles, and his hand touched the top of her head to comfort them both.

"Is Amethyst up there?" That was Leeds.

"Yes," said Charles. He moved then, toward the bed. Brave Charles.

Amethyst was silent, no breathing, no heartbeat. Anna whined at Charles. If he touched Amethyst, he'd be contaminating the scene. The other children were decades dead. Amethyst was the Doll Collector's most recent victim. The one most likely to provide clues.

"Is she alive?" asked Marsden.

"She's not breathing and her heart isn't beating," said Charles.

"I take that as a no," said Marsden. "Damn it. Just once I'd like to be in time."

"Don't be too hasty." Charles drew his boot knife. "It's hot up here. She isn't rotting. All the putrefaction I can smell is old. Death and heat equal rot. Either he killed her less than a half hour ago, or she's not dead."

Or she's dead and the fae has found a way to preserve her body.

Charles nodded at Anna, but he didn't relay her comment to anyone else. He used the blade of his knife to push the fabric aside, petals falling down like leaves in autumn, leaving Amethyst exposed. He put the back of his hand against her skin and pulled it back with a hiss, shaking it out.

"If the Doll Collector didn't know we were here before, he does now," said Charles.

"What's going on?"

"I touched Amethyst and tripped some sort of magic," Charles told them. "I'm going to try something."

"Wait," said Leeds. "We have an expert in fae magic who is flying in from Oakland tonight."

"Might be too late," Charles said. He rolled his knife in his hand.

Anna had had it custom-made for him last Christmas. It was a san mai knife, high-carbon steel sandwiched in stainless steel. The high carbon meant that it held an edge better, and should be effective against fae magic because it was closer to "cold iron" than straight stainless steel was.

He pressed the edge of the knife against Amethyst's arm. It rested against her skin for half a breath and then cut through. As the first drop of red smeared the knife, Anna's ears popped as if the air pressure dropped. Then Amethyst sat up and screamed in terror.

It wasn't a pretty sound, raw and pitched like nails on a chalkboard. It hurt Anna's ears. She hadn't been happier to hear anything in a long time.

Charles gathered the girl into his arms and held her, face pressed against his shoulder. Anna wasn't sure that was a good idea. A stranger, a male holding her? Who knew what the fae had done to her in the months since he took her?

"Shhh," said Charles as the other three came boiling up the ladder. "Shh. It's over. It's done. We won't let anyone hurt you again. *I* won't let anyone hurt you."

And, perhaps because it was Charles, the little girl grabbed his T-shirt with both hands and buried her face against him. Her screams became sobs that were even worse than the screams. Anna whined, remembering the garden fae, the wearden, saying that the child the people in Scotland had saved had died anyway.

Leslie took a good look around and climbed back down out of the attic. After a few moments she said, "Hey, Hemmings, this is Fisher. Can you go pick up the Millers and bring them to this address in South Scottsdale"—she read them the address—"tell them we found her, but not until you have them in the car. I don't want any tragic traffic accidents on the way here. There are enough dead people haunting this place already. Tell the team—FBI, Cantrip, and Scottsdale PD. Tell them to get down here ASAP: we have a crime scene to process. And tell someone to find out who owns this damned place."

"Will do," said a man, presumably Hemmings, on the other end. "And I have good news on the ownership. We have a name. A dozen officers are at his address as we speak. Sean McDermit. He's mostly retired, but he works ten hours a week at Sunshine Fun Day Care."

Charles took one good look around, skipped the ladder altogether, and jumped down to the main floor. He absorbed the fall by bending his knees. Anna was pretty sure Amethyst never noticed their descent at all. Anna jumped down after him. It was easier for her to jump than to climb down in the wolf's body.

She followed Charles out of the house. Watching his body language, she suddenly was reminded of something she already knew. Alphas fancied themselves responsible for the safety and well-being of everyone around them. Charles wasn't an Alpha—he ceded that rank to his father—but he was more dominant than any Alpha other than his father. The way he held Amethyst Miller said that he felt responsible for her.

At that moment something clicked, and she understood his reluctance to have children of his own. She'd noticed it herself, hadn't she? That the people he cared about he could count on the fingers of one hand: herself, Bran, Samuel, probably Mercy. This trip had allowed her to add one more person to that list: Joseph. Five people, because he could not keep any more than that safe. And Joseph was dying.

Oh, Charles.

CHARLES HELD AMETHYST until her parents came to claim her. It was a little like holding a puppy. Hot and wet and shivering, she breathed in ha-ha-ha jerks. He sang "Froggy Went a-Courtin' " because it was long, repetitive, and something his father had sung to him when he was Amethyst's age. He didn't know what parents sang to their children these days, but there was a fair chance that she might find it familiar.

He rubbed her back and walked in the shadows of the wall, hidden from the public and away from the noise and sirens. Anna paced beside him, cloaking herself in pack magic so that he was the only one who could see her. He didn't think she was doing it on purpose. Pack magic didn't always wait for someone to ask it to do something. He wondered, belatedly, if those photos Ms. Jamison had taken would come out, or if Anna would just be a blurry figure.

Amethyst was asleep by the time her parents arrived, and Leslie escorted them to the isolated corner of the yard where Charles paced. Dr. Miller hesitated when he saw the limp bundle cradled against Charles's chest, but his wife made a low, moaning sound and pulled her daughter away from Charles.

"Baby?" Tears spilled down her cheeks.

"Mommy?" Amethyst blinked at her mom, who held her awkwardly because she was not a big woman and Amethyst was not a toddler. "Mommy? He said, he said you wouldn't miss me. That you had a new daughter who looked like me only was better."

"No," said her father, picking her up without really removing her from her mother's arms, so they were all in one little huddle. "He fooled us for a little while, but we knew all along that something was missing. The one he left in your place wasn't our baby girl. It just took us a while, too long, to find you."

"I want to go home," she said. "Daddy, I want to go home, please?"

"Dr. Miller," said Leslie. "I recommend you call her own doctor and have him meet you at the emergency room. One of my guys, the bald guy in the FBI jacket, is waiting to take you all there. He'll make sure you get back home safely, too."

They started to go, but then Dr. Miller stopped. He

turned, releasing his daughter into her mother's care. He wiped his face, then met Charles's eyes and held them.

"Thank you."

"It wasn't just me," said Charles, the gratitude in the other man's expression strong enough that even Brother Wolf couldn't see a challenge in that gaze. "It took a lot of people to find her. And we don't have the one who took her yet. We are not done until he's out of business." He'd heard what Leslie's agent had said on the phone. But it was too soon to declare Amethyst's kidnapper captured.

Dr. Miller looked at the house and said, "I'm a physician, sworn on my honor to do no harm. But I could kill him myself and never lose a wink of sleep over it. Not just for my daughter, but for all the daughters and sons. I heard what you found in that attic."

Charles nodded once at him, then let Brother Wolf out so Dr. Miller could see the predator lurking in his eyes. "I'll take care of him if I get the chance."

Mrs. Miller said, "You are a werewolf."

"Yes," Charles said. He hadn't intended for her to see the wolf, too, but he wasn't going to lie to her.

"Good," she said. "Kill him."

"I intend to," he told her, ignoring Leslie's indrawn breath. Some people needed to die.

Dr. Miller looked down at his daughter. "I thought . . . She's been gone months and we didn't know. I thought it would be months and months more and . . . You found her in one day."

He'd thought they'd find her dead. He'd said as much. Charles understood; he'd mostly thought that, too. It had been Anna who had hoped for them all.

"It's not over," Charles told him. "It's going to continue to be bad for a long time."

Amethyst's father gave Charles an expression that wasn't really a smile; there was too much experience in it. "I'm a doctor. A pediatrician. That's usually my line. I know someone, a really good someone, who picks up the pieces and helps people put themselves back together. Amethyst will be all right." He looked at his daughter, and when he looked up again, his eyes were wet. "It'll take years of therapy. Probably for all of us: a long uphill battle. But we're still on the field fighting the good fight, battered and beaten though we are, and I understand just what a great gift that is."

BY THE TIME Leslie drove them back to their car, it was nearly dinnertime.

"We don't get that all the time," Leslie told Charles as she turned onto the highway. Anna grunted as she slid from one side of the car to the other. It wasn't a pained grunt, so Charles made do with a glance over his shoulder to make sure she was all right. "It's why I joined up, you know, saving people."

"She isn't saved yet," Charles told Leslie.

"I know, years of counseling and medication even, but much better than I thought they were going to get."

"Yes," he said, "but she isn't going to be safe until that fae is dead."

Leslie sucked in a breath. "We have the man who owns that property in custody. He lawyered up immediately, but my man on the ground says he is definitely fae. He couldn't bear the touch of metal."

"The current justice system is not up to handling a fae of this caliber. Not if the Gray Lords have removed his restrictions. If he is not killed, that poor pile of bodies in the attic won't be a drop in the bucket. Fae don't die on their own; you have to help them along."

"I think," she said, "that we're going to have to agree to disagree."

"Just make sure you don't let him slip through your fingers," said Charles.

ANNA CHANGED IN the back of the car, while Charles leaned against it and made sure no one got close enough to look in the back window. When she was human again and dressed, she got out of the car and just hugged him.

He hugged her back and let himself admit just how much he needed her touch.

"All those children," she said. "All of those children dead. And that was just here, in this town. How long ago did he start? One a year for what? A thousand years? Two thousand years? And Amethyst? Do you think . . . ?"

She couldn't even make herself say the words. All he could give her was the truth.

"I don't know. Probably." He kissed the top of her head and found that he was comforting himself as much as he was her. "But we stopped him and she'll grow up strong and true. Her parents will see to it. And she's tough."

Amethyst had grabbed on to him, he thought. Grabbed on with both hands, and held on because she had known he'd keep her safe. She wanted to be okay, and that was a good step.

"She'll survive, Anna. He won't win—we have him now. Let the human justice system do what it can. When he leaves it, I'll hunt him unto the ends of the earth if I have to." Cliché words—and they sounded hollow to him, though he absolutely meant them.

Absurdly, they seemed to be what Anna needed. She took a deep breath and said, "Yes. Yes. That. How fortunate for the world that you are in it." She pulled back, wiped her eyes, gave him a smile.

He didn't know what she meant. He was a killer with bloodstained hands. He was necessary, though. Maybe that was what she meant.

"Part of the solution," she said. "My dad always told us to be part of the solution, not part of the problem. You are always part of the solution."

"Solution to what?"

"Anything. Everything. Me." Her smile brightened and then died. Her voice was dead serious when she spoke again. "There is evil in the world, Charles. I know I'm not telling you anything that you don't know. But those people out there?" She swept a hand out toward the bustling rush-hour traffic on the road running past the parking lot where they stood. "Those people have no idea. And the reason they have no idea is because you are around to keep them safe. You and Bran and Leslie—and Leeds and Marsden, too. But mostly you. Where you are, there hope is also. The hope that good is strong enough to prevail." She took a big breath and let it out. "I want your child."

His stomach plummeted. He didn't know that he could have that conversation right now. Not when his shirt was still damp from Amethyst's tears and the stink of the dead was still in his nose.

Anna turned away from him, rocking up on her toes and back. He wondered if she was thinking about running away. Or wishing she could run back to the Anna she had been before she learned about the evil in the world.

"I understand now, I think," she told him in a low voice, her back still turned. "You know what's out here. You think that if you, if we, have a child, then they will come after him or her. Those who serve evil. You see a child as a hostage to fate. Isn't that Shakespeare? Evil *always* goes after the innocents, Charles. But no innocent will be safer than one under your protection. You brought hope into my world when I had given up."

She turned back to him, and she was wiping her cheeks again. She hesitated, her eyes widening—and then she reached up and gently wiped his, too.

"But I saw you today," she whispered. "I *do* think you are wrong. I think your child would be the safest person in the universe. But I'm done hurting you. I saw your face and I know why you're scared. That was a lot of pain you felt for her. It's okay. I don't like the way this discussion has come between us. When you are ready, you just let me know, okay? Don't wait until forever."

Children die, he thought. He was pretty sure he kept those words to himself and hadn't given them to Anna.

She stood on tiptoe, waiting for him to duck down to her. When he did, she kissed him, first on the nose and then, hotly, on the mouth.

"Get in the car, sweetcheeks," she said briskly, though her voice was husky. "I have horses to look at."

"Anna," he said as he buckled himself into the passenger seat.

"Yes?" She hit the gas and drove out of the parking lot headed north.

"Don't ever call me sweetcheeks."

She grinned at him, then paid strict attention to her driving. As she took them out to the Sanis' ranch, he wondered that she could look at him, who had hands that would never, could never come clean, and she saw hope.

HOSTEEN WAS THERE when they got back. He frowned warily at Anna. But Anna had seen terrible things today. Having a grumpy old werewolf who freaked out because she could send his wolf to sleep was barely a blip on her radar. Not when she was worried about Charles, who hadn't said a single word all the way to the ranch.

His hand was on the small of her back, though. So they had to be good, right?

"Wade told me that Cantrip and the FBI are *letting* you help go after the fae who tried to kill my great-grandchildren," Hosteen growled.

He was talking to Charles, but it was the wrong attitude to throw at her husband just now. Anna said, "We worked with the FBI and Cantrip today. We found the girl who'd been replaced by the changeling. She's alive, and I think she'll be okay. Wade or Kage told you about the changeling, right? Also, the FBI think they have the person who took her and spelled Chelsea in custody. He was the janitor at the day care."

She waited, the tension in the air rising as her husband started to get angry. It was like the whole hallway started to smell of ozone—the smell was imaginary, but the energy crackled.

"You know what?" she said suddenly. "This is not the time for this. We just found the bodies of dozens of children stacked up like forgotten dolls. You two go ahead and have your fight. This is not my problem to fix."

Charles's hand curled around the nape of her neck.

Hosteen said, "Feisty, isn't she?"

"Tired of drama today," said Charles. "So am I."

Something happened between them; Anna was sure of it. Something she missed because Charles was behind her, or maybe it was some guy thing. But the air cleared.

Charles said, "Are we going to have drama here?"

Hosteen rubbed his face with both hands. "Hell, Charles, there is always some sort of drama going on here. If you think wolf packs are big on drama, you should try the horse crowd for a while." He looked at Anna. "My problem with you is just that, my problem. I've never met a real Omega before. I didn't understand what that meant. I don't like making a fool out of myself; my father was a drunkard and I swore never to be one."

He wasn't the first werewolf to freak out about what Omega really meant. She suspected he wouldn't be the last. He was being gracious, so she could be gracious, too.

"Yes," she said. "It hits the dominant wolves harder, I'm told. For what it's worth, I didn't do it on purpose. I didn't know I could affect someone like that; if I had, I'd have warned you." She'd have apologized earlier, but he hadn't given her the chance.

She was hungry. Changing always left her starving, and so did drama. "I smell food. Is there any left?"

Hosteen smiled, and bowed. She saw some martial arts training in that bow. "I think they left you some," he said, his face lit with mischief. "We could go see."

CHELSEA CAME OUT of her room to eat with them, making it a late supper for four. Kage was out working in the stables with all three kids. They had taken some horses to the show grounds that night and were planning on taking more in the morning. Maggie and Joseph had eaten in Joseph's suite earlier in the day. Ernestine was in her room taking a break.

Chelsea had accepted the news that they'd found Amethyst and, probably, the fae responsible for all the trouble with a faint smile and a quiet "That's good."

Anna worried that she was being too quiet, like the calm before the storm.

Bran had developed a method designed to minimize the problems of the Change as much as they could be minimized. People who wanted to become werewolves petitioned Bran, the Marrok. They would fill out questionnaires, get testimonials from people they knew (werewolves), and write essays on why they wanted to be werewolves. Those with good enough reasons and stable personalities (although Anna had argued that anyone who wanted to be a werewolf on purpose could not be deemed "stable" on any level) were granted their petition.

The actual Change was done at the same time every year, complete with a set of ceremonies intended to weed out the bad seeds and the weak willed, the latter of whom would not survive the Change they were seeking.

Bran's intention was to increase the survivability of werewolves. And it worked. Those who attended Bran's version of the Change were much more likely to live, long-term, than those who were simply Changed by accident or attack.

They knew what to expect, they knew the costs, and they understood what they were getting into. The others, those like Anna and Chelsea, had to deal with the reality of being a werewolf on the fly. Chelsea looked as though she was having trouble adjusting. Maybe Anna could help with that.

She took a bite of very good lasagna and said, in as conversational a tone as she could manage, "I was trying to gently tell this guy that I had decided that we shouldn't go on any more dates when he attacked me and turned me into a werewolf." She looked at Hosteen. "This is very good; did Ernestine make it?"

He shook his head. "No. I did." He smiled. "Part of my penance for riding off in the middle of things."

"I'd love your recipe." She took another bite.

"I'll write it down for you before you go," he said.

She nodded. "I'd like that." She looked at Chelsea. "They had been looking for some time for an Omega wolf, because Omegas, among other things, can calm werewolves. The

Alpha in Chicago, where I lived, was desperately in love with his mate. She was getting more and more violent; that sometimes happens to old werewolves. Anyway"—she forced herself to eat another bite and swallow it—"this was before werewolves had come out. I didn't even know they were real when I turned into one." The next bite stuck in her throat and she couldn't talk.

"They kept her prisoner," Charles said in a low voice. "Abused her because that was the only way they could control her. You know that packs are very hierarchical. An Omega is outside the pack structure like that. She—or he— doesn't feel the same need to obey."

Charles gave Chelsea a compassionate look, though Anna didn't know if anyone but she could read him well enough to see the sympathy in his eyes. "Like the way that you felt you needed to come here and eat with us, only because Hosteen asked you to."

Chelsea looked down at her plate, her jaw tight. Anna had thought she had a handle on what Chelsea was going through, but she'd missed that part of it. Maybe because, as an Omega, she'd never felt that *need* to obey someone more dominant. Yeah, she thought, that would rankle a woman like Chelsea.

Charles continued. "The Alpha is, or should be, the one most capable of protecting his pack. Not just the safety of the pack, but the well-being of each of its members. But Anna's first Alpha only cared about his mate. He needed Anna to keep his mate from attracting my father's attention. He knew that my father would have her killed because Isabelle was a danger to everyone around her, human and wolf alike. He couldn't dominate Anna as he did all the other wolves, so he brutalized her. He taught her to fear him in an effort to keep her under his thumb." Charles and Hosteen exchanged a look.

It was Hosteen who said, "That was a betrayal of everything an Alpha is supposed to be."

"Yes," said Anna. "I'm telling you this story, not as a one-upmanship kind of thing." She dropped her voice and added a little radio announcer. "You think you have it bad, you have it easy compared to me." And then returned to her own voice. "Because that isn't true. You have it different. But you need to know that you aren't alone; I do understand what you're going through."

She set down her fork because eating was beyond her. "Yesterday you woke up and were just grateful you were alive. That your kids were okay. Tonight you are beginning to understand the price that you are going to pay for that. You aren't entirely sure it is worth it."

"Dying is easy," said Hosteen. "Living is brutal."

"There are a lot of downsides," Anna said. "You probably know what most of those are." She wasn't going to enumerate them. Nothing like taking a person who feels bad already and telling them how horrible their life might be to turn mild depression into suicidal. "The people who go to Bran to be Changed know what they're getting into and they have time to make a choice. You and I? We didn't get time to make a choice. But the downsides are only there because you're alive. You have people who love you. And you have what will hopefully be a very long time to come to terms with what you are."

Under the table, Charles put his hand on her knee. She swallowed hard. "You're going through a period of mourning what you once were because there is no going back. Just keep in mind that there are good things, too."

"One of the good things is that you don't have to be afraid of the dark witches anymore," said Hosteen casually.

Chelsea stiffened and looked up at him.

"You're not dumb. Of course you are afraid of them." He turned his coffee cup around between his hands, watching it instead of Chelsea. "If you're born a witch and you don't want to kill and torture for power, then you're ripe for being killed and tortured yourself. That's why you worked so hard to keep what you are secret. Kage worried for you. He didn't talk to me about it, but he told Joseph, who came to me. I'm ashamed to admit that I didn't offer my help."

"Maybe I am a dark witch," she said hostilely.

"No," said Hosteen, raising his eyes. "I can smell a dark witch from a mile away. No. You were hiding. But now you belong to a pack, and our pack can and will protect you from the dark witches."

"Why now?" she asked, her blue-gray eyes lightening to near-Arctic white, like those of Charles's brother, Samuel. "Wasn't I worthy of protection when I was just Kage's wife?"

"Yes," said Hosteen slowly. "But I was not worthy of protecting you."

"What does that even mean?" asked Chelsea, pushing away from the table abruptly. She stood up, clenching her hands into fists.

"It means that I am a stubborn old wolf," Hosteen said. "And maybe I am more interested in my own opinions than listening to my grandson, who is a smart man. That is my failure. Perhaps one of the things that will be a good thing about your becoming a werewolf is that it has changed me, too. And that will mean our family is more welcoming, as it should have been from the beginning."

"I can't think," said Chelsea, breathing hard. "Why can't I think?"

"Mom?"

Anna had been so distracted by Chelsea that she hadn't heard Max until he spoke from the doorway.

Chelsea turned wild eyes to her son and fell to the ground, convulsing.

Anna got up and put her hand on Max's shoulder to keep him from going to Chelsea. "It will be okay," she said. "But she wouldn't want you to see this."

Chelsea cried out, her voice hoarse and guttural.

"Mom," Max whispered, resisting Anna.

She quit trying to move him, just put her shoulder between him and his mother so he couldn't get to her without going over Anna.

"Changing hurts," Anna told him. "It hurts every time, but the first time is the worst. Almost all werewolves awaken from their first change completely out of control. There is nothing you can do to help or stop it. And I guarantee you that with Hosteen and Charles in there, your mother will be fine." She waited and said, "You need to be out of here before she changes. If she hurts you, it will break her."

He stood firm for a moment more, muscles twitching with the desire to help. Then he nodded once and let Anna tug him out of the room. She took him into the big living room and led him to the far side of that before she let him stop.

They listened to Chelsea's pain from there for a few minutes, Max flinching and fisting his hands as the noises his mother made changed from human to something else.

"Would it be easier with three werewolves in there?" he asked.

"You mean me?" Anna shook her head. "Not while she's changing. Charles will call me in when she's done. My wolf has a calming influence on other werewolves. Right now she needs to keep her fighting edge. As soon as she's found the wolf shape, I'll be more useful."

Someone knocked at the front door just as Chelsea's voice roared out again. Before Anna could decide how to handle visitors, the door opened and Wade started in at a run.

He saw Anna and Max and paused in his dash.

"Chelsea?" he asked Anna.

She nodded. "In the kitchen."

Wade glanced at her. "Are you coming in?"

"No," she told him. "We've found that having an Omega too close slows down the first change."

He grimaced; no one wanted to slow down a change. Then he sucked in a breath. "Omega?" He blinked at her a moment. "That's what it was." He gave her a smile. "Thanks. I've never had such a weird reaction to a wolf before."

Chelsea made another noise and he bolted for the kitchen. After fifteen minutes or so, the sounds all died down.

"Have you seen Hosteen in his wolf form?" Anna asked Max, though her eyes were directed at the kitchen. She had a vivid memory of how alone she'd felt the first few months she'd been a wolf.

"Yes," he said.

"Scare you?"

"Not after the first time," he said.

She turned to him. "Truthfully. No judgment at all on you. Even a normal wolf makes most people want to find a door to hide behind, no matter how often they see them."

He smiled. "He's beautiful," he said, and there was no fear in him.

"Anna," Charles called out quietly.

"That's my cue," she told Max. "Wait here and if everything is okay, we'll introduce you to your mother's wolf."

When Anna got back to the kitchen, Chelsea had pushed her butt into the corner between the fridge and the wall. Her head was half-lowered, but her nose kept wrinkling into a snarl.

Like Charles's older brother, Samuel, she was icy white with bluish-white eyes, but the tips of her ears and her eyes were lined in the same medium brown that covered her belly and the underside of her tail.

Wade was the closest to her. He was on one knee with his head bowed. Yeah, Anna had been pretty sure Chelsea was going to come out dominant. They were going to have issues trying to put her down on the bottom of the pecking order with the females who had no wolf mate to gain rank. Not when the pack's second was already acknowledging her dominance over him.

"Hey, Chelsea," Anna said cheerfully. Silver eyes met hers and the snarl slid off the new wolf's face. Anna kept talking. "It's okay if things are a little mixed up right now. Just wait a second and it will all come back." She walked in front of Wade and let her wolf bring the tension in the room down.

"Having warning doesn't help at all," said Hosteen.

"Sure it does," Charles said. "You aren't giggling this time."

Hosteen made an odd noise, a half growl, half laugh that attracted Chelsea's attention. The new wolf's hackles rose and she let out an unhappy whine.

The Alpha left his post leaning against the sink and walked up to Chelsea. He took her muzzle in his hand, meeting her eyes and holding them. If he worried that she had insufficient control to keep her wolf from biting him, Anna couldn't see it.

Slowly, shivering with stress, Chelsea dropped to the ground and rolled over, giving Hosteen the unprotected vulnerability of her belly. He held her there a moment, then let her up.

"Good," he told her. "Begin as you mean to go on, Chelsea. You are in charge and the wolf must listen to you."

"Max is waiting," said Anna. "Do you think it's safe, Hosteen?"

Chelsea gave a panicked yip and scrambled back into the corner.

"Chelsea," Hosteen said. "I promise you won't hurt him."

She held his eyes for three heartbeats.

"It will be okay," he said.

She dropped her eyes and took two steps away from the corner, still looking unhappy.

Max, summoned by Anna's call, stopped in the doorway, and for a moment Anna thought it was going to be bad. But then he grinned. "Wow, Mom. Kage is going to have a heart attack, you came out so pretty. He's going to have to carry a silver-loaded shotgun to keep off the wolves in Hosteen's pack. You've gotta see this in a mirror. Come on, there's a full-length one in the main bathroom."

THEY HAD ABOUT an hour of light left when they got to the barn. Anna was tired and stressed. She was pretty sure that Charles was in worse shape even though he didn't show it.

Hosteen had taken a good look around the kitchen and decided that what everyone needed to "heal the spiritual wounds of the day" was a ride out into the desert. That he could deliver phrases like that and not sound hokey was impressive, Anna decided.

Chelsea came down with them, running beside the four-wheeler with Charles, who was also in his wolf form. They'd driven around back this time, where there were tie posts outside the back of the barn. Four horses were tacked up with western saddles. A harried-looking Teri was hastily brushing out one horse's tail with a hairbrush.

"New dogs?" she asked Hosteen as they all disembarked from the four-wheeler, looking at Chelsea. "Sure are pretty."

Pack magic let people see what they expected to see.

Otherwise werewolves could never have stayed hidden as long as they had.

"One new dog—the white female. The red one belongs to Anna, our guest," Hosteen told the woman.

"What's her name?"

"We haven't decided yet. Would you go get Kage? I'll take over here. We'll put them away properly when we're done."

Teri gave him a bright smile. "Sure thing. He said to tell you he'd be right out, but I'll let him know you're here anyway."

As soon as she disappeared inside the barn, Charles returned to human form, a little more slowly than was usual for him. This was his second change of the day, Anna thought. If he had to do another one, it would be slower yet. Charles stretched, trying to loosen cramped muscles.

"Chelsea," said Hosteen. "The horses won't care as long as you don't stare them in the eye for very long. If you make eye contact, they recognize you as a threat." He turned to Anna. "Let me introduce you to Portabella while we're waiting for Kage."

Chelsea stayed close to Hosteen as they walked over to the horses. As promised, none of the horses seemed particularly bothered by her.

"Here she is," Hosteen said, then stood back and let Anna look.

Portabella was a big mare. Anna had to stand on tiptoes to look over her back. Her color was not dark enough to be black, but very dark just the same. Bay, Anna thought, though the characteristic black points—legs, mane, and tail—were really very close to the same color as her body. A white streak dropped from a star between her big eyes to another splash of white on her nose. She was polished and beautiful. Even Anna, amateur that she was, could see that she was spectacular.

Anna couldn't help but put her hands out to touch and found herself stroking steel clothed in silk. She ran her hands down the horse's legs, and the mare lifted her front hoof to

Anna's asking. She wasn't shod and the bottom of her feet looked—like the bottom of a horse's foot. She laughed inwardly at herself, because she didn't know enough for the examination to tell her anything except that the mare would stand quietly while an idiot ran hands all over her.

Somewhat to her own surprise, Anna's fingers found a bump on her neck that struck her as odd. She was more surprised by her understanding that it was out of place than she was at finding something wrong with this paragon of a horse.

She glanced at Hosteen.

"From a vaccination," he told her. "Some horses just do that sometimes. I have a vet report on it in her file."

"Is she a mare you bred?" she asked, after looking for a question that wouldn't make her sound too stupid.

Charles was being very quiet, even for Charles. He must have been as exhausted as she was. Hosteen was right: it was a tiredness of spirit rather than body. Even so, she was pretty sure she should have insisted that they retire to their room.

Hosteen shook his head. "Three years ago, Joseph was out at a trainer's barn looking for interesting horses," Hosteen said. "And he found this mare. She'd been soured in the ring so they'd put her in the breeding barn, but she wasn't sound for breeding. So they'd sent her back to the trainers. But sour didn't even touch on how much she hated arena work. She put the trainer's assistant in the hospital and he was done with her."

Hosteen shook his head. "My son is magic on a horse, and game for any challenge. He wanted to retrain her himself. We got her for more than we should have paid for her, but a lot less than she'd be worth if he could fix her. Before he could start working with her, his health started going downhill again."

Hosteen turned away and ran a hand down the mare's shiny neck. The smile he gave Anna when he turned back was unhappy, but not, she was sure, because of the horse. "Anyway, since then she's been one of our trail horse band. We keep them in shape and ready to go for buyers or clients who want to take a ride out in the desert. So she's been ridden steadily since she came, but not in the arena."

"Portabella," Anna said, having thought about the name and come up with an alternate theory for it, instead of the one attached to the mare's pedigree. "Because someone fed her BS until she turned into a mushroom."

Hosteen laughed. "Kage tried working with her last spring and he wanted to call her Soyuz."

Anna frowned.

"After the Russian single-stage-to-orbit rocket," said Kage dryly as he emerged from the barn. "I've never been dumped so fast with such authority in my life. It was a lesson in humility, especially since my eighty-year-old father had ridden her in the arena a couple of times before . . ." His voice trailed off as he caught sight of the wolf standing next to Hosteen.

Chelsea regarded him warily and, well versed in dealing with skittish animals, he stopped where he was and crouched down. "Oh, honey," he crooned. "I'd have known you if you had six legs and scales. But I had no idea what a beautiful wolf you'd be."

She leapt toward him—and misjudged, knocking him right off his feet. Portabella jumped back and Hosteen yanked at the rope that attached the horse to the tie post. A single jerk and she was loose from the post, her lead held in Hosteen's hand instead. She took a couple of steps away and then settled, regarding the pile of wolf and man with pricked-ear disdain.

Chelsea backed off and looked distressed. Kage laughed and leaned forward until he could rub her neck. "Don't worry, sweetheart. You'll get the hang of it."

Anna thought he hesitated a little as he got to his feet, but if he was hurt he wasn't showing any other sign. Smart man. If Chelsea thought she'd hurt him, it would unsettle her, and unsettled was a bad thing for a werewolf in her first time out.

"If you get Anna taken care of," Kage looked at Hosteen, "I'll introduce Charles to his horse."

A little snorty after the excitement, Portabella still let

Hosteen bridle her with little trouble. She mouthed the bit and then stood, ears up and muscles quivering, while Anna mounted. She didn't move, but Anna got the feeling it was an effort for her to remain still while the others got on their horses.

Charles's horse was a rawboned gelding with a long, flexible neck and a Roman nose.

"I didn't think Arabs ran to convex noses," Anna said.

"Not a purebred Arab, anyway," said Kage, seeing where she was looking. "Though I could show you a few pictures . . . But Figaro is a national show horse that's half-Arab and half-saddlebred. He turned out all saddlebred in looks and Arab in gait. That's pretty much the opposite of what we're trying for when breeding national show horses. He's a terrific jumper, though, and loves the trail." He looked at Charles. "He's for sale, too. He's big enough to carry you."

Charles patted the gelding. "We're shopping for Anna."

Charles's gelding was a little smaller than Portabella, Anna found when she started out riding next to her husband.

The big mare had big gaits, too. She quickly outpaced the rest of the horses. Anna was forced to circle her to stay with the others. Like Heylight, the gray gelding from her first day, the mare was very sensitive to cues. Anna finally quit using the bridle for anything except speed control and just shifted her weight from one hip to the other to turn.

"Comfortable?" asked Hosteen, coming up on her left side. He rode a short chestnut gelding with a wide blaze and a friendly demeanor who trotted to keep up with Portabella's quick walk.

"Very," she said, straightening her back a little and making sure her heels were down. Portabella slowed.

"Ah," Hosteen said, effortlessly keeping his horse next to hers, "don't worry about me, just relax. Charles would never teach anyone the wrong way to ride. You ride better than a lot of the people you'll see at the show tomorrow. Ready for a trot?"

"Sure," she said. Were they going to the show tomorrow? She'd have to ask Charles.

"Go ahead and ask her, then," he said. "We'll follow. Just

keep her on the trail. There's a fork ahead, take either one you want."

Portabella's trot was lilting, but not heavy, so Anna didn't bang into her back, but she had to really relax to keep her seat. As she did so, the mare's ears perked up and her gait softened.

"Canter," called Kage.

And before Anna cued her, Portabella broke into a blistering run, head up and tail flagged. Anna laughed and sat back, slowing her with a light hand on the reins until she was cantering. This was a lot different from riding Jinx. Chelsea ran beside them, stretching out with her tongue lolling in pleasure.

See, thought Anna, *there are some things that are amazing about being a werewolf.*

As soon as Hosteen tried to ride even with them, Portabella put on an extra burst of speed. The trail forked and Anna took the left, which was up a little hillock. At the top of the hill, she asked her to walk. Willingly the mare dropped speed and let the others catch up.

"We're going to lose our light," said Kage. "We ought to turn back soon."

"I'd like to see what she does in the arena," Charles said. Maybe there was something to what Hosteen had said, because Charles looked better. He had expressions that Anna could read again, which was an improvement.

"A challenge," said Hosteen, laughing. "You always were up for a challenge. Okay, fair enough."

They walked back to the barn. Anna ended up beside Hosteen again.

"I just remembered," Anna said. "It's not important to help us find the fae anymore, but I'd like to know, I guess. Do you know a werewolf named Archibald Vaughn who was here back in the seventies?"

"Archie?" asked Hosteen, startled.

"He's dead," said Charles, riding up beside them. "Killed by a fae . . . at least thirty years ago, now. Why do you ask?"

"Killed by a fae?" she asked. "Are you sure?"

Charles just looked at her, but Hosteen said, "I found the body. Yes. I'm sure. It was in the fall, 1979."

The hair on the back of Anna's head stood up. "Did he ever tell you that he saved a little boy from a fae creature? June of the year before. We're pretty sure it's the same one who built the fetch that tried to make Chelsea attack the kids."

"Not that I heard," Hosteen said. "After his mate died, he went to live with his family for a few years. We hoped it would help, but then I found out he'd stayed in his wolf shape the whole time. So I picked him up and brought him back to the pack and made him change to human. He never did go back to being his old self. When I felt him die, I was sure he'd found a way to kill himself. I thought it was suicide by fae."

"I think," Anna said, "that maybe it was revenge because he stopped this fae from stealing his grandchild. Or great-grandchild. Great-something-grandchild, anyway. It's an awfully big coincidence otherwise."

"Maybe he went looking for the fae," offered Charles thoughtfully. "And both of you are right."

"Any way you look at it," said Anna, "the fae we're chasing is powerful enough to kill a werewolf."

"Tore him to pieces with magic," said Hosteen thoughtfully.

"Makes you wonder," Charles said slowly, "that such a fae let a handful of federal agents and police officers escort him off to jail."

"Do you think they have the wrong fae?" Anna asked.

He didn't quite answer. "I think . . . I think, Hosteen, that we need to borrow your wolves. This is not a fae that is going to let Amethyst, the little girl we rescued, stay rescued. We probably should send wolves out to protect Dr. Vaughn, too. And we'll keep a weather eye on Chelsea and the kids."

"Who is Dr. Vaughn?" Hosteen asked.

"The little boy that your wolf rescued back in 1978."

"How many do you need?"

"All of them. On our victims, and on the FBI agent and the Cantrip agents who found his latest victim with us. At least two werewolves at all times. And they'll have to stay out of sight," he said. "I know that'll put a strain on the pack. You can tell them that the Marrok will make sure they don't suffer financially and that I don't think it will last long."

"Maybe they do have the right fae," said Hosteen. "With them, it's sometimes hard to predict why they do things."

Charles's horse snorted and Charles tilted his head sideways, closing his eyes, and murmured, "Can't you feel it in the air? There's a storm coming." When he opened his eyes, they were yellow. He straightened and, though Anna couldn't see that he moved again, his horse broke into a gentle canter.

THEY PUT THE other horses away before taking Portabella into the same smaller arena that Anna had ridden in the day before. The mare didn't look any different than she had before Anna had gotten on her outside. Or if she did, she looked even calmer, because she'd still been a little huffy about Chelsea when Anna had hopped on.

Charles lengthened the stirrups a lot, checked the cinch, and then swung up on the mare. Her head went up, her eyes rolled until Anna could see the whites that were normally hidden, she shifted her weight to her haunches, and she danced uneasily from foot to foot.

Charles just sat there, his body loose and easy; the only motion he made was the motion generated by the horse's movement. She shuffled a few steps forward, two backward, a hop sideways. He made no move to correct her, just stayed balanced and light on her back.

They fit each other, Anna thought: big dark man, big dark horse, both elegant and strong. The idea made her lips quirk up, even with the worry that the janitor wasn't the fae they were really looking for.

"You coming to the show tomorrow?" Kage asked. "Michael's riding in the lead-line and Mackie's taking the little gray you rode yesterday in the English walk/trot class."

"I'll ask Charles," she said, watching as the mare, left mostly to her own devices, finally stopped moving except for the unhappy swish of her tail. "I think we're going to try to get in to see the guy the FBI has locked up if we can. But I'd love to come see the kids ride." And to make sure that they were safe.

After five minutes more (Anna checked her watch), Charles still having done nothing but sit there, the mare lowered her head and began to chew her bit. Immediately, Charles slipped off. He patted her neck and led her out of the gate. "If you want to put her on your list of possibles," he told Anna, "that would be okay."

And she knew for sure that he really liked her. Anna liked her a lot, too. "Okay," she said. She looked at Kage. "She's on our list of possibles, but not on the price list you gave us. Do you have a price for her?"

"Ten thousand," said Hosteen.

Kage snorted. "Not anywhere near that, Hosteen. Five thousand for a pretty horse, well broke for trail. Twenty-five hundred for the well broke plus twenty-five hundred for the pretty. But don't make up your mind yet, there's some nice horses you haven't seen."

And as Kage and Hosteen left to put the mare away, Anna heard Hosteen chortle, "Did you hear him? She's a challenge. He wants her. He'd have paid ten thousand for her."

"We don't overcharge for our horses, old man," said Kage. "That's a good way to get a bad reputation. And I suspect that Charles knows just exactly how much that horse should cost." He paused. "I shouldn't have said anything at all. I could have just told Dad what you tried to do; then you'd be in real trouble."

Hosteen made a reply, but Anna couldn't hear what he said. His voice sounded happy.

"I like them," Anna said, very softly.

Charles's lips quirked. "Hosteen was watching Kage when he gave us that price, did you see?"

"He was right, though," Anna observed. "You'd have paid ten thousand for her because she's a challenge."

He smiled, eyes soft. "I already have a challenge," he told her in a gravelly voice.

She shook her head with mock sadness. "I'm not a challenge, Charles. I'm just another woman panting after you like that teacher with the hungry eyes at the day care."

He laughed out loud. "Sure you are," he said, putting an arm around her shoulders. "Sure you are."

Well, she knew it was true, even if he didn't believe her. His arm pulled her a little off balance, and paradoxically it steadied her at the same time. That was what Charles did to her heart, too. He knocked it off balance into what felt like the right position, a safe place that was still exciting, exhilarating, and terrifying.

What if I lost him?

ANNA CALLED LESLIE in the morning.

"No, I can't get you in to see Sean McDermit," she said in a distracted voice. "His lawyer is a shark, and he's not saying anything. Apparently all we have on him is that the bodies were found in his house, a house that he's never lived in. And that he's a fae. Which makes this all the more politically hot, given the current tension with the fae."

"We're not sure you have the right person," Anna said.

There was silence on the other line.

"I found Archie Vaughn," Anna told her. "He was killed a year and a half after he stopped that kidnapping. Torn to pieces by a fae. Why would someone who could tear apart a werewolf let human police officers pick him up without a fight?"

"I'll take your concerns to our fae expert," she said. "I hate to say it, but I'm suspicious about how easy this was, too. So I've got people doing background checks on anyone who was ever employed by or used the day care and everyone *they* knew." She paused. "We're also searching records of missing children, trying to identify the bodies. Some of that is on computer, some of it on microfiche, and still more of it is in paper files scattered all over the city. We've got a pair of poor flunkies wading through microfiche of hundred-year-old newspapers, too. It doesn't help that it's not just Scottsdale, it's Phoenix and all the rest of the suburbs, too. We'll be decades identifying the bodies in that attic."

Anna made a sympathetic noise.

"Anyway," Leslie continued, sounding more grounded and less frantic, "you'll be as happy as I am that it looks like that poor baby we rescued yesterday wasn't raped. She's still traumatized, scared of the dark, terrified of dolls—and who could blame her—and she cries every time her parents aren't in the room with her."

"What did he do?" she asked.

"Dressed her like a doll, sang to her, hurt her. She said his touch hurt like a bee sting all over her body. Made her so she couldn't move. She wasn't asleep, she just couldn't move."

"Terrifying," Anna said.

"Yes," agreed Leslie, sounding tired.

"Since you have your manpower focused on research, you'll be happy to know that we have werewolves guarding Amethyst's parents, Dr. Vaughn, and his partner and his mother. Also, you and Leeds and Marsden. You won't know they are there."

Anna kept speaking over the top of Leslie's indignant protest. "This one killed a werewolf, tore him to pieces with magic. A human simply doesn't stand a chance. The werewolves will be wearing black Converse sneakers, so you'll know not to shoot them or react to their presence. They are doing this because we feel it necessary, Leslie, putting their lives on the line. They are, all of this pack"—Hosteen had clarified this—"living as human. If you reveal what they are to the public, it might ruin their lives."

Leslie made an unhappy sound. "I will keep their secrets, and make sure Marsden and Leeds are apprised, too. How long are we going to be protected?"

"Thank you," Anna said, air leaving her in a whoosh of relief at Leslie's agreement. "Until we are all convinced you have the right fae. If you need us, we're going to the Arabian horse show at WestWorld in north Scottsdale. If we don't pick up the phone, text us."

"The horse show?" said Leslie. "Let's see. Ms. Newman's

four-year-old class is going to be there in the morning and Miss Baird's five-year-old class in the afternoon. Apparently they do it every year. Tomorrow it will be the two-year-olds and then Mrs. Hepplethwaite's three-year-old class. Do you want any of the classes' daily schedules by day? The music teacher on Monday and Wednesday is also the swimming instructor Tuesday and Thursday. Did I tell you we are taking a very close look at that day care?"

Anna laughed.

"Why do the two-year-olds have a teacher?" Leslie asked. "Don't you think they should have a babysitter? Or even an entertainer? Can't they just be toddlers and not students?"

"Students pay more for school than toddlers pay for baby-sitters," Anna suggested.

"Hmm," said Leslie. "Okay. That makes more sense. Thank you."

"Just don't talk too much to Ms. Newman," Anna suggested, "or you might be overcome with the temptation to steal all of her students out from under her iron rule and take them outside to run around and have fun like normal four-year-olds."

Leslie laughed. "Look," she said. "There is no way I can get you and Charles in to see McDermit before our expert has a go. But call me this afternoon."

"We'd appreciate it," Anna told her.

"No promises, but I'll try," Leslie said, and ended the call.

Anna pulled on her socks and boots and trotted down the stairs through the empty house; everyone else, including Maggie and Joseph, was already at the horse show. Both of the little kids were riding today and no one wanted to miss it.

No one. A chill ran down Anna's spine. The fae were tricksy. They were also supposed to be all locked up in reservations, but one fae had been in Kathryn Jamison's garden. Presumably, because neither she nor Charles had seen him, the janitor was a second. The bodies had been found in a house he owned. But Anna had learned to listen to her instincts; they told her there was a third fae, the real

Doll Collector, complete with ties to the day care, the fetch, and the janitor.

Happily Anna wasn't the only one whose instincts were on edge. Hosteen had claimed guard duty on the kids for himself, and Wade was assigned to Chelsea. But Anna thought it was a good thing that she and Charles were going, too. Two more werewolves keeping an eye on four victims who had escaped, mostly escaped anyway. Their job would be floating security, looking for any signs that the fae was stalking the Sani family. She found it very interesting that Sunshine Fun Day Care was scheduled so that the whole day care, staff and students alike, was going to be at the show at one time or another.

Charles was down in the kitchen finishing his breakfast. The family and most of their staff had left before dawn. Hosteen had suggested she and Charles come after the show opened to the public.

"I warned Leslie," Anna told him. "She told me that the whole day care is going to be at the horse show today and tomorrow. She also said there wasn't a chance of us getting in to see their captive fae today. She's going to try to get us in this afternoon."

He had set his silverware down as if he were finished eating. She sat on his lap and ate his last piece of bacon. "So I guess you get to take me to my first horse show."

"The last time I went to this show it was at Paradise Park. I think it was about 1965, long before you were born." He quit speaking, frowning a little at her.

"Are you planning on worrying about how much older you are than I am when you are four hundred and I'm only two hundred?" she asked him in an interested voice. "I'm only asking because my father said it was dangerous when you start tuning out your spouse, but I don't know how long I can worry about it."

He laughed; his arms surrounded her and pulled her tighter in a brief hug.

"Besides," she said airily, sliding off his lap, "I've heard that Vlad the Impaler established without a doubt that having a stick up one's ass was detrimental to one's health. And I am very interested in keeping you healthy."

She didn't make it to the door before he had her, one arm wrapped around her shoulders and the other around her middle, pulling her back into his body.

He put his mouth against her ear and growled playfully, "So I'm in danger of suffering the fate of Vlad's victims, am I? Maybe you should do something about rescuing me?"

The vibration of his voice against her ear made her shiver, but she tried to keep her voice steady anyway. "Why, sir, what could you possibly mean? Are you propositioning *moi*?"

He growled in her ear and she squeaked because it tickled, and caused a more interesting sensation in her stomach. Then he moved his right hand down to cup her breast and his left hand slid south. He said a few sentences in French, his voice rough and hungry. She thought maybe he'd forgotten she didn't really speak French.

"Charles," she said, her own voice husky with need, because her mate was hard to resist at any time. But he was never sexier than when he was feeling playful.

He picked her up and took her to their room, his steps slow and deliberate—and that was its own kind of foreplay.

IT WAS A while before they actually got to the show grounds. They were still early. Kage had said that crowds didn't get really big until the last three or four days. That being said, the place they finally found to park was a quarter-mile walk to the entrance.

Armed with a map, Charles led the way briskly through what felt like miles and miles of kiosk shopping in the huge main building. He ignored the surreptitious attention he was garnering, for both his looks and, Anna thought, his air of dangerous intent.

Michael's class was getting its fifteen-minute warning call as they finally found the seats the Sanis' ranch had reserved in the indoor arena. Anna had been beginning to despair when Charles spotted the mobility cart bearing the ranch's logo in silver and brown parked tightly behind the rows of blue stadium seats. From there it was easy to find familiar faces.

Anna and Charles found seats next to Mateo and Teri, just behind Maggie, Joseph, Max, Chelsea, and Wade. Max twisted around and grinned at Anna.

"Mackie is a little tyrant," he said. "She declared that everyone had to see her ride." He raised his voice to a squeak that was supposed to sound like his little sister. "Ev-er-ee-bo-dee." He grinned. "And then Michael, not to be outdone, declared that we all had to be here to watch him, too. So Dad and Hosteen are getting the kids and horses ready for the class so that the rest of the crew can watch from the rail."

Anna thought it seemed reasonable to her: children ought to feel comfortable demanding an audience if they were going to ride in this huge building. The bleachers were empty, but the stadium seating along the arena railing seemed to be pretty full.

"Where's Mackie, then?" Anna asked. "Her class isn't until this afternoon, right?"

"She seems to think that Michael might need some coaching," said Joseph. If his voice was hesitant, the twinkle in his eye wasn't. "Bossing, more like. It's a good thing that boy is laid-back or Kage's household will be hell until they both grow up and go out on their own."

"She's got a good heart," Maggie said repressively.

Joseph looked at her, and Anna saw that he adored the woman who sat beside him. "She's just like her grandma," he said, patting her hand. "Tough, straightforward, and determined. You didn't turn out so bad, Maggie my love. If she's half the woman you are, the world better watch out."

"Joseph," said a stranger who came down the short stretch of stairs until he could stand next to Joseph's chair, which was on the aisle. "I didn't expect to see you here."

"My grandson's riding," Joseph said with dignity. "Where else would I be?"

And the two men started talking about other days and other shows. Horses they'd owned, horses other people had owned. They were joined by an older woman who could have stepped out of the Grand Ole Opry of the '80s. She glittered in gold and black tiger stripes, wore too much makeup, and had a voice that decades of smoking had roughened to Marlene Dietrich level. She was bawdy and made both of the old men laugh. Maggie leaned sideways and added a sharp remark that showed that she, too, was a welcome part of this group.

They tried to include Chelsea, and she smiled on cue, but she was noticeably tense in the big, noisy crowd. Anna glanced at Charles, who was watching Chelsea, too.

He didn't look worried, so she sat back and looked around. Directly in front of them, a large group of very well-groomed and glittering horses circled the arena at a very, very slow canter. As soon as she started watching them, Charles whispered in her ear, "Half Arab, Anglo-Arab western pleasure, amateur owner to ride, section one. This is an elimination round. The best of them will go on to the semifinal round. That's why no one in the audience is too excited about it, except for the cheering sections for each horse and rider."

"They are very slow," she said after a moment. "Shouldn't they be going faster? What if something was chasing them? I think Portabella *walked* faster than this yesterday. What's an Anglo-Arab?"

"Half Thoroughbred, half Arab. It was the first of the half-bred Arabs to gain popularity. The Thoroughbred added size, so bigger people could ride. These are almost all quarter-horse or paint crossbreeds, except for the Appaloosa down there." He paused. "That's a really nice Appaloosa."

Joseph, still chatting with his buddies, had apparently been paying attention to them, too. "Still got the eye. That mare won this class the past two years running. If this is a fair sampling of her competition, she's got a good chance of winning it again. If Helen's daughter-in-law doesn't take it with her Shining Spark gelding."

Anna quit trying to parse the horse talk (for instance, what in the world was a Shining Spark gelding?) and just settled in and watched pretty horses moving very slowly with pretty riders wearing sometimes garish colors and lots and lots of glitter. The men were better off than the women, coming off conservative in comparison.

All the while, Anna breathed in deeply, paying attention to what her nose could tell her. Mostly it told her that at least two people around here were wearing too much perfume, and there were lots and lots of horses around.

The riders were called into the center, those advancing to the next level were announced, and then they cleared the ring. Almost instantly the stadium seats filled and the nosebleed bleachers saw some use. Joseph and Maggie's gossip partners wandered off to find their seats.

Over the loudspeaker, the announcer said, "This is class one-sixteen, lead-line ages two through seven. First in is Candice Hart, riding Little Joe Green by Mister Vanilla out of Desert Wind Doll, with handlers Josie Hart and Karen Tucker."

And a tiny girl who was younger than Michael came into the ring wearing a tiny pink cowboy outfit that glittered with pink rhinestones under the lights. She wore itty-bitty pink boots and bright pink fringed chaps. She sat on a very small black saddle that looked utterly ridiculous and precious at the same time. Instead of a cowboy hat, she wore a bright pink riding helmet. The horse, a very pale palomino, carried his tiny burden with solemn majesty. The two adults walked on the left side, one holding a lead clipped to the bridle, the other with a hand on the tiny girl's leg.

"That is the cutest thing I've ever seen," said Anna seriously.

"Just wait," said Maggie. "It's not over yet."

And one at a time, each little rider was announced and led in. There were English riders, western riders, and one who looked like an extra from *The Sheik* in what the announcer called traditional costume. The costume was a bright-colored flowing thing with enough tassels, jewels, and bangles to leave any self-respecting Bedouin tribesman running for the hills.

"Next in we have Michael Sani on three-time national champion SA Phoenix by Xenophonn out of SA Rose Queen. Leading them in is Kage Sani."

Michael couldn't compete with the little fairy doll in pink. Instead, like some of the men Anna had seen in the last class, he was wearing a perfectly respectable blue western-cut shirt with a black shoestring tie. Like his father and Hosteen, Michael looked very much at home on top of the big bay gelding his father led.

When Michael rode past them, he gave his grandfather a solemn nod and patted his horse. Joseph returned the nod but added a grin as he held up both hands clasped together in the traditional victory sign. When the last rider was in, the announcer asked the group to reverse at a walk. They paraded for about five minutes, so that everyone had time to take photos, and then they were taken to the middle of the ring.

Anna couldn't help a ridiculous twinge of anxiety. Michael looked awesome. But who could compete with a toddler in pink? Or a princess dressed in tassels on a white horse with a tail that dragged the ground? She clenched Charles's hand, and he clenched her hand back, looking so serious that she knew he was having fun. She had the suspicion that it might be at her expense.

"Well, ladies and gentlemen," said the announcer. "Our judges have been very impressed with this group this morning. What do you say?"

The crowd exploded in a chorus of clapping and whistles. Charles covered Anna's ears to protect them and winced a little. It was loud. Chelsea had covered her own ears. Good for her.

When the crowd quieted, the announcer said solemnly, "That's exactly what our judges said. With this quality of competition they have been unable to pick a clear winner. If this were a race, they'd have to declare it a dead heat. Because of this, we have decided to award first place to every child in the class." More applause followed.

Anna sat back and gave Charles an indignant look. "They all get first prize," she said.

"That's right," Charles said.

"Every time."

"Could you have picked out a winner?"

She smacked his thigh lightly and then rubbed it to wipe away any hint of sting in case she'd hit too hard. When the last child was led out of the ring, Anna gave a happy sigh as the group of Sani stablehands, trainers, and riders stood up and began shuffling out.

"Joseph and I will watch from here," said Maggie. "You should go out and walk around. Mackie's class isn't until just before the lunch break. We'll keep Max here to run for food and drink."

The arena they had been in, despite its size, was not a tenth of the Scottsdale show grounds. Their program guide promised them more than two thousand horses, and Anna supposed that many horses could not be contained in a small area.

And Charles was interested in them all. Anna soon gave up watching horses for the pleasure of watching her husband watch the horses. Once in a while he'd grunt in approval, and she knew he'd found something he really liked.

They stood for a while by a covered arena (there were lots of arenas) where people were doing some last-minute training or warming up or whatever. English horses with big shoes trotted rapidly around, lapping the western horses whose oh-so-slow gaits seemed almost Zen-like. Women riders outnumbered men, but not by a huge margin except in the ten-to-eighteen-year-old crowd, which seemed to be mostly girls. One horse was foaming with sweat, and his mincing western gait was stiff and uncomfortable looking. His rider kept pulling back on the bit and spurring at the same time. Charles grunted and walked away from the arena.

"What was she trying to do?" asked Anna.

"I don't know," Charles said unhappily. "And I can tell you that poor horse didn't know, either."

They stopped for a bunch of young horses crowded in front of yet another arena, clad only in narrow-banded halters designed to show off their exotic heads. They sidled and snorted and looked pretty. A few of them were frightened—Anna could smell it—but most of them were just bouncing around with happy energy, preening when they noticed some-one looking at them.

Charles bought Anna an ice cream cone, taking a good-humored lick himself when she offered it to him.

And nowhere did they smell fae.

The buildings where the horses were stabled were set in parallel lines along the outer edge of the show grounds. Some of them were strewn with banners belonging to one stable or another. They found the Sani stables more by luck than because they were looking for them.

A crowd of children were gathered around the horse Michael had ridden in the lead-line class. He was bare of tack except for his halter and stood half-asleep while one of the Sani handlers held him so that the children could pet him.

Kage stood by the horse's hindquarters, gently directing the kids toward the front of the horse instead of the rear and patiently answering questions. Mackie seemed to be helping, showing the younger children how to pet gently. She was dressed in a white button-up shirt tucked into dark gray stretch pants that were tucked into tall English riding boots.

"Anna, Anna," caroled Michael, breaking free of the crowd and running up to her. "I won, I won, did you see me?"

She smiled. "I did. Did you have fun?"

"I like riding Nix," he said, bouncing happily in a way that reminded her of the bunch of young horses they'd just seen. "He is Grandpa's horse and he likes kids. The kids from my school are here. They saw me win, too. I'm letting them pet my horse."

"I see that."

Ms. Newman was mostly too busy admiring Kage to look their way, though she managed one sly look at Charles that stopped as soon as Anna caught her eye. Ms. Edison smiled sharply, an *aha* smile, but didn't leave her post at the rear of the herd of children.

Anna didn't know if it was good or bad that the principal had figured out just who had clued them into the trouble at the day care. None of them, children or teachers, smelled of fae magic, either. She could smell Ms. Edison's perfume and Ms. Newman's shampoo, and one of the kids had a cat, but she didn't smell fae.

Charles walked them around the kids, nodding to Kage as they passed, and into the stable building. Hosteen was drinking from a bottle of water and chatting with Wade. Beside them, sitting hunched over on a straw bale, Chelsea had her eyes closed.

Anna left Charles's side and sat down beside Chelsea. She finished the last of her ice cream cone, licked her sticky fingers, and tried to radiate calm. She was rewarded by Chelsea's gradual relaxation, though the other woman didn't open her eyes.

"Too many people," Chelsea murmured. "Too many sounds, too many smells."

"Yeah," Anna agreed. "It hits all of us like that once in a while. Do you need to go home?"

Chelsea shook her head, took a deep breath, and opened her eyes. "Not until after Mackie's class. Then a whole bunch of us will go back to the ranch. All the kids and me. We'll take Nix, too. He's twenty-eight, ancient of days. One day of excitement is enough for him."

"How long until Mackie's class?" Anna asked.

Hosteen said, "About an hour."

"Then why don't I wait with you here?"

Chelsea smiled tensely, but it was Hosteen who said in a gentle voice, "I think that would be very useful. Thank you."

About then Ms. Edison came into the stables to thank

Chelsea for letting the four-year-olds pet Michael's mount.
She was smiling, gracious, and brief.

MACKIE'S CLASS WAS a lot smaller than the lead-line class
had been. There were three girls, one of them nearer to ten
and the other girl about Mackie's age.

"This is English pleasure," said Joseph for Anna's benefit.
"The horses have more elevated gaits; that means they pick
their feet up higher and are generally more excitable. There
aren't a lot of horses who can be English pleasure horses
and be safe enough for someone under ten to ride."

The riders rounded the ring at a trot, Heylight looking a lot
bigger with Mackie riding him. Anna leaned forward and paid
attention. The other younger girl looked a little off balance,
and her horse, a sweet-faced chestnut, didn't have the action
of the other two horses.

This time, Anna noticed, the family was tenser than they
had been for Michael, leaning forward in their seats. The
horses walked for half the arena, reversed, and trotted.

Max groaned and Maggie sat up straighter. "Change
diagonals, Mackie," she said under her breath. "Come on,
notice what's going on. Quit paying attention to the crowd
and watch what you're doing."

Anna leaned toward Charles in silent query.

"When you're posting, you rise and fall with one front leg
instead of bouncing with every footfall," Charles said.

It was like music, and Anna understood music. "Like cut
time instead of four-four."

"Right, it's easier on the horse and on the rider. But when
you are riding in a circle, you want to rise and fall with the
outside leg; the inside leg on a circle is already taking more
weight. Mackie is on the wrong leg. She'll have to bounce a
beat to change. There she goes. Good girl."

"She'll make reserve," said Joseph. "That's just fine. Not
the first mistake she's made in the ring, and it won't be the
last."

"Any class that you end up still on top instead of eating dirt is a good class," said Max, deadpan, but obviously quoting someone.

"She's got the hands and the seat," said Maggie. "Just like her grandfather. She'll be one of the good ones."

"If she wants to be," said Chelsea.

She'd come to the stands with Wade, Anna, and Charles to watch while her husband was in the paddock behind the in-gate to make sure Mackie got into and out of her class okay. She was, Anna noticed, doing a lot better with the crowded arena than she had earlier. The hour in the quiet of their section of barn with Anna radiating calm had given her the respite she'd needed to regain her control.

Max laughed. "No one is capable of making Mackie do anything she doesn't want to, Mom. You know that."

The riders lined up in the middle, and the places were announced. Mackie did indeed take reserve, which apparently was second place. The horses trotted one more time all the way around the arena and then out of the gate.

Chelsea stood up as if she had springs. "I'll go gather the children. Max, can you help your grandparents get home when they are ready?"

"Will do," he said.

Charles got up, too. "Let's take a break from the horse show. If there is someone who is fae here at the show grounds, we aren't having any luck finding them."

THEY ENDED UP eating at a Chinese restaurant that was fairly decent—better than anything in Aspen Creek, anyway. It was late for lunch and early for dinner—so there was only one other couple in the place. Charles relaxed and listened in on Anna's phone call with Special Agent Fisher.

Leslie sounded frustrated and unhappy. "Our expert was in with McDermit for two hours this morning, but he wants another crack at him this afternoon. Sorry."

"Tell her," Charles said thoughtfully, "to see if she can figure out if Mr. McDermit was gone for a couple of weeks in November, when the fae all disappeared into the reservations. He shouldn't be one of the ones who hid out like the wearden in Ms. Jamison's garden. If she's checking the background of the other people associated with the day care, she should look at that for them, too."

When Anna relayed the suggestion, Leslie sighed. "Already working on that, but it was right around Thanksgiving. A lot of people left to visit relatives. We are, my flunkies are, confirming that people actually went where they say they did. So far we found one wife who was supposed to be visiting her parents who was actually sleeping with a married man. And another who was in rehab. It is understandable that he told his work that he was taking an extended vacation. I promise I'll call when I get something, or if I can get you in to talk to Mr. McDermit."

THEY DROVE BACK to the Sanis' ranch about two hours after they left the show, only to find it deserted. Anna called Kage.

"Chelsea's hanging out with Michael, Mackie, and the girl who was last place in Mackie's class," Kage explained, a smile in his voice. Charles wondered why no one had called them to let them know that everyone was staying at the show. But Hosteen had his family well guarded, even without Anna and Charles.

"Mackie was feeling pretty bad until she saw that the little girl on the chestnut was crying," Kage said. "She gave her the same pep talk Hosteen gives everyone. Did you do your best? Well, okay then. Any class where you don't end up on the ground is a good class." Charles could hear the smile in Kage's voice. "Chelsea took them both to get ice cream with Hosteen."

"I told you not to worry," Charles said after she hung up.

"If I were a fae trying to steal children, that horse show with all of its distractions would be just the place to do it," she said.

"He'll have to get past Hosteen, Wade, and the handful

of werewolves working the crowd because they aren't going to be distracted from their job. And it's pretty public. So far this one has gone out of its way to avoid detection."

"Handful?" Anna frowned. "I only spotted two."

"They mostly stayed out of range of your nose," he said. "No use them running over the same places in the crowd where we were already looking. If we didn't pick up on any fae, neither would they. But I know most of the people in Hosteen's pack by sight."

Charles settled in with his laptop on the only chair in their room to work on pack finances. Just because the fae were out terrorizing Scottsdale didn't mean the rest of his work stopped.

Anna pulled out a paperback novel with a half-naked man holding an improbably long sword. He wondered if the sword was meant to be metaphoric. Then he wondered if he should be concerned that his mate was reading a book with a naked man on the cover. Anna stretched out on her stomach to read. Her feet were toward him. Her position gave him a nice view when he needed a break from studying numbers, and he quit worrying about naked men.

A couple of hours later they heard a car drive up and the front door opened. The chatter of happy voices told Charles that the younger children were home—and so was Max. He didn't sound as happy as the kids. Charles was already logging off and shutting down his laptop when there was a quiet knock on their door.

Anna hopped off the bed and pulled the door open.

"Um, excuse me," Max said. "But Granddad is down in the car and he's too tired to get out. Grandma sent me up to get you."

Charles brushed past him and leapt down the stairs. He was worried, though he knew that was ridiculous. Joseph was dying. He might die tonight, waiting for someone to help him out of the car. He might die a week from now in his bed.

Ridiculous or not, Charles rushed out to the car, where Maggie stood with the door open.

"Don't you die on me, old man," she said. "We have some fighting left to do."

"And arguing, too," Joseph said, the humor coming through the breathlessness just fine.

"I told you we should go after Mackie's class," she snapped.

"But we needed to see how good that stallion Conrad's been bragging about really is. And then Lucy was riding in the amateur class on that filly she bought from us two years ago."

"I know why you stayed," Maggie said. "And it had nothing to do with Lucy's filly and everything to do with stupid pride. You couldn't admit you were feeling poorly."

If she was yelling at him, Joseph was all right. As Charles bent down to lift his old friend, Maggie put her hand on his arm and leaned her head against his shoulder; he could all but feel her pain himself. Maggie was always sharpest when she hurt.

"Let's get you inside," Charles said.

"If I die after a day of watching beautiful horses, that would be okay," Joseph said.

The spirits that seemed to be always hovering around Joseph, even if Charles was the only one who could see them, hit Charles so hard he could barely breathe. Their impact forced him to hesitate, stop walking altogether, and spread his legs a bit to keep his balance.

"You have a task yet," he murmured when he could. He headed for the house. "Let me see if they'll give you a little more strength to do what is necessary."

"Tell those spirits that if they want him so badly, they might cure his cancer," said Maggie tartly.

"It's worth my life to tell the spirits anything," Charles said. "You know better than to ask."

He was starting to get an odd notion about those spirits. The spirits who petitioned him were not human, they were spirits of the earth and air. That didn't mean there weren't spirits of the dead. Usually the dead had a weight to them, a feeling of wrongness. The spirits surrounding Joseph burned with purpose, a heat that made Charles's heart pound in his chest and called to Brother Wolf. There was nothing twisted or wrong in them.

Still. This incident he and Anna were unraveling involved so many dead innocents: children killed before they had a chance to decide who they were going to be. Unfinished.

The innocent dead . . . he'd only met one of those and if Mercy, who could see ghosts better than anyone he'd ever met, had not been with him, he'd never have connected that spirit to the child who'd been killed on that stretch of road a dozen years before. Mercy had seen the boy quite clearly, but Charles had only felt a hot sizzle on his skin, like a sunburn, only deeper.

Maybe this heat he felt from these spirits was like that child, only multiplied by all the dead who were owed balance because of the loss of their chance at life. Not rage, but vengeance.

Still, what service could an old man dying of cancer provide for dead children?

"Charles?" Anna asked hesitantly. "Are you going to keep Joseph out here all afternoon?"

He wondered how long he'd been standing still. Without replying he carried Joseph into the house.

"Anna?" he asked. "Could you come with me?" He thought again. "Maggie, it would be best if you stayed with Mackie and Michael."

"Where do you want me?" asked Max. "I know how to hook up all of Granddad's machinery."

Max was like Samuel, Charles thought, a good man to have at your back. And he brought nothing with him that might change the nature of what Charles wanted to do.

Maggie . . . he didn't quite trust what Maggie wanted. Maggie was never happy where she was, always looking elsewhere for happiness, for fulfillment. As much as she loved Joseph, and she did, she was not a restful person.

"Yes," he told Max. "Come with us."

Maggie looked at him with stricken eyes, and he felt as though he'd struck her.

"Strength and purpose are useful qualities," he told her. "But for what I'm going to attempt, we need quiet souls."

He didn't know if it was enough, but he left Maggie and the kids in the living room and headed up to Joseph's rooms.

He and Max helped Joseph into the bathroom to take care of the necessities of living, while Anna pulled back the bedding and generally made herself scarce so as not to embarrass Joseph. Charles hadn't had to say anything to her. His mate was one of the most perceptive people he'd ever met.

They laid the old man, who had once been one of the toughest men Charles had ever met, on the bed, and he struggled to draw breath enough to talk. It made Charles's heart hurt to see him this way.

"Shh," said Charles.

He looked around the room for . . . something. "I don't suppose there's still a cello around here someplace, is there?" There used to be. Kage had played cello.

Max frowned. "Actually, I think there is. Kage's old cello is still in his room here. Grandma makes him play it every Christmas. He starts sneaking practices in along about November. He says he doesn't take it home because it just sits there and makes him feel guilty for not practicing an hour a day like Grandma used to make him do. Hold on."

As soon as he was gone, Anna said, "You want me to play?"

"We need music," he said, knowing it was true. "I think I need you to start it, and the cello is where your music lives."

"They're talking to you today," she said. "The spirits. What are they saying?"

"That's the problem," he said. "Usually I know exactly what they want me to do. All I have to do is decide if I'm going to accommodate them or not. This time . . . all I can do is follow my instincts."

"Good enough for me," she said as Max came back into the room with a cello in a canvas carry bag.

Anna took the instrument, stripped away the wrappings, and gave it a cursory examination. "New strings," she said as she tuned it. "Not a bad instrument." She took the bow, rosined it briskly, and drew it across the strings.

Her eyebrows rose at the tone. "Better than I thought. Not as good as the one you got me, but it's better than most student instruments. Do you have a song in mind?"

"Something . . . beautiful, but still upbeat." He tried to put his feelings into words.

She nodded and then started playing.

"*Lord of the Rings*," said Max, startled.

Charles closed his eyes, listening, and it was all right. He raised his voice in answer to the cello. No words, just music, until the words became necessary. By that time he was so lost in music, which he and Anna had morphed into their own song, that he didn't even know what language he sang in, let alone what the meaning of the words were. They were just a shape in the music he and Anna made together.

The music built and the power burned down his arms into his hands, so he placed those hands on Joseph. When it was over and the heat was gone, Joseph slept comfortably. The heat, the fire in his veins, was gone. The room was silent, and he knew that his earlier theory was right.

For some reason, the dead, the children killed by the fae who'd attacked the Sani family, were very interested in Joseph. That was something he wasn't going to share with Maggie and her very Navajo view of the dead. Maybe he should tell Joseph.

He covered the sleeping man while Anna put the cello back in its case. Max took it without a word and they all left, shutting the door quietly. Max started down the hallway farther into the depths of the house and stopped.

He turned back to them and met Charles's eye.

"Anyone hearing that," he said, "has to believe in magic."

He left them. Anna took Charles down the hall in the other direction, toward the main part of the house.

"What did you do?" she asked.

"I have no idea," he told her. "I find that somewhat unsettling."

She took a deep breath, like an actress going onstage, pasted a big smile on her face, and said, "I find it *somewhat* reassuring that I'm not the only one who feels like I should be running around shouting, 'Where's the script? Where's the script? If only I had a script, I'd know what the freak I'm supposed to be doing.'"

WHILE CHARLES HAD been making magic, Maggie, Mackie, and Michael had made sandwiches for everyone, since Ernestine had the day off. Maggie had also made a huge effort at cheer for the sake of the children.

"Where's Chelsea?" Charles asked. Anna remembered that Chelsea was planning on coming home with the kids.

"Teri ate something that disagreed with her, so Mom borrowed an outfit and she's going to take over Teri's ride in the western pleasure futurity elimination round," Max said.

"Ánáli Hastiin said she should," added Mackie.

"Eat," said Maggie, setting a giant plate of sandwiches down at the table where she'd already set a stack of dishes.

"What are your plans for the rest of the afternoon?" asked Max. "If you aren't busy, Hosteen suggested I take you for a ride around the ranch. He said to remind you that you are guests, not guards. He had two of his pack follow us from the show grounds. They're patrolling the grounds."

Anna looked at Charles.

"Fine with me," he said.

"What horses is Hosteen having you look at?" Max asked.

"I left the list upstairs," Anna said. "Let me go get it."

ANNA AND MACKIE did the dishes while Max looked over the list with a pencil he used to make notes.

"We could go out for a ride, Anna," he suggested when he was done scribbling. "Merrylegs is here. We're not showing her at the big show this year. She's more of a trail horse than an arena horse, though she's not nearly as bad as Portabella that way."

And, Anna thought, it would get them out of the house and her out from under Maggie's glower. It was Charles who'd made her stay downstairs. So why was Anna getting the cold shoulder? Maggie hadn't so much as looked at her since they'd come down the stairs.

Okay, she had to be honest. She understood. She didn't like it, it upset her sense of justice, but she understood. Charles had explained his reason for leaving Maggie downstairs, which Maggie could accept. But Anna had gone up with him and with Joseph. Anna, young and werewolf Anna, had taken Maggie's place.

"A ride sounds like fun," Anna said, and Charles nodded.

"Can I come?" asked Michael.

"Sure," said Maggie.

Mackie started to say something, but she looked at her grandmother and hesitated. Anna saw the moment she made the decision.

"Grandma? I'm tired of horses today. I don't want to go for another ride."

"You can stay with me, then," Maggie said. "We'll go play some Candy Land."

THIS TIME THEY tacked up their own horses while Max found saddles that fit and bridles that would work.

"First time I ever rode a horse, I was eight," he told them, helping Michael brush the horse he'd picked for him, a short, stout, brown-and-white-spotted half Arab named Romeo. "Kage was dating my mom and he was like, 'Come ride some horses.' When she and I got home that night, I said—"

"'You gotta marry him, Mom,'" said Michael. "'He has *horses*.'"

Max laughed. "That's right, pipsqueak. Maybe if I didn't like horses so much, Mom wouldn't have married Kage. And then you wouldn't even be around."

"Yes, I would," Michael answered. "Because Daddy says I'm his penance for past sins."

Anna hid her grin as she picked up Merrylegs's foot to clean it. Merrylegs was a seven-year-old mare of indifferent breeding (Max's words) who'd come to the Sanis as a training prospect. When her owner discovered boys, she'd turned over the mare's registration and ownership in return for back board and training fees.

"She's sweet as pie," Max said. "Not a show horse of any kind. But she'll try her heart out for you and take care of you. Mackie rides her a lot on the trails."

For Charles, Max brought Portabella.

"She's on your list," Max said. "And she's a fun ride on the trails."

Merrylegs, as promised, was sweet and responsive. She also had a trot that made Anna glad she'd inherited her mom's teeth and not her dad's because if she'd had any fillings they'd have been gone by the time the ride was over. Merry's canter was better and her walk was brisk, but that trot was horrible.

"Yeah," said Max, though Anna hadn't said anything. "It's those really short and straight pasterns. She's like riding a jackhammer. But she'll canter forever, and her canter is lovely."

They rode past the hill where Anna had turned Portabella around the day before. Max led them on by it and out into the desert.

"Okay," he said. "You might as well see her strengths, right? And she's best out here where common sense and willingness mean more than pretty."

So they rode, and as a sort of camaraderie settled over them, Max gave Charles a half-shy look. "How did you meet Granddad?" he asked.

Anna wondered if he was going to answer Max. He didn't often speak about the past unless it was important to something going on in the here and now. It was, Samuel had told her once, how the old wolves coped with the passing of time. Samuel was a lot older than Charles.

But the magic of riding in the last of the afternoon sun, the smell of horses, and the rhythm of the ride had, she decided, caught him up in the magic of the shared experience. Or maybe he didn't have the heart to shut Max down with one of his usual conversation-killing two-words-or-less answers.

"I first saw him when he was about Michael's age," said Charles. "Really met him when he was barely a teenager in a bar fight in Phoenix—it can be a hard thing to be a different color when men get together and get drunk. I was walking by and I heard a war cry." His horse snorted and shook her head; Charles patted her. "And then a whole lot of cursing and glass breaking. But it was the war cry that made me wade into that bar fight and start clearing it out. At the bottom of a pile of battered veterans—it was just after World War Two—was this skinny little Indian kid of about twelve or thirteen."

Charles's face lit with the sudden grin he had sometimes. "I said, 'Takes a real man to hit a kid.'" His grin widened. "One of the guys—he was sporting the start of a real beauty of a shiner—he said, 'Hell, mister, all I said was that he should get his butt out of here because he was too Indian to be safe with all the rough stock in here drinking like fishes. And the kid lit into me like I punched him.'"

Charles ran his hand down the shiny long neck of his horse and then said, "Joseph never did have any quit in him. Though he learned, eventually, to pick his battles. I'd been up conducting my father's business with Hosteen when someone told him that Joseph was missing. His mother had found out what Hosteen was and picked up and left. I guess Joseph overheard one of the hands saying that she'd probably run down to Phoenix to earn a living on her back in the bars there, which she hadn't. Hosteen had followed her all the way back to her sister's home out in the Four Corners area to make sure she was safe. But he told Joseph he wouldn't talk about her to him, and Joseph took him at his word, so Joseph didn't know where she'd gone. When he overheard the cowboys, he decided he couldn't leave his mother in trouble. So he stole one of the ranch trucks and drove it into Phoenix with the intention of finding his mother if he had to go to every bar in town to do so. When Hosteen figured out what happened, and those two cowboys never worked on the Sanis' ranch again, he took the whole pack, and me, to Phoenix to find Joseph."

Charles was quiet for a little while, and Anna thought he'd finished the story, but he picked it up again. "So I looked down at that boy and said, 'Are you Joseph?' He got to his feet, dusted himself up, wiped the blood off his chin, and said, 'Yes. I got twelve more bars to go.' I said, 'You need to be more careful who you get your information from. Your mom is living with her sister over near Monument Valley.' That gave him pause. While he was still thinking, I said, 'You need to remember one other thing. If you're going to face someone bigger and stronger than you, kid, make damn sure you are better armed.' I gave him my knife and sheath. We stopped to give the bartender Hosteen's address so that Hosteen could settle the bill, because by my reckoning it was Hosteen's pride that had caused the whole mess."

"You used to run around with him," Max said. "Kage said you and he got into a lot of trouble."

"That was later," Charles said. "Started, I suppose, when your grandfather was about seventeen. He'd run away again and was punching cows for a Navajo rancher. He and Hosteen locked horns over every little thing in those days. Hosteen asked if I'd stop and check in on him and see if I couldn't talk him into going home. Might not have worked, but he sent me out with an Arab Hosteen had bought from a breeder in California. Joseph could resist almost anything except pretty mares."

"That would have been in the fifties, right?" asked Max. "Why were you on horseback?"

"The ranch was out in Navajo country," Charles said. "I don't think there was anything with four wheels that could have made it there. I had a truck and horse trailer parked about twenty-five miles from the ranch." He paused. "My da and I were having trouble seeing eye-to-eye about then. It gave Joseph and me something to talk about on that trip back. I didn't go home. We worked Hosteen's ranch until the next fight. Then Joseph and I went out on our own. Mostly working cows and increasing our cash flow with the occasional rodeo. Your granddad could ride anything with four hooves. On one memorable, almost-fatal occasion, that included a moose. I think I have a photo of that one somewhere; if I find it I'll send you a copy."

"That's when he met Maggie, right?" Max said. "Grand-dad says he was working at her ranch."

Charles huffed a laugh. "Her ranch was two hundred acres of the nastiest country I've ever tried to run cows on. It had a spring, though, pure and clean and cold at high summer. We were at the nearest town . . . I don't remember the name of it, though it might come to me. Joseph and I had just finished up the fall roundup and were flush with money and time, because we'd been let go like most of the other hands after the drive. She'd come into town driving a beat-up old truck to buy supplies and ran into trouble at the store."

"Because she was Navajo—I mean, Diné?"

Charles shook his head. "Most of the people there were Navajo—Diné if you'd prefer. No. It was that she was a woman trying to be a man. That kind of attitude about women wasn't very Navajo, really, but it was very 1950s. Anyway, Joseph and I stepped in. Joseph being Joseph, it wasn't long before fists were flying, and Maggie was pretty good with her fists. She was smarter than the rest of us, though, because she hiked back to her truck and pulled out her shotgun. And that was the end of that fight. We worked for her all that winter." He looked at Anna. "Not that winter in Arizona, except for the really high country, is very cold compared to Montana. I lit out that spring, but Joseph stayed and married her. I think she still owns that patch of ground, but they moved back here after a few years when Hosteen's dedication to the Arabians started to pay off and he really needed more help."

"Why a moose?" Anna asked. She'd seen a few moose since moving to Montana. Even the werewolves were wary of them.

"You'd have to be male, eighteen, and trying to impress a girl to understand," said Charles.

Max laughed. "Sixteen works," he said.

First Anna's phone rang and then Charles's.

"McDermit was a fetch," said Leslie as soon as Anna

answered the phone. "I'm looking at a pile of sticks sitting in the chair where he was sitting not ten minutes ago."

Charles, his attention caught by Leslie's conversation, answered his own phone, and though Anna could hear the voice on the other side, she couldn't understand a word he said.

"English," said Charles. "My Navajo was never that good and I've hardly spoken it for twenty years."

"The fae," said Joseph, "the fae can look like anyone. She's here."

"I'll get back to you," Anna told Leslie, and ended the call.

14

Joseph Sani woke up feeling as though he were eighteen again. Nothing hurt. He sat up in his bed and wondered if he had died and this was what happened afterward. But his body looked like the body of an old man, and his breath was still too short.

He got up gingerly, expecting at any moment to feel as he had sitting trapped and helpless in the car. Aging, he knew, was part of living—a part of living that he'd chosen over the arguments of his father and his wife. That didn't make the frustration of being dependent easier, he'd found.

But on his feet, his body was still obeying him as it had not in years. Not only didn't it hurt, but he picked up a heavy potted plant that was set on the ground near the window; he had most of his old strength back.

There's something you need to do, Charles had said, or words almost like that.

Joseph wasn't a particularly spiritual man. Not like Charles, his brother-by-choice, and mostly he'd been grateful for that. Men who saw the spirits had to listen to them—though Charles only listened to them when he wanted to.

But even a man who wasn't spiritual could tell that something was up when the wear and tear of eighty-odd years of life were lifted from him: it must be time for him to do that something. Too bad he had no idea what that was.

Still, a man who was doing something ought to do it with clothes on. And an old cowboy who ought to do something would do it with his boots on. So he pulled out a pair of new jeans . . . and set them aside for a faded and broken-in pair. He took out a good shirt, though, that snapped up the front like any shirt that belonged to a cowboy ought to. Cowboying was hard on the hands. Any cowboy who handled ropes for very long soon had knuckles that didn't like fussing with tiny little buttons.

After a moment's thought, he didn't put on a hat. This didn't feel like something a hat would help with. He took a good look at himself in the mirror in his bathroom.

"You are old," he told his reflection. But he didn't feel that way. Not at all. He tightened his right hand in a fist.

He could still see the crooked finger that he'd broken when that four-year-old stallion decided to get the old Indian off his back. He hadn't stayed off and hadn't realized his finger was broken until twenty minutes later, when the adrenaline had worn off.

That finger had hurt for ten years, but it didn't hurt now.

He turned away from the mirror and met the bright blue eyes of a little red-haired boy.

"The fae can look like anyone," the boy said. "He's coming."

"Who are you?" Joseph asked—but the boy, who had been standing in the doorway of the bathroom, was gone.

"Chindi," said Joseph—though the boy hadn't felt evil. Maybe he'd been imagining things. But he still was careful to twist around so he didn't go through the space where the boy had stood as he walked through the doorway back into his bedroom.

He decided to go downstairs and find Charles. Charles would know . . . the right questions to ask, maybe. He could at least expect that Charles would believe him.

He stopped as he passed his chest of drawers and opened up the small drawer on the upper left side. And there was the old knife Charles had given him after rescuing him from a bar fight. It was a very good knife, six inches of pattern-welded steel. How good, he hadn't realized until four or five years later when someone had tried to buy it from him for four hundred dollars. That had been at least sixty years ago. He had no idea what it might be worth now. But it was an old friend. Until very recently, he'd carried it every day of his life since the day Charles had given it to a skinny Indian kid with a chip on his shoulder.

It took him a minute to find the sheath and belt. Dressed properly, he opened his bedroom door and started down the hall. Mackie and Maggie were playing Candy Land. He could tell because Maggie exclaimed, "I get to go to Gum-drop Mountain!" while Mackie cheered her on.

That Mackie did not care whether she won or lost was not a fault of the game. Joseph thought that twenty years from now, when it was Mackie and not Kage competing in the rarefied atmosphere of the best equestrians of their genera-tion, Mackie would still cheer on her opponents.

For a moment Joseph was deeply saddened by the thought that he would never get to witness that. But his time here was nearly past, and he really did not regret it. So much had changed, and so much had not. He was ready to go on to—how did Peter Pan put it? *An awfully big adventure.*

"I wanted to stay with you, Grandma," Mackie was saying. "But I'm worried about Michael. Nix is too tired to ride and Michael is very little. Who do you think he's riding today?"

"I don't know," Maggie said. "Max knows the horses who will be good for Michael. One purple. Your turn."

"Orange," said Mackie. "Do you think Anna will buy Merrylegs? I like Merrylegs."

Evidently Max had taken his brother, Charles, and Anna out riding, Joseph thought.

"I hope she buys Hephzibah," said Maggie. Joseph, unseen, still in the hall above the stairs, grinned. Mackie might not care about winning or losing, but her grandmother certainly did. If Anna had been what she had at first appeared, a too-young, too-innocent weakling, Maggie would have pitied her. But she would have taken her under her wing, too, and tried to teach her how to deal with strong-minded men.

But Anna was, in her own way, as strong-minded as Maggie. The two of them would never have been able to be friends. Maggie would always view her as competition. That Anna had Mackie's appreciation of competition, except where Charles was concerned, didn't make Maggie like her any better.

"Hephzibah is pretty," said Mackie in a doubtful voice. "But Daddy calls her Hellbitch. I don't think Anna should buy a horse called Hellbitch, do you? It's okay, though. Max will help Anna find the right horse. Two reds. It's your turn."

A car drove up outside. Joseph, who had taken a step forward, hesitated. He backed up a few feet and went into one of the guest bedrooms that overlooked the parking area. The car wasn't one of theirs, and it wasn't one he knew.

He knew the woman who got out of it, though. Why was the owner, she could call herself a principal if she wanted to, of Michael and Mackie's day care showing up at their door?

The hair on the back of his neck stood up suddenly.

She's here. The soundless whisper was hot in his ear.

He knew that the feds had the person they thought had hexed Chelsea and killed all those kids. He also knew that Charles hadn't been convinced.

If he knew his father, and he did, Hosteen would have wolves watching the place. So why hadn't they stopped her? A fae can look like anyone. Maybe he could look like a woman, like the principal of Mackie's day care. Instinctive certainty gripped him, and Joseph had learned to pay attention to his instincts. The woman approaching the house was the fae who'd tried to kill his grandchildren.

Charles had told him that this fae had taken down a werewolf—Joseph remembered Archibald Vaughn. He'd been a big, mean, scary old wolf, and this fae had torn him apart. One old Indian wasn't going to stop him very easily.

There was a phone in the bedroom. He picked up the receiver and dialed Charles's cell phone. As soon as Charles picked up, he told him what was going on.

The doorbell rang as Charles said, "English. My Navajo was never that good and I've hardly spoken it for twenty years."

Downstairs Maggie got up and went to the door. How well did the fae hear? Were they like his father?

"The fae," said Joseph in an urgent whisper, "the fae can look like anyone. She's here." And then he had to hang up because the door opened.

If she was here for Mackie, she would want to take her away from the ranch. One of the things that living with werewolves had taught him was that just because someone was supernatural didn't mean that cars didn't make getaways faster.

He pulled off his boots and ran stocking-footed down the hall to the other end of the house. He slipped out the window, dropped onto the back porch roof, and slid off as far as he could before jumping to the ground, hoping that his rejuvenation would keep him from breaking his knees on the landing. When he was eighteen, he'd have thought nothing of making such a drop.

He was almost surprised to land on his feet. He ran to the cars and pulled his knife. He sank the blade into one tire of every car in the lot. Maybe Hosteen's people would see him. But usually Hosteen didn't like guards that close to the house. They were probably out by the main road somewhere.

If he'd had a cell phone, he could have called his father and alerted him. He could have called him from the house instead of Charles. But Charles was closer . . . and Charles had a better chance of coming out on top. His father was tough, but Charles . . . was *Charles*.

It took him less than a minute to disable the cars and the pair of four-wheelers—buying time for Charles to return and save Mackie. The knife had a real sharp edge; Charles had taught him how to sharpen it.

No getaway car. What would the fae do?

Kill Maggie.

His heart clenched and his teeth bared in a silent growl. The fae didn't need her, didn't want her, and his Maggie wouldn't let anyone take Mackie without a fight.

He faced the fact that the fate of the woman he had loved for over half a century was entirely out of his hands. All he could do was go into that house and die beside her.

He'd do that willingly, except for Mackie.

There was nothing he could do to affect Maggie's fate. Live or die, she would do it without him. He swallowed hard. Maggie would be happy to die if it gave someone a chance to save Mackie.

So.

The fae would come out of the house with Mackie and discover that it could not use the cars to run. If it tried to walk out of here, Hosteen's wolves would notice that. If they were still alive to notice anything.

The horses . . . maybe.

There was a truck in the back of the barn. They never left the trucks hitched up overnight, so it would be parked next to the trailer they'd brought Nix back in. Mackie would know that.

Probably the fae could get Mackie to talk.

Another fact, like Maggie's fate, to absorb and not react to. He had to use his head if Mackie was to be saved.

Instead of running into the house as his heart wanted to do—*oh, Maggie*—Joseph ran toward the barn as fast as he could. Which was plenty fast. He couldn't run like one of his beloved horses, or a werewolf, either, but he had run everywhere when he had been a young man.

He stabbed the tire of the truck and then ducked back inside the barn. There were a lot of empty stalls because the barn was where they kept the show horses. The breeding barn was a quarter of a mile down the road, along with the paddocks where the rest of the horses were kept.

He stared at Hephzibah, who stared back at him with wicked eyes. He caught her and saddled her. Then he put her back in her stall and hung her bridle next to the stall door.

They did that sometimes with horses they were planning on taking out or showing to clients so that they could move from one horse to another quickly.

The rest of the horses in this part of the barn were yearlings and two-year-olds—none of them trained to ride. He was trying to figure out his next move when he heard Mackie's screams.

MACKIE LIKED MOST of the people at the day care. Miss Baird was her current favorite, but she liked Michael's teacher, Ms. Newman, too. She was predictable and strong—like Ánáli Hastiin. When she said something, she followed up on it. She'd told Michael that. Michael didn't like being away from his family at day care, but Ms. Newman made him feel safe so he didn't get scared and make them get Mackie for him anymore. He was glad when Ms. Newman brought his class to the horse show so that everybody saw him ride.

Mackie wished that Miss Baird had come to see her ride.

Ms. Edison was scary. She would smile and say nice things, but Mackie didn't think that her eyes were nice at all. Grown-ups liked her, though, so she seldom said anything about it—except to Max. Max listened to what Mackie said, and even if he disagreed, he didn't make her feel stupid.

When she had told Max she didn't like Ms. Edison, Max had said, "Listen to your instincts, pipsqueak. I trust them. She's not your teacher, right? Okay. If she does something that makes you feel uncomfortable, you make a lot of noise. I mean, really scream. That one you have that makes Hosteen grab his ears. People should come running and when they do, you make them get Mom or your dad or me, right? You don't shut up until you are happy with the situation."

Max had given her a plan of attack. So when Grandma had fallen against the wall and Ms. Edison grabbed her arm, she did what Max said and screamed and screamed.

She screamed when Ms. Edison carried her out to the car, and kept screaming when the principal changed her mind and carried her down to the barn. Even when she knew that there was no one who could hear her. Max had said to scream—so she did.

She screamed right up until the thing wearing Ms. Edison's face and body made her stop.

CHARLES GAVE ANNA a wild look and hopped off Portabella, tossing his reins to Max.

"If I told you the fae was a woman," he asked her, "who would you pick?"

"Ms. Newman," she said. "Or Ms. Edison."

"Mackie thinks Ms. Edison is bad," said Michael. "She said I shouldn't be alone with her."

"Did she?" Charles breathed. "We should have talked to Mackie." He changed then, in one of those instantaneous changes he could do when the need was great enough, and then he was off and running.

"What's going on?" asked Max.

"Joseph called to tell us that the fae is here and *she's* after Mackie," Anna told him. "The man that they have in jail was a fetch, like the one who took Amethyst's place."

"She's after Mackie?" Max said, and his horse settled back on his hind legs, ready to go.

Anna swung off her horse and took a good hold on Max's gelding's bridle. She kept an eye on him and one on Michael.

"Both of you stay right here. Mackie has your grandparents and Hosteen's wolves, and Charles is on his way."

"We're miles away," said Max.

"She's going to get Mackie like she got Amethyst," Michael said, sounding frantic. "We've got to stop her."

"Charles is fast," she assured them. "Max, do you have your phone?"

He nodded.

"You call Hosteen and you tell him that the fae is here. That its human shape is female. Probably one of the teachers"—she looked at Michael—"probably the principal from Mackie and

Michael's day care. Then you stay here and keep Michael away from that thing so we can minimize the damage it might do, okay? It's not going to find you out here."

Max took a deep breath and let it out. He hopped off his horse and took Michael's reins. "All right."

"I'm going to help Charles. I can't change like Charles. No one changes like my husband. I'll take Merrylegs and head back. You have the worse task, but it is the most important one. Stay here until someone calls you. Or until you talk to your dad or Hosteen and they say it's safe."

Max nodded soberly. Then he said, "Take Portabella, not Merry. Bella's a lot faster. If you ride up the trail a hundred yards that way"—he pointed opposite the way Charles had run—"and take the left marked by a white flag, you'll be on one of the maintenance roads. I'm not supposed to, but I run her on that road all the time. There are three gates across the road. You can dismount and open them; you can't open those kinds of gates without dismounting. But she'll jump them. I jump them with her all the time. You do much jumping?"

"No," Anna said. She handed Merry over and took Portabella from Max. "A couple of times, but there were two-foot-high logs on the trail." She shortened the left stirrup six holes and did a quick measure against her arm. It looked about right, so she rounded the horse to do the other side as she absorbed Max's instructions.

"These are about four feet high and, fair warning, jumping in a western saddle sucks. Just make sure your butt is out of the saddle when she goes up. Keep it out until she's all the way down. Keep your weight in the stirrups and your knees and not your butt. She won't run out—just give her her head and don't hit her in the mouth when she lands."

"Got it," Anna said, mounting up and gathering her reins. "Don't hit her with my butt or my hands while she's doing what she can to get over the fence."

"That's it," said Max.

"Stay safe," she told them.

"You, too," he said.

She asked Portabella to go. The mare took three short strides as if to ask, *Do I have to leave my friends?*

When Anna asked her a second time, she *ran*.

She was turning at the white flag before Anna asked her, obviously used to the path. Four strides and the trail connected to a narrow road, groomed and flat, and the mare put her mind to getting down the road.

At first Anna tried to ride this new gait like Charles had taught her to do, sinking her rump into the saddle and taking the movement with her back so her hands stayed steady. But a particularly hard stride pushed her up over the horse's shoulders, where the ride was smooth as glass. She balanced there on her feet and knees and thought, *So that's how jockeys can stay on a racehorse.*

She didn't even think about slowing for the gates. The first jump was a disaster, except that she didn't fall off. Portabella pinned her ears and gave a half buck to complain about the way Anna had landed on her back. The second jump was better, even though the saddle horn hit her in the stomach. The third jump . . . was magic.

CHARLES RAN FLAT-OUT for the house. He hit the front door and broke the door frame so the heavy old door swung free. He staggered a couple of steps and saw Maggie.

She was crumpled up against the wall, a small figure for such a big personality. It took no time at all to see that she was already gone.

Her knuckles were split; she'd hit her attacker at least once. He took one hard breath that hurt—but there were Joseph and Mackie to think about. He would mourn Maggie later, when her loved ones were straightened out.

He wasted a minute checking out the house, and when he didn't scent the fae anywhere except the living room, he followed Joseph's trail out a window in the back of the house. When he encountered the disabled vehicles, he thought, as he had once before, *You'll do to ride the river with, Joseph.*

Following the scent trail the fae had left, Charles ran for the barn.

IT WAS HARD to hide in the shadows and listen to Mackie scream. Joseph bit his lip and hunkered down in the empty stall. The staff had been busy and this stall hadn't been properly cleaned. He was pretty sure that if the fae did have a good nose, the scent of horse urine would disguise the scent of one old man.

He caught a glimpse of them as the woman hauled Mackie out of the barn to the truck. He'd flattened the tire on the far side so she had to go all the way out to see. He heard the door of the truck open, and suddenly Mackie wasn't making any noise.

The little girl had been like that when Charles and Anna had found her, he knew. It was magic, not death, that had silenced his Mackie. He held that thought close to him. He . . . she . . . *it*. He could think of the fae as *it*. It didn't want to hurt Mackie, yet—not until it could use her. Left to its preferences, it kept its victims for a year and a day, Charles had told him.

Shaking and sweating, tucked behind the door of the horse stall, Joseph prayed that magic was why Mackie had quit screaming. After a few minutes a new noise filled the air, a woman's frustrated cry.

"Where are you?" She—she sounded like a she—roared the words out.

Yeah. Sure he was coming out, like he was still that dumbshit kid in that bar in Phoenix. He'd learned a lot that day; some of it Charles had taught him. But most of it he'd learned from those World War II veterans who'd risked their lives for their country and came back to learn that their promises had to mean that they changed how they treated people who didn't happen to look like them. They hadn't learned that lesson until he'd taken them on and Charles had come to his rescue. His fists hadn't taught them anything, but that soft-spoken, laconic Charles? His words, what few there had been, had *flattened* them and left them bleeding by the wayside. He'd bet that they never beat up on someone because they were a different color or different anything again.

Charles had had words for Joseph, too.

If you're going to face someone bigger and stronger than you, kid, make damn sure you are better armed. He could hear Charles's dry voice as though it were yesterday instead of seventy-odd years ago.

The only weapons he had were the knife in his hand and the brain in his head, and the knowledge that Charles would be coming as fast as he could. Between the knife and Charles, Joseph was well armed, as long as he picked his fight.

That woman came back into the barn with Mackie slung over her shoulder like a leg of beef. He tightened his hand on the knife but stayed still. She paused beside Hephzibah's stall and growled, "Horses." She didn't sound happy, and she didn't sound very female anymore, either.

He had a pretty good view of her as she dropped Mackie to the ground—his granddaughter's staring eyes met his through the crack of daylight between the half-open stall door and the door frame.

The fae grabbed the bridle he'd left hanging on the hook and opened the door. "Come 'ere, nag," the thing growled.

He'd worried a little about making Hephzibah a target—what if the fae had been one of those who could ride anything? Hephzibah was quick and strong. If that fae could ride her, they'd have had a fine time trying to run her down— since he'd effectively disabled all the motorized vehicles in the place, except for the lawn mowers.

But no one who could ride like that would ever use the word "nag" to describe Hephzibah, at least not until she'd made them kiss dirt a time or ten. Kage had no trouble calling her a nag.

Hephzibah walked out of the stall quietly, her ears up. That was what caught everyone the first time. She looked happy to have someone saddle her up. She was quiet and well mannered until she wasn't.

The fae grabbed Mackie by a leg and got on the mare.

He'd given it a fifty-fifty chance whether the fae would ride out the back of the stables or go through the big arena and out the front. Hephzibah stopped right in front of his hiding place. She lowered her head and snorted at him.

Anyone would know she was telling them that there was an old man hiding behind the door. But the fae jerked Hephzibah's head up with the bit. The mare didn't even flick her ears. Yep. This was not going to last long. He wished he had moved Nix over where he could get to him, but there had been too great a chance that it would be Nix the fae grabbed. And on Nix, she might actually have escaped.

Joseph would just have to make sure that he stayed with them. His chance to grab Mackie would come. He'd grab Mackie and run and hope that Charles had had enough time to make it down here.

Charles could be watching them right now, biding his time like Joseph was. He'd believe that. It gave him hope.

The fae rode Hephzibah on past Joseph's stall and out toward the big arena that lay between them and the front door of the barn. Joseph counted to five after the sound of the mare's hooves on the hard-packed sand of the aisle gave way to soft thumps in the arena. Then he slipped out of the stall and followed them.

He figured that mare would trot peacefully about halfway down the arena, the better to sucker her rider, and then it would be all over but the crying. About a 30 percent chance she'd decide to stomp the fae, about a 68 percent chance she'd just bolt for the hills, and a 2 percent chance he didn't want to think about that she'd go after Mackie if the fae dropped her while trying to stay on.

One of the times Hephzibah had dumped Kage, she'd gone after his hat, which had rolled off his head when he hit. She'd chomped down on it, tore three or four times around the ring carrying it in her mouth. Then when she had everyone's attention, she dropped and trampled it until there wasn't anything left except a sad bundle of straw. Mostly, though, after she dumped her rider, she either ran for freedom or went after the person who'd had the gall to get on her back in the first place.

Joseph would be ready for either of those.

CHARLES BOLTED THE rest of the way across the big arena when he heard the fae scream from somewhere in front of him. He thought she said, "Where are you?" but he couldn't be certain. As soon as he was past the open space, he dropped to the slinking walk he used when he was hunting deer. His body lowered and his fur served to hide some of the movement that might attract the wary eye.

He turned into the corridor that ran between the rows of stalls and immediately quit moving. He found a place in the shadows of a pair of rubber barrels set right at the corner where he could gather the pack magic around and disappear. He saw Ms. Edison striding back into the barn from the big white truck parked in plain view through the big opening at the end of the run of stalls.

Ms. Edison had Mackie slung over her shoulder. The child was as still as a brace of dead ducks, and the fae was hopping mad, snapping her teeth together in a way distinctly inhuman. She paused as she passed a stable.

He could smell Joseph. He was in here somewhere. Was he in the stall?

She growled, *"Horses."* Spat on the walkway. Then dumped Mackie on the ground. She fell limply and Charles had a flash of Maggie in a limp mound on the floor of the house. His lips curled to expose his fangs, but he kept the growl silent.

Ms. Edison grabbed a bridle and slid open the stall door. She wasn't in there very long before she led out a horse saddled with a worn western saddle.

Who had saddled the horse and left her in the stall?

And such a horse. Her pale tail dragged on the ground, and her thick mane—it was unusual for a chestnut to have such a thick mane—hung six inches below her slender, well-shaped neck. Huge dark eyes looked out at the world with an air of gentle sweetness. Her legs were strong and square-jointed. This was a mare who could run a hundred miles and emerge from the ride entirely sound and ready to go again.

Why wasn't this horse at Scottsdale or in the breeding barn? He'd seen a lot of horses in his long life, and this mare was among the top three or four. Maybe even the very best.

The fae grabbed Mackie and tossed her back over her shoulder. Ms. Edison crawled onto the horse with enough competence that he could see it wasn't the first or the twentieth time she'd been on a horse. That made sense. Until the twentieth century the horse was the prevalent method of transportation.

The horse snorted at an open stall door. *That's where you are, Joseph. Stay quiet. You've done your part, forcing the fae to stay until I could get here. This isn't a good place for a fight when there's an innocent bystander or two. We need a nice open place.* The arena or the dirt lot behind the barn. Either would do.

The fae jerked hard at the bit and Charles winced for the mare's soft mouth. The sweet-natured mare just lifted her head and started obediently for the arena. She walked right past Charles without pause, but he was hidden, so that wasn't strange. Even if she'd noticed him, Hosteen and his pack ran all over this farm in wolf form. She wouldn't view him as a predator.

He was just getting ready to leave his place when Joseph emerged from the stall and, moving like a young man, started after the mare.

Charles let the magic fall and trotted out to block his way.

Joseph stopped, gave him a tense smile, and pointed out to the arena with five fingers open. *Five,* he mouthed. *Four. Three.*

He didn't know what the countdown was, but he trusted Joseph and followed the horse out into the arena and planned on something happening in two seconds. An explosion. The big arena lights turning on suddenly. A loud noise.

Well, the explosion was pretty close.

That sweet-faced mare stretched her neck and pulled

herself about six inches of slack in the reins. Then she levitated without gathering herself. Charles, horseman though he was, didn't even see her move until she was four feet in the air with her front end going sideways one direction and her rear end the other in a catlike twist. When she landed, she planted one front foot, dropped her shoulder, and launched her rear end so high he'd have sworn it was briefly in front of her front feet before it snapped back down.

Mackie flew off one direction, and the fae fell the other. Without making a sound, without anything that might warn the thing that had been Mackie's principal, Charles landed on her and dug his jaws and his claws into her flesh. He ripped, holding her body down with his paws while he jerked back his head.

She screamed, the noise starting as low as a big cat's growl and then reaching a pitch that was a weapon in and of itself. High-pitched and sharp, sound traveled painfully from his ears right down his spine. He released the torn meat and bit down again—or he meant to. His jaws didn't work. When she rolled, he fell off her as limp . . . as limp and unmoving as Mackie and Amethyst before him.

His first reaction was disbelief. Never had his body failed him before, not like this. His magic—wolf, witch, and shaman—had never left him defenseless. Charles felt a breath of panic that was knocked aside by the storm of Brother Wolf's frenzied rage. He lost a moment or two to Brother Wolf. He hadn't allowed the wolf to take over to the extent of losing time since he had been a child. When he took hold of Brother Wolf and dragged control back, the fae was already on her feet again. Her left shoulder drooped until she grabbed her left arm with her right and made a sharp movement. With a snap, the shoulder slipped into place and reknit itself.

She dropped the appearance of being human entirely then. Green mottled skin crawled up her body—*his* body, demonstratively, for he wore no clothes. Limbs elongated and, as if someone had put a hook in the back of his neck, his body jerked upward, unfolding into a form that was seven or eight feet tall.

He stood upright like a gorilla stands upright, with his knuckles dragging the ground. He twisted the upper part of his body until he could look at Charles, his face now covered with knobbly green skin and populated with tiny red eyes and a mouth that opened like a leech's, complete with narrow, long, sharp teeth and a yellow-and-red-spotted tongue.

And Charles was helpless. His frustration and anger burned and sizzled, a tithe on Brother Wolf's fury. Charles sought to push that emotion, all of that power, into magic that might combat the spell that held him helpless.

The fae creature roared at him; this time there was no magic at all in its cry, only triumph and rage. At that moment, two werewolves landed on the creature's back, one from each side as if these two had fought together before.

Charles recognized the raccoon-masked face of the leftmost one as a wolf who'd belonged to Hosteen when he had come to see the Alpha of the Salt River Pack the first time, near enough to a century ago. His fur was dark with dried blood. Evidently this was not the first encounter that wolf had had: Ms. Edison had not driven up to the house unchallenged.

The fae grabbed one wolf with a move that proved him to be double-jointed. His hand was big enough to surround the wolf's head and tear him off, flinging him out of Charles's line of sight. He simply touched the other wolf and that one dropped like a stone. Like Charles.

Charles realized that it hadn't been sound that had echoed through his body earlier, it had been magic. The second wolf landed half on Charles, half off. The remaining wolf, the one who'd been thrown, was back. He moved like a cattle dog working an angry bull, nip and run and nip and run.

For a moment, Charles thought that wolf had a chance. But he went for a throat grab. The fae's joints didn't work like a human's joints—or those of any other animal Charles had seen. His head just moved with the wolf's motion, neck emerging from his shoulders like a Slinky pulled out of a box. He swiveled and bit down on the wolf's neck. The wolf cried out, red blossoming around the fae's closed mouth.

Charles broke out in a sweat and curled his paw.

JOSEPH LET CHARLES take the lead. He was amazingly glad to see Charles. The relief of it left him light-headed. Watching Hephzibah, the Evil One, dump the fae on her head was just the icing on the best zucchini bread he'd ever had.

But the fae didn't follow the script. Charles just collapsed. A pair of his father's wolves cleared the arena fence and joined in the battle. Two werewolves, and one was down in under a minute. That was when he knew his role wasn't finished here.

He had no idea why Hephzibah hadn't taken one of her famous exits. The arena gates were open at both ends, but she just kept circling around at a leisurely canter, her eye on . . . Mackie, he thought. He waited until Hephzibah started around again, and used her body to hide when he entered the arena. He ran beside her, keeping her between him and the fae.

He caught her reins and was grateful that it was Hephzibah he had to work with. Any other horse in the stable wouldn't go anywhere near a thing that looked as deadly as the creature Ms. Edison had turned into. Hellbitch she might be, but Hephzibah had yet to meet something she was scared of.

She eyed Joseph warily but had no objection to him running at her side, not even when he started pushing her to get closer. A glance under her neck told him that the second werewolf was down, with the fae chomping on his neck.

Joseph thanked goodness that he'd tightened the cinch himself and that Hephzibah had the withers to hold the saddle straight as he pulled the old trick of jumping halfway into the saddle. One foot in the stirrup, one hand holding the horn. He pulled her nose tight, aiming her right at the fae as he kicked her in the haunch with his free toe. All of it at the same time, or none of it would work.

She launched herself sideways at the fae, landing smack

on top in an ungraceful movement she'd never have made if he hadn't knocked her off balance. The fae was shoved off the wolf. The horse scrambled hard to keep her feet and kicked the monster good a couple of times in the process.

Joseph, unnoticed, dropped to the ground behind the creature's back. He pulled out his knife and with his full weight behind the blow, just as Charles had taught him, punched the blade through the fae's back while it was still disoriented from Hephzibah's surprise attack.

The fae-thing's arm swung around improbably and hit Joseph in the chest. He heard the ribs crack before he felt them, and then he was down on the dirt next to a wolf who was bleeding out from the wound in his throat.

He had failed.

WHEN THE CHESTNUT mare charged the fae, Charles felt a moment of stunned disbelief. There was no reason . . . and then he saw Joseph. It was an old Indian trick, hanging off the side of your horse so you could get close to your enemy.

He spared an instant of admiration. There was nothing Joseph couldn't do with a horse. The horse landed on the fae, both of them equally surprised by it. And the fae's hold on Charles weakened.

He pulled himself to all four feet, snarling silently with the effort. As Joseph stuck his knife into the fae's back, Charles took two stumbling steps forward as the magic released him— just for a moment. Then the magic was back and his body was once again unwilling to follow his command.

But the fae's hold wasn't as strong as it had been. He couldn't pay attention to the way Joseph was lying on his back, blood foaming from his nose and mouth. Charles had to get to his feet, had to kill the fae while it was still down.

The chestnut mare ran up toward Joseph, stopped about ten feet away, and then snorted, gave a half jump sideways, and trotted off again.

Joseph had severed the fae creature's spine with the knife. As Charles dragged himself closer, he watched it try to reach the blade. But Joseph had, by luck or intent, found a place it couldn't get its hands. The flesh around the knife moved as though there were something under the mottled and bumpy green skin that was both repelled by and attracted to the steel.

The fae gave up trying to reach the knife. Instead it focused on . . . Mackie. It levered itself up on its arms and began crawling toward the helpless girl at a speed roughly twice what Charles could manage.

The chestnut mare whinnied shrilly and galloped between the fae and the girl. She'd been running all over the place, so Charles didn't pay her any more attention than the fae did. Until she did it a second time, blasting past with more attitude than speed, ears pinned and feet hitting the ground with extra force.

She did a pretty little rollback, her left rear planted in the sand as she rotated her body around, crossing her right front leg over her left in approved reining style. Then she trotted back across the fae's path, her tail flagged over her back, her head up, and her tiny ears sharply forward. She did a roll-back in the other direction.

And this time she planted herself between Mackie and the fae, pinned her ears flat, and ran past it. She snaked her long neck down, snapped her teeth at the creature, spun, and caught it with a nasty full-force kick right under its shoulder blade.

The fae let out a high-pitched cry, falling away—and the mare was back. This time she struck with her front feet. She pulled the fae underneath her and stomped it twice before hopping over it and bolting away with a triumphant squeal.

She came back again, snorting and side-passing until she stood between that thing and Mackie. Then she flipped her head in the classic warning that meant *go away or die*. She half reared and squealed—like a mare protecting her baby. Protecting Mackie.

ANNA DIDN'T NEED to go to the house. She could feel Charles in the barn and she sent Bella that direction. The big mare was laboring; by Anna's reckoning they'd run about four miles. But she ran willingly through the dark doorway that opened into the arena, and she cleared the huge arena fence by six inches.

Anna kicked both feet free of the stirrups then and jumped off as the mare gathered herself to keep running. She took in the scene of the arena in one comprehensive look: Mackie down, Joseph down, two werewolves down and unmoving, Charles on his feet but not by much, and the fae thing: huge, hideous, with a knife sticking out of its back. It was going, slowly, after Mackie. The only thing in its way was a big red mare.

Anna had no weapon, so she aimed herself at the knife sticking out of the fae's back. She put one foot on its back and grabbed the knife. She twisted it until the blade was parallel to the creature's spine. Using the strength of the wolf, she dragged it, still embedded in bone, up the body of the fae. At first the flesh healed behind the knife and it was hard to keep her balance because the fae wallowed and writhed underneath her. But as Anna continued dragging the knife forward, the healing slowed and then stopped and so did the fae's motion. Its stillness deceived her and as she approached the creature's head, its neck elongated, allowing it to bite down on her bicep. Anna just shifted her grip to the hand with the good arm and forced the blade all the way up until the point rested inside the fae's skull. The fae was still again. Limp. But Anna remembered the rapid way it had healed itself at first, remembered Brother Wolf telling her that fae were tough. She took a better hold on the now-slippery handle. She thought about Mackie, about the bodies littering the arena sand and those that had been stacked in the hot attic of that little house, and she cut the monster's head all the way off.

As soon as its teeth released her arm, she flung the head all the way across the arena. As quickly as it had healed its spine, she wanted no chance that it would repair the damage she'd done.

The body buckled unexpectedly, and Anna lost her balance at last. She rolled right underneath the feet of the chestnut horse, who reared and bolted away to join Portabella, who was standing, head down, on the far side of the arena.

Brother Wolf landed on the fae's body and began savaging it. All that she could feel through their mating bond was a red haze. The other wolves were getting up, none too gracefully. Joseph didn't move.

About that time, Mackie sat up and began to scream. Anna managed a half run, half hobble toward her. She wrapped her arms around Mackie and turned her, gently, because one arm was bent wrong, so that the child was facing away from the monster who'd tried to steal her away and the other monster who was trying to destroy the corpse.

"Charles," she said, but the wolf continued his attack on the dead fae. "Brother Wolf? I need you."

The wolf froze, let out a single savage growl, and then changed. Charles stood atop the dead thing's body looking as clean and collected as he had when they'd left the house this morning. He wasn't. She could feel his white-hot rage, his need to destroy. That he'd come to her call while feeling like that . . .

Well, she loved him, too.

"I have Mackie," she said. "You need to check Joseph."

ANNA HAD COME. When she cut off the abomination's head, he and Brother Wolf would have howled in pride and triumph. But he didn't regain his ability to do that until the deed was already done.

Brother Wolf thought the creature might still live. Very old fae could live for quite a while without their heads. He was determined to make sure that it didn't survive its beheading. Charles let him out to do what he wanted.

That thing had killed all of those children. They'd died horribly and very, very slowly. If the spirits of the dead joined Brother Wolf's savagery, he was inclined to allow it.

Until Anna called him.

She sat in the sand holding Mackie against her.

"Check Joseph," she said.

First he went to her. She'd taken damage, but the wound in her arm was already healing over.

"I'm okay," she told him. "Mackie will be okay. Listen to her healthy lungs. Go check Joseph."

Charles knelt beside Joseph. To his surprise, the old man was still breathing.

"Dead?" Joseph asked in a breathy whisper.

"It's dead," Charles told him. "You severed its spine. It won't be killing any more children."

Joseph's eyes closed and he concentrated on breathing, not that it was doing him much good.

"Maggie?"

Charles closed his eyes, too. When he opened them, Joseph was looking at him.

"Thought so," he said. "Will see her soon. She'd be happy to die for our girl." A half smile crooked his lips. "I hear she'll be fine."

"Good lungs," acknowledged Charles. Mackie was still screaming.

"Better'n mine," agreed Joseph with a smile. "Give knife to Max."

"I will," Charles said.

"Show him. Show."

"I'll show him how to use it. As I showed you."

Joseph nodded. "Good. That's good." He took another painful breath and then grinned. "It was fun to be . . . to be *me* again."

Charles sat beside him, holding Joseph with his eyes while his ears told him that Hosteen and a whole slew of other people were accumulating in the arena. Mackie quit screaming. Kage sat on Joseph's other side. Joseph couldn't talk anymore, but he held out his hand and Kage took it.

Charles had known this moment would come, ever since he'd understood that Joseph had no intention of becoming a werewolf like his father. Every moment spent in his company had been a moment closer to this. Had it been worth it in the face of Joseph's death?

He thought of all the experiences they'd shared. He felt the huge hole that Joseph's death was carving in his spirit, a hole that was even now filling with pain. Had it been worth it?

"I am so grateful to have had you as my friend," he told Joseph. He would not have given up any of those times to avoid this pain of separation, let alone all of them. Yes, it had been worth it.

Eventually the arena got quieter. Max came and said good-bye. Kage got up, put an arm around his son, and left. Hosteen sat down in his place. Anna came and sat close to him.

Joseph tried to say something to Hosteen, but he didn't have the voice. The hand that Charles held was very cold.

Hosteen said, "I love you. I will miss you. I am so proud to have been your father—and prouder to have been your friend. You have enriched the world with your spirit, my son. Don't be afraid to let go." He kissed his son's forehead, and then, like Charles, settled in to wait.

Night fell.

Joseph took one breath. Let it out. And then he took no more. Charles opened his mouth and let Brother Wolf howl his grief.

CHAPTER

15

There was no funeral. Charles and Anna loaded the dead fae into the trunk of Ms. Edison's car and tucked the dead fae's head into a box and put it in the backseat. They drove it to the day care parking lot, locked it, and drove away. Then they called Leslie and told her where to find it.

She wasn't happy with them, but she called back after they'd retrieved the body. "Better you than us," she said. "That body is going to keep Leeds happy for the next five years."

"Better him than me," Anna told her.

"Be well," Leslie said.

"You, too," Anna told her. "Give your husband a hug from me. I expect we'll see each other again. Charles thinks that there will be worse to come."

"Cheerful, isn't he?" Leslie said grimly. "I expect that you both are right. However, I, for one, intend to celebrate this victory. There may be all sorts of horrible fae in our future, but this fae isn't going to be killing any more children."

They stayed a few days more. There was no funeral, but the family mourned and they were willing to share their grief with Charles. It seemed to help him, but he was more uncommunicative than usual, so Anna couldn't be sure. Anna baked, babysat, and did anything she could to make things easier for the rest.

Bran came and he brought Moira the witch and her werewolf Tom. Moira came to help Chelsea and to make sure Amethyst was free of the fae's magic. Anna was pretty sure that Tom came because no one wanted to tell him to stay home, not even Bran. Anna and Charles flew back to Montana ten days after they'd left.

KATIE JAMISON SURVEYED the ruin of her house ruefully. If she hadn't been drunk, would she have had the brains to tell the FBI special agent and her friends the werewolves to go to hell? And if she had, would they have listened and spared her the headache of dealing with more construction in her house?

But they'd found that fae, the one who'd been killing children. She'd seen it in the news. And she'd seen a werewolf in his—and her—natural state. Too bad those photos hadn't turned out. *Magic could be odd that way,* her garden fae told her.

So she didn't have photos of the big wolf running amok in her living room, the ones she'd taken without permission. But the photos of the black wolf in her garden were lovely. Not as interesting as the ferocious and angry werewolf had been, but beautiful.

The cleaners had come and gone. Her favorite contractor had called this morning to tell her he was sending a guy down to replace her front window today. "And this time," he'd told her dryly, "don't marry him."

Yes, well, she admitted to herself. That had been a mistake—and she admitted it. But he'd been so pretty.

This one was pretty, too. His smile was warm—and his muscles were hard. He didn't have a ring on his left hand. She admired that hand, thinking about what it would feel like to have it touch her skin. He was awfully young for her.

"Are you married?" she asked.

He smiled. "I was. She took off with the bank account, my best friend, and my dog. I sure do miss that dog."

Too young, she thought, watching him work.

"Hey," she said. "Would you like some lemonade? It's fresh-squeezed from lemons I grow in my garden."

"That sounds really good," he said, and she noticed he had dimples.

Maybe not *too* young, she decided. Then she went to pour him some lemonade.

TRENT CARTER HUNG up the phone and thought seriously of getting into his car and driving off a cliff. But that would leave his daughter alone. Five years old was too young to be alone.

"Daddy?"

He loved his daughter with all of his heart. She was the only thing he had left of her mother. But he didn't know how to save her. Didn't really know how to save himself.

"You look sad," she said.

Sometimes, like now, she acted like a normal kid. She'd play with her toys and dress her dolls and invite him to make-believe tea parties.

Last night her babysitter had called him and told him that she could no longer watch Iris. "She was torturing our kitten," she said. "Pulling out her whiskers with tweezers. I can't do this anymore. I am sorry. You need to get her into therapy."

He didn't argue, didn't tell her that he already *had* her in therapy. That hadn't worked with the last babysitter. It probably wouldn't work with this one, either.

He'd called in to work today and told them he had to stay home because he didn't have anyone to take care of Iris. His boss had just called to let him know he didn't need to come back to work at all except to collect his things. That was his second job in six months.

"Daddy?"

"No worries, sweetheart," he told her. "I'm just not feeling good today."

"How about I get Mr. Blanket and we'll watch some TV until you feel better?" she asked.

Someone rang the doorbell. "You do that. I'll see who is at the door and then we can watch some cartoons."

He opened the door without checking through the spyhole. On his doorstep was a very average man so nondescript that he ought to work for the CIA. The woman was small and curvy, with black hair and wraparound sunglasses so dark he couldn't see her eyes behind them. There was an unfamiliar car—a black Mercedes—parked just outside his building. A scar-faced man who looked dangerous was leaning against the fender of the car.

Maybe this was the CIA. He thought back, a little anxiously, to his interview with the Cantrip agents. Had he said something wrong?

He'd kind of expected to be visited by Child Protective Services—it would be his third visit. Somehow the bruises always were gone before CPS came. Both her bruises and his.

"Mr. Carter," said the man, holding out his hand. "I'm Bran Cornick. We were in town on some related business. It was suggested to me that we should stop in to help you with your problem while we were here."

His hand was very warm.

"This is my associate, Moira."

"Daddy?" said Iris in her not-Iris voice. "Tell them to go away."

The woman brushed past him and into his house, her hand reaching down and closing on Iris's wrist. She touched his daughter's forehead and murmured a few words he didn't catch. Iris, who'd been fighting her, suddenly stood still.

"Yes," she said. "He was right about her, Bran. This is definitely a case of demonic possession." She turned her head toward Trent, and for the first time he realized she was blind. "This won't take very long. Demons have a hard time getting a good hold on innocents."

Bran Cornick urged Trent into the house and shut the door, closing them in together. "Mr. Carter," he said. "My associate is very good at what she does."

"Who are you people?" he asked.

"The good guys," said Moira. "We're here to help."

ANNA DREAMED THAT it was summer and she and Charles were riding in the mountains. The air was fresh and clean and the sun was warm on her back. Heylight trotted down the trail with the same enthusiasm he'd demonstrated in the arena. She turned to see how Portabella was doing and frowned at Charles.

"That's a moose," she told him. "Why are you riding a moose?"

"Because Portabella won't be here until the spring," Joseph told her. "Charles would never bring horses up from Arizona to Montana in the winter."

"That's right," Anna said. "We're bringing them up in March."

"You should have bought Hephzibah," Maggie told her, and laughed, but there was no malice in her laughter.

The sweet sound of it rang in Anna's ears as she woke up. It was still dark, so it was early. Charles wasn't in bed, which was probably what had woken her up.

She threw on socks because the floor was cold, and a robe because the house was cold, too. Then she shuffled out to the kitchen, where Charles was putting on the kettle. She shuffled right up to his back, warming herself on him.

"Good morning, sunshine," he said.

"I dreamed of Joseph and Maggie," she told him. "Maggie told me we should have bought Hephzibah instead of Portabella and Heylight."

"Kage won't part with her, not after she saved Mackie," Charles told her.

"Hey," she replied. "I'm just telling you what Maggie said."

He finished what he was doing and turned around so she was plastered against his front instead of his back. "I've been thinking," he said.

"A dangerous pastime," she warned, and was rewarded by the happy laugh that belonged only to her.

"It was Joseph," he said. "When he was dying, I suddenly realized all that I would have missed if I hadn't known him."

"I liked Joseph," she told him. "I wish I'd had a chance to know him better."

Charles smiled at her. "Love," he said, "is always a risk, isn't it? I've always thought that there were no certainties in life, but I was wrong. Love is a certainty. And love always gives more than it takes." His hand was running up and down her back. "I think we should adopt. What do you think?"

Adopt? She had wanted his children. His and hers.

She thought of his face as he'd cradled Amethyst and crooned a silly children's song, and Anna knew that any child who came to live with them would be his. His and hers.

"That would be okay," she told him, slowly, a smile growing with the words. "That sounds right."

Read on for an exciting excerpt from
the next Mercy Thompson novel

FIRE TOUCHED
by Patricia Briggs

Coming March 2016 from Ace Books

I sat up in bed, a feeling of urgency gripping my stomach in iron claws. Body stiff with tension, I listened for whatever had awakened me, but the early-summer night was free of unusual noises.

A warm arm wrapped itself around my hips.

"Mercy?" Adam's voice was rough with sleep. Whatever had awakened me hadn't bothered my husband. If there were something wrong, his voice would have been crisp and his muscles stiff.

"I heard something," I told Adam, though I wasn't certain it was true. It *felt* like I'd heard something, but I'd been asleep, and now I couldn't remember what had startled me.

He let me go and rolled off the bed and onto his feet. Like me, he listened to the night. I felt him stretch his awareness through the pack, though I couldn't follow what he learned. My link to the Columbia Basin werewolves was through simple membership: but Adam was the Alpha.

"No one else in the house is disturbed," he told me, turning his head to look at me. "I didn't sense anything. What did you hear?"

I shook my head. "I don't know. Something bad." I closed my fist on the walking stick that lay against me. The action drew Adam's eyes to my hands. He frowned, then crouched beside the bed and gently pulled the walking stick away.

"Did you bring this into bed last night?" he asked.

I flexed my fingers, frowning with annoyance at the walking stick. Until he'd drawn my attention to it, I hadn't even realized that it had, once again, shown up where it shouldn't be. It was a fae artifact—a minor fae artifact, I'd been told, if very old.

The stick was pretty but not ornate, simple wood shod in etched silver. The wood was gray with age, varnish, or both. When it had followed me home like a stray puppy the first time, it had seemed harmless. But fae things are rarely what they seem.

It was very old magic and stubborn. It would not stay with the fae when I tried to give it back to them. I didn't know what to do with it, so I'd given it to Coyote.

My life has been a learning experience. One thing I have learned is: don't give magical things to Coyote. He returned it, and it was . . . different.

I opened and closed my hands several times; the fierce knowledge that something was wrong had faded. Experimentally, I reached out and touched the walking stick again, but my fear didn't return.

"Maybe I just had a nightmare," I told him. Maybe it hadn't been the walking stick's fault.

Adam nodded and set the walking stick on the top of my chest of drawers, which had become its usual resting place. Shutting it up in a closet had seemed rude.

"Let me just take a look-see around the place," he told me after a quick kiss. I nodded and he left.

I waited for him in the dark. Maybe it had been a nightmare, or maybe something was wrong.

Maybe something was wrong with Tad and Zee. The walking stick would be concerned about them—they were fae. At least Zee was fae.

When one of the Gray Lords who ruled the fae had

declared independence from the human government, all of the fae had retreated to their reservations. Zee, my old friend and mentor in all things mechanical, had been forced to go to the Walla Walla reservation, which was about an hour away.

The fae barricaded themselves inside the walls the government had built for them. For a month or so, they'd let the humans figure out that the walls weren't the only things that protected the reservations now. The Walla Walla reservation had all but disappeared. The road that used to go there went somewhere else now. And I'd heard that when people tried to find it by airplane, the pilots forgot where they were going. Satellite photos were a gray blur.

Then some things started to get out. Fae that had been held in check by their rulers had been set upon us, one by one. People died. The government was trying to keep a lid on it, to avoid panic, but the media was starting to notice.

I closed my hands again on the gray wood of the walking stick, the one that Adam had just set on the top of the chest of drawers. I hadn't worried about Zee a whole lot—he can take care of himself. And Tad and I had been able to contact him now and then.

Tad was Zee's son. Half-fae, the product of a mostly failed experiment by the Gray Lords to see if fae could reproduce with humans and still be fae, Tad hadn't been required (or asked) to retreat to the reservations. The fae had no use for their half-bloods, at least not until Tad had demonstrated that his magic was powerful and rare. Then they'd wanted him.

Seven weeks he'd been gone. Without Tad, I hadn't been able to activate the mirror we'd been using to contact Zee. Seven weeks and no word at all.

"Is it Tad?" I asked the walking stick. But it sat inert in my hands. When I heard Adam on the stairs, I got up and put it back on the chest.

SITTING AT THE kitchen table the next morning, I paged through yet another catalog of mechanic's supplies and made crabbed notes on the notebook beside me with page numbers and prices.

I hadn't forgotten last night, but I could hardly sit and do nothing, waiting for something dire to happen. I had no way to contact Zee or Tad. I also had no way to tell if the walking stick had caused my panic over something real, or if I'd had a nightmare and that had called the walking stick.

If something dire was going to happen, in my experience, it would happen whatever I was doing—and waiting around was singularly useless. So I worked.

The wind rustled the pages gently. It was early summer yet, cool enough to leave windows open. A few more weeks, and the heat would hit in full force, but for now we only had the occasional windstorm to complain about. I flattened the page and compared the specs of their cheapest lift to the next cheapest.

We'd managed to scavenge some tools out of my shop when a volcano god toasted it, but a lot of things got warped from the heat—and other things got demolished when the rest of the building collapsed. It would be months before the shop was up and running, but some items were going to take a few months to order in, too. Meanwhile, I sent a lot of my customers to the VW dealership. A few of my oldest customers—and a few of my brokest customers—I had bring their cars out to the big pole building at my old place. It wasn't really tooled up, but I could take care of most issues.

Music wafted down from upstairs out of Jesse's headphones. Her door must have been open or I wouldn't have heard them. The headphones were an old compromise that predated me. Jesse had told me once, before her father and I got married, that she suspected that if she were playing big band music or Elvis or something, her dad wouldn't have minded her playing it on a stereo. He liked music. Just not the music she liked.

She also told me that if she hadn't told him that her mother let her play whatever she wanted (true—you don't lie to a werewolf, they can tell), he probably wouldn't have been willing to compromise on the headphones. Werewolves can hear music played over headphones, but it's not nearly as annoying as music over speakers.

I like Jesse's music, and I hummed along as I sorted through what I didn't want, what I wanted and didn't need, and what I needed. When I finished, I'd compare the final list with my budget. After that, I expected that I'd be sorting through what I needed and what I absolutely needed.

Above Jesse's music, I could hear male voices discussing the pack budget and plans for the next six months. Today was, apparently, a day for budgets. Our pack had money for investments and to help support the wolves who needed help. *Our* pack because though I wasn't a werewolf, I was still a member of the pack—which was unusual but not, as our newest member proved, unique.

That we had money (not all packs did) was very good. Werewolves had to work to control their wolves, and too much stress made it worse. Lack of money was stressful.

It was a fine balancing act between helping the people who needed help without encouraging slackers. Adam and his second, Darryl, and Zack, our lone submissive wolf who was the one most likely to hear if someone in the pack was in trouble (in all senses of that word), were upstairs in the pack meeting room—Adam's office being too small to accommodate two dominant wolves.

I couldn't hear Lucia, the sole human in the room. She was there because she had taken over most of the accounting for the pack from Adam's business's accountant. She was quiet because she wasn't yet comfortable enough with the were-wolves to argue with them. Zack was pretty good at catching what she didn't say and relaying it to the others, though, so it worked out.

Lucia's husband, Joel (pronounced Hoe-el), sighed heavily and rolled over until all four paws were in the air and his side rested against the bottom of the kitchen cabinets a few feet away from where I sat at the table. Joel was our newest pack member.

He was black, but in the strong sunlight, I could see a brindle pattern. Like me, he wasn't a werewolf. His induction into the pack was my fault—it had saved my life and probably his. Instead of turning into a werewolf—or a coyote like me— he sometimes regained his human form and sometimes took on the form of a giant, very scary beast that smelled like brimstone and had eyes that glowed in the dark. Mostly, though, he looked like a large Pressa Canario, a dog only slightly less intimidating to most people than a werewolf, especially if the people weren't familiar with werewolves. We were hoping that someday he'd get control of his change and be able to be mostly human instead of dog.

Someone drove in front of the house and stopped. Joel rolled over and took notice. Upstairs, the men's voices stopped. There was no doubt the car was for us because our house was the last one on a dead-end, very rural street.

It wasn't the mail carrier or the UPS lady—I knew those cars. I marked my place in the catalog and told Joel I'd check it out. Adam would hear me say that, too. I was halfway to the front door when someone knocked.

I opened the door to see one of Jesse's friends and her mom, who was carrying a large, teal canvas bag.

"Hey, Ms. H," said Izzy, not meeting my eyes. "Jesse's expecting me." She slid around me and—escaped was the only word that would fit—up the stairs. As soon as she spoke, Adam and his budget brigade (as Darryl called them) went back to work—they knew Izzy, too.

"Mercy," said Izzy's mom. I couldn't for the life of me remember her name. While I was fighting with my memory, she continued speaking. "I wonder if you have a few minutes. I'd like to talk to you."

It sounded ominous—but Izzy had just run upstairs, so it couldn't be one of those "I'm sorry but I just don't feel safe with my daughter coming over here knowing there are werewolves in the house" talks. Those usually happened over the phone, anyway.

"Sure," I said, taking a step back to invite her in.

"We'll need a table," she said.

I led her back to the kitchen, where Joel had stretched out, big and scary-looking, across the floor, until the only way to the kitchen table was over him. I opened my mouth to ask him to move, but Izzy's mom stepped over him as if he'd been a Lab or a golden retriever.

Joel looked at me, a little affronted at her disregard of his dangerousness. I shrugged, gave him a small apologetic smile, then stepped over him, too. Izzy's mom sat down at the kitchen table, so I sat down beside her.

She pushed my catalogs away to clear a space, then pulled out a slick, teal-colored spiral-bound book the size of a regular notebook with "Intrasity Living" scrawled in gold across the front.

She placed it gently, as if it were a treasure, on the table and said, in an earnest voice, "Life is short. And we're not getting any younger. What would you give if you could look ten years younger and increase your energy at the same time? That's what our vitamins can do for you."

Holy Avon, Batman, I thought, as worry relaxed into annoyance-tinged humor, *I've been attacked by a multilevel marketer.*

Sounds from the upstairs quieted again, for just a moment, then Darryl rumbled something that was nicely calculated to be just barely too quiet for me to pick up. Adam laughed, and they went back to talking about interest rates. They had abandoned me to face my doom alone. The rats.

"I don't take vitamins," I told her.

"You haven't tried *our* vitamins," she continued, blithely unconcerned. "They've been clinically proven to—"

"They make my hair fall out," I lied, but she wasn't listening to me.

As she chirruped on enthusiastically, I could hear Izzy's voice drifting down from Jesse's room. "Mercy is going to hate me forever. Mom's gone through all of her friends, all of her acquaintances, all of the people at her gym, and now she's going after my friends' parents."

"Don't worry about Mercy," said Jesse soothingly. "She can take care of herself." Jesse's door closed. I knew that with the door shut, the kids were too human to hear anything that went on in the kitchen short of screams and gunfire. And I wasn't quite desperate enough yet for either of those sounds to be an issue.

"I know there are other vitamins out there," Izzy's mother continued, "but of the twelve most common brands, only ours is certified by two independent laboratories as toxin- and allergen-free."

If she hadn't been Jesse's best friend's mom, I'd have gently but firmly (or at least firmly) sent her on her way. But Jesse didn't have that many friends—the werewolf thing drove away some people, and the ones it didn't weren't always the kind of people she wanted as friends.

So I sat and listened and made "mmm" sounds occasionally as seemed appropriate. Eventually, we moved from vitamins to makeup. Despite rumors to the contrary, I do wear makeup. Mostly when my husband's ex-wife is going to be around.

"We also have a product that is very useful at covering up scars," she told me, looking pointedly at the white scar that slid across my cheek.

I almost said, "What scar? Who has a scar?" But I restrained myself. She probably wouldn't get the *Young Frankenstein* reference anyway.

"I don't usually wear makeup," I told her instead. I had an almost-irresistible need to add "my husband doesn't want me attracting other men" or "my husband says makeup is the work of the devil" but decided that any woman whose name I couldn't remember probably didn't know me well enough to tell when I was kidding.

"But, honey," she said, "with your coloring, you would be stunning with the right makeup." And she was off and running, again.

Izzy's mom used "natural" and "herbal" to mean good. "Toxin" was bad. There was never any particular toxin named, but my house, my food, and, apparently, my makeup were full of toxins.

The world wasn't so clean-cut, I mused as she talked. There were a lot of natural and herbal things that were deadly. Uranium occurred naturally, for instance. White snake root was so toxic that it had killed people who drank the milk from cows who had eaten it. See? My history degree was useful sometimes—as a source of material to entertain myself with while listening to someone deliver a marketing speech.

Izzy's mother was earnest and believed everything she said, and so I didn't argue with her. Why should I upset her view of the world and tell her that sodium and chloride were toxic but very useful when combined into salt? I was pretty sure she'd only point out how harmful salt was, anyway.

She turned another page while I was occupied with coming up with more toxins that were useful—and I was distracted from my train of thought by the picture on the page. A mint leaf lay on an improbably black and shiny rock in the middle of a clear, running stream with lots of water drops in artistic places. It made me a little thirsty—and thirsty reminded me of drinking. And though I don't drink because of an incident in college, I sure could have used something alcoholic right then.

Come to think of it, alcohol was a toxin—and useful for all sorts of things.

"Oh, this is my favorite part," she said, caressing the dramatic photo, "essential oils." The last two words were said in the same tone a dragon might use to say "Spanish doubloon."

She reached into her bag and pulled out a teal box about the size of a loaf of bread. In metallic embossed letters, "Intrasity" and "Living Essentials" chased each other around the box in lovely calligraphic script.

She opened the box and released the ghosts of a thousand odors. I sneezed, Joel sneezed. Izzy's mother said, "God bless you."

I smiled. "Yes, He does. Thank you."

"I don't know what I would do without my essential oils," she told me. "I used to have terrible migraines. Now I just rub a little of our Gaia's Blessing on my wrists and temples and 'poof,' no more pain." She slid out an elegant, clear bottle that held some amber liquid and opened it, holding it toward my nose.

It wasn't that bad. I admit my eyes watered a little from

the peppermint oil. Joel sneezed again and went back to sleep. But from upstairs came a gagging noise and loud coughing. Ben wasn't here, and I didn't think Zack was the type. I'd have thought Adam and Darryl would both have been more mature. If I had any doubt that they were teasing me, it would have been dispelled by the way they were careful to be just quiet enough that Izzy's mother couldn't hear them.

Joel looked at me and let his tongue loll in an amused expression. He stretched, got up, and trotted up the stairs, doubtless so that he could join in the next round of fun. Deserter.

"Gaia's Blessing contains peppermint oil," Izzy's mother said unnecessarily because that was the one making my eyes water, "lavender, rosemary, and eucalyptus, all natural oils, blended together." She capped it. "We have remedies for a variety of ailments. My husband was an athlete in college, and for twenty years, he's battled with jock itch."

I blinked.

I tried to keep my face expressionless, despite the laughter from upstairs, as Izzy's mother continued, apparently unaware of the meaning of TMI. "We tried everything to control it." She dug around and pulled out a few bottles before coming up with the one she wanted. "Here it is. A little dab of this every night for three days, and his jock itch was gone. It works for ringworm, psoriasis, and acne, too."

I looked at the bottle as if that would keep inappropriate images from lingering. It helped that I had never met Izzy's father, but now I hoped I never did.

The bottle label read: "Healing Touch." I wondered if Izzy's mother's husband knew that his jock itch was something that his wife brought up in her sales pitch with near strangers. Maybe he wouldn't care.

She opened that bottle, too. It wasn't as bad as the first one.

"Vitamin E," she said. "Tea tree oil."

"Lavender," I said, and her smile wattage went up.

I bet she made a mint on her multilevel marketing. She was cute, perky, and very sincere.

She pulled out another bottle. "Most of our essential oils

are just one oil—lavender, jasmine, lemon, orange. But I think that the combination oils are more useful. You can combine them on your own, of course, but our blends are carefully measured for the best effect. I use this one first thing every morning. It just makes you feel better; the smell releases endorphins and wipes the blues right away."

"Good Vibrations," I commented neutrally. I hadn't been pulled back to the sixties or anything; that was what the label on the bottle read.

She nodded. "It's just a rumor, mind you, but my manager says that she thinks it does more than just elevate your mood. She told me she believes it actually makes your life go a little smoother. Helps good things to happen." She smiled again, though I couldn't remember her not smiling. "She was wearing it when she won a thousand dollars on a lottery ticket."

She set the bottle down and leaned forward earnestly. "I've heard—but it hasn't been confirmed—that the woman who started Intrasity"—she pronounced it "In-TRAY-sity"— "Tracy LaBella, is a witch. A white witch, of course, who is using her powers for good."

That made me reach out and pick up the bottle of Good Vibrations. I opened it and took a careful smell: rose, lavender, lemon, and mint. I didn't sense any magic, and mostly if magic is around, I can tell.

LaBella wasn't one of the witch family names, as far as I knew, but if "Tracy the Beautiful" was her real name, I'd have been surprised.

"Now this little gem"—Izzy's mother pulled out yet another bottle—"this is another of my favorites, guaranteed to improve your love life. Does your husband ever have trouble keeping up?" She held up a finger, then curled it limply downward as her eyebrows arched up.

The silence from upstairs was suddenly deafening.

"Uhm. No," I said. I tried to resist, I really did. If Darryl hadn't said, "Way to go, man—for a moment I was worried about you," I think I could have held out. But he did. And Adam laughed, which clinched it.

I sighed and picked an imaginary string off my pant leg. "Not *that* way. My husband is a werewolf, you know. So *really* not, if you know what I mean."

She blinked avidly. "No. What do you mean?"

"Well," I said, looking away from her as if I were embarrassed, and I half mumbled, "You know what they say about werewolves."

She leaned closer. "No," she whispered. "Tell me."

I had heard the meeting-room door open, so I knew that the werewolves could hear every word we whispered.

I let out a huff of air and turned back to her. "You know, every night is just fine. I'm good with every morning, too. Three, four times a night? Well . . ." I let fall a husky laugh. "You've *seen* my husband, right?" Adam was gorgeous. "But some nights . . . I'm not on the right side of thirty anymore, you know? Sometimes I'm tired. I just get to sleep, and he's nudging me again." I gave her what I hoped would come out as a shy, hopeful smile. "Do you have anything that might help with that?"

I don't know what I expected her to do. But it wasn't what happened.

She nodded decisively and pulled out an oversized vial with "Rest Well" written on the label. "My manager's father, God rest his soul, discovered the 'little blue pill' last year. Her mother just about divorced him after forty years of marriage before she tried this."

"God rest his soul" meant dead, right? I took the vial warily. Like the others, it didn't *feel* magical. I opened it and sniffed. Lavender again, but it was more complex than that. Orange, I thought, and something else. "What's in it?" I asked.

"St. John's wort, lavender, orange," she said briskly. "This isn't quite chemical castration, but it will bring your life into balance," she said, and she was off on her sales pitch as if the phrase "chemical castration" was a common concept—and something one might consider doing to one's husband.

And she looked like such a nice, normal person.

I sniffed the vial again. St John's wort I knew mostly from a book I'd once borrowed about the fae. The herb could be used to protect yourself and your home against some kinds of fae when placed around windows, doors, and chimneys. If it protected against the fae, maybe I should see if we could get it somewhere and stockpile. Maybe we could grow it. Lucia had our flowerbeds looking better than they had in years, and she was talking about putting in an herb garden somewhere. St. John's wort was an herb.

Eventually, Izzy's mother finished her sales presentation and began the hard sell.

I have a strong will. I didn't join up to sell Intrasity products to all my friends. She could say it "wasn't a pyramid scheme" all she wanted, but that's what it was. When she offered a 10 percent discount for names and phone numbers of friends, I thought about giving her Elizaveta's name. But I wasn't all that keen on sending a perfectly nice woman to the scary witch. I also wasn't sure that the witch really counted as a friend.

I would let Elizaveta know that Tracy LaBella was styling herself a witch to sell her products and let the old Russian deal with it herself.

So I paid full price for one normal-sized and one over-sized bottle of Rest Well, which was Izzy's mother's entire stock. I mostly bought it because it was funny, but also because I intended to see what kind of an effect the St. John's wort would have on a fae.

With Zee and Tad stuck on the reservation, I might need something to use against the fae.

I also bought a small vial of Good Vibrations. I hadn't intended to, but Izzy's mother gave me five percent off because she'd used it as a demo. I could give it to Elizaveta to make sure it wasn't really magical. It wouldn't hurt anything if I tried a little of it myself first.

It was when I bought some orange oil that I acknowledged that Izzy's mother had beaten me. But the orange oil smelled really good. Izzy's mother told me it was supposed to promote calmness—and it worked in cookies. I'd used orange extract in brownies before, but Izzy's mother said the oil worked better.

I saw her out and put my back against the door once I closed it. Adam cleared his throat. I looked up to see him halfway down the stairs. He was leaning against the wall, arms folded as he did his best to appear disgruntled. But there was a crinkle of a smile at the edge of his eyes.

"So," he said, shaking his head. "I'm too much for you. You should have said something. We might be married, Mercy, but no still means no."

I widened my eyes at him. "I just haven't wanted to hurt your feelings."

"When I give you that little nudge, hmm?" His voice took on a considering air. "Come to think of it, I'm feeling a little nudge coming on right now."

"Now?" I whispered in horrified tones. I looked up toward Jesse's room. "Think of the children."

He tilted his head as if to listen, then shook it. "They won't hear anything from there." He started slowly down the stairs.

"Think of Darryl, Zack, Lucia, and Joel," I said earnestly. "They'll be scarred for life."

"You know what they say about werewolves," he told me gravely, stepping down to the ground.

I broke and ran—and he was right on my tail. Figuratively speaking, of course. I don't have a tail unless I'm in my coyote shape.

I dodged around the big dining table, but he put one hand on top and vaulted it. So I dove under the table and out the other side and down the stairs, laughing so hard I almost couldn't breathe.

He caught me in the big rec room, tripped me, and pinned me against the floor. He kissed my chin, my neck, my cheek, and the bridge of my nose before he touched my lips. He put our game right out of my mind (along with any ability to form a coherent thought), so when he said, "Nudge," it took me a second or two to figure out what he was talking about.

I dragged my thoughts from my enervated and trembling body and thought about how many people would know what we were doing down here. "No?" I said hesitantly.

"What happened to not hurting my feelings?" he asked. Even though his body was evidently as excited as mine, and his breathing harder than our little chase merited, there was amusement in his eyes.

"Izzy, Jesse, Darryl, Zack, Lucia, and Joel happened," I said. And if my voice was husky, well, I think anyone in my situation would have had trouble keeping her voice steady.

He rolled off me but grabbed my hand as he did, so we lay side by side on our backs with our hands clasped. He started laughing first.

"At least," he said finally, "being a werewolf means I never have to worry about jock itch."

"Every cloud has a silver lining," I agreed. "Even being a werewolf has its upside."

I expected him to laugh again. But instead his hand tightened on mine and he sat up and looked at me. He pulled my hand to his lips and said, "Yes."

Of course, I had to kiss him again.

WE WENT UPSTAIRS after that kiss, so I didn't end up embarrassing myself. Sure, there were sly grins from the peanut gallery, but since nothing happened, I was able to keep from blushing as Darryl and Zack got ready to leave. Adam and the others had apparently concluded their business while I was finishing up with Izzy's mother.

Darryl kissed my hand formally and said, "You are endlessly entertaining."

I raised my eyebrow and gave him a "who me?" expression. Of course, that only made him laugh, his teeth flashing whitely in amusement. Darryl was a happy blend of his African father and Chinese mother, taking the best features of two races and combining them. A big man, he could do scary better than anyone in the pack, but with a grin on his face, he could charm kittens out of trees.

Zack gave me a hug good-bye. Our only submissive wolf, he had been really . . . skittish and worn when he first joined the pack a few months ago. But as he'd gotten used to us, he touched us all a lot. Some of the guys had been taken aback when he'd started, though his touch had nothing to do with sex. But no one wanted him sad: a happy submissive wolf balanced the dominants and lowered tempers. So they'd learned to accept Zack's ways.

I returned Zack's hug, and he slipped something into my pocket that felt like one of the vials I'd just bought. He stepped back, looked me earnestly in the eye, and said, "To protect you from the nudge."

Darryl high-fived him as he stepped out on the porch. It made Adam laugh.

After I shut the door on the miscreants who didn't live here, I turned around to see Lucia, Joel at her side, standing in the doorway to the kitchen with her arms crossed and a big grin on her face.

I frowned at her.

"Don't worry," she said earnestly. "I didn't hear the whole thing, but Zack courteously kept me apprised as it was happening, so I wouldn't feel left out. Why didn't you tell her to go away before she got started?"

"Because she's Izzy's mother—and that sort of thing can have repercussions for Jesse," I told her.

"And because you didn't want to hurt her feelings," said Adam. "Which is why multilevel marketing works. And you bought the oil because you want to see if there's real magic involved because you're worried about her," said Adam.

I met his eyes solemnly. "No." I patted my pocket. "I bought the orange oil for brownies, and I bought that other as a shield for the nudge attack."

He raised an eyebrow. "So, do you wear it, or do I?" he asked.

I frowned at him. "I couldn't actually tell from her story, but I'm afraid it might be fatal for you." Her manager's father had gotten a "rest in peace" after his name when she was talking about him, after all. "I figure the way it works is that I put it on me. Then I'll smell so strongly that you'll stay away until you are really desperate."

He threw his head back and laughed. Adam . . . Adam

tried to downplay it with a military haircut and clothes that were subtly the wrong color—I'd just figured that one out—but he was beautiful. Like magazine-model beautiful. I didn't always see it anymore, the inside being more interesting than the outer package, but with his eyes sparkling and his dimple flashing . . .

I cleared my throat. "Nudge?" I said.

Lucia laughed and turned back toward the kitchen. "Get a room," she said over her shoulder.

Adam? He took a predatory step toward me, and his phone rang.

So did mine.

I checked the number on my phone, intending to let the voice mail catch it, but when I saw who was calling, I answered it instead.

"Tony?" I asked, walking away from Adam so my conversation wouldn't get mixed up in his. Adam was talking to Darryl, whose voice sounded urgent.

"I don't know if you and Adam can help us," Tony said rapidly. In the background, sirens were doing their best to drown out his voice. "But we have a situation here. There is something, a freaking-big something, on the Cable Bridge, and it is eating cars."

"You and Adam" was short for "please bring a pack of werewolves out to take care of the car-eating monster." If they were asking for the pack, they must be desperate.

"Mercy," said Adam, who, unlike me, apparently had no trouble keeping track of two conversations at the same time, "tell him we're on our way. Darryl and Zack are almost on-site."

I repeated Adam's words, and then said, "We'll be right there."

I hung up and started out the door. The Cable Bridge, which had another name no one remembered, was less than a five-minute drive from our house.

"Mercy," said Adam tightly. The last time we'd faced down a monster, I'd almost died. It had taken me six weeks to stand on my own two feet, and it hadn't been the first time I'd been hurt. The werewolves were two-hundred-plus pounds of fang and claw who mostly healed nearly as quickly as they could be hurt. I was as vulnerable as any human. My superpower consisted of changing into a thirty-five-pound coyote.

He still had nightmares.

I looked at him. "You're going to be a werewolf. Darryl is going to be a werewolf, and I'm assuming Joel is going to be a monstrous tibicena, spitting lava and looking scary. I think you need someone on the ground with the ability to shout things like 'Stop shooting, those are the good guys.'" I took a deep breath. "I won't promise not to get hurt. I won't lie to you. But I do promise not to be stupid."

His cheeks whitened as he clenched his jaw. His eyes shadowed; he nodded slowly. That was the deal that we had, the thing that allowed me to give up my independence and trust him. He had to let me be who I was—and not some princess wrapped in cotton wool and kept on a shelf.

"Okay," he said. "Okay." Unself-consciously, he stripped out of his clothes because it would be easier to do that here than in the car. "Joel? Are you coming?"

The big black dog, who already looked a little bigger, padded out of the kitchen. I wasn't certain how much control Joel had about what shape he wore except that it wasn't much. We needed to get to the bridge before he started melting things in the car—the tibicena was a creature born in the heart of a volcano.

I opened the door, stopped, and ran up the stairs. I opened Jesse's door without knocking.

"Monster on the Cable Bridge," I said. "Police are requesting assistance. Stay home. Stay safe. We love you."

I didn't give her time to say anything, just bolted back down the stairs to Adam's black SUV, where the others waited.

We were going to fight monsters.